Taken by
the Millionaire

KATE HARDY
ROBYN GRADY
NICOLA MARSH

Published in Great Britain 2013
by Mills & Boon, an imprint of Harlequin (UK) Limited,
Eton House, 18-24 Paradise Road, Richmond, Surrey TW9 1SR

TAKEN BY THE MILLIONAIRE
© by Harlequin Enterprises II B.V./S.à.r.l 2013

Hotly Bedded, Conveniently Wedded, Naughty Nights in the Millionaire's Mansion and *Big-Shot Bachelor* were first published in Great Britain by Harlequin (UK) Limited.

Hotly Bedded, Conveniently Wedded © Kate Hardy 2008
Naughty Nights in the Millionaire's Mansion © Robyn Grady 2009
Big-Shot Bachelor © Nicola Marsh 2007

ISBN: 978 0 263 90568 7
ebook ISBN: 978 1 472 00141 2

05-1013

Harlequin (UK) policy is to use papers that are natural, renewable and recyclable products and made from wood grown in sustainable forests. The logging and manufacturing processes conform to the legal environmental regulations of the country of origin.

Printed and bound in Spain
by Blackprint CPI, Barcelona

HOTLY BEDDED, CONVENIENTLY WEDDED

BY
KATE HARDY

Kate Hardy lives on the outskirts of Norwich, with her husband, two small children, a dog—and too many books to count! She wrote her first book at age six, when her parents gave her a typewriter for her birthday.

She had the first of a series of sexy romances published at twenty-five, and swapped a job in marketing communications for freelance health journalism when her son was born, so she could spend more time with him. She's wanted to write for Mills & Boon since she was twelve, and when she was pregnant with her daughter, her husband pointed out that writing medical romances would be the perfect way to combine her interest in health issues with her love of good stories.

Kate is always delighted to hear from readers—do drop in to her website at www.katehardy.com.

For Chrissy and Rich—the best aunt and uncle
in the world—with love

CHAPTER ONE

'RUN that by me again.' No way could Isobel have heard him correctly. She was used to Alex asking if he could sleep on her sofa while he was in London between digs or on a flying visit—his own flat in London was let out to tenants—but this request...

She must've been hearing things.

'Will you marry me?' Alex repeated.

Exactly what Isobel thought he'd said.

Was this some kind of joke?

Unlikely, because he looked serious. Besides, Alex didn't make that kind of joke. She frowned. 'I don't understand. Have you gone temporarily insane, or something?'

'No. I just need to get married. And I think you'd be the perfect wife.'

Oh, no, she wouldn't. She'd already failed spectacularly with Gary. 'You get women posting their knickers to you. You could get married to any woman you wanted.'

He laughed. 'They don't post their knickers to me, Bel. That's a vicious rumour started by Saskia.'

Saskia was Alex's baby sister and had been Isobel's best friend since they were toddlers. Though Isobel wasn't so sure the comment was just sibling teasing. 'I know for a fact you get asked out by more women than most men even dream about.'

'Women who fantasise about The Hunter—not about me.'

'You're one and the same, in their eyes.' In hers, too: Alex had presented three series of a popular television archaeology programme, based on a series of articles he'd written for a leading Sunday newspaper, and when Isobel had curled up to watch the programmes she'd thought he came across just as he was in real life. Clever and extremely well read, but with a bit of flamboyance that had women dropping at his feet and the kind of easy charm that meant he made friends effortlessly and couldn't go anywhere without half a dozen people hailing him by name. It had been like that even before he'd been catapulted to fame as 'The Hunter', an explorer who delved in ancient places and found treasure; but nowadays, with national television exposure, he was recognised by people he'd never even met.

'Just let it slip to one of your gossip-column friends that you're looking for a wife and there'll be queues for miles,' she suggested.

'Gossip-column journos aren't anybody's friends except their own,' he corrected. 'And none of those women would be like you—sensible and settled.'

She coughed. 'You're digging yourself deeper into that hole, Alex.' He wanted to marry her because she was *sensible?* Give her a break. That wasn't why people got married.

Then again, marrying for love hadn't exactly worked for her, had it? Her marriage hadn't survived its final crisis.

'Why do you need to get married anyway?' she asked.

'Because I need to get a job.'

'This is beginning to feel like *Alice Through the Looking Glass*. The harder I try to understand this, the weirder it seems.' She shook her head. 'Apart from the fact that you don't need to get married to get a job, why do you even need a job in the first place? You're loaded.'

Alex waved a dismissive hand. 'It's got nothing to do with money.'

'So what, then?'

'It's complicated,' he hedged.

She leaned back against the sofa. 'You're not getting out of it that easily, Alex. Explain. Why do you need to get married?'

'Because of this job. It's perfect, Bel—Chief Archaeological Consultant for a firm that works with all the big property developers. When the developers plan to build on a site and discover remains of some structure they hadn't even known existed, or we already know there are remains in the area that need to be conserved or recorded before any development work can start, I'd be in charge of a team of archaeologists who'd excavate the site.'

'A desk job, you mean?' She shook her head, scoffing. 'No way. You'd last five minutes before you came down with a case of terminal boredom.'

'It's not a desk job. I'll be doing the initial site visits and setting up the exploration, liaising with planning officers and talking people into giving us more time than they really want to for excavation work. Plus I'd be talking to the press, explaining the significance of the find.'

Put that way, it sounded just the sort of thing he'd enjoy doing. Alex would love the chance to be the first one in maybe hundreds of years to discover something. And the time pressure to excavate the site as thoroughly but as quickly as possible, so the builders could finish their job on schedule, would just add to the thrill for him. He thrived on being too busy.

'I still don't understand why you need a job. Aren't you going to do the Hunter stuff any more?'

'Of course I am.' He shrugged. 'But it's only for a few weeks a year.'

She understood where he was coming from. Alex was a workaholic—it was the only way to explain how he managed to pack more into two days than the average person did in a working week—and he liked it that way. 'In other words, not enough to keep you busy and out of mischief.'

He laughed. 'Exactly. I could do more TV work, I suppose, but I've talked to my agent and I agree with him that over-exposure would be a mistake. It's better to keep the series the length it is and leave people wanting more, rather than them seeing my face and thinking, Oh, no, not *him* again, and switching off. So I need something else to keep me occupied.'

'What about your articles?'

He shrugged. 'As you say, a desk job would drive me crazy. I need something with a lot of variety.'

'Lecturing, then? If you had tutorial groups as well, that'd give you the variety because your students would all be different.'

He wrinkled his nose. 'I've had offers, but to be honest I don't really want to teach.'

Isobel frowned. 'What's wrong with what you do now?'

'Nothing. I love freelancing. But I'm thirty-five, Bel. I need to be realistic about the future. In ten or twenty years I'm not going to want to spend hours at a time on my knees in a trench in the pouring rain. So I want to make the right career move now, while all my options are still wide open.'

It was a fair point, although Isobel thought Alex had enough strength of personality to make his own opportunities. She had a feeling there was a bit more to it than what he was telling her, but she couldn't work out what. A relationship that had gone wrong? Surely not, because Alex kept his relationships light and very casual and in all the years she'd known him she couldn't remember a girlfriend lasting more than half a dozen dates.

Maybe she was asking the wrong questions.

'I still don't understand where the married bit comes in.'

'Apparently, the guy who owns the company wants a married man for the job.'

She snorted. 'No way. That's discrimination. It's against the law, Alex.'

'They're not going to be able to ask me outright about my marital status,' he agreed. 'But it seems the last two guys they hired lasted all of six weeks before they got an offer they couldn't refuse for—I quote—a really glamorous dig abroad.'

They both laughed, knowing that real archaeology wasn't glamorous in the slightest. The stuff Alex did on TV accounted for a tiny fraction of the hard graft behind the scenes, and certainly didn't take account of being on your knees in a muddy trench for hour after hour, or the long gaps between finds.

'So third time around they want someone settled,' he continued. 'The word is they're looking for someone who'll commit to the project for at least two years. And, you know as well as I do, a married man's seen as more dependable than a single guy because he's already made a commitment.'

She flinched. 'Marriage doesn't always mean commitment.'

He winced. 'Sorry, honey. I didn't mean to rip open old wounds.'

'I know you didn't.' Alex didn't always think. Mainly because he did things at a hundred miles an hour and his head was stuffed full of the past—just like her own. Which was one of the reasons why she'd always got on so well with him.

He took her hand and squeezed it briefly. 'But you know what I mean. My reputation's going to count against me. The Hunter, a gypsy vagabond.'

She rolled her eyes. 'You're hardly a vagabond, Alex.' Even though he did have itchy feet and didn't tend to stay long in one place.

'But I'm part gypsy. My mother says I'm a throwback to her grandfather—'

'Who met your great-grandmother when she accompanied your great-great-grandfather to a dig in Egypt in the nineteen twenties, and your great-grandfather fell in love with her,' Isobel finished. She knew the story, and she'd always privately thought it really romantic.

Archaeology was in Alex's blood. And so too was the gypsy heritage. Which was why 'The Hunter' was his perfect screen persona: dressed in jeans with a white shirt, and a battered Akubra hat worn at a rakish angle, Alex Richardson made women swoon. That and his dark curls, his hair worn slightly too long, his exotic olive skin, and those piercing light grey eyes, completely unexpected with the rest of his colouring.

'Look, I've spent the last few years travelling the world. On digs or for the show, admittedly, but still travelling.'

'Which shows commitment to your job,' she pointed out.

'It's not *enough*.' He shook his head in apparent frustration. 'The series played me up as the sort who won't obey orders—a maverick who'll go his own way regardless.'

She couldn't argue with that. Besides, that was exactly what Alex was like—not that there was any point in telling him.

'So that's why I need a wife. To prove I'm settled.'

'I still think it's a crazy reason to get married. And why ask *me*?'

'I already told you. Because you're settled.'

That stung, and she couldn't help sniping, 'You mean I'm staid and boring.'

He laughed. 'No. Just I've known you for ever. You're the girl next door.'

'Strictly speaking, I haven't lived next door to you since I was thirteen and you went to Oxford,' she said dryly. 'Which is the best part of seventeen years ago.'

'You were still there when I came home for the holidays,' he reminded her.

The girl next door. As familiar as wallpaper. Alex hadn't noticed her as a *woman*.

At her continued silence, he sighed. 'Look, I never planned to get married. Archaeology's my life—just as the museum is yours. There isn't room in my life for another relationship.'

She raised an eyebrow.

He winced. 'Sorry, Bel. That came out wrong. Mouth in gear, brain not. What I mean is, if I'm going to get married, I want to marry someone I like a lot. Someone I've got a lot in common with. Someone I trust.'

It should've warmed her that he felt that way about her. Trusted her. Liked her a lot. Exactly the way she felt about him. But she couldn't help asking, 'What about love?'

He lifted one shoulder in a half-shrug. 'I don't believe in it.'

She knew where he was coming from. She didn't believe in love any more, either. She'd loved Gary, but it hadn't been enough to make their marriage work. Though at the same time, marriage without love seemed…wrong, somehow. 'All three of your sisters are married,' she remarked. 'And if they weren't happy and in love with their husbands—'

'I'd take their husbands apart,' he admitted. 'Very slowly. And remove their hearts with a rusty spoon.'

Although Alex rolled his Rs and his eyes, she wasn't sure that he was being entirely dramatic.

'But it's different for the girls.'

Sexism? From Alex? Now that she hadn't expected. 'Since when did you turn into a chauvinist?'

He frowned. 'I'm not. It's got nothing to do with gender. Just that…' he lifted one shoulder in a half-shrug '…I'm not like them.'

'So this marriage business—you're looking for someone you like, someone who shares your interests, and who's not going to tie you down.'

'I'm not planning to have a string of girlfriends or be unfaithful to my wife, if that's what you're asking.'

Alex dated a lot. Which meant he had a lot of sex. If he was giving that up…did that mean he was planning to have sex only with his wife?

With *her*?

Oh, Lord.

The last twelve years suddenly unravelled, back to when she'd been eighteen and Alex had kissed her. Just once. But what a 'once' it had been. He'd actually taken her breath away. For one mad moment she'd thought that Alex had noticed her—that instead of seeing her as just his little sister's best friend, the girl he'd known for years, he'd seen her as a soul mate. Someone who shared his interests. Someone he was attracted to. And then she'd realised he was being kind. Showing her that just because her rat of a boyfriend had dumped her, it didn't mean that she'd never be kissed again.

He'd even said as much. Said that she'd soon find someone else. Added that she had a whole world to conquer.

That kiss hadn't meant the same thing to him as it had to her. And Isobel was pretty sure things hadn't changed since then. Alex saw her as a friend—a close friend, but *just* as a friend.

So no way would this marriage work.

She couldn't do it.

She'd already ended up in one loveless marriage, and she really couldn't face starting another on the same basis. She dragged in a breath. 'I'm sorry, Alex. I can't marry you.'

CHAPTER TWO

ALEX schooled his features into neutral. 'Why not?'

'Because it's wrong to get married without loving each other.'

He flapped a dismissive hand. 'Of course I love you, Bel.'

'But not in *that* way, Alex. And I'm not putting myself through that again.'

Alex stared at her. 'Hang on. Are you telling me Gary didn't love you? That he was unfaithful to you?'

She shook her head. 'He didn't break his marriage vows, no. Let's just leave it that our marriage turned into a mess.'

She looked uncomfortable, and Alex knew Isobel wasn't telling him the whole story—but he also knew not to push her. She'd talk to him when she was ready. She always had.

'Though it didn't take him very long to find someone else.' Isobel dragged in a breath. 'His new partner's just had their first baby.'

That had clearly hurt her. He'd never asked Isobel why she'd split up with Gary—because it wasn't any of his business and he didn't want to rake open any painful wounds—but he'd always supposed that Gary had wanted a baby and she hadn't been prepared to make any compromises with the career she loved.

So had his guess been completely wrong? Was Isobel the one who'd wanted children?

No, of course not. She adored Saskia's daughter, Flora—her god-daughter and Alex's niece—but Alex had always assumed that it went with the territory of being Saskia's best friend. Isobel liked children, otherwise she wouldn't have been able to do her job—but she really, really loved what she did. A museum interpreter who worked with hands-on exhibits, dressing up as a Roman matron during school holidays or at weekends and giving cookery demonstrations and showing people what everyday life was like in Roman Britain, as well as working behind the scenes as a curator on the exhibitions that toured other museums.

So if it wasn't the baby, maybe she was upset because the baby signalled that things were well and truly over between her and Gary. That they could never go back to how things were.

According to his sister, Isobel had rarely dated since her marriage ended two years ago, so maybe she was still in love with Gary. Alex had never thought Gary was good enough for her—for starters, the man had a feeble handshake and no imagination—but he also didn't like seeing Isobel hurt and miserable. 'Come here.' He slid his arms round her and held her close. 'I'm sorry.'

'What for?'

'That it didn't work out for you. That he let you down.' He stroked her hair. 'I know it's probably not what you want to hear, but he was never good enough for you.'

'But he didn't ask me to marry him just because I'm staid and sensible.'

Alex pulled back slightly and looked her in the eye. 'I asked you because I want this job and being a married man is going to give me the edge I need.'

'Rubbish. You can talk your way into anything.'

'Apart from getting you to marry me, you mean,' he parried. 'And you didn't let me finish. Whatever I said about you being sensible—which you are—the main reason I asked you is because you're my friend. I've known you for years and years. I enjoy your company and I trust you. And that's a much, much stronger basis for a marriage than being "in love" with someone.' Thinking of Dorinda, Alex curled his lip. She'd been his biggest mistake ever. And she'd taught him all about the misery of love. A lesson that meant he wasn't going to repeat that mistake. 'Being "in love" is just temporary. It's hormonal. Whereas what we've got has a much more solid foundation and it's not going to change.'

'Isn't it? Because that's what worries me, Alex.' She bit her lip. 'I don't want to lose your friendship when it all goes pear-shaped.'

He sighed. 'Apart from the fact that it's not going to go pear-shaped, things aren't going to change between us.'

'How do you know? Unless you're talking about a marriage in name only—and as you said you weren't planning to have a string of girlfriends, I have to assume you're…' Her voice tailed off and she actually blushed.

He'd never seen her colour like that before.

And even though he knew he wasn't playing fair, he couldn't resist teasing her. 'Assume what, Bel?'

'That getting married means having sex with each other.' Her flush deepened.

Alex felt as if his skin were suddenly burning, too. *Sex with Isobel.* Right now, he was holding her. Loosely, admittedly, but he was still holding her. All he had to do was move forward a fraction, dip his head, and he could kiss her.

His mouth went dry.

He could remember the last time he'd kissed her, other than

the usual peck on the cheeks that accompanied their welcoming hugs when they hadn't seen each other for a while. The night she'd come round to their house, crying her eyes out because her boyfriend had dumped her for someone more glamorous and less studious, and he'd answered the door. Saskia had been out, so he'd taken Isobel into the summer house in their garden for a heart-to-heart. He'd told her that the boyfriend was an idiot and it didn't matter because there was a whole world out there just waiting for her to conquer it.

And he'd kissed her.

Just once.

Before remembering that Isobel was eighteen to his twenty-three, much less worldly-wise, and he really shouldn't be kissing her like that.

Now he wondered what would've happened if he'd kissed her a second time. Would they have ended up making love in the summer house? Would he have been the one to introduce her to the pleasures of love-making?

And what shocked him even more was that his body was reacting even now at the thought of it.

Making love with Isobel.

He became aware that she was speaking.

'And besides, I'm not your type.'

'I don't have a type,' Alex protested.

'Yes, you do. You always go for tall, skinny brunettes with legs up to their armpits.'

'You have dark hair.' The colour of a chestnut that had just slipped out of its prickly case, it was soft and silky when he ran his fingers through it. 'And you're not short.' She was curvy rather than skinny, though with three younger sisters he knew much better than to discuss a woman's weight or body shape.

'I'm five feet four. That makes me slightly shorter than the average woman.'

He smiled at her. 'It also makes you two inches taller than the average Roman woman in the fourth century.'

She rolled her eyes. 'Trust *you* to know that.'

He laughed. 'Actually, you were the one who told me. When you were researching your first talk about Roman women.'

She stared at him in obvious surprise. 'You remember that?'

'Course I do. We must have sat up half the night talking about it. Well, after I'd bored the pants off you with all those photographs of the dig I'd just come back from.'

'I wasn't bored.'

'See? We have things in common. Lots of things. And we like each other. Getting married would work, Bel.'

The colour was back in her cheeks, even deeper this time. 'Supposing we're not, um, compatible?'

'Compatible?'

'In bed,' she muttered. 'What if I'm rubbish at sex?'

'If that's what Gary said, he clearly wasn't doing it right— and his ego made him blame you.'

'Mmm.'

'Look at me, Bel,' he said softly. She had huge brown eyes that had topaz glints when she laughed, and a perfect rosebud mouth. Why had he never really noticed that before? 'I think we'd be…' he paused as his heart gave an unexpected kick '…compatible.'

'I can't believe we're even discussing this!' She pulled back from him. 'So why didn't you ever get married, Alex?'

He let her go. 'Because my job meant a lot of travelling— and that meant either living apart from my wife most of the time, or dragging her around the world with me. Neither option's a fair one.'

'And you never met anyone who made you want to stay in one place?'

Once, but that had been a long time ago. In the days when he'd still worn rose-coloured glasses. Before he'd discovered that Dorinda was a liar and a cheat and had played everyone for a fool, including him. Since then, he'd never quite been able to trust anyone. He'd held back in his relationships, unwilling to risk his heart again and have it ground beneath a stiletto heel. Keeping things light and fun had worked for him, until now. 'I told you, I don't believe in love. But I do believe in friendship. In honesty. And if you marry me, Bel, I'll be a good husband to you.' A much better one than Gary had been.

'I can't get married. Ask someone else.'

There wasn't anyone else he'd trust enough to marry. He shrugged. 'Look, forget I asked. Come on, I'm taking you out to dinner.'

'Why?'

He rolled his eyes. 'It's not an ulterior motive. You've said no and I'm not going to bully you into saying yes. Bel, you're putting me up for a few days, so taking you out for dinner to say thank you is the least I can do.'

'Alex, you don't need to do that. You know I never mind you staying here.'

He smiled. 'I know. But I like having dinner out with you. I like talking history and arguing over interpretations and laughing too much and eating half your pudding—because I'm greedy and you're always nice to me.'

She rolled her eyes. 'You're impossible.'

'Uh-huh.' But to his relief she was smiling and relaxed with him again. 'Is that Moroccan place we went to last time still open?'

'I think so.'

'Good. Let's go.'

* * *

It always surprised Isobel slightly that Alex liked taking the tube rather than a taxi. Then again, on the tube people were careful not to catch anyone's eye, so although he'd probably be recognised it was unlikely that someone would ask for an autograph or a photograph with him taken with the camera on their mobile phone. Besides, without the hat, people were more likely to think he was a guy who just happened to look like the archaeologist from the show, rather than being the man himself.

It was practically impossible to talk on the tube; there were just too many people squashed onto the train. During late spring and summer, rush hour seemed to last a lot longer; the office workers crushing onto the train were quickly replaced by tourists.

Isobel wasn't sure whether it made her more relieved or uptight—or both at the same time. Relieved, because she didn't have to make eye contact or conversation with Alex. And uptight, because it gave her time to think about what he'd said.

Getting married—to Alex.

Having sex—with Alex.

Oh, Lord.

She'd enjoyed her friendship with Alex. She always had. And she'd married Gary because she'd loved him.

But a little bit of her had always wondered: what if Alex hadn't had his string of glamorous girlfriends? What if he'd repeated that kiss when she was twenty-one? What if she'd ended up with Alex instead of Gary?

Panic skittered through her. She had to be insane even to be considering this. Marriage wouldn't work. She'd had one serious relationship before Gary, so she was hardly experienced—whereas Alex had practically had a girlfriend at every dig, not to mention the ones in between. She'd never be able to live up to his expectations.

His words echoed in her head. *I enjoy your company and I trust you. And that's a much, much stronger basis for a marriage than being 'in love' with someone.*

Was he right? Were friendship and trust a better basis for a marriage than love and desire? Should she have said yes?

A note appeared in front of her eyes. In Alex's spiky, confident handwriting.

'Stop brooding. "Dinner" means dinner.'

The last word was in capitals and underlined three times.

She faced him. Sorry, she mouthed.

He smiled, and it gave her a weird sensation—as if her heart had just done a somersault. Which was anatomically impossible and completely ridiculous. Especially as, at the age of thirty, she was way, way past the teenage heartthrob stage.

And then it was their stop.

The crowds of people swirling round them meant it was still impossible to talk. But she was aware that Alex was behind her on the escalator. So close she could have leaned back against him.

What would it be like to feel Alex's arms round her?

What would it be like to feel his hands against her bare skin?

What would it be like to feel his mouth touching her body intimately?

'OK?' he asked when they were through the ticket barrier and standing outside on the street.

'Fine.'

'Liar.' He caught her hand and squeezed it briefly.

The lightest contact…and it sent a shiver all the way through her. Woke nerve-endings she'd forgotten she had.

No.

It wasn't possible for her to feel like this about Alex. And even thinking about it meant she was storing up trouble for herself. She'd loved Gary. Deeply. But it hadn't stopped everything going wrong. So she had to keep some kind of distance between herself and Alex, not let her heart get involved.

Or her libido.

'I'm not lying,' she mumbled, but she didn't look him in the eye until they got to the Moroccan restaurant.

Alex insisted on holding the door open for her. 'I don't care if it offends your feminist nature. It's good manners and it's how I was brought up,' he informed her.

It was how she'd been brought up, too. 'Thank you,' she said, meaning it.

Stepping inside the restaurant was like stepping out of London and into a souk. The air smelled of cinnamon and cardamom, and the décor was as beautiful as she remembered it; the walls were painted shades of saffron and terracotta and deep red, there were rich silks everywhere, the wrought iron chairs were covered with bright silk cushions toning with the walls, and the silk hanging from the ceiling gave the place the effect of being in some rich prince's tent. Tea-light candles flickered on the glass tabletops, and rose petals were scattered everywhere.

The waiter ushered them to the table and handed them each a menu.

'Red wine OK with you?' Alex asked, glancing down the menu.

'Fine.'

'Good. *Meze* to start, I think. Anything in particular you fancy?'

'I'll let you choose.' Not that she wasn't capable of choosing her own meal, but she knew how much Alex enjoyed it. And, as he'd said, his tastes were very similar to her own, so she knew she'd like whatever he chose.

'What do you want for your main course?'

'Chicken tagine. The one with preserved lemons.'

'I think I'll have the same. We'll choose pudding later,' Alex decided.

And after pudding…he'd go home with her.

And if she'd said yes to his proposal, he would have taken her to bed. Proved how compatible they were.

Her concentration went completely, and she was reduced to saying, 'Mmm,' and nodding in the right places as Alex talked to her about the dig he'd been on in Turkey before his return to London. And it was even worse when the *meze* arrived—a selection of dishes to share. Traditionally, Moroccan food was eaten with fingers and pitta bread was used to scoop up the dips, and every time she reached for one of the stuffed vine leaves or the aubergine and cumin dip or the felafel, her fingers brushed against Alex's. In the past, it wouldn't have bothered her, but tonight the lightest contact made her tingle. A sensual awareness that spread through every part of her body and made her wish that she'd been wearing a thick concealing sweater rather than a thin T-shirt that revealed her body's reaction to his touch.

If Alex said one word about being able to see her nipples, she'd kill him.

She ate her chicken tagine in silence.

And then Alex sighed.

'Would it really be so bad?'

'What?'

'Going to bed with me.'

She felt the colour shoot into her face. 'Alex!'

'You've been quiet ever since I suggested getting married.'

And having sex. 'It's just…I never thought about you in

that way before.' It wasn't the strict truth, but she didn't want him thinking that she'd been secretly lusting after him. Their friendship had been genuine.

'Not ever? Not even when you were...I dunno... eighteen?'

When she was eighteen? The only time she remembered him kissing her on the mouth. 'No.' She looked curiously at him. Did he remember that, too? And was he saying that, all those years ago, he had seen her as more than just the girl next door? 'Did you?'

'Not when I was eighteen—of course not.' He flapped a dismissive hand. 'Bel, you were still a child when I was eighteen. And when you were eighteen and I was twenty-three, there was still a huge gap between us.' He paused. 'But now you're thirty and I'm thirty-five. The gap's not there any more.'

She knew she was going to regret asking, but she couldn't help the question. 'And?'

'And...' he paused '...I'm thinking about you in that way right now.'

There was a gleam in his eyes she'd never seen before. A purely masculine gleam that told her he was interested in her. As a woman, not as a friend.

Her breath hitched. 'Oh.'

'You're thinking about it, too, aren't you?' he asked, his voice sounding husky.

'Yes,' she admitted, before she could stop herself.

'Good,' he said softly. 'Hold on to that thought.'

It still seemed like some weird parallel universe. The idea of becoming Alex's lover. Yesterday it would've been unthinkable. Today...the possibilities sent heat all the way down her spine.

She found it hard to concentrate when the waiter offered

them the dessert menu, and eventually went for the safe option: *bagrir*, a light pancake served with honey and ice cream and nuts. Alex, just as she could have predicted, went for the selection of chocolate and cardamom ice cream.

'Oh, yes. Best ever,' Alex said when he tasted it. 'Open your mouth.'

Oh, Lord. The pictures that put in her mind.

It must have shown in her expression, because she saw colour bloom along his cheekbones. 'I meant, you have to try this. And it's the cardamom one—I know you loathe chocolate ice cream.'

So he wanted her to lean forward and accept a morsel from his spoon? But her T-shirt was V-necked. Leaning across the table would give Alex a full-on view of her cleavage.

The thought made her nipples tighten even more.

'Bel, it's melting. Hurry up.' He held the spoon out towards her.

She leaned across the table. Opened her mouth. Let him brush the cold, cold spoon against her lower lip before she ate the morsel of ice cream.

'Good?' he asked.

She had a feeling he didn't mean just the ice cream.

'Good,' she whispered.

He smiled—a warm, sensual smile that made her catch her breath.

'My turn,' he said.

They'd done this so many times before—shared a pudding, tasted each other's meals, filched buttered toast from each other's plates or a swig from each other's mug of coffee with an ease born of long familiarity.

But tonight it was different.

Tonight they were feeding each other like lovers.

And when he ate the proffered piece of her *bagrir*, she could see that he looked as distracted as she felt.

She had no idea how they got through the rest of their dessert, or the mint tea afterwards. Or when Alex had ordered a taxi, because one was waiting for them outside practically as soon as he'd paid the bill.

He didn't say anything on the way back to her flat; he simply curled his fingers round her own—reassuring and yet incredibly exciting at the same time.

Holding hands with Alex was something she'd never really done. She was used to him giving her a friendly hug—almost a brotherly hug. But there was nothing remotely fraternal in the way he was holding her hand right at that moment. His touch was gentle—and yet firm enough so that she could feel the blood beating through his veins, in perfect time with her own.

When the taxi pulled up outside her building, Alex paid the driver and opened the car door for her. Isobel's hands were shaking slightly and she fumbled the entry code for the security system; it took her three goes to press the right buttons in the right order. By the time she unlocked her front door, she was a nervous wreck.

Alex paused, leaning against the doorway. 'Bel, let me reassure you that I'm planning to sleep on your sofa tonight. I'm not going to push you into anything you don't want to do.'

That was what worried her most: what she wanted to do. The more she thought about sex with Alex, the more she was tempted to do it.

Except she didn't want to risk ruining their friendship.

And she definitely didn't want to tell him her deepest, darkest secret—the thing she'd only told Saskia after extracting a promise from her best friend that Saskia wouldn't tell anyone else and wouldn't ever talk about it again.

She couldn't possibly marry Alex. Even though she was

pretty sure he didn't want children, what if he changed his mind? If anyone had asked her before today, she would've said straight out that Alex would never get married. And yet today he'd asked her to marry him. Tomorrow he might want to start a family. Something she wasn't sure she could do.

Her worries must have shown on her face, because he said softly, 'Have I ever let you down before?'

'No.'

'That's not going to change.'

Maybe. But if she married him, she'd be letting him down. Taking a choice away without telling him. Which was morally wrong.

Even though she knew she was being a coward, she muttered, 'I've got a bit of a headache. I need an early night.'

'I'll make sure I don't disturb you. Do you want me to bring you a glass of water and some paracetamol?'

'Thanks, but I'll manage. I'd better sort the sofa bed out for you.'

'I'll do it.' He reached out to stroke her cheek. 'See you in the morning, Bel. Hope you get some sleep.'

CHAPTER THREE

TRUE to his word, Alex didn't disturb her. And when Isobel got up the next morning he'd already put the sofa bed back to rights, tidied up and made coffee.

'Morning. How's your head?'

'Better, thanks.' The fib had blossomed into the truth, and she'd ended up taking paracetamol.

'Here.' He passed her a mug of coffee—hot, strong and milky, exactly the way she liked it. 'Toast?'

'Yes, please.' She sat down at the little bistro table in the kitchen. This was the Alex she knew best. Her friend who knew her so well that he could practically read her mind. Though usually she was the one making toast and he was the one filching it from her plate.

'So what are you doing today?' he asked.

'Roman kitchens,' she said. 'How about you?'

He joined her at the table after he'd switched on the toaster. 'A bit of research.'

But nothing that really excited him, from the flatness of his tone. And he still seemed faintly subdued when she left for work.

Alex really needed a new challenge, she thought. Like the job he'd told her about yesterday; his eyes had been almost pure silver with excitement when he'd described it. But she still didn't see how getting married would make any difference to whether he got the job. There was no reason for her to feel even slightly guilty about turning down his proposal. She'd done the right thing for both of them.

Though she couldn't stop thinking about him all day. And when she walked in her front door that evening and smelled something gorgeous cooking, guilt bloomed. 'Alex, I didn't expect you to cook for me.'

'No worries.' He shrugged. 'It's as easy to cook for two as it is for one.'

She scoffed. 'You mean, you were that bored.'

He handed her a glass of red wine. 'Go away and let me have my mid-life crisis in peace.'

'It's my flat. I'm not going anywhere.' But she sat down at the table. 'What mid-life crisis? Alex, you're thirty-five. That's hardly middle-aged. And you don't have a conventional desk job, so you can't exactly take a six-month sabbatical and grow your hair and ride a motorbike round the world in search of adventure. That's what you *do* for a day job, for goodness' sake!'

'I don't have a motorbike.'

'Don't nit-pick. What I mean is, for you to do the opposite of what you normally do, you'd have to cut your hair short and get an office job and wear a suit and date the same person for more than three consecutive evenings. For most people, your life would be an adventure.' She looked at him. 'What mid-life crisis, anyway?'

He wrinkled his nose and turned away to pour himself a glass of wine. 'Just forget I said anything.'

She shook her head. 'You've been quiet for you, today. Something's obviously bothering you. Come and sit down and talk to me.'

'I'm busy cooking dinner.'

She sniffed. 'Chicken casseroled in red wine, baked potatoes and salad?'

He smiled wryly. 'All right. So most of the cooking's already done. How did you know what I was cooking, anyway?'

'Apart from the fact it's your signature dish? Educated guess,' she said dryly. 'You just emptied that bottle into a clean glass.'

'I could've been swigging straight from the bottle,' he pointed out.

They both laughed, then he shrugged. 'Anyway, I've been quiet because this is what happens when I have too much time on my hands. I start thinking—and that's dangerous.'

'Talk to me, Alex,' she said softly. 'What's wrong?'

'This is going to sound mad.'

'Tell me anyway.'

He sighed and joined her at the table. 'I'm thirty-five, Bel. My little sisters are all settled, married with a family. All the people I was at university with have settled down—some of them are on their second marriage, admittedly, but they're settled. And although I love my life, I'm starting to wonder if what I've got is really enough for me any more. If it's what I really want.'

'So you're saying you want to settle down and have children?' Isobel asked carefully.

'Yes. No. Maybe.' He took a sip of wine. 'I suppose what I'm saying is that I'm starting to think about what I do now. I'm doing something about my job, but what about the rest of my life? Do I want be one of these eternal bachelors who still behave as if they're in their twenties when they're pushing sixty?'

She smiled. 'I can't quite see you doing *that*, Alex.' He'd still be immensely charming when he was almost sixty. He'd still turn heads. But he'd also have dignity and wouldn't try to pretend he was still young.

'But time goes by so fast, Bel. It seems like yesterday that Helen had the boys, and now they're seven. Next thing I know, I'm going to be forty-five and I'll be the spare man invited to dinner parties to make up the numbers, sitting next to the woman who's just got divorced and either hates all men or is desperate for company.'

She frowned. 'Alex, this isn't like you. And this whole thing about looking to the future…oh, my God.' A seriously nasty thought clicked into place. The reason why he suddenly wanted to settle down. 'Is there something you're not telling anybody?'

'Such as?'

Well, if he wasn't going to say it, she would. This needed to be out in the open. Right now. She swallowed hard. 'You're seriously ill?'

For a moment, there was an unreadable expression on his face, and Isobel felt panic ice its way down her spine. Please, no. Not this.

'I'm fine. In perfect health,' he told her. 'But I did hear some bad news about a close friend while I was on my last dig.'

Someone else. Not Alex. Relief flooded through her, followed by a throb of guilt. Bad news was still bad news. 'I hope your friend's OK now.'

He shook his head. 'He didn't make it. It didn't seem right, standing at Andy's graveside only a couple of years after I'd been in that same church for his wedding. He's the first one of my friends to die, and it's made me realise how short life can be. How I shouldn't take things for granted. And I got to thinking, maybe it's time I did something about settling down.' He looked thoughtful. 'That's one of the things I really liked about the specifications for this job. There's enough travelling to stop me getting itchy feet, but not so much that I can't have a family life as well. It's the best of both worlds.'

A family life.

So he *did* want children.

Which meant, Isobel thought, that he needed to marry someone who could definitely have children—not someone who had a huge question mark hanging over her. After her miscarriages, the doctor had reassured her that the statistics were all on her side, that plenty of women went on to have healthy babies afterwards. Miscarriages were so common that the hospital wouldn't even begin to look into the causes until a woman had had at least three.

But Gary hadn't wanted to take the risk. He hadn't wanted to stick around and wait.

And although Alex wasn't like Gary—she knew he had the integrity to stand by her—he wanted a family. Something she might not be able to give him.

Telling him the truth was out of the question. If she did, she'd see pity in his face and she'd feel that she was no longer his equal. No way did she want that to happen.

But not telling him… If he was serious about settling down, if he'd meant that proposal and intended to ask her again, she'd have to refuse. It wouldn't be fair to accept. If it did turn out that she couldn't carry a baby to term, that she couldn't have children…she didn't want their relationship to go the same way as her marriage had. Down the tubes.

She pushed the thoughts away. This wasn't about her. It was about him. 'Hey, you'll be a shoo-in for the job. And once you actually stay in one place for more than three seconds, you'll find Ms Right,' she said brightly.

She suppressed the wish that it could've been her.

They spent the rest of the evening talking shop, the way

they always did. And Alex behaved the next morning as if everything was just fine, so she followed his lead and pretended he hadn't opened his heart to her, the previous night.

She'd been at her desk for an hour when a courier arrived. Odd. She wasn't expecting a delivery. But when she opened the parcel, she discovered a box of seriously good chocolates. And there was a note in familiar spiky script: *'Thanks for listening.'*

Alex might be a whirlwind, but he never took anything for granted.

She flicked into her email program.

Thanks for the chocs. Unnecessary but very, very nice. Bel x

A few moments later, her monitor beeped. Mail from Alex.

Least I could do. Don't eat them all at once.

Ha. As if she would. She smiled, and carried on with the report she was writing.

A few moments later, her monitor beeped again.

Doing anything tonight?

Nothing special. Why?

It was a while before he responded. And then:

Consider your evening annexed. Meet you from work. What time do you finish today?

Six. Do I need to change first?

If you're dressed as Flavia, yes! Otherwise, fine as you are. Ciao. A x

Which told her absolutely nothing about what he had planned. Typical Alex.

But she was busy and it was easier to go along with him, so she didn't push the issue.

He was waiting for her in the foyer at six, wearing a casual shirt and dark trousers and looking absolutely edible. For a moment, her heart actually skipped a beat.

But this wasn't a date. This was just two friends meeting up while one of them was briefly in London. The fact that he was staying with her was by the by. They weren't living together and it wasn't that kind of relationship.

And that marriage proposal hadn't been a real one. She really needed to get a grip.

'Hi.' His smile did seriously strange things to her insides, and she strove for cool.

'Hi, yourself. Good day?'

'Not bad.' He slid a casual arm round her shoulders and ushered her down the steps. 'How was yours?'

'Fine.' She was glad her voice wasn't as shaky as she felt. This was crazy. She and Alex had always had a tactile relationship. So how come this didn't feel like his usual hug?

'Good. You hungry?'

She grinned. 'Considering I've been eating chocolate all day…'

'What, and you didn't even save one for me?'

She laughed. 'No. But I did share them in the office.'

'Hmm. So was that a yes or no to food first?'

'Food before what?'

'Before…' He took his arm from her shoulders, fished in his pocket for his wallet, then removed two tickets and handed them to her.

She felt her eyes widen. Two tickets to that evening's performance of *Much Ado about Nothing* at the Globe. The best

seats in the house. 'These are like gold dust, Alex!' And to
get them at short notice he must've paid a fortune to one of
the ticket agencies.

'I wanted to see the play, and it's more fun going with
someone who actually enjoys it, too.'

'At least let me pay for my own ticket.'

'No. But you can buy me a drink in the interval, if you
insist.'

'I do insist.'

'"My dear Lady Disdain,"' he teased.

'I did that play for A level,' she reminded him.

'I know.' He rolled his eyes. 'I used to have to listen to you
and Saskia murdering it in the summer house when I was
home in the holidays.'

'Murdering it?' She cuffed his arm. 'I'll tell her that, next
time I talk to her. And then you'll be in trouble.'

'No, I won't. I'm her favourite brother.'

'Her only brother,' Isobel corrected.

'Still her favourite,' Alex said. 'So. Food first or later?'

She glanced at her watch and at the time on the ticket.
'Better make it later. Unless you want to grab something
from a fast-food place?'

'I'd rather wait and have something decent.'

'Later it is, then.'

The tube was so crowded again that they didn't get a chance
to talk on the way over to Southwark. And the bar at the
Globe was so crowded that they were forced to sit incredibly
close together to have any chance of hearing each other speak.

Odd.

Alex was used to touching Isobel—giving her a hug hello
and a kiss on the cheek when they said goodbye—but this was
different. Now, he was aware of her in another way. Of the

softness of her skin. Of the sweet scent of her perfume—a mixture of jasmine and vanilla and orange blossom. Of the shape of her mouth.

And it shocked him how much he suddenly wanted to kiss her.

'Alex?'

'Sorry. It's a bit noisy in here. I can barely hear you.' Acting on an impulse he knew was going to land him in trouble, but he was unable to resist, he scooped her onto his lap.

'Alex!'

She was protesting—but she slid one arm round his neck to stop herself falling off his lap.

'It's easier to hear you if you talk straight into my ear,' he said, his mouth millimetres from her own ear. 'That way you don't have to shout. And I don't get backache from leaning down to you.'

She cuffed him with her free hand. 'That's below the belt.'

And maybe this hadn't been such a good idea. Because the whisper of her breath against his ear sent a peculiar sensation down his spine. A feeling he really didn't want to acknowledge.

He took refuge in teasing. 'I apologise… Shorty.'

'Huh.' She rolled her eyes.

He knew she wasn't upset with him; this was the kind of banter they'd always indulged in. The kind of banter that was safe because their friendship was deep and it had been practically lifelong.

When she'd finished her glass of wine, he glanced at his watch. 'We'd better find our seats.'

'Sure.' She slid off his lap, and Alex was shocked to discover he actually missed the warmth of her body against his.

The production was fantastic. And as soon as Benedick

spoke his 'dear Lady Disdain' line, Alex glanced at Isobel—
to see her glancing straight back at him. He curled his fingers
round hers, acknowledging that he knew what she was remembering. To his pleasure, she didn't pull away. But all the
way through the play, when Beatrice and Benedick were
fencing verbally, he found himself thinking of himself and
Isobel.

*'I do love nothing in the world so well as you. Is not that
strange?'*

His fingers involuntarily tightened for a moment round hers.
This was crazy.

Of course he wasn't in love with Isobel. She was his *friend*.

But it didn't alter the fact that he was holding her hand.
Treating this like a date, when it wasn't one at all.

He needed to regain his composure.

But for the life of him he couldn't let her hand go.

At the end of the play, he released her hand so they could
clap. And his arm was only round her on the way out of the
theatre so he could protect her from the crowds.

At dinner afterwards, they chatted animatedly about the
play until their meal arrived.

'Next time we'll have to take Saskia as well,' he said. 'And
Mum—if she's up to it.'

'How is she?' Isobel asked.

'You know my mother. She almost never admits to feeling
under the weather.' He sighed. 'This lupus thing... I worry
about her.'

Isobel reached across the table and squeezed his hand.
'She'll be fine, Alex. Saskia was telling me about it—I know
they haven't found a cure for lupus, yet, but they can keep it
under control with medication.'

'But it's going to take a while for them to find the right
treatment to help her.' Alex grimaced. 'I've read up on it. I

was in Turkey when Helen rang me and told me—and although I came home straight away, a snatched weekend here and there isn't enough. I need to be around a bit more. Living in the same country as my family would be a start.' He smiled wryly. 'I'm not planning to move back in with my parents, because I'm used to doing things my own way and I'd drive them crazy, not fitting in with their routines—but I want to do my bit. It's not fair to leave everything to the girls. I'm the oldest, and our parents are *my* responsibility.'

Isobel raised an eyebrow. 'I think your parents would say they're their own responsibility.'

'Maybe.' Alex frowned. 'Mum's putting a brave face on things but I know she hates it when I'm away so much, and she worries every time she turns on the news and hears of some kind of political unrest which might be somewhere near wherever I am at the time. It's extra stress she doesn't need.'

'Alex, it's not your fault she's got lupus.'

'No?' He raised an eyebrow. 'It's stress-related.'

'And my money's on most of the stress being caused by her job. Saskia says she's been feeling a lot better since she changed her hours and went part-time.'

'Even so, it doesn't help if she's worried about me.'

'She'll be pleased about your new job, then,' Isobel said.

'Hey, I'm not quite arrogant enough to count my chickens—I know I'm in the running, but if they decide that my career to date makes me too much of a risk, that I'll stay in the job for all of five minutes and then leave them in the lurch when I get a better offer…' He shrugged. 'Well, something else'll turn up.'

She frowned. 'Alex, do you actually have to be married to make them think you're settled, or would being engaged be enough?'

He thought about it. 'Engaged would probably be enough.'

* * *

Alex needed her. And of course she wanted to help him. He was too proud to ask her again, she knew, so there was only one thing she could do. 'Alex. I want to help you. I really want you to get this job and be happy.' She took a deep breath. If she got engaged to him, it wasn't the same as being married, was it? It wasn't the same as tying him down to someone who might not be able to give him what he wanted in life. 'Look, if we get engaged—after you get the job we can quietly break off the engagement and go back to being how we are now.' And because they weren't getting married, she wouldn't have to tell him the truth about herself—about the miscarriages. Everything would be just fine.

'You'd get engaged to me?'

'Until you get the job, yes. If it'd help.'

She could see the relief in his eyes. 'Thank you, Bel. I really appreciate this.' He took her hand, raised it to his mouth and kissed her palm before folding her fingers over where his lips had touched her skin. 'Any time I can return the favour, do something for you, you know I will.'

'Hey. That's what friends are for,' she said, striving for lightness despite the fact that the touch of his mouth had sent desire zinging through her veins.

Though his words made her heart ache. Yes, there was something Alex could do for her. But it wasn't going to happen, so there was no point in even letting herself think about it. A real marriage and babies weren't on his agenda. Besides, the fact that Gary had a baby now proved that the problem was with her, not him.

'To you,' Alex said, lifting his glass. 'My lucky charm.'

'What was that you were saying about not counting your chickens?' she asked wryly.

'With you by my side,' Alex said, 'I could conquer the world.'

Oh, help. He sounded serious. She reverted to some child-hood teasing. 'Alexander the Great, hmm?'

He laughed. 'Hey. I'm not going to make you change your name to Roxana. Though if you really want to…'

'No, thanks!'

'And this is an engagement of convenience.'

'Exactly. Until you get the job. Which you will.' She raised her own glass. 'To you.'

'To us,' he corrected. 'And to teamwork.'

'Teamwork,' she echoed.

CHAPTER FOUR

ALEX spent the weekend in the Cotswolds visiting his parents, and Isobel was shocked at how much she missed him, how empty the flat seemed without him.

Don't get too used to this, she warned herself. Alex would move out once he'd got the job and decided where to settle. If he decided to move back to his own flat, he might stay for his tenants' notice period, but he wouldn't stay any longer than that. And their engagement was one of convenience, which wouldn't last very long; there was no point in getting a ring.

She went out for a long walk on Hampstead Heath on the Sunday; when she let herself back into the flat, she was surprised to see Alex already there. And she was furious with herself for the fact that her heart actually missed a beat. 'You're back early,' she said, keeping her voice deliberately light.

He looked grim. 'Mmm.'

There was only one thing she could think of that would've made him look so upset. 'Is your mum all right?'

'She's fine.'

'Then what's wrong?'

He raked a hand through his hair. 'Things didn't go quite according to plan.'

'How do you mean?'

He sucked in a breath. 'I took my parents out to lunch today. I was telling Mum about the job—and that you'd agreed to be my temporary fiancée, to give me the right profile. Except she didn't hear the word "temporary".' He sighed deeply. 'She thinks we're really getting married, Bel. And her face… She looked so happy. As if a huge weight had been lifted from her. I just didn't have the heart to correct her—not in the middle of the Partridge, anyway. I was going to wait until we were back home and then explain without having an audience listening in. But then I got out of the car and Dad was shaking my hand and slapping me on the back and telling me how pleased he was that I was finally settling down and about time it was too—and the next thing I knew, my mum had already gone next door to see your mum.'

Isobel blinked. 'Marcia told my mum we were engaged?'

'And Saskia. And Helen. And Polly. And half the street. I've only just managed to persuade her not to stick a notice in the local paper.' He looked rueful. 'I tried to ring your mobile to warn you, but your voicemail told me your phone was unavailable—and your landline went straight through to your answering machine.'

'I went out for a walk—I must've been in a bad reception area.'

'I sent you a couple of texts. Maybe they went AWOL.'

Or maybe she'd accidentally left her phone in silent mode. She took it out of her bag and checked the screen. There were three messages from Alex, all telling her to ring him urgently and not to listen to any of the messages on her answering machine until he got back to London.

She glanced at the answering machine. 'Messages.' The light was still flashing, so clearly he hadn't listened to them.

'I'm really sorry, Bel.'

'Better find out what they have to say.' She pressed 'play'. The first message was from Alex. 'Houston, we have a problem. Call me when you can—and if you've got other messages on the machine after this, don't take any notice of them, OK? I'll explain everything when I get back.'

Next was her mother. 'Bel, Marcia just told me. It's fantastic news—but why didn't you tell me yourself, love? Get your diary and call me when you're back. Your dad and I want to take you both out to dinner to celebrate. Love you.'

Then it was Alex's mother. 'Bel, we're so pleased to hear the news—I wish Alex had waited until you were back from your course, so you could've told us together, but I know what my son's like. He can't wait for anything. See you soon, love. And we're *so* pleased. We couldn't have hoped for a better daughter-in-law.'

And then Saskia. 'Oh, my God, you're actually going to be my sister! Isobel Martin, how could you keep something like *this* quiet? And from *me*, of all people! Ring me the second you get this. I want *details*.' She laughed. 'And congratulations. This is brilliant. It's the best news I've heard all year.'

Isobel sat down and looked at Alex. 'Oh, blimey. They're all so pleased.'

'I know.'

'And *what* course? Why does your mother think I'm on a course?'

He lifted a hand in protest. 'She asked why you weren't with me to share the news. I had to think on my feet. So I said the first thing that came into my head—that you were on a course. Which I know was a lie, and I know you hate lying, but what else could I do?'

'You could've told them the truth.'

'How?' He sighed. 'I've been racking my brain all the way

here to work out how to fix this. Look, if you don't mind going along with it for a while, then we can say I've done something terrible—I dunno, got drunk and disgraced you and gone off with another woman at a party or something— and you can break off the engagement in high dudgeon. And then we can just go back to normal.'

She shook her head. 'Alex, that's a hideously bad idea— it'll hurt everyone. Your parents will never forgive you if they think you've treated me badly, mine will never forgive you either, and it'll cause rifts all over the place. And I'm not going to tell even more lies. It's enough of a mess as it is.'

'Bel, you heard them all. They're delighted that we're together. It's as if we've given them Christmas, a milestone birthday and a huge lottery win all rolled into one. If I tell them the truth, they'll be so disappointed, so upset that it's not happening. At least if we tell them it didn't work out, it'll let them down gently.'

'By you being unfaithful? That's hardly being gentle, Alex.'

'Then I hope you've got a better idea, because I can't think of any other way.'

Her mind had gone completely blank. 'I can't, either,' she admitted.

'Mum said she wondered how long it would take me to see what was right under my nose, and she's glad I finally realised.' He raked his hand through his hair. 'She thinks I've been in love with you secretly since for ever.'

'Of course you haven't.' Isobel shifted guiltily. Though could she say the same for herself? The fact that she could still re-member how a kiss had felt twelve years ago…' This is crazy.'

'And it's my fault. I'm sorry, Bel.' He looked grim. 'I'm just going to have to call everyone and put them straight. I apologise if it's going to cause any awkwardness for you.'

'Hey. I'll get over it,' she said lightly.

'I just hate bursting Mum's bubble. Especially as Saskia called me on my way back here and told me it's the brightest she's heard Mum sound in months.'

'I know where you're coming from. My parents have wanted to see me settled down again, too, after Gary. I think it's because they're...' She bit her lip. 'I was a late baby. Their only one. And although Mum's a young seventy-two, she's been talking lately about...' She swallowed. 'About getting old.'

'And the fact that they're your only family.'

Trust Alex to see straight into the heart of things. And to voice what she couldn't bring herself to say—that when her parents died she'd be completely on her own.

He paused. 'You know, this could be a solution for both of us.'

'What could?'

'Getting married. For real.'

It was a moment before she could speak. 'But, Alex, you said you want to settle down and have a family.'

He shrugged. 'A wife counts as family.'

'So you don't want children?'

He spread his hands. 'Bel, if you want children, that's fine by me—if you don't, that's also fine. No pressure either way.'

'But...' Panic skittered through her. If only he knew. They might not have a choice. 'We can't do this.'

'Yes, we can.' He took her hand. 'Think about it. Our parents get on well. I like your parents and you like mine— we're both going to have great in-laws.'

Something Isobel definitely hadn't experienced with Gary, whose mother had always resented her. Nothing had ever been said overtly, but there had been plenty of pointed comments; Gary's mother hadn't taken well to the idea of his wife being the most important woman in his life. Isobel knew she wouldn't have to put up with anything like that from Marcia, who had always treated her as a much-loved part of the family.

'Both lots of parents are going to be relieved we're settled down,' Alex continued, 'and they'll stop worrying about us and nagging us. And we've got the basis for a brilliant marriage—we like each other.'

'But liking isn't *enough*,' she protested.

'Yes, it is. It's better than love, Bel. It's honest. It's permanent—something that's not going to change and we don't have all these false ideals and rosy-coloured glasses, so we're not going to get hurt. We're going into this knowing exactly what we're doing. Eyes wide open.'

'I…'

He sighed. 'Bel, if you're worrying about what I *think* you're worrying about…there's only one way to prove it to you.' He bent his head and kissed her.

It was the lightest, sweetest, most unthreatening kiss, and Isobel felt herself relax. Alex cupped her face in both hands and bent his head again. His mouth moved against hers, soft and sweet and gentle.

And then suddenly it was as if someone had lit touchpaper and heat flared between them. Her hands were fisted in his hair, their mouths were jammed together, and his tongue was exploring hers.

She couldn't remember the last time she'd wanted someone so much.

And it was as scary as hell.

He broke the kiss for a moment, just to warn her, 'Stop thinking—just feel.' And then he was kissing her again, making her head spin.

The next thing she knew, Alex had swung her up in his

arms and was carrying her to her bedroom. He set her down on her feet next to the bed. 'Wow, Bel, you're a real hedonist. I've never seen so many pillows.'

Of course. It was the first time he'd ever been in her bedroom. He'd always slept on her sofa bed whenever he'd stayed over at her flat. He walked over to the wrought-iron footboard and ran his fingers along it. 'This is beautiful. And I'm very glad you have a double bed.' He smiled. 'Especially because you have all those pillows.'

'I read in bed,' she said defensively. 'It's more comfortable with lots of pillows.'

'Other things are better with lots of pillows, too,' he remarked.

And when colour shot into her face he laughed, stole another kiss, and went over to her bedside table. He switched on the lamp, closed the curtains, then frowned. 'This light's a bit bright.'

'I told you, I read in bed.' She rolled her eyes. 'I don't see the point of giving myself eye strain.'

'True. But I want something softer. Don't move. And whatever you do, don't start thinking.'

'Why?'

He sighed. 'Because… Look, there's an easier way.' He walked back over towards her, slid his arms round her and kissed her—sensual, demanding, and it actually made her knees weak. She couldn't remember ever feeling this turned on by just a kiss.

'Whatever's put that look in your eyes, hold that thought,' he said, his voice huskier and deeper than usual.

He left the room and she could hear him moving things in her living room. He returned a few moments later with the pillar candle she kept on her mantelpiece, placed it on the bedside table next to the lamp, lit the candle and then switched off the lamp.

'Better,' he said in approval.

Then he sat on the bed and patted the space next to him. 'Come here,' he said, his voice soft.

'Alex, I…' How could she tell him she was scared she'd disappoint him? That she was out of practice? That no way would she match up to the leggy stick insects he normally dated?

In the end, she didn't have to, because he took her hand and tugged her towards him, then scooped her onto his lap. 'It's going to be OK, Bel. And you don't have to be shy with me. I've seen you naked before.'

She stared at him in surprise. 'Since when?'

'When you were about…oh, I dunno. Two? It was a really hot summer that year and we almost always had the paddling pool out. You and Saskia used to splash about all afternoon.' He laughed. 'Mum's probably got a photo somewhere.'

When she was *two*? She rolled her eyes. 'That doesn't count.' But she found herself laughing, relaxing.

'That's better,' he said softly. 'Stop worrying. This is going to be fine.'

And if she were honest with herself, it was something that had been simmering between them for years. Unfinished business. An attraction she'd never admitted to because she'd been so sure Alex didn't think of her in that way…but he'd brought it up himself a few days ago. Told her that he saw her as a woman.

Maybe—just maybe—this was what they both needed.

To get it out of the way and go back to being sensible.

Though there was still a problem. She took a deep breath. 'Alex, I haven't done this for a while.'

'Good.'

'Good?' Now that was a reaction she hadn't expected.

He smiled, and rubbed the pad of his thumb against her

lower lip. 'Very good, in fact. Because it means I get to remind you what pleasure's all about.'

When her lips parted involuntarily, he dipped his head again to kiss her; by the time he broke the kiss, her head was spinning. He slid his hands under her T-shirt, stroking her abdomen with the tips of his fingers. 'Your skin's so soft.' He nuzzled the curve of her neck. 'You smell of orange blossom. I want to touch you, Bel. I want to look at you.' Gently, he tugged at the hem of her T-shirt and she let him pull the material over her head.

He sucked in a breath. 'You're beautiful. How come it's taken me all these years to notice?'

'Because you've dated a string of women who were practically models?' she suggested.

He gave her a mock-affronted look. 'Isobel Martin, are you calling me shallow?'

'Yup.'

He grinned. 'Better hope I have hidden depths, then.'

He traced the lacy edge of her bra with the tip of one finger. The light touch made her quiver, and her nipples were tightening again.

Although he didn't make a comment, he'd clearly noticed, and rubbed the pad of his thumb across them; the friction of her lacy bra against her sensitive skin sent a thrill through her.

'You're still fully clothed,' she said.

'Do something about it, then,' he invited.

She undid the buttons of his shirt to reveal a broad, muscular chest, olive skin and dark hair. Such perfect musculature. She ran her fingertips over his hard pectoral muscles, his ribcage. And when she looked him straight in the eye, she could barely see his irises, his pupils were so huge. Meaning that he was as turned on by this mutual exploration as she was.

He slid the straps of her bra down, then kissed her bare shoulders; Isobel felt a sharp kick of excitement in her stomach. His mouth drifted along to the curve of her neck; when she closed her eyes and tipped her head to one side, he began a trail of tiny, nibbling kisses all the way along the sensitive cord at the side of her neck. His lips were warm and sure and incredibly sexy, and he was finding erogenous zones she hadn't even known existed. Isobel shivered when he lingered in the sensitive spot behind her ear and her mouth parted involuntarily.

Then she became aware of the lacy fabric of her bra falling away from her skin; he'd unfastened it with one hand, so deftly she hadn't even realised what he was doing. And now her breasts were spilling into his hands; he cupped them, lifting them slightly, teasing her nipples with his thumb and forefinger and making her quiver with arousal. From the hard pressure through his jeans against her thigh, she knew that he was just as turned on.

'I love having you sitting on my lap,' he whispered, 'but it isn't enough for me, Bel. I need more. *Now.* I need to touch you. Taste you.'

She needed it, too. 'Yes.'

Gently, he shifted her off his lap and lay her back against the pillows. Kneeling between her parted thighs, he dipped his head, took one nipple into his mouth and sucked.

Oh, Lord.

So many sensations at once.

The soft silkiness of his hair against her skin, contrasting with the beginnings of spiky stubble on his face. The movement of his tongue and lips. The warmth of his mouth. The pressure of the suction. The tingling that started in her nipples and seemed to flood through every nerve-end.

'Oh, yes, Alex,' she whispered, arching her back against

the softness of the duvet. She slid her hands into his hair, wanting more.

He lifted his head a fraction and looked up at her, his eyes dark in the candlelight. 'Do you like that?'

'Yes.' The word came out slurred with pleasure.

'Good. So do I.' He paid attention to her other nipple, teasing it with his teeth and his tongue until she was wriggling, then slowly kissed his way down her abdomen. 'I wish you were wearing a skirt.'

'Why?'

'Because these are in the way.' He stroked his hands down the denim of her jeans, then slid one hand between her thighs, cupping her sex through her jeans. 'If you were wearing a skirt I'd be closer than this.' He rubbed one finger along the seam of her jeans, pressing against her clitoris. '*Much* closer.'

And right now she needed him much closer. She shivered. 'Alex. You're driving me crazy.'

'That's the idea.' He shifted back onto his haunches, keeping his gaze firmly fixed on hers as he undid the top button of her jeans.

They were getting nearer and nearer the point of no return.

Slowly, slowly, he lowered the zip. The air felt cool against her heated skin, and she shivered.

'Cold?'

'And hot,' she admitted.

'Good.' He leaned forward and kissed the skin he'd just uncovered. 'And you're going to get hotter still by the time I've finished with you.'

And wet.

God, she was wet. So ready for him.

Gently, he encouraged her to lift her buttocks, and pulled her jeans down over her hips. He made short work of removing them after that, taking off her socks at the same time so she was left wearing only a tiny pair of knickers. He looked at her, lying against the pillows, and sucked in a breath. 'Wow. How come I never noticed you're a pocket Venus? All curves.'

Curves. She flushed and wrapped her arms round herself.

He groaned. 'I didn't say "fat".'

'I am compared with the stick insects you normally date.'

'I might date them,' he said softly, 'but it doesn't necessarily mean I sleep with them. And, for the record, I happen to *like* curves. And yours are gorgeous.' He slid the tips of his fingers underneath hers. 'Don't be shy with me. I want to see you, Isobel.' Gently, he prised her hands away from her body. 'You're lovely.'

She dragged in a breath. 'This isn't fair. You're still wearing your jeans.'

'I'm all yours, honey. Do with me what you will.' He spread his hands in invitation.

It had been a long, long time since she'd played this sort of game with anyone. Towards the end, with Gary, sex had been primarily to make a baby, not an expression of love. And when that had all gone wrong…

'Touch me, Bel,' he said, his voice sinfully inviting.

Isobel reached out and undid the top button of his jeans. And the next. And the next. She could feel his erection straining against her fingers as she continued unbuttoning his fly. What was sauce for the goose, she thought with an inward smile, and traced the outline of his penis with one fingertip.

He shivered. 'I think I should warn you not to tease me.'

'Is that a threat?'

He shook his head. 'You can tease me as much as you like, later. But I want this first time to be for you.' He took her hand and kissed it, sucking each fingertip in turn.

The movement of his mouth against her skin made the pulse beat hard between her legs. If he could make her feel like this just by playing with her fingers, what was it going to be like when he touched her more intimately?

She sat up again and pulled his jeans down over his hips. On impulse, she pressed her mouth against his abdomen.

He groaned. 'I warned you about teasing me.' He rolled to one side and ripped off his jeans and socks, then joined her on the bed.

'I half expected you to go commando.'

He laughed. 'No.' Then his expression went serious. 'Bel, just for the record, I don't sleep around. I date a lot, I have a good time, but I'm fussy about who I take to bed. And in the past I've always used protection.'

She nodded, appreciating his candour. And she believed him absolutely. 'I haven't—' she dragged in a breath '—slept with anyone since I split up with Gary.' Two years. More, if you counted the last disastrous months of her marriage. She'd dated a couple of times but she'd never gone further than a goodnight peck on the cheek.

He stroked her cheek. 'Then we'll take this slowly.'

He was going to stop? Now?

She must've said it aloud, because his eyes darkened. 'I'm not going to stop, Bel.' His voice was deep and husky and sexy as hell. 'And, as much as I feel as though I'm going to implode if I'm not inside you in the next nanosecond, I want this to be good for you.'

He wanted her that much? Oh-h-h. 'I need you inside me, too,' she whispered. And she couldn't remember the last time she'd felt that needy. The last time she'd wanted sex for its own sake and not to make a baby.

Gently, Alex removed her knickers and slid one hand between her thighs. She felt the long, slow stroke of one finger against her sex, a movement that had her quivering and needing more. As if he could read her mind, he did it again. And again.

'This is taking it slowly?' She could hardly get the words out.

'Uh-huh.'

'You're driving me crazy, Alex. I want…'

'This?' He pushed one finger inside her.

She gasped. 'Yes.' The word came out as a hiss of pleasure.

He continued circling her clitoris with his thumb, and she wriggled against him, wanting more.

'You're so warm and wet for me,' he whispered. 'Just how I want you.'

'Alex. Now. Please,' she said huskily. 'I need… I want…' Why couldn't she even string a sentence together? She was never this inarticulate.

He smiled. 'Guess what? I want you all the way back.' He stripped off his jockey shorts, then took a condom from his discarded jeans and rolled it on before kneeling between her thighs again and kissing her. She felt the tip of his penis nudge against her entrance—and then he was inside her with one long, slow, deep thrust.

She shuddered.

He stilled, letting her body adjust to his. 'Are you all right, Bel?'

'Yes—I just wasn't expecting this to… Oh-h-h,' she said as he began to move again.

She could feel the pressure growing, warmth curling at the soles of her feet and spreading up through her body into ripples, then waves.

She'd known Alex would be good at this—Alex was good at everything he did—but she really hadn't expected it to be this good, taking her to a completely different world.

'Bel,' Alex demanded softly. 'Look at me.'

She opened her eyes—and saw the same wonder she was feeling reflected in his own eyes as her climax hit her.

It was a while before she could even think, let alone speak. And she was cradled in Alex's arms, her head resting on his shoulder.

'I think,' he said softly, 'that proves we're pretty compatible.'

'Yes.' More than she'd ever expected.

He stroked her face. 'So. We like each other. We have a lot in common. And the sex is good.'

She had a nasty feeling she knew where this was heading.

'So how about we don't burst anybody's bubble?' He shifted so he could kiss her lightly. 'If we get married, it's going to solve all the problems at a single stroke.'

No, it wasn't. Because she was going to have to tell him about the miscarriages. 'Alex—about the baby business…'

'It's fine.' He pressed his forefinger lightly against her lips. 'Stop worrying. I know you love your job and you're good at it. I'm not expecting you to give it up. If we do have children, we'll work something out. If we don't, then we'll carry on exactly as we are.'

He said that now, but how would he feel later?

'It's a win-win situation.'

Hardly. Because Alex didn't love her. Which meant their marriage would be one-sided—and if he had any idea that she was falling in love with him, he'd back off straight away. He made no secret about the fact he considered himself allergic to love.

'Bel. Stop panicking.' He stole a kiss. 'It's going to be fine.'

'Is it?'

He smiled. 'I think I'm going to enjoy spending the rest of today proving it to you. Very, very slowly.'

Her face felt hot. 'Alex!'

'I'm going to get us something to eat.' He climbed out of bed. 'Stay put. And I mean it, Bel. No worrying. This might just be the best idea either of us has ever had.'

CHAPTER FIVE

THE alarm shrilled; Isobel rolled over to hit the snooze button and collided with a body.

A warm, hard and very obviously male body.

'Good morning, Bel,' Alex said quietly.

How could he possibly be awake already? They'd spent much of the previous night making love, after Alex had returned to bed with a platter of fruit and cheese and crackers and insisted on feeding her. They'd explored each other's bodies so completely that neither of them had anything left to hide.

And right now all Isobel wanted to do was snuggle back under the duvet, wrapped in his arms, and go back to sleep.

'Hello? Earth to Isobel? Anyone home?' he teased.

He sounded bright and chirpy. But that was Alex, able to burn the candle at both ends. He could stay up late—or, in the case of last night, spend a fair part of it making love—and still be wide awake and ready to go at the crack of dawn.

'Uh,' she said.

He must've hit the snooze button because the alarm stopped shrieking; then he rolled her onto her side and curved his body round hers. 'Good morning, sleepyhead.' He kissed the sensitive spot behind her ear. 'I take it you have to be up for work this morning.'

'Uh.'

He chuckled. 'I always thought you were a morning person.'

'I am,' she mumbled, 'if I get enough sleep first.'

He traced a lazy circle round her navel with his fingertip. 'Ah. That. I guess we were a bit…busy, last night.' His hand flattened against her stomach, then slid upward to cup one breast. 'Any regrets, this morning?'

Apart from aches in muscles she'd forgotten she had… She twisted round to face him and pressed a kiss into his chest. 'No.'

'Good. So you're going to marry me, then.'

He hadn't actually asked her, the previous night. None of the traditional down-on-one-knee stuff, no declaration of love, no four little words.

She suppressed the sting of hurt. He *had* asked her, a few days before—and she'd refused him. So this time round he hadn't asked and she hadn't accepted. Which, in a weird sense, made them quits in this marriage that wasn't a marriage.

'Bel?'

She forced herself to sound light-hearted. 'Depends.'

'On what?'

'I need coffee.'

'I can take a hint.' He laughed. 'Go and have a shower, and I'll make us some breakfast.' He stroked her hair. 'I'm tempted to join you in the shower…but then you'd be seriously late for work, and I don't want to get you into trouble.'

'Trouble?'

'For spending the morning in the shower with me instead of doing what you're supposed to be doing.'

She could just imagine the water beating down on them as Alex eased into her body, and desire flooded through her. 'Oh-h-h.'

'Tempted?' he teased.

She slid the flat of her palm down his side, curving round his buttocks. 'Mmm.'

The alarm shrilled again, and she groaned. 'I have to go to work.'

'We'll take a rain check. Just keep thinking about whatever put that incredibly sexy look on your face just now—and tell me tonight. In detail. So I can act it out.'

Oh, Lord.

How was she supposed to concentrate on anything for the rest of the day, after a promise like that?

He shut off the alarm and climbed out of bed, pausing only to pull on his boxer shorts, and headed for the kitchen.

By the time Isobel had showered and dressed for work, Alex had made a pot of proper coffee, set the table and was halfway through buttering some hot toast.

'Breakfast,' he said with a smile.

Sitting there at her kitchen table, bare-chested, he looked utterly edible.

She'd never breakfasted like this with Alex before. Sure, they'd had breakfast together plenty of times. But not when he was practically naked. And not when they'd spent most of the previous night making love, and his hair was all mussed, and she knew just what that sexy mouth felt like against her skin. All she wanted to do right now was sit on his lap, make his hair even messier, kiss him stupid and drag him back to her bed.

God, she really needed that coffee.

She couldn't fall in love with Alex. This wasn't part of the deal.

'Thanks,' she mumbled, reaching for her mug. He'd made the coffee just the way she liked it—hot, strong and milky. 'Mmm. Perfect.'

'Me or the coffee?' he enquired with a lazy grin.

'The coffee, of course.'

'Huh. Tomorrow, Isobel Martin, you can make your own breakfast,' he retorted. Though the gleam in his eye told her he was enjoying the banter as much as she was.

'House rules—you stay here, you make breakfast,' she teased back.

His eyes glittered. 'I can think of some much more interesting house rules. But then you'll be very, *very* late for work.' He moistened his lower lip. 'Want me to tell you?' His gaze slid lower. 'Mmm. Looks as if you can guess.'

She folded one arm across her breasts. 'Alex. That's not fair.'

He laughed. 'Sorry, Bel. I shouldn't tease you. Not when I can't carry it through to its proper conclusion.'

'No.' She paused. 'Alex, about last night… I wasn't expecting it to be so…' How could she say this without insulting him? 'Well, so good,' she ended lamely.

'Neither was I,' he said. 'I mean—I've always liked you. A lot. But last night wasn't just going through the motions, was it? It wasn't just perfunctory sex.' He reached over and took her hand. Kissed her palm and folded her fingers over his kiss. 'Maybe we should've done this a long time ago.'

'You weren't ready to settle down.' She wasn't so sure that he was ready now. Alex wasn't a settling-down kind of man. He was more like a meteor shower that made a spectacular appearance in your life for a brief while and then vanished— until the next time.

So although sex with Alex had been a revelation—of the nicest possible kind—she wasn't going to let her heart get involved. Wasn't going to rely on him.

'What are you doing today?' she asked.

'A bit of research. You?'

'Probably working up a handout for the touring exhibition.'

'Want to do lunch?'

She shook her head regretfully. 'Sorry. I've got meetings that I know are going to end up going through lunch.'

'Admin. Bleugh.' He pulled a face. 'My least favourite bit of any job.'

'Says the man who's planning to get a desk job.'

'I'll be negotiating for an admin assistant.'

She laughed. 'You *would*.'

'I don't want to spend my time on tedious paperwork when I could be doing something much more interesting.' He smiled at her. 'I'll see you back here tonight, then. And I might even cook you dinner.'

'Yeah, right,' she scoffed. 'Once you're in the archives, you only leave when they chuck you out at closing time.'

He gave her a speaking look. 'As if you don't do exactly the same.'

She shrugged. 'I love my job.'

'I know. Which is why you understand me so well.'

She finished her toast. 'I'd better be off. See you later.'

'You're leaving me to do the washing-up? Not fair,' he complained teasingly. 'I made breakfast.'

'I'll pay you back tonight.'

He raised an eyebrow. 'I'll hold you to that.'

Over the next few days, life just seemed to get better and better. Alex was right about an affair not affecting their friendship; he still talked to her as much, argued with her and teased her. But at the same time their love-making gave an added dimension to their relationship. One Isobel hadn't expected. She couldn't remember being this happy before, even in the early days with Gary—in the days before they'd tried for a family. Before Gary had accused her of putting her job before their baby, the last time she'd miscarried. An accusation that was so far beyond unfair, it was untrue. She'd wanted a baby just as much as he had. And if the midwife had put her on bedrest for her entire pregnancy, she would've done it for the sake of their child.

She shook herself.

Not now.

Though now she'd agreed to marry Alex, the question of babies rose uppermost in her mind. He'd been so casual about it, saying that if it happened, it happened, and he'd be guided by her. But when she told him just how much she wanted a baby, would it make him run?

And there were no guarantees she could even have a baby.

Then there was his new job. Although he was based in England, it would still involve a fair amount of travelling. So his lifestyle wasn't really going to fit in with being a dad.

She needed to talk to him about this. Before the engagement and wedding plans went too far. It was just a matter of finding the right time.

The following Thursday morning, Alex was not only up at the crack of dawn, he was wearing a suit.

Isobel blinked. 'Blimey. You really are trying to impress the interviewers.'

'No. I'm giving them a chance to see me as a consultant,' he corrected. 'Someone who can talk to the money people— they already know I can do the other side of the job.'

'The last time I saw you in a suit, it was Flora's christening.'

'It's the same suit,' he said with a grin. 'I only possess one. And it usually gets dragged out for just christenings and weddings.'

'Uh-huh. Well, you look professional. Just check your pockets for confetti.'

'Good point.' He checked his pockets. 'No confetti.'

'Good.' She kissed him lightly. 'And I'm buying you dinner tonight to celebrate.'

'You really think I'm going to get the job?'

'Of course I do. You're the best candidate.'

'You don't actually know any of the other candidates,' he pointed out.

She shrugged. 'I don't need to.'

He smiled. 'Thanks for the vote of confidence. So what are you doing today?'

'Being Flavia.'

He laughed. 'You love all that dressing-up stuff, don't you? It's just like when you and Saskia were little—pretending to be a princess or a bride or what have you.'

'Don't knock it,' she said with a grin. 'It's a lot of fun. I know you proper archaeologists have a bit of a downer on living history, but it gets the kids interested, and that's a good thing.'

'Living history's OK as long as you're not too *earnest* about it.' He rolled his eyes. 'And you know exactly what I mean. So what's today's topic? Roman food?'

'Domestic stuff. Beauty,' she said.

'Mmm. Well, if you need someone to oil you and get the strigil out…'

She laughed. 'Don't you dare. You'll mess up your suit.' She paused. 'Will you know today?'

He nodded. 'Assessments this morning and then interviews, and then they'll tell us.'

'Text me when you hear?'

'Course I will.' He glanced at his watch. 'I'd better go. See you tonight.'

'I'm not going to wish you luck. Just go and be yourself. That'll be more than enough to get you the job.'

'Especially as I'm a nice, settled, about-to-be-married man.' He kissed her. 'Thanks, Bel. I owe you.'

She patted his shoulder. 'Go and show them what you're made of.'

When he'd gone, Isobel tidied up the kitchen and then headed for work. Although she normally loved the days when she did the hands-on displays, today she found herself itching for her lunch break so she could check her mobile phone.

But there was no message from Alex. He must still be in the interview, or waiting round while the other candidates were being grilled, she thought. Well, she'd just have to wait until the end of her shift.

She was partway through getting the children to guess what all the items were on the little manicure set she kept on her belt, and was right at the point where they were gleefully disgusted by the earwax remover when she became aware of someone walking into the gallery, dressed in a toga with a broad purple stripe. Odd. She didn't think they had anyone playing the part of a senator today. Maybe they'd changed the schedules round a bit without telling her and were doing politics in the next gallery.

As the man in the toga drew nearer, she realised who it was.

He'd oiled his hair back to give the impression of a short Roman crop.

And he looked utterly gorgeous.

But what on earth was Alex doing here, dressed like this?

'Sorry I'm late. Politics in the Forum,' he said with a smile, coming to join her.

What?

But—

She didn't have time to ask any questions because he stood next to her and took her hand, before turning to the audience. 'I'm Marcus, the senator in charge of the emperor's entertainment. I order the elephants and the gladiators for displays in the circus, so I'm very busy—and I really need someone at home keeping my domestic affairs in order, running my household.'

He was ad-libbing, Isobel knew. But his knowledge of the historical period was sound and he was used to performing to a TV camera or lecturing at conferences, so their audience would no doubt think he'd played this role for years.

'One of the important customs in Roman times was betrothal. If I wanted to get married, I'd have to negotiate with my intended bride's family. And if they approved of me, we'd have a betrothal ceremony.' He produced something from inside his robe; it glittered in the light. 'The Roman wedding ring used to be made of iron in the early period, but betrothal rings like this one could be more opulent.' He let the audience pass it round, then made sure he got it back. 'Now, what did you notice about it?'

'It's gold and shiny,' one little girl piped up.

He smiled. 'Absolutely right. It's a new one, so my bride's parents will know that I'm wealthy enough to buy her jewellery and I haven't just borrowed it from my mum. Anyone else notice anything?'

'There's a pattern on it,' another child offered.

'That's right.' He smiled at Isobel, then showed the audience the pattern on the front. 'What sort of pattern?'

'Two hands,' one of the children said.

'It's a claddagh ring,' one of the mums offered.

'Not *quite* a claddagh—though that also has two clasped hands, it usually has a heart between them to represent true love, and a crown or fleur-de-lys carved over the top for loyalty,' Alex explained. 'There's a very pretty story behind that—about three hundred years ago, a fisherman from Claddagh in Ireland was captured by Spanish pirates and sold into slavery. His new master taught him how to be a gold-smith, and every day he stole a speck of gold from the floor and after many years he had enough to make a ring to remind him of his sweetheart back in Claddagh. Eventually he escaped and made his way home—to find that his sweetheart was still waiting for him. And he gave her the ring to prove his love.'

Oh, Lord. She could practically see various hearts melting right before him. He definitely had this audience in the palm of his hand. Half the women in the audience were clearly imagining that he was the Irish fisherman about to give her a gold ring.

And Alex was on a roll.

'This is actually a replica of a Roman betrothal ring, and the hand clasped at the wrist represents Concordia, the goddess of agreement,' he said. 'But, as with the claddagh ring, the design also symbolises love and fidelity. It's sometimes called a "fedes" ring.' He smiled. 'Does anyone know why an engagement ring is put on the third finger?'

A chorus of no—and now practically all the women in the audience were gazing longingly at Alex, Isobel noticed. Hardly surprising: in a toga and sandals, he looked fantastic.

He lifted Isobel's left hand and stroked his fingertip along the length of her ring finger. 'The Romans followed the Egyptian belief that there was a vein in this finger that led straight to the heart, so it was important to capture it within a ring—a symbol of unbroken eternity.' He slid the ring onto Isobel's finger. 'Like so.'

A shiver went down her spine. He was acting...wasn't he?

'Aren't you the guy from the telly?' one of the women asked. 'You did that programme on Egypt last year. *The Hunter*.'

'Uh, yes,' Alex said.

'So you work here now?' she asked.

He smiled. 'No. My fiancée does.' He draped one arm around Isobel's shoulders. 'I just hijacked her exhibition. But that's how people got engaged in Roman times—exactly as we got engaged just now.' He took Isobel's left hand and raised it to his lips. 'Sorry about that, Bel. I mean, Flavia.'

'He's... I...' Isobel squirmed. 'Sorry, everyone. This wasn't planned. And he isn't supposed to be here.'

'Don't worry, she's not going to get into trouble,' Alex said in a stage whisper. 'I talked to her boss first.'

He'd talked to her boss? What? When?

'Oh, that's so romantic,' another of the women said, sighing. 'To surprise you at work like that.'

'Given what she does for a living, I couldn't really do anything else,' Alex said. 'And if you'll excuse us, Flavia has finished work for today.'

'Alex, I—' she began.

'Shh.' He placed his finger on her lips. 'I cleared it with your boss. Thank you, everyone, for being our witnesses today in a genuine Roman betrothal ceremony.'

Everyone started clapping and calling out their congratulations. Alex smiled back, then simply picked up all the elements of Isobel's display, took her hand, and shepherded her out of the gallery.

'Alex, I can't believe you just did that!' she said in a low voice.

'Stop worrying. I really did clear it with your boss. Rita also let me borrow the outfit—which I need to return, so let's go and change.'

'You borrowed the senator's outfit?'

'I wanted to surprise you,' he said with a grin.

'You did that, all right. I thought you were in the interview this afternoon?'

'I was.'

'And you were going to text me to let me know how it went.'

He shrugged. 'I decided to come and tell you in person.'

'So did you get the job?'

'This morning, you were very confident in my abilities.' He tutted. 'Clearly I'll have to take you home and remind you just how able I am.'

'Alex,' she said warningly, 'if you don't tell me right *now*, I'll stab you with these tweezers. They might be replicas, but they'll hurt.'

He laughed. 'Yes. I got the job. And I'm taking you out to dinner to celebrate—that, and our engagement.'

'Our engagement?' She glanced at the ring. 'I thought you were…I dunno…hamming it up.'

'No. You just got engaged to me, Bel. In public, so you can't back out—and, besides, we're meant to be seeing the parents at the weekend. They're expecting to see a ring.' His eyes glittered. 'Do you like it?'

'It's gorgeous. And it's a perfect fit—but how did you know my size?'

'Give me some credit for resourcefulness.'

'No, I want to know.'

'While you were in the shower a few days ago, I borrowed one of your rings and drew round it. I took the drawing to the jeweller's and asked them to size it for me—and I gave them a photograph of exactly what I wanted them to make for me. I picked it up on the way here. It's eighteen-carat so it's more durable.' He paused. 'I know it's not exactly a modern engagement ring, but I thought this was more you.' He smiled at her. 'Though if you want a diamond, that's fine—we can go shopping for one whenever you like.'

'No. This is perfect.' She shook her head. 'I can't quite

believe this just happened. You borrowed the senator's robes and hijacked my show—'

'With factually correct information,' he cut in.

'Skimpy, but I suppose it'll do.'

'Skimpy?' He scoffed, then bent his head to whisper in her ear, 'But, seeing as you brought it up…skimpy can be good. Are you dressed *completely* as a Roman woman?'

'What do you mean?'

'Because, if you are, then I know you're not wearing very much underneath that robe. And in that case I sincerely hope your office has a blind at the window and a lock on the door.'

'It's open plan.'

'Pity.' He nibbled her ear lobe. 'Looks as if we'll have to go home before dinner…'

CHAPTER SIX

WHEN Isobel walked into the office, she was surprised to see a large card propped up in the middle of her desk along with a beautiful bouquet of flowers; the card attached to the flowers made tears well up in her eyes when she read it. *'Isobel and Alex. Congratulations and much love.'* It was from the whole department—and they could only have known about this a few minutes ago. Someone must have organised a collection at record speed and gone straight out to buy the flowers even as Alex had been striding towards her in his toga.

'Congratulations, Bel.' Rita, Isobel's boss, came over to her and hugged her. 'I'm so pleased for you, love.'

'Though you kept it very quiet,' Siobhan, the department secretary, said. 'I thought you two were just good friends?'

'Not any more,' Alex said, smiling back at her and draping his arm round Isobel's shoulders.

'Let's see the ring.' Rita looked at it, then nodded her approval at Alex. 'It's lovely. And very much our Isobel.' She smiled at Isobel again. 'And don't you dare sneak off and get married in secret, do you hear?'

'We won't,' Alex promised with a smile. 'In fact, I want to have a chat with you about that.'

Isobel could guess exactly where this was heading. 'No,

Alex, we're not having a Roman wedding in the middle of the Roman gallery. Apart from the fact it's not licensed for weddings… *No.*'

'Spoilsport,' Alex grumbled, but he was laughing. 'Rita, I know it's a bit of a cheek, but would you mind if I sweep my new fiancée off for dinner right now rather than waiting until the end of her shift? We've got a few things to celebrate.'

Rita smiled broadly. 'It's not every day someone gets engaged around here. Of course I don't mind. Shoo. Go and have fun.'

'I'll stay late tomorrow night to make up the time,' Isobel offered.

'No need, love. Apart from the fact that you already put in more hours than you should, I believe a happy staff is a pro-ductive staff.' Rita smiled. 'Though you two *might* want to change back into normal clothes before you leave the building.'

'We'd turn a few heads, dressed like this,' Alex agreed, laughing.

By the time Isobel had changed, Alex had ordered a taxi, which was waiting outside for them.

'That's so *extravagant*,' she said.

'It's also much easier than carrying a bouquet on the tube in the rush hour,' he pointed out as he opened the taxi door for her, then placed the flowers on her lap before climbing in beside her.

'I can't believe they managed to do all this between you asking Rita if you could hijack my display, and you taking me back to my office.'

'Everyone likes you, Bel,' he said simply. 'Of course they'd want to do something for you—and not wait until tomorrow, either.'

She opened the card. 'Everyone in the department's signed

the card. Look at all these messages wishing us luck and so much happiness together.' She blinked back the threatening tears. 'This is all wrong. I feel such a fake, Alex.'

'You're not a fake. And it's not wrong. We've been through this, Bel. This marriage is going to work, because we're very, very good friends.' He moved slightly closer, and whispered, 'Plus we're having great sex. Which in my book is a million times better than falling in love and being as miserable as hell.'

She frowned. 'What happened, Alex? Who was she?'

'Who?'

'The woman who made you so bitter about love.'

He shrugged. 'It was a long time ago.'

'She must've hurt you a lot,' Isobel said softly, curling her fingers round his, 'for you to avoid a relationship for all these years.' She couldn't even remember him bringing anyone back to meet his parents.

'As I said, it was a long time ago.'

'And if you're still hurting…'

'I'm not. I'm over it.' Alex sighed. 'All right. If you have to know the gory details, I was working on my PhD. I was on a dig down on the south coast, and Dorinda lived in the next village. Like most of the locals, she'd come to take a look at what we were doing at the dig. She was the most beautiful woman I'd ever seen—glamorous, with all that long dark hair and legs that went on for ever.'

So that was why he always dated stick-insect brunettes. Because he was looking for another Dorinda. Right at that moment, Isobel wished she'd never asked.

But Alex was still talking.

'I was a geeky student who still practically had teenage spots, and I thought she was way out of my reach. But then I found out that she liked me, too.'

Geeky?

Alex had never been geeky, as far as she could remember. Or covered in spots.

'We had a drink together, and it snowballed from there into a mad summer affair. I spent every second with her I could. And, yeah, a lot of it was in bed.' His expression turned grim. 'She told me she was divorced, or I would never have started seeing her.'

Isobel believed him. Alex had a strong code of honour.

'I was actually planning to ask her to marry me. I hadn't got as far as choosing a ring and working out a romantic place to propose, but I was close to it. But then her husband came back. It turned out I was just a diversion because she was bored.' His smile was tinged with bitterness. 'I was twenty-two, remember. Still didn't have a clue how the world worked. And would you believe I was actually stupid enough to say to her that I'd thought she loved me? She just laughed and asked me why on earth she'd want to go off with a student who had no money and no prospects of having any, when her husband was practically a millionaire.'

'Sounds as if you had a lucky escape.' She tightened her fingers round his again. 'Alex, she wasn't worth it. And if you've been hurting all these years over her…'

'I haven't been brooding on it, exactly. But it left a nasty taste in my mouth.' He grimaced. 'She'd cheated on her husband with me. She'd lied to us both, played us both for a fool. And I hated the fact that she'd used me to hurt someone else.'

'Not everyone's like that.'

'I know. But her husband was away for long periods—just like I was. So it made me stop and think. Supposing I'd got married and left my wife on her own all the time…'

'Your wife wouldn't necessarily have cheated on you.'

'Maybe not *intentionally*, Bel. But these things happen. With me being away so much, she would've been lonely. Vulnerable. An easy target for anyone who showed her the affection she wasn't getting from me because I wasn't there. And I didn't want to take that kind of risk. It was easier to stay single and keep my relationships short and sweet—and to focus on my job.'

'You're still going to be away a lot with this job. So do you think I'm going to be unfaithful to you?' she asked.

'Of course I don't.' His eyes glittered. 'Apart from the fact that you're not a liar or a cheat, we're not going into this all hormonally charged and with rose-coloured glasses on and declaring all the hearts and flowers stuff. And I hope you know that I won't be unfaithful to you, either.'

'This feels more like a business arrangement than a marriage.'

'It's not a business arrangement. It's a sensible arrangement,' Alex said as the taxi pulled up outside her flat. 'And you and I will never lie to each other, so it's going to work out just fine.'

Guilt flooded through her. Lies didn't have to be direct; lies could also be caused by omission. And she was keeping something important from him.

She really had to tell him.

Soon.

He paid the driver, then let them in—almost, she thought, as if he'd lived there for ever and wasn't just using her spare set of keys. 'I need to get changed,' he said.

'You look good in a suit.'

'But I hate wearing it. It makes me feel…' he clenched his fists and paced up and down the room '…"cabin'd, cribb'd, confin'd."'

'Ooh, get the drama king,' she teased. 'Though you're more of an Antony than a Macbeth.'

'What, an ageing roué whose brains are in his trousers?' He pulled a face. 'Which makes you a middle-aged tart who doesn't have the courage of her convictions—and takes a whole act to die, while talking about making the briefest end.'

'Oi! I *like* that play,' she protested.

He smiled. 'Next time it's on at the Globe, we'll go. But before you dive for the what's on listings, I really need to wash my hair.'

She laughed. 'You're being prissy about your hair? Don't tell me you're planning to get a haircut, now you're officially a consultant.'

'Am I, hell,' he scoffed. 'My hair's fine as it is. Well, when it's not oiled back so I can fake a Roman haircut.' He raised an eyebrow. 'Hey, you didn't happen to bring that strigil home from your Roman beauty kit, did you?'

'No,' she said, guessing what he had in mind, 'and I'm sure you wouldn't like traditional Roman hygiene.'

'I dunno.' His eyes glittered. 'I quite like the idea of sauntering into a caldarium and having you scrape me off with a strigil.'

She laughed. 'Alex. You're impossible.'

'Who, me?' he deadpanned. 'Look, I don't want to get olive oil all over this suit, so would you mind giving me a hand undressing?'

'That has to be the most trumped-up excuse I've ever heard.'

'I thought it was quite a good one, actually.' He gave her a wicked smile. 'Come and have a shower with me.'

'Now there's an offer,' she said, rolling her eyes. But she slid his jacket from his shoulders and hung it over the back of a chair. He hadn't put his tie back on when he'd changed out of the toga, and he looked incredibly sexy in dark trousers and a white shirt with the top button undone.

She unbuttoned his shirt, and ran her hands lightly over his chest. 'Mmm. The barbarian look. I like it.'

'Do you, now?' Alex's response was to make short work of her clothes and the remainder of his own; then he picked her up and carried her into the bathroom.

Isobel laughed. 'You really are a barbarian, Alex.'

'Just living up to your view of me.' He set her on her feet in the bath, stepped in next to her, and switched the water on.

Isobel shrieked. 'That's cold!'

'Don't be a baby.' He grabbed the shower gel. 'All righty— you're Flavia the patrician matron and I'm your barbarian slave.'

She laughed. 'Shouldn't you have scented oil and a strigil if you're my barbarian slave?'

'This is much more civilised,' he said loftily.

'You? Civilised?'

'I can be.' He gave her a lascivious wink, then poured shower gel into his palms, lathered it, and glided his fingers over her skin. 'Mmm. Bel. Your skin feels nice. Turn round.'

She did so, and he lathered her shoulders and her back, then drew her back against his body. She could feel his erection pressing against her; then he fanned his fingers across her abdomen and then stroked gently upwards until he could cup her breasts.

'Better still,' he whispered, kissing the curve of her neck as his thumbs and forefingers played with her nipples.

She wriggled against him. 'Barbarian.'

He nibbled her earlobe. 'At your command, my lady.'

She turned round again to face him. 'I don't think you'd be at anyone's command except your own, Alex.'

He kissed her lightly. 'You could command me to make love with you. I'd obey you.'

She slid her fingers down to grasp his erection. 'Only because it's what you want to do.'

'It's a win-win situation, Bel. Apart from the fact that

you've turned round, which means we switch roles,' he added with a grin.

'We do?'

'Uh-huh. You have to obey me, because I'm the patrician now.'

She gave him a wicked grin. 'But you look like a barbarian. I'll just get the tweezers to sort you out, my Lord.'

'Don't you dare.' He lifted her up and pinned her against the tiles.

She yelped. 'Alex, that's *freezing*!'

'I'll warm you up, then.' He kissed her hard, his mouth urgent against hers. Her hands were locked round his neck, holding him close, and he'd moved so he could push one hand between her thighs, stroking her and teasing her until she was quivering.

'Now?' he asked softly.

'N-now.' She could barely speak, she was so turned on.

He lifted her slightly so he could fit the tip of his penis against the entrance of her sex, then slowly pushed into her.

'Alex,' she whispered, and jammed her mouth over his.

The water was pouring over them and Isobel was so aware of every single movement Alex made—the slow, deliberate thrusts as he brought her nearer and nearer to the edge, the way his body fitted hers perfectly—and she knew the exact second his self-control snapped and his body surged into hers. Although her eyes were tightly closed, she could see starbursts; and all she could do was hold on tightly to Alex as her climax rocked through her.

Finally, he eased out of her and set her on her feet. 'Um. When did the hot water run out?'

'No idea,' she said.

'Sorry.'

And he really did look contrite. She smiled. 'I'm not.' She

reached up and touched his hair. 'Except for this. You still need to get rid of that olive oil. I'll go and boil the kettle so you've got some hot water to do your hair.'

'Thanks. I wouldn't want to look a total scruff when I take you out to dinner.'

She raised an eyebrow. 'Are you telling me you're going to wear your suit again tonight?'

'No. Suits are overrated.' He kissed her again. 'I'm not wearing a tie, either.'

But by the time she'd dried her hair and he'd dressed, she had to admit he looked good. Black trousers and a turquoise silk shirt that, on Alex, just heightened his raw masculinity.

'You scrub up rather nicely—for a barbarian.'

'Watch it, or the hat goes on,' he teased back. 'Come on, beautiful. Let's go celebrate my new job—and our engagement.'

The endearment warmed her. Alex thought her beautiful? Probably just a figure of speech.

But she was glad he'd made the effort.

And she was starting to believe that he was right. This was going to work out just fine.

CHAPTER SEVEN

ON SUNDAY, Alex drove Isobel to the little market town in the Cotswolds where they'd grown up. They'd arranged to meet their parents at the local hotel, along with Alex's sister Saskia and her husband Bryn and baby Flora. Alex's twin sisters, Helen and Polly, were both away for the weekend, but he'd said wryly that their parents wouldn't wait any longer for them to turn up as an engaged couple—if they didn't go to the Cotswolds, their families would come straight to London and besiege the flat.

The second they walked into the dining room, their respective mothers spotted them and started waving. And it was a good ten minutes before the hugs and the congratulations and the official inspection of the engagement ring were over.

'What a welcome,' Isobel said, smiling as she sat down.

'Well, of course! This is a celebration. It's not every day my daughter gets engaged.' Stuart made what was clearly a pre-arranged signal to the waiter, who immediately brought over champagne.

'Getting engaged to the boy next door after all these years. It's so *romantic*,' Marcia said, smiling at them.

Saskia rolled her eyes. 'This is Alex we're talking about, Mum. Your son doesn't do romance.'

'Of course I do,' Alex protested.

No, he didn't, Isobel thought. But they were meant to be putting on a show for their parents, so she didn't correct him.

He nudged her. 'Bel, tell them how we got engaged.'

She smiled. 'He hijacked my talk on Roman beauty—came strutting up in a toga, told everyone all about betrothal customs, and then put the ring on my finger.'

'You got engaged in the *museum*?' Anna asked.

'It was romantic,' Alex protested.

'That's so you, Alex,' Marcia said ruefully.

'And so Isobel, too,' Anna added, laughing. 'You've got a rival for my daughter's affections in her job, you know, Alex.'

He laughed. 'You could say the same about me. But we'll put each other first, won't we, Bel?'

'Of course,' she chipped in.

'So you bought her a Roman betrothal ring and you had a Roman engagement.' Saskia raised an eyebrow. 'Does this mean you're going to have a Roman wedding, too?'

Isobel groaned. 'Don't encourage him, Saskia.'

'No. It'll be an ordinary civil wedding,' Alex said. 'Close family only. As in you lot plus Helen and Polly and their husbands and the boys.'

'Well, congratulations,' Stuart said, raising his glass. 'And welcome to the family, Alex.'

'Thank you,' Alex said, smiling.

'Welcome to the family, Bel,' Tom echoed, raising his own glass. 'We've always thought of you as family anyway, but it's good to make you officially one of us.'

Isobel swallowed the lump in her throat. 'Thank you. I think I'm going to cry.'

'No, you're not.' Alex, who'd made sure he was sitting next to her, scooped her onto his lap and wrapped his arms round her waist, holding her close.

'So have you set a date or anything?' Saskia asked.

'No,' Alex admitted, 'but as we've known each other for years, there's not much point in having a long engagement. As it's a small wedding, it won't take long to organise—so are you all busy in three weeks' time?'

Isobel almost choked on her champagne. 'Alex, I can't possibly organise a wedding in three weeks!'

'But I can,' he said. 'I'm twiddling my thumbs for the next month until I start my new job. Three weeks to the wedding, a week's honeymoon—and this will give me something to do in the meantime and keep me out of mischief.' He smiled. 'Actually, it'll be fun.'

'Why does that set all the alarm bells ringing in the back of my head?' Isobel asked.

'Because you know what my brother's like,' Saskia said. 'He could be planning anything.'

'Alex, maybe we'd better wait until you've been in your job for a few months,' Isobel suggested. And it would buy her some time, too. So she could find the right moment to tell him about what had happened with Gary. Explain about the miscarriages. She was marrying him under false pretences as it was. She couldn't do it under double false pretences.

'No, he's got a point,' Anna said, surprising Isobel. 'You've known each other for years. Why wait? And a summer wedding will be lovely.'

'I think so, too,' Marcia said. 'Don't worry that he's going to go over the top, Bel. We'll keep him under control—won't we, Anna?'

'Absolutely,' Anna said. 'I foresee daily phone calls and updates.'

'I'll text you,' Alex said, laughing at the horrified look on his mother's face.

Saskia dug him in the ribs. 'Don't be mean. You know

Mum hardly ever switches her mobile phone on and gets in a knot over texting.'

'All right, all right. Daily updates. In a phone call,' Alex promised.

'I think we need a toast,' Marcia said, beaming. 'To Isobel and Alex. And may they have a very long, very happy married life.'

'Isobel and Alex,' everyone echoed.

Alex bent his head to whisper in Isobel's ear, 'Stop worrying. It's all going to be fine.'

'No snogging at the table, you two,' Saskia directed. 'Let the poor girl go back to her seat, Alex. It's lunchtime. Flora's been really patient but if we don't feed her in the next ten seconds she's going to start screaming.'

'Just like her mother,' Bryn said.

Alex laughed. 'You can say that again.' He lifted Isobel's hand, kissed her palm and folded her fingers over the place he'd just kissed. 'As my little sister's being bossy...'

'Yes, dear.' Isobel fluttered her eyelashes at him, laughed and slid off his lap to reclaim her seat.

It was the perfect lunch. Everyone was laughing and talking and smiling, and Isobel's heart gave a funny little throb as she thought how much she loved all the people there.

Including Alex.

But Alex didn't feel the same way about her. If she wasn't very, very careful, she was going to get her heart broken all over again. And this time she wouldn't be able to put the pieces back together.

Isobel was really quiet on the way home, Alex noticed.

'Are you all right?' he asked.

'Yes, of course.'

But her smile was fixed rather than genuine. He reached

across to take her hand and squeeze it. 'No, you're not. What is it? The wedding?'

She sighed. 'Yes.'

'Going to tell me about it?'

'I've been married before,' she said softly. 'I've done the church and the partying and it all went wrong.'

'Because you trusted in love,' he said. 'This time, we're going for something that lasts—we like each other and we get on well, so it'll work. And I can guarantee this wedding's not going to be anything like your first one.' He slid her a wicked look. 'For a start, the groom will be wearing an Akubra.'

'You're *kidding!*'

Oh, he loved this. She was so easy to tease. 'You don't want me to wear my Hunter stuff? OK. We'll make it a Roman do and I'll sweet-talk Rita into lending me that toga again.'

'Alex…'

He could hear in her voice that he'd just pushed her over the edge into worrying again. 'I was teasing, Bel. As our mothers are both keeping an eye on me, I can't do anything too outrageous, can I?'

'I suppose not,' she admitted. 'Though I'd be happier if you actually planned it with me.'

'Bel, you're up to your eyes at work. The last thing you need when you get home is to have to go through all the hassle of choosing this and booking that and seeing if there's an alternative if we can't have our first choice.' He rubbed the pad of his thumb across the backs of her fingers. 'Whereas I'm not officially at work for another month. I don't have anything pressing to do, so it makes sense for me to be the one making the arrangements and chasing things up. And, actually, I'd get a huge kick out of giving you a surprise wedding. A day to remember for all the right reasons.'

She swallowed hard. 'Alex, I really need to talk to you about something.'

'Bel, it's going to be fine,' he said softly. 'I'm not going to plan anything you'll hate. Just trust me.'

'I do trust you. It's not that. It's…' She sighed. 'Now isn't the right place. But there's something you ought to know. About me.'

'Your divorce never came through properly?'

She shook her head. 'No, that's sorted. Gary made sure of that when his—' for a moment, her voice cracked '—when his partner became pregnant.'

'So there's no legal bar to us getting married. Good. So do you want a church wedding or a civil wedding?'

'I'm divorced,' she reminded him. 'I can't marry in church.'

'You could still have a blessing, if you want one.'

'Civil's fine. And something quiet, Alex. Not a media circus.'

'It won't be a media circus,' he promised. 'So the mums and Saskia are coming to help you find a wedding dress, next weekend?'

'Yes.' She dragged in a breath. 'But this is all happening so fast.'

'Relax. We have three weeks. And whatever I say about loathing admin, I'm actually quite good at organising things. I'm not going to skimp any of the little details—or anything major, come to that.' He gave her a sidelong look. 'So I take it you're not going for the meringue dress?'

'Been there, done that.'

'That's a no, then.' He paused. 'Tell you what would look good. A little shift dress—you know, like the one Audrey Hepburn wears in *Breakfast at Tiffany's*.'

'A *black* wedding dress?'

'No.' He rolled his eyes. 'I was talking shape, not colour. White would be good, because it would go with your flame-coloured veil.'

'What flame-coloured…?' She groaned. 'Oh, no. Saskia put the idea in your head. We're not having a Roman wedding and I'm *not* wearing a flame-coloured veil.'

He pursed his lips. 'It'd look stunning in the photographs.'

'Alex!'

He laughed. 'All right, all right. I'll leave the dress up to you. But just remember the mums and my sister will all be sworn to absolute secrecy about the finer details, so when you go shopping there's no point in even asking them what I'm planning.'

'You're impossible.'

'If what I have in mind is doable, you're going to enjoy it, I promise you that much.'

She was silent for a while, and he was aware of her fidgeting next to him.

'All right. What now?'

'Nothing.'

He sighed. 'Bel, don't pull that girly stuff on me. What's the matter?'

'Are you at least going to tell me where we're going on holiday?'

He noted her choice of word: holiday, not honeymoon. Good. So she wasn't about to go sentimental on him. 'Nope.'

'So how do I know what to pack? Or if I need any vaccinations?'

'You don't need any vaccinations—and we're not going anywhere that involves mosquitoes or even the tiniest possibility of malaria. As for packing…wear what you want.'

She sighed. 'Will you at least tell me if it's going to be cold or hot?'

'Better than that. I'll pack for you.'

She growled in frustration. 'I hate you.'

'No, you don't. Just humour me, Bel. I want to do something nice for you—and I like giving surprises.'

'I don't like receiving surprises.'

'Because you're a control freak,' he teased.

'I'm not. You're a steamroller.'

'Insulting me isn't going to make any difference. I'm still not going to tell you anything.' He chuckled. 'Though you could try seducing it out of me.'

'Maybe I'll do a Lysistrata on you,' she fenced.

He got the reference to the ancient Greek play immediately. 'Go on a sex strike? You can try, honey.' His luck was in, because there was a lay-by ahead. He signalled, parked the car, then removed his seat belt. 'But that's not going to work.'

'Oh, really?' She lifted her chin at the challenge.

'Really. Let me show you why.' He undid her seat belt, yanked her into his arms, and kissed her. Teasing, nibbling kisses along her lower lip until she gave in and opened her mouth, letting him deepen the kiss. He slid one hand underneath her top, stroking her skin in the way he knew she liked; she slid her arms round his neck and drew him closer.

He moved one hand up to cup her breast, rubbing the pad of his thumb against her hardening nipple through the lace of her bra, then broke the kiss.

'That,' he said softly, 'is why a sex strike wouldn't work. Because it's good between us, and your body knows it. Right now, your nipples are hard, just as right now I'm hard for you and I really, really want to be inside you.'

Her cheeks flamed. 'So you're saying I'm easy?'

'No. Just that it's good between us.' He stroked her face. 'And if it makes you feel any better, I'm not going to be very comfortable while I'm driving us home. Right now, I can't think of anything I'd like more than to carry you out of the car, lay you down on the nice soft grass and wrap your legs round my waist.'

She shivered, and he knew she wanted it, too.

'But as having sex in public could get us arrested, I'll go for option two.'

'Which is?'

'To drive home as fast as possible without getting a speeding fine. And then I'm going to take all your clothes off. And then…' He gave her a wicked grin. 'Then I'm going to make you beg.'

She scoffed. 'In your dreams, big boy.'

He kissed her again. 'No, honey. In ours.'

CHAPTER EIGHT

THE next week simply flew by. Isobel was really busy at work; so she had to admit that no way would she have had the time to organise the wedding herself, or even help Alex much.

But by Friday night she knew she had to talk to him. Before she went shopping for a wedding dress. Before things went too far. Because once he knew the truth, he might change his mind about getting married.

As she walked up the steps to her flat, her feet felt like lead. This was a conversation she really didn't want to have. But if she didn't speak up now and things went pear-shaped in the future, Alex would never forgive her for lying to him.

One of the reasons he'd reacted so badly to Dorinda's betrayal was that she'd lied and cheated.

Right now, she was no better. She could be cheating him out of a future.

And hadn't Alex himself said that their marriage would work because they'd never lie to each other?

When she reached the front door, she dragged in a breath. Nerved herself. And walked indoors to face Alex.

'Hi.' He looked up from his laptop and smiled at her. 'How was your day?'

'Fine.' Lord, how she wanted to back out of this right now. To pretend that nothing was wrong. But she couldn't do that to him. 'Alex, we need to talk. I need to tell you something.' Forestalling his interruption, she held up a hand. 'There's no easy way to say it, so I'm going to just come out with it. And I don't want you saying a word until I've finished, OK?'

He frowned, but nodded. 'Hit me with it.'

'It's why Gary and I split up. And I'll understand if you want to walk away now.' She closed her eyes, unable to bear looking at him and seeing the pity in his face. 'We…we tried to start a family. Except I lost the baby. Both times. And…' she gulped '…you said you maybe wanted a family. I might not be able to give you that.'

He was silent.

Just as she'd expected.

And now he was going to walk away. Just as Gary had.

She dragged in a breath, still with her eyes closed—and the next thing she knew, she was in Alex's arms and he was holding her really, really tightly.

'Alex? What…?'

'I agreed not to say a word until you'd finished,' he reminded her.

'I—I've f-finished now.' To her horror, her voice was actually wobbly.

'Oh, Bel. I had no idea you'd been through something like this. I'm so sorry.'

Sorry, because he didn't want to marry her any more?

But then why were his arms still round her? Why was he still holding her close to him, as if she were the most precious thing in the world? This was Alex—the man who didn't even believe in love.

'I'm sorry,' he said softly, 'that you had to go through something so heartbreaking. I just assumed that he wanted kids and you didn't, because you've always been so dedicated to your job.'

She swallowed hard. 'I wanted a baby. I wanted a baby so *much*, Alex. And when Gary and I couldn't…' She closed her eyes again. 'When he left me, I thought I'd never have another chance to have a child of my own. I've tried so hard to suppress it—so hard to make my job, my life, be enough for me. And it's got worse since Saskia had Flora. Every time I hold my god-daughter…' The wave of longing was so strong, she could hardly breathe. 'I never thought I'd be the broody type, but it doesn't seem I have a choice in the matter. It's her weight, the perfect size to cradle in my arms, her warmth, that new baby smell. Everything.'

'So what happened? Did the doctors say why you miscarried?'

'Just that it's really common before twelve weeks. It happens to lots and lots of women.'

'Did they do any tests?'

The question hurt, but his voice was so gentle. No judgement. No blame. 'They don't even consider looking into the causes until you've had at least three miscarriages.' And that was the worst part. She tried to swallow the tears. 'Gary didn't want to take the chance of losing a third baby. And I guess I was a becoming a bit difficult to live with.'

'What?' Alex shook his head, as if trying to clear it. 'Are you telling me he walked out on you, and said it was *your* fault?'

'I…' She let her head rest against his shoulder. 'Yes,' she admitted brokenly.

'Right at this moment, I'd like to break every bone on his body, then peg him out in the desert in Turkey, smear him in honey and leave him to the ants.'

Isobel pulled back and stared at Alex in shock. She'd

never, ever heard him sound angry like this before. Coldly, *viciously* angry.

'But that's not going to change the past—or the fact he hurt you. That he let you down when you needed him.' Still keeping one arm wrapped round her, he stroked her cheek. 'Here's what we're going to do. You want a baby.'

She dragged in a breath. 'Yes.'

'You helped me get what I want, Bel, so I'm going to do the same for you. After we get married, we're going to try for a baby.'

'But what if…?' She couldn't bring herself to ask the rest of the question.

But he seemed to guess what she couldn't say. 'We'll see how things go. And if it doesn't work out, we'll talk to the doctors. Get tests. Find out what the problem is and see what our options are.'

She swallowed hard. '*I'm* the problem.'

'And how do you work that out?'

'Gary has a baby now. So it can't be him, can it?'

Alex smoothed the hair off her face. 'I'm not a medic and I don't know anywhere near enough about miscarriages to give an informed opinion. But things are never that clear-cut, Bel. Don't blame yourself.'

She made a noncommittal murmur.

'Seriously, Bel. Don't blame yourself.' He paused. 'When you told me about Gary's new partner and the baby, I thought you were upset because you were still in love with him.'

She shook her head. 'My love for him died a long time ago. I don't envy her because she has him. It's because…' Because of the baby. The baby she'd wanted so much herself. She paused. 'Look, I understand if you want to call the wedding off.'

His eyes glittered. 'Two weeks tomorrow, Isobel Martin,

we're getting married. And we're going on honeymoon. And we're going to make a family of our own.'

The tears she'd been trying so hard to hold back were suddenly too much for her. She could feel her eyes brimming, feel the wetness leaking down her face even though she tried to stop it.

With the pad of his thumb, Alex wiped the tears away. 'This doesn't change anything about our marriage, Bel. It just proves I'm right about love. It lets you down.' He dipped his head to kiss her very lightly on the mouth. Gentle and unthreatening. 'But I'm not going to let you down. That's a promise.'

And Alex was the kind of man who always kept his promises.

'Come on. Give me a smile,' he coaxed.

She tried. And failed.

He rubbed the tip of his nose against hers. 'I think you need food. Though I can't cook because there's nothing in the fridge. I'd planned to take you out to dinner, tonight.'

'Alex, that's lovely of you, but I'm really not hungry.' Right then she felt as if food would choke her. And after baring her soul to Alex, she felt too raw, too exposed even to go out of the flat.

He stroked her cheek. 'OK. I understand. So let's stay in.' He stroked her hair. 'What I want to do right now is hold you close—just you and me, skin to skin. I'm not going to lie to you, Bel. I can't promise that I'm going to make everything all right for you—but I can promise that I'm going to try my hardest.'

She let him draw her to her feet. Let him strip away her clothes, the way she'd stripped away her emotional barriers. He just held her in silence for a while, his arms wrapped protectively round her. And when they made love, later that night,

Alex was so tender, so cherishing, that just for a while she allowed herself to believe that he felt the same way about her as she was beginning to feel about him. And maybe, just maybe, her dreams were going to come true.

The following morning, Isobel woke to an empty space beside her. Judging by how cold the sheets were, Alex had been gone for a while.

She pulled on a dressing gown and padded into the living room. Alex was curled up on the sofa, working on his laptop and nursing a mug of coffee. He looked up when she walked in and quickly saved whatever file he was working on. 'Morning, Bel. I was going to wake you in about half an hour.'

'It's Saturday. How come you're up so early?' Because he'd had time to think about what she'd told him last night, and changed his mind?

'I'm always awake early.' He shrugged. 'And you needed some sleep. I thought I'd work out here so I didn't disturb you.' There was a distinct twinkle in his eye. 'Besides, I can hardly give you a surprise wedding day if you're able to look over my shoulder and see what I'm doing.'

The knot of tension between her shoulders loosened slightly. 'What's to stop me doing that now?'

'I've closed the file. And the whole lot's password-protected, so it's pointless you even *trying* to open it.'

'I could,' she said, pursing her lips, 'hack my way in. I have friends who are good with computers and they'll tell me how to do it if I ask them nicely.'

He laughed. 'But you're not going to, or I'll tell the mums and they'll nag you stupid. What time are they getting here?'

'They're not. I'm meeting them at the train station.' She glanced at the clock on the mantelpiece. 'Oh, help. I didn't realise it was that late!' She frowned. 'But my alarm didn't go off.' She hadn't bothered looking at the clock before she got out of bed, assuming that she'd woken before her alarm went off.

'I turned it off,' he admitted, 'because I thought you could do with some sleep.'

'I'm going to be late now, and they'll worry.'

'They won't. Go have your shower and I'll text Mum to let her know.'

'Alex, she never picks up texts. Better ring her or text Saskia instead,' Isobel called from the bathroom door.

It was the quickest shower on record and for once she didn't bother washing her hair. But by the time she was ready, Alex had a cup of coffee waiting for her. 'I added enough cold water so you can drink it straight down,' he said. When she'd done so, he handed her an apple and a banana. 'Breakfast to go.'

'Is this what you do when you're on a project?'

He grinned. 'Hey, it's healthy. At least I wasn't suggesting what some of my colleagues used to do—doughnuts and coffee with four sugars. Carb overload.' He kissed her lightly. 'See you when you get back. Have a good time.'

'Thanks, Alex. And, um, about last night…' She swallowed hard. 'I wanted to say thank you. For understanding.'

He laid his palm against her cheek. 'Stop worrying. This is me you're talking to. There are no pedestals for either of us to fall off. Go and find yourself a nice frock.' His lips twitched. 'And a flame-coloured veil.'

Isobel met their mothers and Saskia as planned at the railway station, albeit slightly late. And although she tried to get some information out of them about the wedding, none of them would tell her a single thing about Alex's plans.

'He'd have our guts for garters,' Marcia said. 'No can do.'

'But I promise you'll love it,' Saskia added.

Anna nodded agreement. 'And I know now just how much Alex loves you—because he's gone to a lot of trouble to make it the perfect day.'

He didn't love her, Isobel thought. Not in the way her mother believed he did. But that was something she didn't want to explain, so she allowed herself to be distracted by dresses.

'This,' Anna said, holding out a cream silk shift dress, 'is perfect.' She made Isobel try it on and come and pirouette for the three of them. 'That's the one,' she said.

Meanwhile, Marcia found the perfect pair of high-heeled cream court shoes to go with the dress. And they had them in Isobel's size.

'That's the difficult bit done, then.' Saskia smiled. 'And I need a coffee break after all that hard work.'

Next were the dresses for the mums. And after the fourth shop, Isobel rubbed the base of her spine. 'Time out. We've been walking for ages. Coffee.'

Marcia looked at her and then at Saskia. 'I've known you two all your lives—and I know full well you can shop all day without a break. Are you doing this because of me?'

'Of course not,' Isobel fibbed, but she couldn't look Marcia in the eye.

'You arranged this between you,' Marcia said suspiciously. 'Breaks practically on the hour. Look, I'm fine. I'm not ill.'

Isobel exchanged a look with her best friend. 'OK. I admit it. We're worried about you, Marcia. You're not an invalid, but you've had a rough time with your health. We don't want to push you too hard.'

'You want to stay well for the wedding, don't you?' Saskia added.

Marcia scowled. 'That's emotional blackmail.'

'But they're right,' Anna cut in gently. 'They're worried about you, Marcia.' She smiled. 'And I'm ten years older than you, so I vote for a rest, too.'

'I give in,' Marcia said ruefully.

'So are you going to humour Alex about the flame-coloured veil?' Saskia asked over coffee.

'So he *is* planning a Roman wedding,' Isobel said.

'No, no, no, no, no!' Saskia, looking panicky, crossed her hands rapidly in front of her. 'But he was going on about it last weekend. You could call his bluff and do it.'

'I'm not sure an orange veil would look right with that dress, love,' Marcia said.

'But if it was made of crystal organza and you wore it more like a stole—actually, that would look stunning.' Anna looked thoughtful. 'Especially if your hair's up and you wear finger-less elbow-length gloves and your bouquet's a simple sheaf of lilies. If you choose the material today, I can hem it for you.'

Isobel spread her hands. 'Well, as none of you will tell me anything, I'll just have to let you decide for me.'

Saskia grinned. 'And don't you just *hate* not being in charge?'

Isobel scowled. 'Alex called me a control freak, too.'

'You are,' Saskia said, laughing. 'You like everything just so.'

'It's called doing your research properly.' Isobel sighed. 'My colleagues all have invitations to the reception, but he's sworn them all to secrecy as well. Nobody will even give me a hint. It's driving me *insane*.'

'He's not going to tell you, so there's no point in stressing about it,' Saskia told her.

'So you've got everything now, apart from the gloves and the veil?' Marcia asked. 'Something old, something new, something borrowed and something blue?'

'I've got a new dress,' Isobel said. 'So that's one of them.'

'And you can borrow my gold bracelet—the one my parents gave me for my twenty-first,' Anna said. 'That takes care of old and borrowed. I'll bring it to you on your wedding morning.'

'And I'll deal with the blue,' Saskia said with a smile. 'Something tasteful, Bel, I promise.'

'Thank you. You've all gone to a lot of trouble over this.' There was a huge lump in Isobel's throat.

'That's because we love you,' Anna said, hugging her daughter. 'And we all want you to have the happiness you deserve. With Alex.'

Alex.

Her husband-to-be.

Who was equally convinced that everything would work out just fine.

She knew Alex was nothing like Gary. And, as Alex had pointed out, they were going into the marriage with their eyes wide open. Practical. Sensible. So why was the fear—the horrible feeling that everything was going to go pear-shaped—still dragging along behind her like a shadow?

Isobel managed to keep it away for the rest of the after-noon—just—while they went shopping for more shoes and the gloves to match her dress. Their last stop was to choose a length of shimmering flame-coloured crystal organza.

'Don't tell Alex about this,' she said. 'As he's keeping me in suspense about everything, I want this to be a surprise.'

'We won't let him see the dress, either,' Marcia promised.

'Thank you.'

'I'll take these,' Anna said, scooping up the bags containing Isobel's dress, the shoes and the material for the wrap. 'I'll be helping you get ready, so I'll bring them with me—that way Alex won't see them before the big day.'

Isobel shivered. 'Mum, I...'

'Shh.' Anna kissed her gently. 'Of course you've got butterflies in your stomach. It's only natural.'

They weren't butterflies. They were elephants, doing the cancan.

'But Alex is the right man for you,' Anna said softly. 'You love each other, so everything's going to be fine.'

Was it?

Isobel wasn't so sure—because they didn't love each other. Not in the way their family seemed to think they did.

But she forced herself to smile. 'Thanks, Mum.'

Over the weekend, Isobel found the perfect wedding present for Alex on the internet—a watch made of black ceramic, with no markers on the dial except for a diamond on the twelve. She discovered there was a stockist for the Swiss manufacturer near the museum, so she dropped in on Monday lunchtime to buy it and have it wrapped. Then she transferred it to a plain bag so if Alex did spot it he wouldn't have a clue what she'd bought.

The next few days went by in a blur. And then it was the day before their wedding: her last day at work for over a week. Isobel ate a sandwich at her desk and used the time to try to get ahead of schedule with her work, but at the end of the day, when she'd planned to slip quietly away, Rita banged a spoon against a bottle of sparkling wine and the whole department focused on Isobel.

'You haven't got a wedding list,' Rita said, 'so we were flying a bit blind here, but I hope you like it.' She handed Isobel a beautifully wrapped box. 'Happy wedding, from all of us.'

Isobel carefully unwrapped it, and stared in delight when she opened the box to discover a fused-glass bowl, shading from light azure through to deep cobalt. 'It's gorgeous, Rita. Thank you. Thank you all so much.'

'Our pleasure,' Rita said, speaking on behalf of the department. 'See you tomorrow night.' She hugged Isobel. 'You've got a good man, there.' She lowered her voice. 'And he'll be so much better for you than He Who Should Not Be Named. You'll be happy with Alex. It shows in your face when you look at him—and when he looks at you.'

If only you knew, Isobel thought, but she smiled. 'Thanks, Rita.'

She went back to her flat, carefully protecting her parcel on the tube. Alex was waiting for her and kissed her hello. 'How was your day?'

'Lovely. Look what everyone in the department gave us as a wedding present.'

Alex inspected the bowl. 'That's gorgeous. I love the colours. And it'll look great in our new house.'

Isobel frowned. 'What new house?'

'The one we'll be looking at when we get back after the wedding. This flat only has one bedroom,' he reminded her, 'and if we're going to start a family we're going to need extra space.'

She lifted her chin. 'What if we can't have a family, Alex?'

'We'll face that if we have to.' He raised an eyebrow. 'My grandmother used to have a saying: "Never trouble trouble, until trouble troubles you." But if you want to think of it another way—with two of us, and the fact that I've got even more books than you have, we need more office space and more storage space. Which means a bigger place.'

'You are going to let me have a choice in this, aren't you? You're not going to steamroller me, the way you have about the wedding?'

'I'm not steamrollering you. I've been trying to *surprise*

you about the wedding,' Alex pointed out. 'I'm giving you a day to remember. Choosing a home's different—the place has to feel right for both of us, so we need to look at it together.'

'So you're telling me I have to put my flat on the market?'

He shook his head. 'Keep it as an investment. You can rent it out—the rent should cover your mortgage.'

She frowned. 'But yours is rented out, too. How on earth are we going to afford another flat between us?'

'Actually,' he said, 'my flat isn't going to be rented out any more. The letting agent rang me the other day and said the tenants wanted to know if I'd consider selling to them. Serendipity,' he said with a smile. 'Obviously I wanted to discuss it with you, first, before saying yes. But a bigger place would be sensible, wouldn't it?'

'I suppose so.' She bit her lip. 'Alex, my life feels as if it's been zooming along on a fairground ride—at a speed I can't control, spinning round just when I think I know where I'm going. A month ago, I was single and I thought you were in Turkey. Tomorrow, I'm marrying you—and in ten days' time you start an office job. And now you're telling me we're going to move house.'

'Right now it might seem we're going fast, but it's all going to be fine,' he told her softly, pulling her into his arms. 'And think of the fun we're going to have, choosing a new place together.'

'Hmm.' Isobel wasn't so sure. What he'd suggested was sensible, she knew—but she liked her flat. Liked it a *lot*. It had been her bolt-hole ever since she'd split up with Gary. And losing that security…

'Just trust me,' he said, holding her close. 'I'll call the trattoria and get them to deliver dinner while you pack—and then we'll go straight after dinner.'

'Go where?'

'To the place where we're getting married tomorrow.' He rolled his eyes. 'Pay attention, Mrs Richardson-to-be.'

'So we're not getting married in London?'

'No.' He smiled at her. 'Pasta, salad and garlic bread OK for dinner?'

It was much easier just to give in and go along with him when Alex was on a roll. And she adored Italian food anyway. 'Fine.'

'Good. Go and pack—I'd recommend just a few light clothes. If it turns cold where we are, then I'll buy you something warmer when we're there,' Alex said.

He was giving her absolutely no clue about where they were going—tonight or after the wedding. Though at least, she thought, he hadn't carried out his threat of packing for her.

She was still none the wiser about their destination when they left London, though when Alex turned onto the M4 she was fairly sure he was heading for the Cotswolds. It made sense that they'd get married near their respective families.

But then he took a different turning. 'Alex? Where are we—?'

'You'll know when we get there,' he said.

'You really are an infuriating man.'

He gave her a sunny smile. 'Indeedy.'

When he drove into Bath and parked outside a beautiful Georgian manor in the middle of the city, she blinked again. '*This* is where we're getting married?'

'Stop asking questions,' he said. 'We're staying here tonight.'

'Alex…' She swallowed. 'I know we're not exactly getting married for traditional reasons, but I'm not supposed to see you on the day of the wedding until the actual ceremony. It's bad luck.' She dragged in a breath. 'I saw Gary on the morning of the wedding.'

'Honey, that had nothing to do with why your marriage broke up. You just married a man who wasn't good enough for you and who let you down.' He stroked her face. 'I'm not Gary. This isn't a rerun of your first marriage, and I'm not going to let you down. But I had a feeling you'd be superstitious about this. Which is why we're having separate rooms—and I'm going to sneak out of your room and go to my own at precisely one minute to midnight.'

'So when do I see our mums and Saskia?' she asked.

'After your alarm call at six.'

'*Six?* Alex, that's the crack of dawn.'

'Just as well you're a morning person, then.' He paused. 'Bel, there's something I need to talk to you about.'

Ice trickled down her spine. 'What?'

'Don't look so worried.' He bent his head and stole a kiss. 'Just that you need to be on time tomorrow. I know it's traditional for the bride to be late, but if you're late tomorrow we'll have major problems.'

She frowned. 'So what time are we getting married?'

'Half past eight.'

'You're kidding! Why so early?'

'Tomorrow,' he said, 'all will be clear.'

'As mud,' she grumbled.

'Everyone else is staying at a different hotel.' He gave her a wicked little smile. 'So they don't cramp our style. But you'll see them in the morning. Our mums and Saskia are bringing your outfit with them.'

He signed them into the hotel, then carried their bags upstairs to her room.

There was a bottle of champagne on ice in her room.

Which had a king-size bed.

'Time for just you and me,' he said softly. 'And there's something I want to give you. A wedding gift.'

'Me, too.' She'd retrieved the watch from its hiding place and packed it in her suitcase before they'd left London.

He turned the lights down low, then opened the champagne and poured them both a glass before raising his own in a toast. 'To us.'

'To us,' she echoed.

He undid his suitcase, then gave her a gold box, beautifully tied with an orange ribbon. Isobel smiled, thinking about her organza wrap: her compromise on the flame-coloured Roman-style veil he'd been so keen on. Alex gave her a suspicious glance. 'What's that smile about?'

'Tomorrow,' she quoted back at him, 'all will be clear.'

'Oh, yes?' He laughed. 'Maybe I'll have to seduce it out of you.'

'You can try.'

'Is that a dare?' His eyes glittered.

She backtracked, fast. 'No.'

'OK. You can open it now, if you like.'

She did—and stared at the string of almost perfectly symmetrical black pearls. 'They're beautiful.' They had an incredible shimmering lustre—and although Isobel didn't know much about modern jewellery, she had a feeling they cost a small fortune. 'Alex. These are amazing. Thank you.'

'Happy wedding day,' he said softly. 'They're Tahitian, by the way.'

She tried them on. 'They feel gorgeous.'

'They look good on you,' he said with a smile. 'Maybe you can wear them tomorrow.'

'I will. They'll be perfect with my dress.' Gently, she took them off and put them back in the box, then retrieved the box from her own suitcase. 'And this is for you.'

He unwrapped it and blinked as he saw the black ceramic watch. 'Wow. This is fantastic.'

'I thought you'd like something high-tech and sophisticated,' she said.

He tried it on. 'It's perfect—thank you. And I'll wear it tomorrow.' He put it back in his box, then went to sit next to her on the bed. 'Come here. Let me thank you properly.'

'I need to thank you properly, too.'

He smiled, cupped her face in his hands and kissed her.

Their love-making was gentle, and so perfect that Isobel was near to tears.

At precisely two minutes to midnight, he climbed out of bed and pulled some clothes on.

And at precisely one minute to midnight, he kissed her goodnight. 'I'll see you tomorrow. Sleep well.' He stroked his face. 'And stop worrying. Everything's going to be just fine.'

CHAPTER NINE

ISOBEL slept really badly that night. Odd how she'd grown used to sleeping with someone again. The bed felt way too wide without Alex curled round her body, his arm wrapped round her waist and holding her close to him.

Every time she glanced at the clock, only a few minutes seemed to have gone past.

She'd just drifted into sleep when the phone shrilled.

Groggily, she reached out and felt for the phone, picked it up, and dropped it back on the cradle again.

The phone shrilled again.

This time she answered—more of a mumbled noise than an actual word, though she put the receiver to her ear.

'Rise and shine, honey. We're getting married in two and a half hours.'

'Alex? But…'

'It's not unlucky to talk to your bridegroom on the wedding morning, before you say it.' He laughed. 'Tomorrow, you can sleep in as late as you like.' His voice went husky. 'Because you might be a little bit busy tonight.'

'Oh, yes?'

'Later,' he promised. 'Later I'll carry you over the thresh-old. And there's going to be some serious ravishing in the bridal bed. But for now…go have your shower. Because I think you have visitors due in twenty-five minutes.'

She glanced at the clock. 'They'll be up already?'

'Their hotel is all of ten minutes' walk away, two minutes by taxi, and Saskia told me yesterday they're getting changed in your room—so I'd say the odds are they're already up or they've just hit the snooze button and they'll be up in five minutes. I'll see you at eight-thirty.'

'Eight-thirty,' she promised.

A shower and washing her hair made her feel a lot more awake. She'd just wrapped her hair in a towel and herself in the thick towelling robe provided by the hotel when there was a knock on her door. She opened it and Marcia, Anna and Saskia were all there, beaming at her and carrying an assortment of bags and cases.

'This is the plan. The mums sort the clothes and order breakfast by room service, I do your hair and make-up, and you're going to be the most beautiful bride ever,' Saskia informed her.

'Room service?' Isobel asked.

'Coffee and pastries. It's our family tradition to have cake for breakfast on red letter days,' Saskia said, smiling.

'In your dreams, you bad child.' Marcia laughed. 'I'm sorry, Anna. My daughter's a bad influence.'

'I hate to tell you this, but cake for breakfast sounds good to me as well,' Anna said, laughing back.

'*Pain au chocolat* and Danish pastries. Oh, and some orange juice so we can claim we've been healthy,' Saskia directed.

'Champagne and orange juice?' Anna suggested.

'Mmm, but we don't want her tipsy in case she falls into the—' Saskia clapped her hand over her mouth. 'I didn't say anything.'

'I could always tell Alex you told me anyway,' Isobel suggested.

Saskia cuffed her. 'Behave, or I'll accidentally on purpose stab you with a hair pin.'

Isobel didn't have a chance to start worrying about the wedding. What with a breakfast of pastries and Buck's Fizz, then the flowers arriving—a simple bouquet of cream Calla lilies that matched her cream silk shift dress perfectly—and her hair, nails and make-up being done, and everyone else getting changed, there wasn't a spare moment.

'Right. Time to get you dressed. Something old—and borrowed.' Anna handed her the bracelet.

'Thanks, Mum.'

'Something new—that's the dress. But before you do, the something blue.' Saskia fished in her bag and handed Isobel a box.

'A blue garter.'

'We won't make you flash your legs. Well, Alex might,' Saskia said with a grin.

'And we'll spare you the sixpence in your shoe—that'd be way too uncomfortable,' Marcia chipped in.

Saskia helped her into the dress and the gloves.

'And I need these.' Isobel took her pearls from the box.

'Oh, Bel—they're *gorgeous*,' Marcia sighed.

'Alex gave them to me as a wedding present,' she said shyly.

'They go perfectly with your dress,' Anna said. She brought out the organza stole and draped it round Isobel's shoulders. 'Oh, love. You look like a princess.'

Marcia took her camera from her handbag. 'Hold your flowers, Bel. That's it. Now smile.'

'You look…' Saskia blinked back tears. 'Oh, Bel. Today, you're really going to be my sister.'

'You used to tell your school friends that she was your twin, like Helen and Polly are twins,' Marcia said.

Anna's eyes were glittering with tears. 'The sister I never managed to give you, Bel.'

Isobel stared at her mother in surprise. It was something they'd never talked about, and as she'd grown up she'd simply assumed that because her parents were older, she'd been a 'happy accident' late in life rather than a planned baby.

So did this mean her mother had wanted more children? Or even that she'd had trouble conceiving—had had miscarriages, the same way that Isobel herself had? 'Mum…'

Anna shook her head. 'This isn't the time and the place to talk about it. But just as long as you know how much your father and I love you. How proud we are of you. And how happy we are that you and Alex are together.'

Isobel swallowed hard. 'I think I'm going to cry.'

'Don't you dare. You'll smudge your make-up. And Alex will scalp us if we deliver his bride in anything less than smile mode,' Saskia said quickly.

The phone rang; Marcia answered, then nodded. 'Thank you.' As the others turned to her in enquiry she said, 'That was the wedding car.'

'Wedding car? So where exactly are we going?' Isobel asked.

'It's more than our lives are worth to tell you,' Marcia said. 'But everyone else is meeting us there.'

Alex had hired an old-fashioned Rolls-Royce. And when the car pulled up outside Bath Abbey, Isobel shook her head. 'No. This can't be right. No way can he have booked the Abbey. They wouldn't marry us, not when I'm divorced.'

'It's not the Abbey,' Anna said gently, squeezing her hand. 'You'll love this.'

'Then where…?'

Enlightenment dawned when they reached the entrance to the old Roman baths. 'I don't believe he managed to organise this.'

'They're open to the public during the day, so the only time you can get married here is half past eight in the morning,' Saskia explained. 'Which is how come you had to be up at the crack of dawn.'

'I… Oh, Lord.' Isobel was lost for words.

'Smile,' Saskia directed, 'or my brother will scalp me.'

'We could've walked here, but Alex wanted to string it out to the last possible second,' Marcia said. She laughed. 'You know my son. He always takes things further than anyone else.'

'You can say that again,' Isobel said fervently.

The torches around the great pool were lit and the steam was rising. The water was pure aqua—the same colour as the bowl her colleagues had bought them. And that, Isobel thought, was probably no coincidence.

And then she saw Alex.

She'd known he was teasing her when he'd threatened to wear his battered Akubra or a toga. But she really hadn't expected this. He was wearing a morning suit: a black tailcoat and pinstriped trousers with a white wing-collar shirt and a gold waistcoat. And his cravat matched her stole exactly. The rest of the wedding party were dressed in similar style, and they all had a lily as their buttonhole.

For a moment, she could believe that she and Alex really were getting married for love. He looked absolutely stunning and, when he walked towards her, smiling, her heart felt as if it had done a weird kind of flip.

'That dress is perfect. Simple and classic and letting your beauty shine through. The gloves are pretty sexy, too. You look amazing,' he said softly.

'You look pretty stunning yourself.'

He smiled. 'Note—no toga, and no hat.'

She indicated her stole. 'And I've got the flame-coloured veil you asked for. Sort of.'

He laughed. 'I like it. And I like your hair up like that.' He leaned forward and whispered, 'And I'm really looking forward to taking it down later tonight.'

A shiver of pure desire rippled through her. 'Later.' She glanced round at the registrar and their family, sitting there with such love and such joy on their faces.

And Alex had been the one to make this all happen.

'Thank you, Alex, for doing this. It's just…' She could feel tears welling up.

He looked alarmed. 'Don't cry, Bel.'

'They're happy tears,' she hastened to reassure him.

'Even so.' He took her hand, raised it to his mouth and kissed it. 'Let's go and get married.'

'I can't believe we're getting married on a two-thousand-year-old warm pavement.'

He smiled. 'I told you it was going to be different.'

'It's perfect, Alex.'

She walked with him over to the table where the registrar was sitting; Alex held her hand very, very tightly as the registrar welcomed them all.

'I declare I know of no legal reason why I, Alexander Tobias Richardson, may not be joined in marriage to Isobel Anna Martin,' Alex said at the registrar's prompting.

She repeated his declaration.

Then he turned to her. Held both hands. Looked her straight in the eye. 'I, Alexander, take you, Isobel, to be my lawful wedded wife.'

She swallowed hard. 'I, Isobel, take you, Alexander, to be my lawful wedded husband.'

Then Saskia came to the front, carrying Flora, who was holding a basket containing the wedding rings.

Alex took the smaller one and slid it onto her finger. 'With my heart, I pledge to you all that I am. With this ring I marry you and join my life to yours.'

And even though he didn't mention love in his vows, she knew he meant what he said.

Just as she meant it when she took the other ring and slid it onto his ring finger. 'With my heart, I pledge to you all that I am. With this ring I marry you and join my life to yours.'

She barely heard the registrar's speech; the only thing that she could focus on was Alex's wide smile when the registrar said, 'You may kiss the bride.'

He did.

When they'd signed the register, it was time for photographs. Then they went back to the hotel, where there were more photographs in the garden and Alex's nephews took great delight in throwing rose petals over them—and then brunch, which Alex had arranged in a private dining room.

'So where are the speeches?' Polly asked.

'We're not doing any. We're together, we're married, we're happy. End of story.' Alex gestured to his nephews, who were busily playing with the train set he'd had put in the room earlier. 'And the kids won't want to sit through long speeches.'

'They won't mind. They're quite happy playing, thanks to their genius uncle,' Helen said.

Alex laughed. 'I can remember sitting through weddings at their age and being bored out of my mind. I thought they'd like something a bit more interesting to do.'

'They love it,' Poppy confirmed.

'Come on. Don't cheat us,' Helen wheedled. 'Speech.'

'No need.' Alex gave her his most charming smile. 'As I said. We're together, we're married, we're happy. Everyone knows how we met—and everyone knows everything about both of us. So there's nothing more to say.'

'Actually, as the father of the bride, I'd like to say something,' Stuart said diffidently. 'I found this lovely blessing on the internet. I'm sorry it's not Roman—it's Apache—but I thought the words were lovely.'

'Go on, Dad,' Isobel said.

Stuart stood up, took a piece of paper from the inside pocket of his jacket, and unfolded it. With a tender look at Isobel, he said:

'May the sun bring you new happiness by day;
May the moon softly restore you by night;
May the rain wash away your worries
And the breeze blow new strength into your being,
And all the days of your life
May you walk gently through the world and know its
beauty.
Now you will feel no rain,
For each of you will be the shelter for each other.
Now you will feel no cold,
For each of you will be the warmth for the other.
Now you are two persons,
But there is only one life before.
Go now to your dwelling place to enter
Into the days of your life together.
And may your days be good and long upon the earth.'

Everyone clapped loudly.

'Hear, hear,' Marcia said. 'Stuart, that's so lovely.'

Isobel had a lump in her throat. She glanced at Alex, who tightened his fingers round hers.

'Thank you, Stuart,' Alex said.

Even his eyes were smiling, Isobel thought. As if he'd married her for real.

Well, it was legally real. Just not the great love match everyone believed it was.

Tom stood up, next. 'I'm more of a figures man than a words man,' he said ruefully, 'so I can't come up with anything anywhere near as pretty as Stuart. So I'm going just to keep it short and sweet. Welcome to the family, Bel—though we've thought of you as part of our family for years anyway, we're so pleased that you're officially ours now. And may you both be very happy. I'd like everyone to join me in raising their glasses in a toast. Bel and Alex.'

'Bel and Alex,' everyone echoed, raising their glasses of champagne.

In response, Alex kissed Isobel. Very, very thoroughly.

CHAPTER TEN

'SEEING as our dads have made such nice speeches,' Alex said, 'maybe I will say a few words.'

'About time, too,' Helen teased.

'I just want to thank you all for being here. For sharing our special day—and for all the help beforehand, especially from our mums and Saskia. I know it's traditional for the bride and groom to give gifts to their parents and ring-bearer and what have you—but I loathe giving gifts in public,' Alex said, 'so you'll find our thanks to you back in your respective hotel rooms. And the train set is for the boys to keep, by the way,' he added to his middle sisters. 'There should be enough track and trains for it to be a decent set each when split in two.'

'Alex, that's so sweet of you.' Polly smiled at him. 'Thank you.'

'And as everyone was up at the crack of dawn,' Alex continued, 'I suggest an afternoon nap before the reception this evening. You're welcome to stay here for more champagne or coffee, but I want some quiet time alone with my bride before tonight.'

'Quiet time alone,' Saskia said, rolling her eyes. 'Yeah. We all know what *that* means.'

Alex laughed. 'I said quiet time, not wedding night.' He

raised his glass. 'To you all. Because Bel and I are lucky to have the best family in the world.'

'Oh, you charmer,' Saskia said, but she was looking misty-eyed. And Isobel had too big a lump in her throat to speak.

Alex had a quick word with the butler, then whisked Isobel off to the garden and found a quiet table and chairs beneath a tree. 'We're going to do a very English thing, now, and have tea in the garden.'

'That's fine by me.' She smiled at him. 'You've made it the perfect day.' And very different from her first marriage. He'd made it so much easier for her, because there were no points of comparison. 'And this ring is beautiful.' A layer of white gold sandwiched between yellow gold.

'I'm glad you like it.'

Something in his eyes made her wonder. 'What aren't you telling me?'

He gave her an enigmatic smile. 'Doesn't matter. Bel, you look amazing in that dress. Especially with the, ahem, orange veil.'

'It's a stole, and you know it,' she corrected with a grin. 'You look pretty amazing yourself. I thought you hated wearing suits.'

'I do.' He shrugged. 'But you nixed the toga and my normal clothes just aren't appropriate today.' He reached over to run his thumb along her lower lip. 'I did think about taking you for a spa this afternoon—but I didn't want to mess up your hair or your make-up before this evening.'

'I don't know if I dare ask what you've planned for this evening.'

He laughed. 'It's a surprise. But one I think you'll like.'

'Continuing the Roman theme?'

'Might be.' He raised an eyebrow. 'Just think yourself lucky they throw confetti rather than walnuts at the bride and groom nowadays.'

'You've gone to so much trouble, Alex.'

'You're worth it,' he said simply.

For a moment, Isobel thought he was going to tell her he loved her.

But she knew that Alex didn't believe in love.

And she didn't, either. She wasn't going to let her heart be broken again. He was absolutely right to be practical about this. Deep friendship and spectacular sex were a good basis for a marriage. Something that wouldn't crumble—unlike love. And if they couldn't have a family…he'd still be there for her. He wouldn't walk away.

'This,' Alex said after the waitress had brought their tea, 'is the life.'

Isobel scoffed. 'You'd far rather be pottering around ruins with a camera and someone who'd talk to you about the history of the place.'

'Well, yes,' he admitted. 'But that's hardly an option today.'

'What time do we have to be at the reception?'

He raised an eyebrow. 'Are you worrying again?'

'No—just wondering how much free time we have.'

He glanced at his watch. 'Ages. We don't have to be there until seven. Which means leaving here about ten to, if you don't mind walking.'

She smiled. 'Walking's fine with me.'

'Obviously we'll be expected to dance together, but we can get away with just the traditional first dance if you really hate it.'

The first dance. That feeling of floating on air—and, despite being in a crowded place, there being nobody there except her husband. 'Just as long as you haven't picked the same song as I had with Gary.'

'Hardly. Apart from the fact we're having a string quartet…'

'A string quartet?'

He laughed. 'They're going to switch halfway through to pop stuff. Don't worry. It'll be fine.'

'I don't think I've ever seen you dance. You didn't dance at Saskia's wedding—or Helen's, or Polly's.' Or her own wedding to Gary, now she thought about it.

He shrugged. 'It's not something I do very much.'

'So you can't dance?'

'I didn't say I can't. Just that I don't.' He raised an eyebrow. 'Worried that I'll have two left feet and ruin your shoes?'

'No.' *Yes.*

Alex stood up, took her hand and pulled her to her feet. 'OK. Practice run.' He held her close, then began to sing a ballad very softly as he danced with her, swaying perfectly in time to the beat.

'I had no idea you had such a nice voice, Alex.' He'd never sung along to the radio whenever they'd travelled in a car together.

'Thank you, Bel.' He pulled back and gave her a mock bow. 'So I take it you're no longer worried that I'm going to bruise your toes.'

She smiled. 'You have a good sense of rhythm—but that wasn't really dancing.'

He laughed. 'If you're expecting Fred Astaire or Patrick Swayze, forget it. That's as much as I do. And only on very, very special occasions.'

So was he saying that today was very special for him?

She didn't dare ask.

When they returned to their table, Alex kept the conversation very firmly on the topic of history. Which suited Isobel just fine: it kept her mind well off dangerous emotions.

But she could see he was looking fidgety. Eventually, she reached over and took his hand. 'Alex. You want to go exploring, don't you?'

'I'm perfectly happy sitting here with you, relaxing.'

'Liar.' She smiled at him. 'We're only a short walk away from the baths. I haven't been there for ages.'

He coughed. 'All of five hours, by my reckoning.'

'I mean as a tourist.'

'Isn't this a bit of a busman's holiday? A busman's honeymoon, even?' he teased. 'Bel, I can't go wandering round Bath dressed like *this*.' He fluttered his fingers at his morning suit.

'How about we go and change? Nobody's going to know.'

'You can get away with staying as you are—leave the stole and gloves here and you look like a wedding guest killing a bit of time before the ceremony.'

'That goes for you, too.'

He ran a finger round the collar of his shirt. 'How about I ditch the jacket, cravat and waistcoat?'

She couldn't be hard-hearted enough to make him stay in an outfit he obviously loathed. 'Deal. Your room or mine?'

'Just hand your stole to me and I'll sort it.'

She frowned. 'What's the big deal about not letting me see the room?'

'Because,' he said softly, 'I want the first time you see it to be when I carry you over the threshold. To our bed.'

The thought sent a shiver of desire through her.

'Hold that thought,' he said, and took the organza stole and her gloves.

He returned a few minutes later, wearing just the white shirt and dark trousers. 'Sure you're OK to walk in those shoes?'

'Would I buy shoes I couldn't walk in?' she asked.

He laughed. 'Course not. Practical to the last, my Bel.' His eyes glittered, and he sang the first verse of 'Michelle', changing the name to 'Isobel'.

She groaned. 'That's *terrible*, Alex. Come on. Let's go exploring.'

They spent the rest of the afternoon wandering round Bath, starting with a tour of the Roman baths.

'Just think. We got married here, a few hours ago,' Alex whispered, sliding his arm round her and holding her close when they got to the Great Bath.

Married. She still hadn't quite taken it in. And despite the ring sitting on her finger, she didn't *feel* married. This felt like playing hookey with her friend and lover to do something they both enjoyed.

Alex insisted on playing tourist afterwards and having afternoon tea in the Pump Room. 'Tea, yes. A glass of warm spa water from the fountain—no,' Isobel said.

'Chicken,' he teased.

'Be my guest if you want to try the water,' she teased back, 'but I've done it before and, I warn you, it's vile.'

After tea, they wandered hand in hand round the Circus, admiring the Georgian houses. 'I'd love a house like that,' Isobel said wistfully. 'All high ceilings and masses of light.'

'We can if you want,' Alex said.

She wrinkled her nose. 'Think of the commute to work every day.'

'You're right—it'd be too much.' He looked thoughtful. 'You know, we could buy a flat in a Georgian town house somewhere like Bloomsbury. High ceilings and lots of light, like these ones.'

'And a price tag to suit.'

He squeezed her hand. 'Actually, we can afford it, otherwise I wouldn't have suggested it.'

'You might be able to, but I can't. And I'm paying half the mortgage,' she added swiftly.

'Bel, don't be difficult. Now you're officially married to

me, what's mine is yours. Actually, it makes sense for us to live in Bloomsbury—it means we both have a reasonable commute. And if you like the area…'

'I do,' she admitted.

'Then let's do it.'

She looked up at the mellow stone houses. 'Are you sure?'

'Yes. We're not in a chain, so once we've found a place we both like we can persuade the vendors to let us have early possession. They win because they've sold—and we win because we have the house we want. Result.'

'Persuasion's your middle name, isn't it?' she asked wryly.

He laughed. 'So that's a yes, then?'

She nodded. 'That's a yes. And thank you.'

He spun her round to face him and kissed her thoroughly. 'We'll get ourselves on some mailing lists in the morning before we go to the airport.'

Finally, they went back to their hotel. Alex glanced at his watch. 'As we ought to be there first to welcome everyone, we'd better leave in a minute. Do you need to freshen up?'

'Just my make-up. I'd guess that I don't have any lipstick left on.'

'You kissed me as much as I kissed you,' he pointed out.

She laughed. 'So are we in my room now or yours?'

He evaded the question. 'Can't you just do what girls normally do and whip a mirror and lipstick out of your bag?'

She spread her hands. 'Funnily enough, I don't have a bag on me. Which means my lipstick is upstairs.'

'I'll fetch it.'

'Alex, it'd be quicker if I—'

'No,' he cut in. 'Not until I carry you over the threshold.'

He returned a couple of minutes later, holding her make-up bag and compact mirror. When Isobel had refreshed her make-up, he took the bag back to their room, then came back downstairs wearing the jacket, waistcoat and cravat again.

'Ready?' he asked.

'Ready,' she confirmed.

And this time she wasn't that surprised when he led her back to the Roman Baths.

'I should've guessed,' she said.

He shrugged. 'I had to carry the theme through, didn't I?'

'So this string quartet…is it going to play Roman music?'

He laughed. 'Considering nobody knows exactly what Roman music was like…no. They're going to play ordinary chamber music. Bach, Vivaldi, some Mozart.'

The musicians were playing a violin concerto when Alex and Isobel walked in. That teamed with the backdrop of the Roman baths in the evening, lit by torches and with steam rising from the water, Isobel found incredibly moving. There was a table full of glasses and champagne bottles in ice buckets, another table laden with food, and smaller tables and chairs dotted around where people could sit and chat.

'It's perfect,' Isobel whispered.

Their family were the first guests to arrive. Stuart shook Alex's hand warmly and hugged Isobel. 'That paperweight was beautiful, darling. Thank you.'

'Our pleasure,' Isobel said, hugging him back. 'Help yourself to champagne, Dad.'

Their mothers and Saskia were equally delighted with their bouquets, and Tom seemed pleased with his paperweight. 'Every time I see it on my desk I'll think of today. Thank you both.'

'Polly and I didn't do anything to help,' Helen said, 'so we didn't really deserve a present.'

'We didn't want to leave anyone out. Besides, I thought if we bought you enough posh chocolate, you might not nag me for five seconds or so,' Alex replied with a grin.

'Oh, you!' She cuffed him playfully. 'Bel, I hope you're going to reform him.'

'She likes me just as I am—don't you, Bel?' Alex retorted.

Isobel rolled her eyes. 'I don't think anyone could change your brother anyway, Helen.'

More and more people arrived to be welcomed, shake hands and wish them well. Some of Alex's former colleagues had flown in from Turkey; others had travelled the length of the country to be there. Most of Isobel's department came from London, as well as old friends of the family from nearby.

The guest list—at least on her side—wasn't much different from her first wedding, Isobel thought. Except this time she wasn't wearing rose-coloured glasses. And this time…this time, she really hoped everything would last.

CHAPTER ELEVEN

ALEX caught the attention of the first violinist, and gave the signal for the first dance. The arrangement he'd asked them to do especially for tonight. A song that definitely hadn't been played at Isobel's first wedding: and one he knew she liked.

'Ladies and gentlemen, I give you the bride and groom,' the first violinist said, and began playing.

He could see in the way that Isobel's eyes widened that she recognised the tune instantly. And even though this was an instrumental arrangement of 'Time in a Bottle', he was well aware that she knew all the lyrics to the song. She'd know how appropriate it was.

'Alex. This is—' Isobel began.

'Shh,' he said, taking her in his arms. Thanks to her high heels, if he leaned forward just a little he could dance cheek to cheek with her.

If he believed in love, he'd say that right now that was the way he felt about Bel. His friend. His lover. His bride.

The thought made him freeze. Last time he'd believed in love, it had gone so badly wrong. That was why he'd never let his heart get involved again—why his relationships had always been for fun, and he'd walked away before they had a chance to get serious.

With Isobel, it was different.

He'd always liked her. Even when they'd been children, she'd been quieter than his sisters, more serious, and he hadn't minded her tagging along behind him. In his teens and twenties, he'd found her easy to talk to, good company—particularly as she shared his love of history. She'd been the one who'd encouraged him to submit his articles to a Sunday broadsheet. And she'd been the first person he'd called to tell about the offer of the television series.

The more he thought about it, the more he realised how important Isobel had been in his life.

And that made it even more essential that he didn't fall in love with her. Because he didn't want this to go wrong. He wanted to come home to her at the end of the day, moan about the paperwork and let her tease him out of his bad mood. He wanted to share his discoveries with her, knowing that she'd be as excited about them as he was.

And he wanted a little girl with Isobel's huge brown eyes and shy smile—a girl he could carry round on his shoulders and who'd adore him as much as he adored her. A girl he could teach to find fossils at the beach and dig trenches in their garden.

It shook Alex that he was actually starting to feel broody—that he wanted a baby as much as he knew Isobel did. So when the song ended, he kissed her lightly on the cheek. He needed space between them. Right now. And there was only one way to do it nicely. 'That's my dancing done for tonight. Better circulate, I suppose, before people start grumbling that I'm monopolising the bride.'

Though even as he worked the room, chatted with friends, he was very aware of exactly where Isobel was—almost as if some invisible cord bound him to her. Every so often, he looked across at her and she'd suddenly glance up, catch his eye and smile at him. And every time that happened, it made him feel odd—as if his heart had skipped a beat.

Eventually, he couldn't stay away from her any more. She was talking to her colleagues when he came to stand behind her, slid his arms round her waist and pulled her back against him. Just as everyone would expect him to. And although Isobel would think that he was playing a part, he knew he wasn't. He needed to hold her. To feel grounded.

'This was an inspired setting for the day, Alex,' Rita told him.

'Considering my wife spends half her working life dressed as a Roman matron, we could hardly have had the wedding anywhere else,' Alex said with a smile. 'Will you excuse me, Rita? I need a quick word with the bride.' He ushered Isobel over to a quiet corner. 'Bel, we've got an early start tomorrow. It might be a good idea to say our goodbyes and sneak out now.'

'An early start? As early as today's?' she queried.

'Not *quite*.' He stroked her bare nape. 'But I've had enough of being sociable.'

She nodded. 'And it's a bit of a strain, living up to everyone's expectations and pretending to be in love.'

It was even more of a strain trying not to fall in love with her, if she only knew it. 'We don't need love. We're better off without it.' And he knew he was trying to convince himself as much as he was trying to convince her. 'We have a solid friendship—' he nuzzled her ear '—and great sex. It's an unbeatable combo.'

'Definitely.'

Was it his imagination, or did she sound a bit wistful?

But weddings did that to women.

Especially brides.

So of course Bel wasn't falling in love with him.

And he'd be very, very stupid if he hoped that she was. Falling in love would be the first step to their marriage falling apart.

They quietly said their goodbyes, then sneaked out of the reception and walked hand in hand back to their hotel.

'So. Just you and me,' Alex said when the lift doors closed behind them. 'There's something I've been wanting to do all day.' And maybe making love with her would clear his head. Bring him back to normal.

Her eyes widened. 'Alex, we're in a lift. It's *public*.'

'I can't see anyone else here.' He spun her round so she was facing the mirror at the back of the lift. 'But I'll defer to your wishes and keep your clothes on. For now.' He ran his finger lightly along the zip at the back of her dress. 'But I'm looking forward to sliding this down. And kissing every inch of skin I reveal—all the way down your spine,' he whispered. 'And then…' He splayed his palms on her abdomen. 'Then I'm going to touch you, Bel.' He slid his hands upwards until he was cupping her breasts. 'I'm going to touch you here.' He rubbed his thumbs over her nipples, feeling them start to harden through her clothes. 'And here.' He slid one hand down until the heel of his hand was just above the opening of her thighs, pressing against her. 'I'm going to touch you. Taste you. Tease you until you're absolutely desperate for me.'

Her mouth had parted, her colour had risen and her eyes were glittering with desire.

Good.

Just how he wanted her.

'Hold that thought,' he whispered as the lift doors opened behind them.

He laced his fingers through hers and led her down the corridor to their room for the night. Pushed the cardkey through the lock. Bent slightly so he could scoop one arm under her knees and lift her up in his arms. 'Tradition,' he said as he carried her over the threshold.

Her eyes went wide as she saw the four-poster. 'I wasn't expecting this.'

'I thought I'd better be traditional about something.' He paused. 'And now it's time for something else traditional. The wedding night. I'm going to make love with my bride. Very, *very* slowly.'

He gently tweaked the stole from her shoulders and dropped it on the bed. Then he spun her round and drew the zip downwards. Slowly. Prolonging the teasing for both of them. He dipped his head to kiss the nape of her neck, then trailed kisses down her spine as he drew the zip downwards. He eased the dress over her shoulders, hooking her bra straps out of the way at the same time so he could bare her shoulders completely, and kissed his way along to the curve of her neck. He let the dress slide to the floor, and she stepped out of it; he picked it up and hung it over the back of a chair, then looked at her. She was wearing only her bra with the straps pulled down, a pair of lace-topped hold-up stockings, a blue lacy garter, and the flimsiest pair of silk knickers. She still had her back to him—and he'd never seen anything so enticing in his entire life. 'Now there's a view,' he said. He'd aimed for teasing, but his voice sounded slightly husky to his own ears. Too breathy. Too desperate. Not good.

He took out the pins from her hair. 'I want this down.' He ran his fingers through it. Her hair was soft and silky, and curled slightly round his fingers. 'And you smell lovely.' He leaned closer. 'Orange blossom again.'

She turned round. 'And you're wearing too much.' Her voice, too, sounded slightly husky. Breathy.

He was pretty sure she needed this as much as he did. 'So you're saying you want me naked?'

She gave the tiniest, tiniest shiver. 'Yes.'

'OK, then.' He took off his jacket and hung it over the back of the chair with her dress. The waistcoat was next; he undid each button before shrugging it off and dropping it on top of his jacket. The cravat…well, hopefully she wouldn't notice that his hands were shaking. And then he stopped. Raised an eyebrow. 'My fingers ache.'

She smiled, clearly picking up on the game. 'So you're saying you want a hand?'

He smiled. 'I'm saying I want you to undress me. Preferably five seconds ago.'

She sashayed over to him, and his heart skipped a beat. When she undid the buttons of his shirt, he couldn't keep his hands off her any longer; he curved his hands over her buttocks, drawing her closer.

Her eyes widened slightly when she felt his erection pressing against her. And then she gave him a sensual smile, and slid one hand across his pectorals. 'Mmm, you feel nice.'

He made short work of undoing his shirt cuffs and dropped the shirt on the floor.

She laughed. 'You've stopped being neat, then.'

'Yep.' He had no intention of doing anything that took him a millimetre away from her or a millisecond longer before he could wrap her body round his.

She undid his trousers, sliding the zipper down as slowly as he'd done with the zip of her dress. Then she drew one fingertip along his length.

'Oh, if teasing's on the menu…' He stepped out of his trousers and removed his socks, then unsnapped her bra with one hand. He had no idea where the lacy garment fell and he really didn't care—what he needed right now was to touch her.

Taste her. He dipped his head and took one nipple into his mouth.

She gasped his name and threaded her fingers through his hair, urging him on.

He didn't need any more hints. He simply picked her up, carried her over to the four-poster bed, and laid her back against the pillows before kneeling between her thighs. He placed the flat of his palms against her waist; Lord, her skin was soft. And he wanted to touch her even more intimately. He moulded his hands over the curve of her hips, her thighs, as if learning her shape for the first time. Then he hooked a finger under her blue garter. 'I'm glad you're wearing stockings.' It was incredibly sexy.

He traced the lacy edges of the hold-up tops with his fingertip. 'I love the contrast between this and your skin. Rough against smooth.' He took her hand and pressed it against his jaw. 'Rough against smooth,' he whispered again and dipped his head to draw a line of kisses along her collar-bone, just below where the black pearls circled her neck, then down between her breasts. He circled her navel with the tip of his tongue, and he could feel her quivering in anticipation; clearly she needed this as much as he did. He slid one hand between her thighs, cupping her sex through her knickers. 'These are too much of a barrier, wouldn't you agree?'

Her beautiful brown eyes grew darker. 'Yes.'

'Allow me a barbarian moment.' Still keeping eye contact, he ripped the sides of her knickers and disposed of them in two seconds flat.

'Oh, my God. Alex, I don't believe you just did that!' She stared at him, looking shocked. 'You actually ripped my knickers off! And they were silk, I'll have you know.'

He shrugged. 'So I'll buy you some more. Not that you'll actually be needing to wear any for the next week…' He stroked her stocking tops again. 'These can stay. And the pearls.'

She shook her head. 'I don't want them spoiled.'

'They won't be.'

She looked pained. 'Alex…'

He smiled. 'You're so practical.'

'That's why you married me. Because I'm settled and boring.'

'Settled, yes. Boring…never.' He kissed her lightly on the mouth, removed the pearls and put them in their box. 'OK now?'

She coughed. 'You've forgotten something.'

'What?'

'Those.' She nodded at his close-fitting jersey boxers. 'Unless you want me to rip them off.'

As he'd just done to her. He laughed. 'Wrong material. It'd take you way too long.' He removed his boxers and came to lie next to her. 'I'm entirely in your hands, *uxor mea*.'

'Are you, now?' She ran the tip of one finger down his sternum, following the line of arrowing hair down his abdomen, then deliberately traced the outline of his erection against his skin, keeping five millimetres away from actually touching his shaft.

She was driving him crazy.

'No teasing,' he warned.

'You said you were in my hands,' she reminded him.

'Your hands aren't anywhere near close enough to where I want them.'

'And where might that be, *maritus meus*?'

'That's more than enough teasing, Isobel Richardson.' He pulled her on top of him so she was straddling him, then shifted so that the tip of his penis was against her entrance. Then he laced his fingers through hers. 'Here will do quite nicely.'

She sucked in a breath. 'Alex.'

'Isobel.' He tilted his pelvis, and gently eased inside. 'Better. *Much* better.' Just where he needed to be. Losing himself inside her, the warmth surrounding him.

She rocked against him and began to move, so slowly that he ached. And just when he could bear it no longer, her control seemed to snap and she gripped his hands, moving over him rapidly.

A shiver of pure bliss spread through him. 'Bel. You feel fantastic. Like silk wrapped round me. And I…'

He just about managed to stop himself saying the words—words that scared the hell out of him, and might scare her well away from him. Instead, he sat up, still inside her, and held her close. Kissed her so that his treacherous mouth wouldn't have the chance to betray him. He felt the very moment that her body went still, poised on the edge of climax—and then his was rippling through him, too. He held her tightly, as if he were drowning and she were the only thing keeping him afloat; her arms were wrapped just as tightly around him.

'And now,' he said softly, when he was able to speak again, 'we're really married.'

CHAPTER TWELVE

ISOBEL woke briefly in the night. For a moment she was disoriented, wondering where she was; then she became aware of Alex's deep, regular breathing. His body was spooned round hers and his arm was wrapped round her waist, holding her close to him. Protected, safe.

When room service woke them in the morning, Alex switched from being her serious, intense lover of the night before to his usual teasing, charming self. He poured her coffee, then buttered some croissants and shared them with her, feeding her alternate bites and deliberately smudging jam against her mouth and leaning forward so he could lick it off.

He carried her to the shower after breakfast and Isobel thought he was going to join her; but then he set her down on her feet and stole a kiss. 'I'd better leave you to it. Because if I do what I really want to do right now, we're going to be late—and that's a bad idea.'

'So where are we going?'

'On honeymoon.'

He refused to give her any more detailed answer than that, and fobbed off every single question until they were actually at the airport.

The moment their flight was called and he stood up, pulling her to her feet, she knew where they were going.

'Naples? We're going to Pompeii?'

'And Herculaneum.' He smiled. 'I told you that you'd love it.'

Just as much as she knew he would. Wandering around ancient ruins was Alex's idea of the perfect holiday—just as it was hers.

When they finally arrived in Naples, she discovered that he'd found them an apartment in an ancient *palazzo* in the old quarter. Again, he insisted on carrying her over the threshold.

The apartment was gorgeous. High ceilings and lots of light, everything painted light colours, with terracotta flooring and voile curtains and white and gold and terracotta roses on the table. She looked out of the window to discover a balcony with a view of the bay and Vesuvius.

'This is wonderful, Alex. Absolutely perfect.'

'Good. Because there's something we need to do before we unpack.' He picked her up again and carried her over the threshold of their bedroom.

'Alex!'

'They eat late, in Naples. And when in Rome—well, Naples...' he quipped. 'So it doesn't matter if we go out late.'

It was very late by the time they went out for dinner. But there was something magical, Isobel thought, about sitting on a terrace overlooking the sea and watching the lights glittering against the night.

And it was the perfect week. They breakfasted on milky coffee and pastries in small cafés, and spent the mornings wandering round museums and churches before having a light lunch at one of the pavement cafés. Then Alex insisted that they needed a siesta, where they'd make love in their room with the afternoon light filtering through the voile curtains.

As Alex had promised, they spent a day at Herculaneum and another in Pompeii—and Isobel wouldn't have wanted to share this with anyone else but Alex. They wandered hand in hand through the village, looking at the frescos and the fountain covered in glass and shell mosaics and the statue of the dancing faun in a courtyard, and talking, talking, talking.

'It's nice to see a couple still like honeymooners after being together so many years,' an elderly tourist said to them with a smile.

Alex and Isobel looked at each other.

'Actually,' Alex said gently, 'we are honeymooners. We only got married at the weekend.'

'Oh!' The old lady flushed. 'I do apologise. It's just that I've been overhearing you talking, and you finish each other's sentences. It reminds me of how it was with my late husband and me—and we were together for forty years.'

'You're right in one sense. We've known each other for a lot of years,' Isobel said, reaching out to touch her hand.

'It just took you a while to realise how you felt about each other, hmm?'

It had taken Isobel a while to realise how she felt about Alex—not that she would tell him, because he'd run a mile. And as for how Alex felt about her... He cared. He just didn't believe in love. Though Isobel didn't have the heart to correct the old lady. 'Yes.'

'Congratulations, my dears. And may you have a very happy life together.'

It was all too easy to fall under the spell of romance in Naples—especially the day Alex took her out to the Blue Grotto at Capri, a fairytale cave bathed in iridescent turquoise light. Although his plans for the next day, a hike up Vesuvius to see the crater, brought her back to earth. 'I didn't realise I was that unfit,' she said when they finally reached the top and took a break from the climb.

'It's a fair bit steeper than anything you're used to in London—unless you take the stairs instead of the escalator on the tube,' he said, 'which you're too idle to do.'

'Idle? Pah. Just because you're used to hauling yourself in and out of trenches, showing off your biceps like some gym gorilla.'

'Any time you want to join me, honey, I could always use a research assistant.' He blew her a kiss.

Their last couple of days in Naples were idyllic. Good food, incredible surroundings and spectacular sex.

And then it was back to London. Back to real life.

Alex started his new job and seemed to love it. But she noticed his hours gradually stretched until he was working late every single night.

But that was Alex. He'd always been a workaholic.

And the fact that he hadn't mentioned babies since they were back from Italy...

She pushed the hurt aside. He'd said they should take it as it came; he'd even talked about his grandmother's saying about not troubling trouble. Maybe she should take her lead from him and forget about it.

But the longing wouldn't go away. Every day, it got stronger.

He took two days off when they moved from her flat to the place they'd found in Bloomsbury—one with high ceilings, lots of light, and vendors who were more than happy to move out early. Though Isobel was the one to go back to the Cotswolds a couple of days later to sort out his stuff in the attic at his parents' house.

'Typical Alex,' was Marcia's response, rolling her eyes. 'I don't think you'll ever change him.'

'He's really busy at work,' Isobel said. 'I'm sorry.'

'It's not your fault, love.' Marcia patted her hand. 'And you get him to ring me a lot more than he used to.' She paused. 'You don't have to worry about making excuses for him. I know what he's like. Just as long as he's treating you properly.'

'Everything's fine,' Isobel reassured her. 'He gave me the perfect wedding and the perfect honeymoon. And the flat's the sort of place where I only ever dreamed about living.'

'That isn't what I mean, and you know it.' As usual, Marcia was straight to the point. 'Is he making time for you?'

'Yes.' Not as much as she would've liked, but he spent time with her. And as for the baby question…it was still early days. At the age of thirty, she couldn't expect to fall pregnant immediately. She'd just have to be patient.

The 'man and a van' Alex had hired was there the next day to load up the boxes and take them to London. Alex had agreed to be there if the driver called him half an hour before arriving, but when Isobel got back to the flat Alex wasn't unpacking the boxes in the hallway as she'd expected him to be doing. And when she went up to the second floor she saw a small suitcase on their bed, almost packed.

'Alex? What's going on?' she asked.

'Something's come up,' he said. 'I have to go up to the Yorkshire coast for a couple of days—they've found what could be a Viking boat under a pub car park. The building work's stopped but I need to do some preliminary work to check out the extent of the site.' He gestured to the boxes. 'If you don't mind them staying there for the time being, I'll sort them out when I get back.'

'Alex, there's hardly room to get past them.' And if he was going to leave the boxes unpacked, why hadn't he put them upstairs in the spare bedroom rather than left them in the hallway?

'Sorry, Bel.' He raked a hand through his hair. 'I was going to start on them this afternoon, but then I got that phone call. You know what it's like. My job's to do the preliminary exploration—so I had a ton of things to set in motion, and I really have to go.' He gave her his most charming smile.

She'd just bet he'd practised that dishevelled, little-boy-lost look until he was perfect at it. She'd seen him use it before to get his own way. And it annoyed her that he was using it on her. She folded her arms. 'I see.'

'Look, if you want to unpack them yourself to get them out of the way, feel free. I don't have any secrets from you and I'm not possessive about my stuff.'

Alex wasn't possessive about anything.

'And how am I supposed to know what you want to keep and what you want to throw out?'

'Anything that duplicates whatever we already have—kitchen equipment and what have you—can go to a charity shop. You keep your books in the same order as mine, so if you wanted to merge our books on the shelves, that's fine by me. And I promise I'll sort out the remaining papers and anything you don't want to tackle as soon as I get back.'

'You're going *now*?'

'It makes sense. Otherwise I'll lose half a day's work tomorrow, travelling up to Yorkshire. And if I leave now it means I'll avoid the rush-hour traffic.'

And also, by her reckoning, he'd be there while it was still light enough for him to do a quick recce of the site. She was lucky he'd stayed in London long enough for her to get home before he left.

'I'm staying at the pub—it's just down the road from Whitby.' He flicked into his PDA, then scribbled down a number. 'That's the number, in case you need it.'

It was pointless being upset about it. She'd always known

that Alex's job came first. Yes, they were married—but it was a marriage of convenience and she'd better remember that. The only thing Alex had changed in his life was ditching the string of girlfriends. She believed him absolutely on that score, because Alex was always honest. 'Thanks. Need a hand with anything?'

'I'm practically done.' He kissed her lightly. 'Thanks, Bel. I knew you'd understand.'

He finished packing—incredibly swiftly, but then again she knew he was used to being on the move and travelling light— and then kissed her goodbye. 'I'll call you when I get there, OK?'

It wasn't OK, but she knew that look on his face. He was raring to go. Anything she said would fall on deaf ears. 'OK. Have a good trip.'

The door closed behind him, but she didn't go to the window to watch him walk down the path outside the flat. There was no point. Alex wouldn't think to look up and wave to her; his mind would be focused on the new site and the possibilities.

The rest of the day stretched out before her. She didn't have anything better to do, she thought, so she might as well tackle the boxes. She unpacked Alex's books and spent a couple of hours rearranging the shelves in the study. Quite a few of his academic books were the same as hers; she flicked through to check and saw that Alex had done exactly what she'd done with her textbooks, so there were notes in the margins in his neat spiky handwriting. She didn't want to throw away her notes either or transfer them to a computer, so she ended up slotting his copies right next to hers.

He didn't have much music, only a few old CDs; again, she wasn't too surprised because Alex had been the first person she knew to get an MP3 player and transfer his music to a much more compact and portable form. There was even less kitchen stuff, because Alex never stayed long enough in one place to need to cook. But she dutifully boxed it up for him to take to the charity shop.

When she opened the next box, it was filled with files and loose papers; a quick scan along the spines told her that these were Alex's notes from his student days. She couldn't resist looking; after all, he'd given her carte blanche. As she'd expected, his undergraduate essays were well reasoned and fluent, and most of his marks were firsts or high upper seconds.

Then a piece of paper fell out of the file she was leafing through, one of the first from his doctoral studies.

Alex's illustrations were usually clear and precise, but this one wasn't of an artefact or a plan of a site or a cross-section. It was a sketch of a woman. A very pretty woman, though she looked a little older than the average student. Odd: Isobel had never known Alex to draw sketches of friends.

There were doodles on the same piece of paper, along with scrappy notes. It looked very much to her as if he'd been studying and let his mind wander to this woman. The initial 'D' appeared several times on the page with a heart drawn around it.

A lump rose in her throat and she wished she hadn't looked at the papers. Hadn't found this. Because even without that tell-tale initial, she knew that this was Dorinda. The woman who'd taught Alex not to trust or to believe in love. Alex had said he was over her—but he'd still kept her picture. So was he still carrying a torch for Dorinda?

As if on cue, the phone rang.

'Bel? I'm here. Well, I got here half an hour ago but I just had to go and take a look at the site first.'

Which was exactly what she'd known he'd do.

'It's incredible, Bel. You'd love it. I've taken some photographs and I'll email them to you tonight when I've downloaded them to my laptop. I wish you were here with me—why don't you call Rita and ask for some time off so you can come up here?'

'Alex, I can't let the museum down. I've already taken enough leave at short notice,' she reminded him. For their honeymoon—which already felt as if it had happened light years ago—and then moving house.

'I know and I'm sorry. I'm being selfish.' He sounded contrite. 'I just wanted to share this with you. Look, I'll be home soon. I'll call you tomorrow, OK?'

He clearly hadn't noticed that she'd been quieter than usual, Isobel thought as she replaced the receiver. Because, as usual, his head was full of his work.

She spent a while pottering round the flat. Even though she'd loved it from the moment she and Alex had viewed it, right at that moment she couldn't settle. She was cross with herself for mooching about, and even crosser with herself for missing Alex.

But the worst was the fact that she'd fallen in love with him. Made exactly the same mistake as she'd made with Gary: fallen for a man who'd never love her as much as she loved him.

Alex turned over for the umpteenth time and fluffed up his pillow. Even though he'd worked until late and his eyes were gritty and sore, he couldn't settle to sleep. And he knew why. Despite this being a single bed, it felt too big—because Isobel wasn't there. He'd become used to curling round her before drifting off to sleep, feeling the warmth of her body and the softness of her skin against him. Without her, it didn't feel right.

And he was feeling guilty about the way he'd packed without a second thought to come up here. OK, so it was part of his job—but he'd just left Isobel to it. Left her to unpack his stuff. Which made him a selfish bastard under anyone's terms.

She'd sounded slightly forlorn on the phone. Again, his fault. He'd uprooted her from the flat that had been her home since she'd split up with Gary. Steamrollered her into this marriage. Promised that he'd support her…and then left her to get on with it, alone.

He needed to make this better. So he'd buy her flowers on his way back to London—and, although he wasn't ready to say the words, he'd show her how he felt. How much she meant to him.

Just as soon as this project was over.

CHAPTER THIRTEEN

ALEX could see the light in the living room window as he climbed out of the car. Good. Isobel was definitely home, then. He took his suitcase, briefcase and the flowers from the back of the car, locked up, and headed for the flat.

'Bel?' he called as he unlocked the front door.

She appeared in the doorway to the living room. 'Hi. Did you have a good journey back?'

'Fine.' Better still because he knew he was coming home to her. Not that he was going to spook her by saying it. He'd already spooked himself enough. 'Have you eaten, yet?'

She shook her head. 'I thought I'd wait for you. I can order in a pizza if you're starving, otherwise dinner will be about half an hour.'

'Let's eat out.' He handed her the flowers. 'And these are for you. To say sorry. I shouldn't have left you to sort out all my stuff, Bel. It was thoughtless and not fair of me.'

'Thanks, but there was really no need to buy me flowers. I didn't mind sorting things out,' she said, but he thought her smile seemed slightly brittle. 'There's a box in the spare room that I've earmarked for the charity shop, so you just need to look through it and check I'm not getting rid of anything you want to keep. And I've left your notes for you to sort out. We really need another filing cabinet for the study, so I've ordered one.'

'Brilliant.' Trust her to see the problem and sort the solution without a fuss. 'Thanks, Bel. I appreciate it.'

'I'd better put these in water.'

Hmm. He'd expected at least a kiss hello. Was this just Isobel being her usual practical self and wanting to put the flowers in water before they started drooping, or was she avoiding him?

He wondered even more when she was quiet over dinner. Something was up. But what?

He found out later that night when he climbed into bed beside her and cuddled into her.

'Sorry. We can't tonight. It's my period.'

'OK. It's not a problem.'

Though it told him why she'd been a bit edgy that evening. Partly possible physical discomfort and partly the fact that it was proof of yet another month when they hadn't made a baby. Given what she'd told him before their wedding, she must be feeling thoroughly miserable right now. Disappointed. And hating herself for not being able to let go and relax.

The last thing he wanted to do was put pressure on her, make her feel bad about not being pregnant. On the other hand, Gary had kept her at arm's length because he hadn't wanted her to risk another miscarriage—which had made her feel even worse. This was a really, really difficult line to tread. It would be so easy to get it wrong. Whatever he did or said would risk hurting her.

So in the end he stayed where he was and kept his arms wrapped round her. 'Just so you know, I'm not trying to pressure you into having sex with me. I'm happy just to hold you tonight,' he said softly.

'Uh-huh.' But her body was tense, and she wasn't relaxing back against him the way she usually did.

'Would a back rub help?' he asked.

'No. Anyway, you've had a long drive. I ought to be the one offering you a back rub.'

'Hey. There are no "oughts" between us. No pressure, OK?'

'OK.'

He sighed. 'Bel.'

'What?'

'We agreed, no secrets. Spit it out.'

'I don't know what you're talking about.'

He switched on the light, then spun her round to face him. So he could see her eyes. 'You're not normally this quiet with me. Is it the baby thing that's upsetting you?'

She swallowed. 'No.'

In other words, yes, but she didn't want to admit it. 'Bel.' He stroked her face. 'We can go and see a specialist, if you want to. Just for a chat, maybe some initial tests. It might help put your mind at rest.'

'It's not that.'

'Then *tell* me. Unfortunately, mind-reading isn't one of my many talents.'

She shook her head. 'It's stupid.'

'Tell me anyway.' He kissed the tip of her nose. 'Better than bottling it up.'

She grimaced. 'All right. I was just checking what was in some of your files so I knew where to put them. And this sketch of Dorinda—at least, I assume it was her, as you'd doodled a "D" in a heart all over the page—fell out.'

'Sketch?' He frowned. 'Blimey. They must have been really old files—I haven't looked at my doctorate stuff in years. And it must've been on the back of some notes I wanted at the time or I would probably have thrown it out.'

'Oh.' She flushed, looking embarrassed.

'Isobel, you don't seriously think I'm still holding a torch for her, do you? I haven't seen her for years and I don't have the slightest interest in where she is or what she's doing now. And besides, I'm married to *you*.' He pulled her into his arms. 'Bel, I'm not Gary.'

'I know.'

'Then give me a cuddle instead of the silent treatment.'

He almost—almost—told her that he'd missed her. That he was glad to be home. That all hadn't felt quite right with his world when he was away from her.

But this wasn't part of the deal.

And they'd both been burned by love before. It was better to keep it the way it was. So he kept his thoughts to himself, and just held her until they both drifted into sleep.

Two more months passed and Isobel's period was regular as clockwork, practically down to the hour. And every time it happened, she bawled her eyes out and then splashed her eyes with water so Alex wouldn't notice when he got home.

Every time they made love, Isobel found herself wishing afterwards that this had been the right time, that they'd made a baby—and every time she hated herself for being so needy, for not being able to emulate his ability to take life as it came. She should be making love with him because she wanted *him*, not because they were trying to make a baby.

She'd even thought about buying an ovulation kit to help them pinpoint the right window for having sex—but then again, she and Alex were having sex regularly. Plenty of it.

So the problem was obviously with her.

Alex had mentioned going to see a specialist, but when she hadn't immediately leapt at the idea he hadn't mentioned it again. He was busy at work and he just didn't seem to have noticed that time was ticking away and they still hadn't made a baby. Or maybe he had noticed that she still wasn't pregnant—and the fact he hadn't brought it up with her meant that he was secretly relieved at not being a father. His job wasn't exactly conducive to fatherhood, was it?

She wrapped her arms round herself. How stupid could she be? He'd told her right from the start that he didn't believe in love. That their relationship was a deep friendship plus great sex. She knew his job was his life. So how on earth had she let herself get to the point where she was wishing he'd put her before his job?

She dragged in a breath.

She knew how she'd done it.

By falling in love with him.

So much for going into this with her eyes wide open. She'd kidded herself that her feelings for Alex were just friendship. Told herself that when he was away and the bed felt too wide, it was simply because she'd grown used to him being there, that it was a habit.

It was nothing of the kind.

She was in love with her husband.

A husband who didn't love her and never would, because he wouldn't ever let himself be that vulnerable again.

How stupid could she be?

She tried taking a leaf out of Alex's book and losing herself in her job, but it just didn't feel the same any more. Every time she did her Roman domestic life exhibition at the museum and saw mothers in the audience carrying their babies around in slings and holding the hand of an older child, she had to bite back the envy.

Another month went by. Isobel had always thought wryly that she could set her watch by her period—practically know the second she'd need to take a coffee break on every fourth Thursday.

So when it reached Thursday lunchtime, she found herself wondering.

The sensible side of her knew that it couldn't be. The stress of wanting a baby and still not falling pregnant had probably thrown her cycle for a loop.

But all the same, hope fluttered in her stomach.

When it was time to leave for the day and her period still hadn't started, the flutter turned into a herd of elephants stomping about in her stomach. She had to know the truth.

There was only one way to find out. She called into the supermarket and bought a test kit on the way home. And she sat in the kitchen with the test kit on the scrubbed pine table before her.

To test, or not to test?

Even though she'd tried to be brave about it, she knew that a false alarm would rip her heart out.

But if she was pregnant, what then? How would Alex react? Right at that moment she couldn't second-guess him.

And what if she miscarried again? That was the point where her last marriage fell apart. Would it be the same with Alex? Although she knew intellectually that Alex was nothing like Gary, she couldn't shift the fear.

'Enough,' she said out loud. 'Calm down. Deep breaths. This isn't *you*, Isobel,' she told herself. 'Stop panicking. Like Alex's grandmother would say, you're building bridges to trouble and that's not good.'

What she really should do was take it step by step. Do the test. And once she knew one way or another, she could take the next step.

She went into the bathroom. The last time she remembered feeling this sick was when a mutual friend told her the news—

that Gary's new love had had a baby. The baby she'd wanted so much herself.

But it wasn't Gary's baby she wanted. It was Alex's. A child with those same amazing eyes and carefree smile and dark curls.

She did the test, and waited. The seconds felt as if they were dragging.

Please, please, please let it be positive, she prayed silently. Please let her have Alex's baby. She really didn't mind if it was a girl or a boy; she just wanted a child to share the world with.

She looked at the clock. How could time move so slowly? Surely it was against the laws of physics?

'Please let it be positive. Please. Is it so much to ask?' she whispered.

Another glance at the clock. Five seconds.

She looked at the test kit. There was a blue line in one of the windows, telling her that the test was working.

She closed her eyes again. Please be positive. *Please* be positive, she willed.

Again, she looked at the clock. Surely it was time, now. Heart thumping, she looked at the test stick and burst into tears—noisy, hot, shuddering sobs. 'Thank you God, fate, whoever's in charge of the universe—thank you,' she whispered when her sobs finally died away.

She checked the test again, just to be sure she hadn't misread it and it hadn't changed; then she bathed her eyes, the cool water soothing her hot, swollen skin.

Pregnant.

She was definitely pregnant

She rested one palm against her abdomen. 'Hang on in there, little one. Everything's going to be just fine now,' she said.

So. Step one. She was definitely pregnant.

Now she had to tell Alex.

She was tempted to ring him, but if he was still in a meeting, it wasn't fair to interrupt him. A text, on the other hand, was something he could pick up at his convenience.

She tapped the message into her phone.

Any idea when you'll be home?

To her surprise, he replied almost instantly.

Hour or so. Why, want to go out for dinner?

She couldn't tell him news like this by text.

No. Just wanted to talk to you.

A few moments later, her phone rang. 'Bel? What's the matter?'

'Nothing.'

'I have three sisters, remember,' Alex said. 'I know that "nothing" doesn't mean anything of the kind. What's wrong?'

'I don't really want to talk about it on the phone.' She wanted to tell him face to face. Where, very briefly, he wouldn't be able to mask his first reaction. She needed to know how he felt about this.

'Do you need me home now?' He sounded concerned rather than irritated.

'No.' *Yes.* 'I'm fine,' she reassured him, knowing she was taking a slight licence with the truth. 'There's nothing to worry about.' That much at least was true. 'See you when you get home.'

'OK, honey. See you soon.'

* * *

It wasn't like Isobel to bother him at work.

Though he had been putting in a lot of hours at work lately. Neglecting her.

Alex made a rough calculation in his head. Hell. Her period had probably just started and she was feeling miserable. And this particular piece of work wasn't desperately urgent. Right now, she probably needed a hug more than he needed to do this. He could catch up later.

He saved the file, locked the office behind him and stopped off for supplies on the way home. Armed with tissues and three large bars of good chocolate, he walked indoors.

'Bel? I'm home.'

She emerged from the kitchen. 'You didn't have to come straight back.'

He took one look at her and knew he'd made the right decision. 'Yes, I did.' He dropped the plastic bag on the floor and enfolded her in his arms. 'You've been crying. Your eyes are all puffy. What's wrong?'

'I...' She dragged in a breath. 'I'm being stupid.'

He could feel wetness seeping through his shirt. 'Don't cry, honey. We'll work something out. Look, I'm not putting any pressure on you here, but maybe it's time we went to see someone about this. We'll get some tests run—on *both* of us,' he emphasised, 'and see what's going on and what our options are.'

'My period hasn't started, Alex.'

'We can try again next month. Maybe we'll go away for a weekend. Somewhere we can both relax and unwind. Take the stress off, and maybe it'll happen.'

'I said,' she repeated, 'my period hasn't started.'

Her words finally sank in and he drew back slightly. So if it wasn't her period... 'Then what is it? Your parents are all right?'

'They're fine. I...um...come and sit down.'

There was a weird sensation flickering down his spine. It took Alex a while to identify it as fear.

Was she telling him this was all over? That she'd met someone else?

He let her lead him into the kitchen and sat down at the table. 'Bel? Talk to me. What's going on?'

'I'm not sure how to say this.'

The flickering grew stronger. 'Whatever it is, I'd prefer you to tell me straight.' Actually, that wasn't true. If she was about to tell him it was over, he didn't want to hear it at all. And that scared him even more: since when had Isobel become this important to him?

She handed him something that felt like a flattened pencil wrapped in a tissue. 'Take a look at this.'

He frowned, and unwrapped it as she went to the opposite end of the table and leaned against it.

And then he realised she'd given him a pregnancy test. He'd never actually seen one before; he'd never been in a position to need to see one before. And he really wasn't quite sure what he was looking at. 'Are you telling me…?'

She nodded. 'I'm late. And I'm always, *always* on time. Practically to the hour.' She swallowed hard. 'I thought I might be late because I was…well, a bit tense.'

Completely stressed out, more like. And he'd been too wrapped up in his new job to notice just how bad she'd been feeling. Guilt made the back of his neck feel hot.

'But I needed to know for sure,' she continued. 'So I bought a test. And, um, it's positive.'

He stared at the test stick and then at her, stunned. 'You're pregnant.'

'Yes.'

She looked worried sick and it was hardly surprising. She'd had two miscarriages, and Gary hadn't exactly been supportive afterwards. She was probably panicking that this pregnancy wouldn't last, either—and that he'd let her down the way Gary had.

Or was she worrying that he'd changed his mind about his promise to her, that he didn't want this baby after all?

Of course he hadn't changed his mind.

But he needed to get his head round what she'd just told him.

Although intellectually he'd expected this to happen eventually, he hadn't been prepared for it emotionally. Hadn't known how he'd feel when she finally told him they were having a baby.

He blinked. 'We're having a baby.'

'Yes.'

'I'm going to be a dad.' There was a lump in his throat a mile wide and a weird sensation in his chest that he couldn't explain. 'Oh, Bel. We're having a baby.'

'You're OK about that?'

He pushed his chair back, walked over to her and wrapped his arms round her. 'More than OK.' That vision he'd had of a little girl like Isobel… It might just be coming true. 'But you shouldn't be on your feet. Sit down.'

'I don't need to—' she began.

He solved her protest by dragging another chair out, sitting down and pulling her onto his lap. 'Bel. I'm so…' He shook his head. 'I can't find the words. It's as if someone's knocked everything I knew out of my head. But it's a good feeling.'

'I thought you might…well…'

'Back out of it? Want to change my mind?' He saw the tear start to slide down her cheek, and kissed it away. 'No. Don't cry, Bel. It's all going to be just fine.'

'I think I'm crying because I'm happy. And I'm so relieved. I thought there was something wrong—'

He placed his finger gently on her lips. 'Shh. Nothing's

wrong. I know we've had to wait a bit, but it'll be worth the wait.' He smiled. 'So do you want to tell your mum first or mine?'

She shook her head. 'Not until twelve weeks. I don't want to tell anyone. Just in case.'

Although she didn't say it, he could read the fear in her eyes. She was terrified that she was going to miscarry again. How far gone had she been when she'd lost her last baby? He hadn't asked her—and now most definitely wasn't the right time to pose the question. 'Try not to worry,' he said, stroking her face. 'The odds are on our side. The chances are that everything's going to be absolutely fine, this time. But you don't take any risks or lift anything heavier than a tissue.'

She coughed. 'That's a bit over the top, Alex.'

'All right. Nothing heavier than a book, then,' he amended. 'And as from now, you're off all housework duties. I'll do them.'

'You're never here,' she pointed out.

He brushed it aside. 'We'll get a cleaner. I loathe ironing so we'll use a laundry service. And—'

'Alex, I'm pregnant, not sick.'

'You're pregnant. And you've had a rough time in the past. So I'm not taking any chances with you.' He took a risk and told her straight. 'You're too important to me.'

Her eyes filled with tears again. 'I'm sorry. I'm being wet.'

'No, you're not. It's just hormones.' He smiled. 'Saskia used to ring me and weep down the phone when she was pregnant. The only way to shut her up was to have chocolate delivered every three days. And then she used to ring me up and cry because I was being nice to her.'

As he'd hoped, the ridiculous story made her smile. 'Alex, you're completely mad.'

'The word you were looking for is "eccentric",' he corrected, and kissed her lightly. 'We're going to have a baby. And I'm going to take care of you, I promise.'

CHAPTER FOURTEEN

IF ANYONE had told Isobel that Alex would start coming home from work at a reasonable time and his bedtime reading would involve a pile of books about pregnancy and babies instead of obscure texts and archaeological journals, she would've laughed.

But he did.

He also insisted on taking over the kitchen while she sat with her feet up. Although he was a great cook, it drove her crazy, having to sit still and do nothing.

When he brought her a glass of water and a multi-vitamin tablet formulated especially for pregnant women, she'd had enough.

'Alex, you're steamrollering me again, like you did over the wedding. I know you're trying to help and be a new man or what have you, but I'm quite capable of looking after myself.'

'Agreed, but all the books say women find strong smells hard to cope with in the early weeks of pregnancy, so you're better off out of the kitchen. And I'm cooking things with as little scent as possible so the kitchen smells don't make you feel sick.'

'I'm not getting morning sickness at the moment. Anyway, you hate bland food.'

He shrugged. 'It's only for a few months. I can put up with it, as long as you're all right.'

Alex was trying his hardest to be domesticated, for her sake. So he really, really cared about her. He might not say the L-word, and he might still say he didn't believe in it, but the way he was acting told her that he cared.

And Isobel had to blink back tears—tears she was glad Alex hadn't noticed, or she would've had to claim they were due to her hormones being all over the place. She just wanted him to learn to trust her. To learn that it was safe to love her—that he could give her his heart and she'd treasure it. That she'd love him all the way back.

To Isobel's mingled shock and pleasure, Alex actually took time off to go take her for the booking-in appointment with the midwife—and he held her hand all the way, including in the waiting room. And he held her hand even more tightly when she explained to the midwife about her previous two miscarriages.

'Normally, my advice is that gentle sexual intercourse is fine in pregnancy—but in this case I'd suggest avoiding intercourse for the first three months,' the midwife advised. 'But there are other things you can do—relax together, massage each other, have a candlelit bath together.'

'Isobel and the baby come first,' Alex said immediately. 'I don't want to take any risks.'

The midwife nodded. 'That's good. Having previous miscarriages doesn't mean you can't carry a baby to term, Isobel, but I would like to see you a bit more frequently so I can keep an eye on you. And if you're feeling worried at all, even if it's something you think is silly, just call me or one of the other midwives on your team—that's what we're here for. Now, I'll book you in for a dating scan, and you'll get a letter with the appointment later in the week—probably for two or three weeks' time.'

When the appointment came through, Alex checked his

diary and made a noise of frustration. 'I'm supposed to be in Chester then—and for the two days before the scan, too. I'll get them to reschedule.'

'What if they can't?' Isobel asked.

'They'll have to, if they want me there. Because no way in hell am I going to miss our first scan.'

While Alex was away, he called Isobel every day. He nagged her like crazy about putting her feet up and getting lots of rest. And when he'd been passing a shopping centre, he'd been unable to resist going into a toyshop and buying the softest, softest teddy bear.

Their baby's first present.

Isobel had been adamant that she wouldn't even look at baby clothes or nursery furniture or a baby book until after the twelfth week, but surely one little bear wouldn't hurt? He'd sneak it into a drawer until she was ready to talk about buying things for the baby.

Isobel was curled up on the sofa, reading, when she felt a familiar dragging sensation in her abdomen.

No.

She froze.

It couldn't be.

Please, don't let it be that.

She forced herself to take a deep breath in. And out. And in. And out. Stay calm, for the baby's sake, even though panic was galloping along every nerve-end.

Gingerly, she walked to the bathroom. Saw the blood.

OK. Maybe it was just spotting. Plenty of women had spotting in early pregnancy.

But she'd been here before. She knew this was too heavy to be just spotting.

She was losing her baby.

Along with her dreams.

Shaking, she called Alex's mobile.

'The cell phone that you are calling is unavailable,' the automated message told her. 'Please try later.'

But later would be too late. She needed him here right now.

It looked as if she was going to have to deal with this on her own. She took a deep breath and called the number her midwife had given her. To her relief, it was Jenny, the midwife who'd seen her at the clinic.

'I'm bleeding,' she whispered.

'All right, love. I know you're worried, but I'll be with you as soon as I can. Just lie on the sofa with your feet up, try to relax and try not to worry. Is anyone with you?'

'No. Alex is away on business.'

'Is there anyone you can call to be with you?'

'My parents are a good couple of hours away.'

'What about friends?'

Isobel took a deep breath. 'We haven't told anyone yet. I—I wanted to wait until I was twelve weeks. Just in case.'

'I'll be there as soon as possible, love.' Jenny double-checked her address. 'Try not to worry. Spotting's very common in early pregnancy—and your hormones will still be all over the place, so if this is around the time when you would normally have had a period, it could just be that.'

'It could be,' Isobel said, trying for bravery. Though she knew this feeling all too well. It wasn't just hormones or spotting.

When Jenny arrived, she examined Isobel very gently, then stroked her hand. 'Isobel, love, we need to get you to hospital.'

'I'm losing my baby.' It wasn't a question. She knew.

'It might be a threatened miscarriage. They'll be able to

tell in the hospital with the scanner—and if that's the case, we'll put you on bedrest for a while and keep monitoring you until the scare's over.'

'Bedrest? But…'

'You're on your own. I know.' Jenny squeezed her hand. 'Don't worry, I'll go with you. Have you managed to get in touch with Alex yet?'

'No.'

'We'll try again in a minute. I'll just call you in.' She glanced at her watch. 'And I'll drive you in myself. It'll be quicker.' Jenny rang the hospital, but Isobel didn't have a clue what the midwife was saying. She was too busy holding onto the tiny fragment of hope that it was a threatened miscarriage. That, this time, her baby would hold on.

'Let's go,' Jenny said softly.

'What if one of your other patients needs you?'

'I'm supposed to be off duty in about three minutes,' Jenny said with a smile. 'So they'll be able to talk to whoever's on the roster.'

Isobel bit her lip. 'I can't ask you to go to the hospital with me in your time off.'

'You haven't asked me. I'm insisting.'

The midwife's kindness made Isobel want to cry. But she was terrified that if she started, she'd never stop. So she forced herself to smile. 'Thank you.'

'Alex and Bel can't take your call right now. Please leave a message after the beep.'

Alex frowned. Isobel hadn't said anything about being out tonight. Not that he was a control freak—just that he wanted to be sure she was all right. From what he'd heard, most new fathers-to-be were a bit overprotective about their pregnant partners. But he was doubly so because of Isobel's past.

Coming here on this job had been wrong. He should've called in some favours and got someone else to do the exploration. Right now Isobel was vulnerable and it had been a bad idea to leave her on her own.

But maybe her friends at work had suggested an evening out. A meal after work, or an impromptu visit to the cinema. Isobel was too sensible to take any risks, he knew. She'd pace herself, and take a taxi rather than the tube if she felt tired. And she'd probably tried to call him earlier to let him know she was out; the mobile phone reception around here was atrocious, and he'd had to wait until he was back at the hotel and could use the phone in his room to call her.

He didn't bother leaving a message on their home phone; instead, he called her mobile.

'The cell phone you are calling is switched off. Please try later or send a text.'

Definitely the cinema, then. OK. He'd call her again after dinner.

On the way to the hospital, the cramps grew worse. On Jenny's insistence, Isobel had kept trying to call Alex, but still there was no reply. 'He's in an area with poor reception,' she told Jenny.

'We'll try again in a bit. Let's go up to the ward. The sonographer might not say anything at first as he tries to find the baby, but don't worry about that,' Jenny reassured her. 'It's perfectly normal.'

As they went through the doors of the ward, Isobel could see her name written on the white board, under the heading 'emergency'.

Emergency.

There was nothing normal about that.

But it didn't send Isobel into screaming panic. Right at that moment she couldn't feel anything.

She let herself be led into the little cubicle, lay on the bed and bared her abdomen for the radioconductive gel. All the while, Jenny was holding her hand and talking to her, but Isobel couldn't take in a single word.

And then she saw the pity in the doctor's face.

'I'm so sorry, Mrs Richardson. There isn't a heartbeat. I'm afraid you've miscarried,' the doctor said gently.

Everything after that just blurred.

How was she going to tell Alex?

'Mrs Richardson?'

'I'm sorry. I…' She dragged in a breath. Now wasn't the time to go to pieces.

'No need to apologise. It's a very difficult thing to have to take in.' The doctor sat next to her. 'You're about nine weeks, according to your notes, so I'd recommend that we just let nature take its course rather than bring you in for a D and C. Do you have anyone who can be with you for the next few days?'

'My husband's away on business.'

'If you'd rather stay in overnight, we can arrange that.'

Cold, clinical hospital. So unlike the bright, sunny nursery she'd allowed herself to plan in her head. But it made no difference. Her baby wasn't going to be there. 'I'd rather go home, please.'

'I'll take you,' Jenny said softly. 'And I can talk you through what to expect.'

Isobel shrugged. 'Same as last time, I presume.'

'I'm so sorry, love.' Jenny squeezed her hand. 'Do you want to wait here for a while?'

Isobel shook her head. 'I'd just like to go home, please.'

She managed to hold herself together on the way back to the flat, mainly because she knew that if she started crying she wouldn't be able to stop.

'Would you like me to ring Alex for you?' Jenny asked.

'No, it's fine. You've done so much for me already this evening, and it's not fair to expect you to stay,'

'I'll wait with you until you manage to get through to him.'

Isobel gave her a tired smile. 'I'll be all right, Jenny. I was half expecting this to happen, anyway. But thank you for being so kind.'

The midwife still looked concerned. 'I'd rather not leave you.'

Isobel patted her hand. 'Honestly, I'll be fine. Thank you.'

She kept the smile on her face until the door closed behind her.

And then she walked into the bathroom, stripped off her clothes, and stood under the shower. Slid down the wall until she was sitting on the floor with the water trickling down over her, her knees up to her chin and her head resting on her knees. Even though the water was warm, she felt as if she'd never be warm again. And she was so, so empty.

She stayed there until the water ran cold, and then dragged herself out of the shower. Wrapped herself in a towel. Went through all the mechanical steps of sorting out clean clothes and a sanitary towel.

White.

The colour of mourning, in some cultures.

But she felt too cold, too empty, to mourn.

She had no idea how much time passed until the phone rang. She answered it mechanically.

'Bel? You're back, then.'

'Back?'

'I rang earlier. There was no answer, so I assumed you were out with people from work. You didn't answer your mobile, either.'

Her tongue felt as if it had stuck to the roof of her mouth. 'No. I must've been in the shower and didn't hear the phone.' It was a complete lie, but to her relief he didn't question her.

'Are you OK?'

No.

Far from it.

And right then she felt that nothing would ever be OK again.

'Just tired.'

That was true. She was tired to the depth of her soul. But if she told him what had really happened tonight, he'd drive straight home. She couldn't do that to him. Knowing Alex, he would've been working since early morning, probably until just before he called her. A four-hour drive on top of that would be unfair. And if he ended up falling asleep at the wheel…

No.

She'd lost their baby.

She couldn't bear to lose Alex, too.

He was speaking again.

'Sorry, Alex. I didn't catch that.'

'I'll be home in two days. Then on Friday morning we've got the scan.'

Not any more. She dug her nails into her palm to stop herself crying. 'I know.' She was trying so hard, but she knew she didn't sound as excited as she should be.

'Are you sure you're all right?'

She could practically hear the frown in his voice. 'Just tired,' she said again.

'Go and have a warm bath and then an early night,' he said. 'Sweet dreams. And I'll call you tomorrow.'

'Goodnight,' she said, still just about in control.

And when she replaced the receiver, she curled up into a ball. Please, somehow, let her get through the next day.

CHAPTER FIFTEEN

WHEN Alex called the following evening, something about Isobel's voice didn't sound quite right. 'Bel, is anything wrong?' he asked

'Why would there be?'

'It's just…' A feeling that something wasn't as it should be. But he couldn't put his finger on it. 'How was your day?'

'Routine. How was yours?'

'Good. I did some geophysics tests today and I think we've got something very interesting.'

It wasn't until he'd said goodbye and put the phone down that he realised what was odd.

Isobel hadn't mentioned the baby or the scan.

Given that the scan meant they'd be seeing their baby on the screen, that it would help her believe she really was pregnant and it really was going to work out, this time, he'd expected her to be all bubbly and happy and hardly able to wait. To be planning how to tell their family, how many copies of the scan photo they'd need.

The more he thought about it, the more he was sure that something was very, very wrong.

She'd answered his questions either with another question or with some anodyne response. So clearly something had happened and she was trying not to tell him because he was miles away and she didn't want him to worry.

Time to call in some favours.

Two phone calls netted him the result he wanted. And then he threw everything into his suitcase, loaded that and his briefcase into his car, settled his hotel bill and drove back to London, not caring that it was late and it would take him four hours to get home and he'd arrive at stupid o'clock, while Isobel was fast asleep. Right now, he had a feeling that she needed him. And he intended to be there for her.

When he arrived back in London, he let himself quietly into the flat and left his luggage in the hallway. He tiptoed up the stairs, and stripped off outside their bedroom so the noise wouldn't wake her. He padded across the carpet to their bed and slid under the duvet beside her, trying not to disturb her. He'd talk to her tomorrow, find out what was wrong then. But for tonight he was happy just to sleep with his wife in his arms.

Although Isobel stirred when he curled his body round hers, she stayed asleep. Alex just held her close, and was asleep himself only a couple of minutes later.

When the alarm shrilled, Alex groaned and reached out to hit the snooze button.

'Alex? When did you get back?' Isobel asked.

'Last night,' he mumbled, not opening his eyes. 'Shh. Go back to sleep. Five more minutes.'

But she'd gone rigid in his arms. Sighing inwardly, he opened his eyes and sat up. 'Good morn—' He stopped abruptly. She looked absolutely terrible. Her face was white and there were shadows under her eyes. But what really shocked him was the way the light had disappeared from her eyes. 'Bel? What's happened?'

'I lost the baby.' Her voice was flat, unemotional.

He stared at her, unable to take it in at first. She'd lost their baby? When?

And then he realised.

'When I called, the night before last. When you were out.'

'Yes.' There was no tone whatsoever in her voice.

'Why the *hell* didn't you tell me?'

She shrugged. 'Apart from the fact you were a four-hour drive away and it wasn't fair to drag you back, it had already happened. There was nothing you could have done.'

'Yes, I could. I could've been there to hold your hand and support you through it.' He shook his head in disbelief. 'Oh, Bel.' He went to put his arms round her, hold her close, but she moved out of reach.

'Don't. I'm OK.'

No, she wasn't. She was very far from it. She looked and sounded so brittle that she'd shatter at any moment. 'Bel.' He raked a hand through his hair. 'I don't know what to say. Except I'm so, so sorry.'

She shrugged. 'It's not your fault.'

'It's not *yours*, either.' He paused. 'If you'd told me, I would've come straight home.'

'Driving for four hours after a long day's work?'

'It's what I did last night,' he pointed out. 'Bel, you didn't sound yourself. I *knew* something was wrong.'

'Well, now you know.'

'And I came straight back.' He reached out to take her hand. 'Don't shut me out, Bel.'

'I'm fine. I need to get ready for work.'

'You're not fine, Bel. And you're in no fit state to go to work.'

When she ignored him and started to climb out of the bed, he moved, wrapping his arms round her and hauling her onto his lap.

'What are you doing?' she snapped.

'Holding you. Because you're not going *anywhere*,' he said, keeping his arms tightly round her. 'Honey, if you put a brave face on it and go to work, you're going to end up in meltdown.'

'I'll be fine.'

Like hell, she would. He refused to let her go. 'Bel, I know you're hurting—and if it's any consolation, I'm hurting, too.'

'Are you?'

It shocked him that she could even question that. Didn't she know? 'How can you think otherwise?'

'You said…' She swallowed hard. 'You said we'd see how things went.'

'Which doesn't mean I was indifferent. You'd told me what happened with Gary, and I didn't want to pile any more pressure on you. I wanted our baby, Isobel. Every bit as much as you did. OK, I admit, before we had that conversation I'd never really thought about having children—but when you showed me that pregnancy test and I realised we were really going to have a baby, it was… I can't explain it.' He shook his head. 'It was as if I'd been let out of a locked room, a room I'd never even realised I was trapped in until I was let out. And then suddenly this whole new world was around me. A world I could share with you and our child. And I was so happy about it, Bel.' He paused. 'Though right now I'm feeling guilty.'

She stared at him. 'Why?'

'Because I should've been here to take care of you.'

She shook her head. 'It wouldn't have made any difference. You couldn't have stopped it happening.'

'But I would've been here with you when it happened— you wouldn't have had to go through this all on your own.' He stroked her face. 'And even though you know I don't believe in superstitions…' He knew that she did. She'd been worried about seeing him on the day of their wedding. And she'd be so upset when she found out what he'd done. But he couldn't lie to her about this. 'Promise you won't hate me for this, Bel?'

'Hate you for what?'

'I know you said you didn't want to tell anyone until twelve weeks. And I didn't tell anyone—I said I had important personal stuff to do on Friday but I didn't say what it was.' He closed his eyes. 'But I bought something. For our baby. I wanted to…' Suddenly he couldn't go on. He buried his head in his shoulder, inhaling her scent. Needing her warmth. Hoping that she'd somehow manage to find more strength in him than he could right at that minute.

'Alex?'

At last her arms were round him and she was holding him back. But it made him choke. He didn't deserve this.

'Alex, you're scaring me.'

He lifted his head. 'I…I bought a teddy bear. I wanted to buy our baby's first toy.' He dragged in a breath. 'I'm sorry. I shouldn't have done it. I shouldn't have tempted fate.'

'You buying a teddy didn't make me lose—lose…' She stared at him, and a tear rolled down her face. Her mouth was working, but no sounds were coming out.

He kept his arms wrapped tightly round her. 'I'm here, Bel. And I know right now this feels like the end of the world…' he rocked her gently, feeling the tears start to slide down his own face '…but it isn't. We'll get through this, I promise. Because we've still got each other. And that's not going to change.'

She buried her head in his shoulder and sobbed her heart out. He held her close, feeling her pain as well as his own.

Eventually she stopped shaking and pulled back from him slightly. 'Alex. I understand if you want to walk away.' Her voice was thick with tears.

Walk away? He didn't understand. 'Why would I walk away?'

'Because I…because I lost our baby.'

He brushed his mouth lightly against hers. 'I'm not Gary, Bel. I'm not going to walk out on you.'

'But I might not be able to have children, Alex. And I can't do that to you.' She dragged in a breath. 'I can't take your choices away.'

'You're not taking my choices away.'

'But you just said you wanted a child.'

'I do. With *you*.' He stroked her face. 'If it turns out we can't have a biological child of our own, there are other ways. Adoption, fostering…we'll still have options.'

'You'd be better off finding someone else. Someone who can give you a family.'

'I'm not Gary, Bel,' he repeated. 'And here's the kicker. I don't want anyone else. I just want you. And I think I always have.'

She stared at him. 'I don't understand.'

'You've always been the one I've talked to.'

'Because we're friends.'

'You're more than that to me,' he said softly. 'And the more I think about it, the more I realise I didn't really love Dorinda all those years ago. I was in lust with her, yes, but I couldn't talk to her—not the way I talk to you. And I didn't tell you about her at the time because…' He shrugged. 'I suppose I was ashamed. I'd been really, really naïve and stupid, and I didn't want you to think badly of me.'

'I've never thought badly of you, Alex.'

'You're the centre of my life, Bel. You have been for a long while. I wouldn't admit it to myself, but when you got married it meant that you were off limits. And I realise now I dated so much because I was searching for someone who'd have that same special relationship with me that you had. Except none of them matched up to you.'

'But…' she shook her head in seeming disbelief '…Alex, I'm ordinary and the women you dated were stunning.'

He stroked her face. 'Number one, Isobel Richardson, you're very far from ordinary. And number two, they might have been physically gorgeous, but they didn't have that certain something about them. There's only one woman like that as far as I'm concerned.' He held her gaze. 'I know my timing's lousy—and saying this is against all my principles— but I need you to know, Bel. I love you. Like nobody else I've ever known.'

'You love me?'

He nodded. 'So there's my other guilty confession. I love you. I adore my job, but I hate being away from you. I miss you like hell when I'm away. And I know I steamrollered you into this marriage and I haven't looked after you properly, but if you'll give me a second chance I swear I'll be the best husband. I'll put you first.'

'You love me,' she repeated, her voice full of wonder.

'Yeah.' He smiled wryly. 'I love you.'

'Alex.' She swallowed hard. 'I thought you'd never let me close. That you'd never trust me enough to let me love you.'

'I trust you with my life, Bel.' He brushed his mouth against hers. 'You *are* my life.'

She shook her head. 'That's not true. Your job comes first.'

'Not any more. And I'll prove it.'

'How?'

'Take off your wedding ring.'

Isobel froze. Why did he want her to take off the ring? Had she misheard what he said earlier? Was he saying that their marriage was over, after all? 'What?'

'Take off your wedding ring,' he repeated. 'I need to show you something.'

She frowned, but did so. He held out his palm, and she dropped the ring into it. He did something clever, and then suddenly the ring fanned out into three hoops.

'It's a gimmel ring,' she said in surprise. Why on earth hadn't she guessed? She'd even remarked on how pretty it was, the sandwich of white gold between yellow. And she'd seen medieval gimmel rings at the museum: interlocking rings that joined into one, symbolising the joining of two lives. There was often a secret message engraved on the middle hoop. She should've realised that Alex wouldn't give her just a normal ring.

'Take a look,' he said.

Engraved on the middle hoop were the initials AT and IA. His and hers. And in between was engraved the date of their wedding.

'Turn it over,' he said softly.

There was a second engraving. *Semper.*

Latin for 'always'.

'Alex…'

'Just so you know I'm not flannelling you now. I guess I've always known I love you,' he said. 'I told myself you were a just good friend. Someone I've always been comfortable with, and the amazing sex was a bonus. But if I'm honest you're the only woman I've ever told my dreams to. And although I told you at the time it was a marriage of convenience—a way of making sure I got the job and staying around a bit more for Mum's sake—I knew in my heart that it was more than that. I meant what I said in my wedding vows.'

'You didn't say anything about love.'

'Because I was still pretty much in denial. But I'm not any more. I love you, Isobel. So very much. And if you can't love me back, it doesn't really matter, because I love you enough for both of us.' He swallowed hard. 'I guess what I'm trying to say is that I'd rather be with you than without you.'

She dragged in a breath. 'I love you, too, Alex,' she whispered. 'If I'm honest about it, I've loved you for years. Ever since you kissed me when I was eighteen. But you always had this string of girlfriends and you never even seemed to notice I was female. So I settled for second-best—being your friend.' She smiled wryly. 'It's one of the reasons why I didn't want to marry you. I'd already been through a marriage where my husband didn't love me. Marrying someone who was up front about the fact that he didn't believe in love… It was going to be a recipe for disaster.'

'Our marriage isn't a disaster. And I do love you,' Alex said. 'Right now we've hit a rough patch—but that's in our life, not our marriage. We'll get through this. *Together.*'

'I wanted our baby so much, Alex.'

'I know, honey.' He drew her close again. 'So did I.'

'All the months of hoping and being disappointed, and then finding I was pregnant and being so scared in case something went wrong…and now it has.' She closed her eyes. 'So much for third time lucky.'

He stroked her hair. 'There's a glass-half-full side to this.'

'How?' How could he possibly see something positive in this, when their world had just fallen apart?

'You said that the doctors wouldn't investigate until after three miscarriages. Now,' he said gently, 'they'll be able to help us. We can have tests, find out why it happened. Find out what our options are.'

Fear flooded through her. 'Supposing we can't have children at all?'

'We'll face that if and when we come to it.' He stroked her face. 'First steps, first. I'll ring the doctor this morning and make an appointment. It might not be easy and it might take a while, but we can lean on each other. Together we're strong.' He kissed her lightly. 'Go have a shower. Though you're not going to work today. I'll talk to your boss—because Rita really needs to know about this, Bel. And it's going to be easier on you if I tell her.'

She shook her head. 'Alex, I can't ask you to do that.'

'You're not asking. I'm offering.' He stroked her face. 'Actually, no. I'm being bossy. But I'm doing it for the right reasons—I'm trying to protect you from being hurt.'

She hugged him. 'Thank you,' she said softly. 'Because I don't think I can tell anyone without bawling my eyes out.'

'Go and have that shower,' she said.

She did so. When she'd got dressed she padded downstairs to the kitchen, her wet hair still wrapped in a towel. Alex was sitting at the kitchen table, a mug of coffee in one hand and the phone in the other, clearly listening to someone talking on the other end of the line. He looked up, saw her and nodded to the cafetière. It's fresh, he mouthed.

'Uh-huh. Right. Thanks a lot. I'll call you next week,' he said, and ended the call.

'Was that Rita?' she asked.

'Nope—my boss. Who sends his best wishes, by the way. Rita sends her love and says on no account are you to even think about coming back to work until the middle of next week. And before you start worrying, she says that if anyone asks, she's going to tell them you're off with a gastric bug.'

'So what now?'

'We've both got a week off.'

'Both?'

'I'm owed some time. My vote is, we get an appointment with a specialist. And then we go away for a few days.'

'Where?'

'Anywhere that doesn't have memories.' His face was grim. 'Right now I don't want to be here—I don't want to walk past the door of the nursery and think of what might have been. So I'm guessing it's worse for you.'

She felt the tears well up again. 'Yes. But going away…isn't that just trying to run from it all?'

'No. It's giving us some space and distance—so when we come back we're feeling stronger and able to deal with the situation. Together,' he emphasised.

'You've taken time off? But you're really busy at work, Alex.'

He shrugged. 'You're more important.' He paused. 'It seems that as of last week, I get private healthcare as part of the package at work, and because you're my wife that includes you. I was thinking, it might be a way for us to get a faster appointment—unless you'd rather talk to your family doctor?'

She thought about it. 'We need answers. The sooner, the better.'

He nodded. 'Then I'll make the call.' He pushed his chair back. 'But I'd be a hell of a lot happier if you were sitting here with me.'

Taking her cue, she sat on his lap. Slid her arms round his neck. Held him close.

Five minutes later, it was all sorted.

'Tomorrow morning. Which in some ways is very, very bad timing. Our appointment's when we should've been somewhere else.' He kissed the end of her nose. 'But in another way, at least we're going to be doing something positive at ten o'clock. Not just sitting here looking at each other, wishing things were different.'

'Thank you, Alex.' She rested her head on his shoulder. 'You're being brilliant about this.'

'I'm feeling pretty helpless, actually,' he admitted. 'Because nothing I do or say is going to change things.'

'You're here,' she said softly. And he'd put her first. Hadn't walked away, as Gary had. 'And that really, really helps.'

'Good.' He kissed her lightly. 'And I'll hold your hand through everything, tomorrow.'

CHAPTER SIXTEEN

THE appointment was a blur. But at least it wasn't at the same hospital they would've been at for the scan, Isobel thought. The doctor asked all kinds of questions about her medical history, took detailed notes and did an internal examination, and all the way through Alex held her hand, letting her know he was there to support her. He was there during the scans—and it took every ounce of strength she had not to bawl her eyes out, wishing they were having the scan they'd been supposed to have—and squeezed her hand comfortingly while phial after phial of blood was taken.

And then all they had to do was wait for the results.

'This is worse than waiting for exam results,' Isobel said when they'd left the hospital.

'Because at least you have an idea how you've done in an exam, and this is out of our control?' Alex asked.

She nodded. 'So I need to go back to work, Alex. I'm going to go crazy if I spend the whole of the next week just waiting with nothing to occupy my mind.'

'I've got a better idea,' Alex said. 'Let's go away for a few days. How do you fancy Florence?'

'What—now?'

'Why not? It's not going to take long to pack. And if we're

wandering round churches and museums and piazzas, we'll be too busy exploring to worry.'

He had a point. 'Thank you.' She paused. 'But, um, it's not going to be like a honeymoon. You heard what the doctor said. No sex for the next month.'

Alex smiled. 'There's more to a marriage than sex. Besides, he didn't actually say "no sex"—just that we shouldn't try for a baby until after your next period. Which, quite apart from the fact we're waiting for your blood test results, is common sense.'

Clearly she still looked worried, because he laced his fingers through hers. 'Relax, Bel. We don't have to have full sex. But we can do an awful lot of other things.' He grinned. 'We can pretend we're teenagers again. Do all the things we maybe should've done twelve years ago.'

'It wouldn't have worked, twelve years ago,' she pointed out.

'You had a world to conquer—and I still had a fair bit of growing up to do. Full of testosterone and not enough finesse.' He stole a kiss. 'I love you, Isobel Richardson. And we don't have to have sex until you're ready. I can be patient.'

She smiled. 'Alex, you've never been patient. You live your life at a hundred miles an hour.'

'For you,' he said, 'I can be patient. Because you're worth it.'

And he proved it. They spent the next week in Florence, wandering round the piazzas, churches and galleries, hand in hand. And on the moments when she went quiet and still inside, thinking of the baby they'd lost and the might-have-beens, he was there to hold her. To whisper that he loved her, and that it was going to work out.

And then it was Friday and they were back for the test results.

Alex paused at the doorway to the hospital. 'Whatever the doctor says to us, remember that I love you and nothing, but *nothing*, is going to change that.' He drew Isobel's hands up to his mouth and kissed the backs of her fingers.

'I love you, too,' Isobel whispered.

The specialist smiled at them when they were ushered in. 'I'm going to need you to have another blood test in about six weeks, Mrs Richardson, before I can give you an absolute diagnosis—but, given what you've told me about your previous miscarriages all being around the ten to twelve week mark and the headaches you had as a teenager, I'm pretty sure that you have antiphospholipid syndrome.'

'What's that?' Isobel asked.

'It's an autoimmune disorder—your immune system is fighting your body and attacking the good tissues, and the antibodies make your blood "sticky" so it clots more than the average person's. It causes miscarriage because clots form in the placenta and the foetus doesn't get enough blood supply.'

'So it *was* my fault.' Isobel swallowed hard.

Alex's hand tightened round hers, telling her silently that she wasn't to blame herself and he still loved her regardless.

'It's not your fault,' the consultant said quietly. 'It's a medical condition. The symptoms are common to a lot of other conditions, so without the antiphospholipid test you wouldn't even know you had it.'

'So what causes it?' Alex asked. 'Is it a virus?'

'We don't know completely,' the specialist said, 'though we do know there's a genetic component. Do you know if anyone else in your family has had recurrent miscarriages, Mrs Richardson?'

'Not for definite,' Isobel said, 'though I'm an only child and, reading between the lines, my parents tried for a very long while before they had me.'

'Then there may be a link there.' He smiled at them both. 'The good news is that it's the most common treatable cause of recurrent miscarriage. As I said, I need you to come back for another test in about six weeks to confirm it, but your other tests are all clear. Your blood pressure's fine and there's no problem with your cervix. So when we've done the second test, if it confirms what I think right now, we'll start treating you and you can go ahead and try for another baby.'

'That's fantastic,' Alex said. 'What's the treatment?'

'One junior aspirin a day.'

Isobel wasn't quite sure she'd heard him right. 'One junior aspirin a day?' she queried.

'That's right. I know it sounds a simple thing, but it works. It'll be enough to thin your blood—and it'll quadruple your chances of having a successful pregnancy.'

'One junior aspirin a day,' she said, just to check.

He nodded. 'And we'll keep a close eye on you throughout the pregnancy. We'll give you more frequent scans so we can keep an eye on the baby, but all the odds are on your side.'

Alex turned to Isobel, his eyes lit with relief. 'Everything's going to be just fine.'

'If the second test confirms it,' she reminded him.

He smiled. 'It will.'

Alex still travelled over the next few weeks, but made a point of not being away for more than one night at a time. And he called her while he was away.

'I miss you,' he said.

'I miss you, too,' she admitted.

'I bought you a present today.'

'Oh?' she enquired, responding to the teasing note in his voice.

'Uh-huh. It's an incredibly sexy nightie.'

She remembered their wedding night. 'It had better not be silk, given what you do to silk things!'

He laughed. 'No, it's the softest, softest jersey. And it'll cling to your curves—have I told you how much I love your curves, Isobel?'

'Indeed, Mr Richardson.'

'Anyway. It's got these little spaghetti straps. And when I get home I'm really looking forward to seeing you try it on.'

'Are you giving me a dirty phone call, Alex?' she teased.

'Might be. What are you wearing?'

She laughed. 'Jeans and a T-shirt. Or is this where I'm meant to do a Marilyn Monroe and say I'm only wearing Chanel No. 5?'

He laughed back. 'That's not the perfume you wear. And I have to say, Mrs Richardson, your perfume is much, much sexier.' He paused. 'If you want to lose the jeans and T-shirt and go to bed while you're talking to me, honey, that's fine by me.'

So he *was* giving her a dirty phone call. 'Where are you, Alex?'

'In my hotel room. With a big empty bed, and I'm missing my wife. Especially as I really, really want to see her in this nightie. Have I told you there's a lot of lace, as well? And the best bit is, because it's jersey, it stretches. I can slide the straps off your shoulders, then push it down, so I can see you and touch you and kiss you and…' He paused teasingly.

She could imagine the scenario and her mouth went dry. 'Oh, yes?'

'Mmm. As I'm miles away, I can't do what I want to do, right now…but I can tell you, Bel.' His voice went husky. 'I can tell you exactly what I'm going to do to you tomorrow night when I come home.'

He did.

In detail.

And by the time he'd finished, she was quivering. 'You'd better deliver on this tomorrow night, Alex,' she warned. 'Because right now I feel as if I'm going to spontaneously combust.'

'Tomorrow night,' he promised, 'we both are.'

The week between her second test and getting the results seemed to stretch for ever. But finally it was confirmed that the problem was antiphospholipid syndrome.

'So tonight we're going to celebrate,' Alex said, holding her close. 'Everything's going to be all right now. You just wait.'

Three weeks later, Isobel called Alex—who was working from home—in her afternoon break. 'Alex, I'm late.'

'OK. Call me when you get to the station and I'll start cooking dinner. Something quick—a stirfry or something.'

'No, not that sort of late. *Late*.'

There was a pause while he digested what she was saying. 'How late?'

'Half a day. But, Alex, I'm regular to the hour.'

'When are you going to be home?' he asked.

'About half past six.'

'Good. And, Bel?'

'Yes?'

'It doesn't matter if it doesn't happen this month. It's still early days and we have plenty of time.'

'Uh-huh.' Though whatever the test said, she knew she was going to be on edge. Horribly disappointed if it was negative, and terrified if it was positive, just in case the specialist was wrong and the aspirin wasn't enough and she'd miscarry again.

When she walked in the door, Alex greeted her with a hug and a warm, sweet kiss. 'OK?' he asked.

'Yes. No.' She bit her lip. 'I've been dying to do a test all day. But I wanted to wait until I was home with you.'

He produced a box. 'Is this one OK?'

She looked at it and smiled. 'Snap.' She produced an identical box from her handbag.

'Great minds think alike,' he quipped. 'Bel—remember what I said. It's early days. If it's negative, that's OK. We just get the fun of trying for another month.'

But she wasn't going to repeat the mistake she'd made in her last marriage. 'I'm not going to make love to you only to make babies,' she said softly. 'It'll be because I love you.'

'Good. I love you, too.' He kissed her lingeringly. 'Now go to the bathroom. I've been clock-watching all afternoon and I can't wait another minute.'

'What was that line you fed me about being a patient man?' she teased.

But she returned two minutes later. 'One line. So we know the test is working.'

Together, they watched the second window. And as the second blue line appeared, Isobel buried her face in Alex's chest and bawled her eyes out.

'It's going to be OK this time,' he said softly, stroking her hair.

'I'm not crying because I'm upset. I'm crying because I'm relieved. Because I'm happy.' But she kept her arms wrapped very tightly round him. 'Alex. I don't want to tell anyone yet.'

'Of course not.'

'Not until twelve weeks.'

He nuzzled her cheek. 'I know you're scared, but it's different this time. We know what the problem was and you're doing everything you should be,' he reassured her. 'But we'll get you an appointment tomorrow and we're going to keep an eye on you. And I promise you, I'm not going to work away from home for the next few months.'

'Alex, that's not fair. You have a job to do.'

'I'm not taking any risks,' he said softly. 'I promised you that you'd come first. And you do.' He held her close. 'And this time everything's going to be fine.'

EPILOGUE

Nine months later

ALEX and Isobel sat on the edge of the bed, watching their daughter sleeping in the Moses basket next to their bed. Her first night home. Their first night in the Bloomsbury flat as a family.

'She's so perfect,' Isobel said. 'I can still hardly believe she's ours.'

'Thea. Gift of God,' he translated softly. 'Dad's still campaigning for us to call her Thomasina, you know. And your dad's desperately trying to find a feminine version of Stuart. And Saskia's put in her bid for the middle name as well as begging to be godmother.'

Isobel laughed. 'Thea isn't being named after anyone. She's just herself.'

'Though she's as beautiful as her mother.' Alex, with one arm firmly round his wife's shoulders, reached out to stroke his daughter's cheek with the tip of his finger. 'My two beautiful girls. Life doesn't get any better than this, Bel.' He rested his head against Isobel's.

'I never knew I could be this happy,' she said softly. 'But with you, I have the whole world. A job I love, the baby I've wanted for so long…and, most of all, you. I love you, Alex.'

'I love you, too,' he said softly. *'Semper.'*

NAUGHTY NIGHTS IN THE MILLIONAIRE'S MANSION

BY
ROBYN GRADY

One Christmas long ago, **Robyn Grady** received a book from her big sister and immediately fell in love with the story of Cinderella. Sprinklings of magic, deepest wishes coming true—she was hooked! Picture books with glass slippers later gave way to romance novels and, more recently, the real-life dream of writing for Mills & Boon.

After a fifteen-year career in television, Robyn met her own modern-day hero. They live on Australia's Sunshine Coast with their three little princesses, two poodles and a cat called Tinkie. Robyn loves new shoes, worn jeans, lunches at Moffat Beach and hanging out with her friends online. Learn about her latest releases at www.robyngrady.com, and don't forget to say hi. She'd love to hear from you!

To Moet and Ebony, with love

CHAPTER ONE

'IT'S settled. You're coming home with me.'

The low murmur at Vanessa Craig's back left her nape tingling, as if her skin had been brushed by an intimate kiss. Drawn from stacking the last of the special diet dog food, she curled some hair behind her ear, then slowly edged around. She tried—but failed—to keep her eyes in her head.

Of course, the attractive man standing nearby hadn't spoken to her. Heck, he didn't know she existed, even if Vanessa was acutely aware of every sensitised cell in her body suddenly glowing with life.

Powerhouse height, pitch-black hair, a strong shadowed jaw and eyes bluer than any Vanessa had seen. The precise cut of his trousers, the immaculate polish of his shoes—everything about this man didn't simply say he settled for the best.

He *was* the best.

When the man-god shifted his weight, the ledge of his magnificent shoulders went back. His attention drifted from the small tank, which contained a single goldfish, and landed on her.

'Afternoon.' His mouth curved up at one side as he quarter-turned to face her. 'You work here?'

Vanessa swallowed the knot of hot desire tugging in her throat. 'I'm the manager.'

'Great. I'm interested in that fish.'

Vanessa studied the goldfish, who was busy studying the man. She smiled over. 'Not half as interested as he seems to be in *you*.'

While she spoke, the light changed in her customer's ocean-blue eyes, as though something in her face or her voice, made him wonder if they'd met before. Not on this side of her dreams.

As his sexy smile returned, he tilted his head at the tank. 'I'm wondering…can you tell his gender?'

Although Vanessa had answered that question regarding fish many times in the past two years, the majority of people who visited her Sydney pet store— Great and Small—seemed content to while away some time fawning over the puppies and kittens. Who could blame them? Cute bundles of fur bouncing around, pressing their squishy wet noses against the window, desperate for a cuddle. Searching for a home.

Caring for her animals was a labour of pure love, but the real joy came when one went to a family whom she knew would truly care. Friends were great: Josie and Tia, her buddies since high school, were the best. But family, *real* family…well, everybody wanted one.

Did this man have a family? Was he an uncle? A father?

She set a hand on a corner of the cool tank. 'Males can have tiny dots on the gills and pectoral fins. Like those.' She waggled a finger at the little guy's fins, then filtered in an interesting detail. 'Did you know that the Japanese have been keeping goldfish as pets for over a thousand years?'

His gorgeous eyes smiled and sparkled. 'Is that right?'

She nodded. 'It's also a bona fide fact that watching fish swim can be soothing to the nerves.'

'Well, that's got to be cheaper than the psychiatrist I'm seeing.'

Vanessa's jaw dropped, but then he lifted a brow and smiled—a sultry *gotcha* smile that burrowed beneath the skin and coddled every inch of her.

'Actually, a friend of mine has a large aquarium,' he admitted. 'He says nothing's more relaxing at the end of a long, hard day. No fuss, no bother. No noise.' The impressive breadth of his chest expanded beneath its dark wool blend shirt as he retrieved his wallet from a back pocket. 'Do you take Visa?'

But before he could extract the card, his attention shifted to a nearby glass pen and its excited scramble of Rottweiler pups. Aware her scent was Perfume de la Birdcage from the tray she'd cleaned earlier, Vanessa swiped both hands down her jeans and moved closer. 'They're pretty special, huh? Only came in this morning.'

When the lines of his classically cut profile intensified, as if he were considering a change of tack, she subtly tested, 'Have you owned a dog before?'

Attention fixed on the pups, the dark slashes of his brows fell together. 'I grew up with dogs…' His Hollywood jaw shifted. 'Kind of.'

She grinned. 'Kind of grew up, or kind of dogs?'

His crystalline gaze met hers again; the contact rippled through her blood like the aftermath of a fiery liquid touch.

'Poodles.' His gaze dipped to her mouth, traced the sweep of her lips, then flicked back to her eyes. 'I grew up with poodles. The tiny, yappy ones.'

Only half recovered from the sizzle of his gaze, she dug her hands into her pockets and rocked back on her Reeboks. 'Whatever size, poodles are a highly intelligent breed.'

'They certainly know how to get what they want.'

'The family pooches were pampered?'

'Like every other female in the house.' His brows crunched together again. 'Sorry. Too much information.'

She didn't mind. She was intrigued.

So he had a mother as well as sisters, sounded like. The fine lines branching from the corners of his eyes said late twenties, early thirties at the outside—too old to live at home with the brood. Had he grown up overrun by female siblings and a domineering matriarch? Perhaps his father had been away often, a foreign diplomat for some exotic far-off land; the dreamy slant to his eyes and coal-fringed lashes suggested a Mediterranean connection maybe.

She smiled at herself.

And maybe she needed to get a life. Whatever his

background, she wouldn't get to know him well enough to hear it.

'These pups are only eight weeks old. They'll grow a whole lot bigger. I'd suggest a good quality bed.' She selected one from a nearby display. 'We recommend this brand.'

Close to where her hand rested, he rubbed and pinched the foam. 'Hmm. Firm yet soft.'

As if on direct dial, the tips of her breasts picked up, tightening to responsive beads beneath her T-shirt. Vanessa surrendered to the delicious undercurrent before managing to shake herself free.

Good Lord, Josie was right. She needed a holiday. But with her most recent business crisis breathing down her neck, sipping piña coladas beneath palm fronds wasn't likely any time soon. She'd take a holiday when she was back on her feet, when her business was back in the black. She wasn't about to give up on her dream.

She set the dog bed down and cleared the thickness from her throat. 'Rotties make great guard dogs as well as companions.'

On cue, the only male pup set his big front paws on the window; his tail whipped around back so hard, the motion almost knocked him over. Anyone who thought dogs didn't smile didn't know dogs.

She weaved around a giggling toddler, who clapped as Mr Cheese went hell-for-whiskers on his mouse wheel. 'He'll need walks. And puppy school to help socialise him.'

'Like kindergarten for dogs.' His arms crossed,

then he scratched his temple. 'How much time are we talking about? I get home late. I work most weekends too.'

Vanessa's heartbeat slowed. She should have guessed. His aura exuded energy and no-nonsense efficiency. Not that 'handsome high-powered executive' was a turn off. Just everyone seemed so busy these days—the twenty-first century treadmill gone mad. No one had time to walk their dogs and smell the flowers any more.

Her gaze flicked to his left hand—large, tanned but no gold ring. Still, not all those who were taken wore bands. As she'd found out.

'Perhaps your wife could help.'

'I'm not married.'

'Girlfriend?'

She was curious—only for the dog's sake. A workaholic man-god descended from warriors wouldn't be interested in an ordinary girl working her way up the ladder…lately one rung up, three rungs back.

'My housekeeper comes in once a week.'

She cut him a wry grin. *Not the same.*

She had a thought. 'If a dog's too much responsibility and a fish maybe isn't enough, perhaps a—'

'Don't say cat.' His chin and its deep cleft came down. 'I don't do cats.'

She almost rolled her eyes. What was it with men and moggies?

'A bird then? We have some lovely budgies. Or a

parrot? You can teach them to talk. Sit on your shoulder.'

The nostrils of his hawkish nose flared. 'I don't think so.'

She indicated a cage. 'What about a reptapet?'

'You mean a *snake*?' He visibly shuddered, a full body shiver. 'Pass.'

He skirted around an elderly man in a grey fedora squeaking at the guinea pigs to return to that tank and scrutinised the fish. Hovering above its yellow and blue bed stones, the fish blew a bubble and stared back. Looking closer, he lifted a hand to knock on the glass.

When she touched the platinum watch on his wrist—fish and tapping was a no-go zone—the fiery sensation of his skin on hers released a crackling zap hurtling up her limb. The scrumptious shockwave carried an arrow straight to her chest and stole the air from her lungs.

He straightened and looked at her oddly—a curious glint in his eye as if he might have felt the charge too. Or maybe that look simply said *hands off*.

Stepping back, she drew her tingling hand away. 'Plenty of people have satisfying relationships with fish,' she said in an unintentionally husky voice.

An intrigued smile swam in the depths of his eyes. 'Do you?'

Her glance took inventory of the wall of tanks behind them. 'We have scores of fish here.'

'But do you have fish at home?'

'No.'

'A dog?'

'I'm not allowed.'

His brows jumped. 'You live with your parents?'

She blinked twice. 'I rent.'

'But you have family close by.'

Her stomach lurched at his assumption. Orphaned at a young age, she'd been brought up by an aunt on the rural east coast of Australia. She had no brothers or sisters, grandparents or cousins. Other than Aunt McKenzie, she had no one.

She swallowed against a flush and regained control. 'I'm not sure that has anything to do with you buying a fish, Mr…'

'Stuart. Mitchell Stuart.' As if annoyed at himself, he waved a dismissive hand. 'And, no, it doesn't. *Totally* off track.' He narrowed his focus on the gaping fish again and slowly grinned. 'I think he'll do nicely.'

She forced her thoughts away from family—or lack thereof—and back onto business.

For a moment she'd wondered if this customer might enjoy a closer connection…someone to walk and have fun with. Guess she'd been mistaken.

But she was pleased for the fish; clearly he was going to a good home. She was sure he'd be fed the finest fish food and have his home regularly cleaned by the housekeeper.

She went to lift the tank. 'Do you have any names in mind?'

Frowning, Mr Stuart took over the weight of the tank. 'Fish have names?'

At the counter, she collected flakes, stabilising drops, a complimentary miniature Poseidon and his trident, then went through everything with Mr Stuart regarding the care of his new goldfish. After he'd scrawled a signature on the transaction slip, she handed back his card. 'I'm sure you'll have no problems.'

'If I do?'

'Call me.'

She whisked a business card from its holder. He gripped it, genuine victory shining in his eyes. 'I feel good about this.'

'Then so do I.'

Mr Stuart collected his bundles. On his way past the puppies, he faltered, but then shot a glance over his shoulder and held up the fish with a smile that said, Right decision.

She winked and saluted. Another satisfied customer. And the puppies would go quickly to homes filled with love and adequate attention. Maybe one day Mitchell Stuart would return when he was ready for a bigger commitment.

Would she still be here? She had to believe tomorrow's appointment with her bank manager would save the day. She couldn't bear to think of the alternative.

Two hours later, she flipped the sign on the door as the phone rang. If that was the feeders and drinkers supplier after a payment, the cheque was definitely in the mail. If it was the landlord reminding her to be out in two weeks…

She held her nervy stomach. Maybe she wouldn't answer.

When it rang again, she buckled and picked up. No hello from the other end, just a straight out, 'I've found a name for my fish.'

That deep voice was even more bone-melting over the phone—low and unconsciously inviting against her ear.

'Mr Stuart. Hello.'

'Kamikaze.'

She stammered. 'B-Beg your pardon?'

'He won't quit jumping out of the tank. He's on a suicide mission.'

She sank down onto a chair and rubbed her brow. Oh, dear. 'That sometimes happens.'

'I filled the tank, added the right amount of drops, set up the filter, gave him a feed. When I turned my back, he jumped out. I put him back in. He jumped out again, and again.' His voice dropped to a growl. 'Clearly he's not happy.'

'Could be a couple of things, like not enough water.'

'I've already put more in.'

'Maybe there's too much.'

His voice cracked. 'A fish can have too *much* water?'

'Only in so far as making it easier to leap out.' She gnawed her bottom lip. 'And then there's the possibility...'

'What possibility?'

'Some fish are just, well, *jumpers*.'

She heard his groan, then a shuffle as if he'd moved and dropped into a seat himself.

A vision flashed to mind: gorgeous Mitchell Stuart dead on his feet after staying up all night, a scoop in one hand, a fist made out of the other, ruing the day he'd ever set foot in Great and Small.

Vanessa gripped the receiver tight. She'd said she'd help if need be. Statistics said people bought pets from shops relatively close to their homes. Doctors made house calls. No reason she couldn't.

'Mr Stuart, I've just shut up shop. Would you like me to drop over and see what I can do?'

'You do that kind of thing?'

She lied. 'All the time.'

A relieved expulsion of air travelled down the line. 'I'll give you my address.'

'You think this is funny?' Mitch manoeuvred Kamikaze off his redwood dining table into the net and, suppressing a shudder, plopped him back into the tank water. 'Well, fun and games are *over*, buddy boy.'

Help was on the way. Help in the form of a petite, twenty-something-year-old whom he had no intention of getting to know beyond, *Thanks for saving my fish*. He wouldn't acknowledge Vanessa Craig's long, glossy hair, iridescent green eyes or the way his blood warmed like syrup on a stove whenever she smiled that *I'm totally harmless* smile. He was on sabbatical from women.

All women.

When his father had passed away fifteen years ago, Mitch had become the man of the house. Although he'd moved out of the stately Stuart mansion seven years ago, he was still the one the females of the family scampered to for help…and it seemed they *always* needed help. Help with their finances, help with repairs, booking flights, computer glitches—you name it, he got the call.

Like a stealthy airborne virus, recently the *helpless female factor* had followed him into more intimate relationships. Up-and-coming lingerie model Priscilla Lawson had seemed independent and resourceful when they'd met at that charity dinner. After three weeks together, their liaison had warmed up nicely, until Priscilla had tickled his chin one night and mentioned her family reunion… Would he mind booking her flight to Melbourne and, while she was gone, clean her pool and take her cat to its monthly check-up? It had liver problems.

His upper lip twitched.

He did *not* do cats.

But damn, he sure had liked that Rottweiler pup.

He was a busy man. His work was his life. However, while he had close associates at the firm as well as friends he knocked about with on weekends when he could spare the time, he'd wanted someone to come home to. Someone *male* who could watch football without a moan, not complain if he put his feet on the coffee table, who didn't flutter eyelashes or resort to tears to get their own way. Someone who didn't demand much time or emotion.

He gazed at his goggle-eyed companion.

A goldfish qualified.

The doorbell rang, echoing through the contemporary two-storey that enjoyed a privileged view of Sydney's magnificent harbour. Mitch rolled the tension from his shoulders, then stabbed a finger at Kami. 'Don't move a fin till I get back.'

He opened the door and there she stood, looking unaffected and fresh, one long leg pegged out in those bun-hugging jeans, conspicuously busty in her white T-shirt with the pink swirly logo that said *Great and Small*. If forced to vote, he would go with *Great* rather than *Small*. In fact, she looked pretty darn hot—

Mitch slammed on the mental brakes.

Sweet blazes, what was he doing? Visualising this woman naked wasn't going to help. In fact, it was highly inappropriate for more reasons than one.

Think 'fish', Mitch. Think 'through with females'.

Clearing his throat, he gestured her in. 'Thanks for coming so quickly. He's over here.'

In the dining room, Vanessa Craig set her hands on her knees and inspected the patient while Mitch stood back, eager for a diagnosis. When the examination went on and her left knee bent more, which meant her right hip hitched up, he scowled and scrubbed his jaw. If she'd done that on purpose, he didn't need the aggravation.

Finally she straightened, one hand on her lower back as she arched to stretch out her spine. Although *Great* jumped out at him, Mitch kept his eyes fixed firmly on hers.

Her question was sombre. 'When was the last time he jumped?'

'Just before you arrived.'

'Before that?'

'Ten minutes ago.'

Pensive, she stroked her chin. 'Could be he's still settling in.'

'Or tomorrow morning I could wake up and—'

Ack. He didn't want to think about it.

She crossed her arms. The letters *G* and *T* met at her cleavage. Not that he was looking. Same way he wasn't looking when she nibbled her lip and searched for an answer. Her mouth was naturally pink and very full. The highly kissable kind with delicate dimples on either side, as he'd already noted with some consternation earlier today.

'What if we try a bigger tank?' she suggested.

Mitch blinked back to the immediate problem. Increased volume equalled decreased risk, which added up to no dead fish in the morning. 'I like that plan.'

She moved towards the door. 'Good. I brought one with me. It's outside on your portico.'

Giving in to a smile, he followed. Clearly Vanessa Craig was intelligent, helpful, prompt as well as prepared. She was also a professional with her own business. Did her profit and loss sheets balance? Of course he was well aware *trouble* was not a gender specific trait. However, for too long now, it sure-as-Jack seemed that way.

He assisted Vanessa in with the larger tank and a few minutes later it was filled with the neutralising drops doing their work.

Hooking up the filter, she nodded almost shyly at the portrait on the wall. 'Is that your family?'

His chest constricted with a familiar sense of fondness tinged with regret. The photo featured his tall, lean father sitting on a red chaise longue surrounded by his wife, their four girls and only son.

His hand slid along the rim of the tank. 'My father passed away not long after that shot was taken.' Only days before Mitch's fifteenth birthday.

When she flicked on the filter, her hand accidentally brushed his. His heartbeat kicked as a live current spiralled up the cords of his arm to his shoulder, much the same heat-generating sensation that had claimed him this afternoon when they'd touched. Instantaneous and perilously pleasant.

Their eyes met—hers filled with perception as well as surprise before she dropped her gaze and edged a little away. 'I'm sorry…about your dad.'

Setting his thoughts straight, Mitch collected his trusty net. 'He was a good but old-fashioned man. A firm believer in tough love.'

Her mouth thinned. 'Spare the rod and spoil the child?'

'Not at all. But, in our house, actions had consequences.' How many talks about responsibility and putting those you cared about before yourself had he listened to? 'We were loved, but you didn't get away with much. In return, he gave us his undivided attention when we needed it.'

Her green eyes took on a sheen, reminding him of the leaves on the pavement this morning when he'd decided to get himself that pet.

'You must all miss him very much,' Vanessa said.

He nodded. *Every day*.

What would his father have done about the current family dilemma? Last night, Cynthia, the youngest at twenty-two, had announced her engagement to the sleaze ball of all time. Their showboating mother had crowed with joy, which had surprised him. Sleaze Ball might be a doctor but he was also a notorious gambler.

How on earth could he protect people who jumped feet first into disaster, tittering prettily as they fell into the abyss?

Groaning, he swirled the new water with the net.

Guess he'd sort something out. Or maybe he wouldn't; maybe this time would be the time he let the women sort it out themselves. He couldn't very well tell his sister who to marry, though he'd certainly like to tell her who *not* to.

Mitch stole a glance at his comely visitor as a gentle reflection from the water danced over her face. Did Vanessa Craig hold high expectations on the business front, or was she focused more on personal matters, like landing a good catch? Seemed his sisters could think of little other than having babies. What was the hurry? He was in no hurry at all.

He set the net down. 'What about you?'

Her bright eyes blinked up from the water. 'What about me?'

'Family. You didn't say whether yours live nearby.'

Her slender shoulders went up, then down. 'I don't have a family.'

None? The idea was alien. And, in some ways, wickedly appealing. No demands. No expectations. No interruptions. 'No one at all?'

She trailed a damp hand down her jeans, leaving a streak on her shapely denim thigh. 'I have an aunt. As well as great friends and my animals—' she flashed an optimist's smile '—so life's full.'

Was that a subtle hint that she wasn't interested in romance? Well, ditto…even if his growing curiosity and flexing libido refuted that statement. There was something about Vanessa Craig—something mesmerising calling to him from beyond those bewitching green eyes.

She checked her large-faced watch, took the net and scooped Kami up to ease him into his new watery home. As his golden scales darted around the relocated trident, Mitch shot out a relieved breath. 'He looks happier already.'

'Hopefully that should do the trick.'

'After all that exercise, he should sleep well.' Which was good news for them both; he had some important paperwork to get through tonight.

'Fish don't sleep,' she pointed out. 'They slow their metabolism and rest.' She knelt down to gather the replacement tank's packaging. 'Dolphins sleep, of course,' she went on. 'But they're mammals. They keep one side of their brain awake while the other half dozes.'

Fascinated, he dropped onto his haunches too. He'd known dolphins weren't fish, but, 'They're awake while they sleep?'

Clearly he was behind in his general knowledge. Maybe he should subscribe to the Animal channel. Or he could cut his more primal instincts some slack and become better acquainted with this expert. Not as if he was taking the plunge and asking her out. He was simply interested in getting to know her mind a little better.

He collected some discarded bubble wrap. 'Did you study marine biology?'

'Zoology. And business as well as some Greek mythology.' Sweeping up more packaging, she tilted her head at him and shimmering hair fell like a silky waterfall from behind her shoulder. 'Did you know that the ancient Greeks believed dolphins were once human? There's a school of thought that says Poseidon was human once too.'

Still crouching, he leant a little closer. The sound of her voice was melodic…soothing. 'Is that right?'

'The more traditional myth says he was one of the supreme Olympian gods,' she continued, grabbing more packaging. 'When Creation was divided between the gods, Hades got to rule the underworld, Zeus dominated the skies, and Poseidon became lord of the water, both fresh and salt. His son, Triton, was half human, half fish.'

Engrossed, Mitch blindly reached for more bubble wrap while she reached the same way. Their hands touched. That sizzle flashed again and this time sparked and caught light. But while the sexual awareness was through the roof, the sense of awkwardness had all but vanished.

They shared a brief *what if* smile, then she pushed to her feet.

He wanted to hear more. 'So the mermaid legend started with the Greeks?'

She nodded. 'But originally mermaids were called sirens, fabled to be half woman, half bird. They had beautiful voices they used to lure sailors and their ships onto the rocks. If a ship got away, the siren would have to throw herself into the sea.'

He slowly pushed to his feet too, chancing to take in the tempting lines of her body as he went. Vanessa Craig didn't smell like birdseed or puppies any more. She smelled soft, sweet and slightly salty, like a fresh ocean breeze.

He rested his hip against the table edge. 'Did any sailors try to resist?'

'One. He'd heard about the sirens hypnotic deadly powers. He had his crew tie him to the mast of his ship so he wasn't able to steer her towards tragedy. But when he saw the beautiful siren on the shore, and heard her song, he begged to be cut free.'

His gaze skimmed her delicate jaw. 'Who won?'

She laughed. 'Depends if you were the siren or the sailor.'

His return smile faded as his gaze drifted to her mouth. Those pink, full, tempting lips. Another few inches and he could taste them. Explore them. Of course this instant attraction could merely be backlash from shunning the dating scene long enough. Vanessa was attractive, intelligent, not to mention incredibly sexy.

Best of all, she was independently minded. A strong but companionable woman. *His* kind of woman.

He broke the trance and bent to sweep the box off the floor. 'Have you had your business long?'

'Two years.'

'Going well?'

Her smile wavered and she shrugged. 'Sure. Aside from being evicted in two weeks from the store I adore and needing to find a new place with rent that's anywhere within my budget. I have an appointment with my bank manager tomorrow and—' She stopped and released a self-deprecating sigh. 'Now *that* was too much information.'

His gut turned to ice as a withering feeling sank through his middle, but Mitch managed a thin smile in return. 'Not too much information at all.'

Rather, just enough. Barring an earthquake in central Sydney or the acting President suddenly losing all faith in his protégé, two weeks from tomorrow Mitch would claim the head chair of the family company, as per his late father's will. If anyone could organise finance, the soon-to-be

President of Stuart Investments and Loans certainly could.

But, realistically, he and Vanessa Craig were little
more than acquaintances. Despite the lure of smouldering embers, he wouldn't ignore the warning signs.
Eviction. Financial disaster. Before him stood a time
bomb about to explode, which translated into a loss for
his company should he choose to invest, not to mention
a hit to his personal armoury if he allowed himself to
become any more intrigued. God knew, he had enough
to worry about without taking on new risks.

He held the box against his ribs and glanced
around. 'Well, that seems to be it,' he announced
cheerily. 'How much do I owe you?'

Reading his terminating social cue, her smile
wavered and her gaze flicked away. 'No charge.'

'There must be some difference between the
two tanks.'

'All part of the service.' She nodded at her card on
the table. 'And if you need any help in the next few
days, you know where to find—'

'Absolutely.' He snatched up the card with his free
hand as if to confirm his commitment. 'I'll see you out.'

A moment later, he swung open his front door
and faced the sunset's dying colours, deepest crimson
and streaks of gold bleeding across the eucalypt hills
in the west.

'Goodnight, Mr Stuart.' She gave him her signature salute. 'Good luck.'

'Yep. Thanks. You too.'

She'd need it.

When the door closed, he emptied his lungs, tossed her business card on the hallstand and made a vow. If he had any more problems with Kami, he'd call a fish expert; *Yellow Pages* were bound to list them. The best way not to get burned was to stay away from the fire, no matter how attractive the flames of that fire might be.

But as he strode towards the living room, a tantalising image swam up to taunt him…those heavenly hips, that amazing T-shirt, her hypnotic voice and come-hither smile.

Damp broke out on his hairline and he wheeled back around. Grabbing the card, he looked at it hard and tore it clean down the middle.

Beautiful sirens. Sailors sinking with their ships. The only rocks he wanted to see were the ones clinking in his pre-dinner Scotch while he pored over those figures for tomorrow's late meeting.

He settled down to that drink and his work, with the new tank and its occupant on a side table nearby. He was trying to banish Vanessa Craig and her lips to the furthermost corners of his mind when the doorbell rang.

He slammed down his glass. *What now?*

A moment later he swung open the door and his heart hit his throat.

'Me again.' An apologetic but upbeat Vanessa Craig curled some hair behind her ear. 'I got down the street before realising I forgot to collect the smaller tank. I bet you don't want it clogging up your gorgeous home—'

Her words ran dry at the same time her face fell.

Her gaze had drifted behind him, to the hallstand at his back.

To the torn business card.

As his insides wrenched into a guilty knot, she blinked several times, then her mouth quivered with a lame smile—a vain attempt to cover her hurt. 'Gee, I didn't realise I'd made such a sterling impression.'

He ran a hand through his hair. *Hell.*

'It's not how it looks.'

Her laugh was short. 'It looks like you can't bear to see my name.'

He groaned. She had it completely wrong, but he couldn't tell her that. He couldn't begin to explain.

Her chin angled up. 'Whatever your opinion of my service today, you're one hundred per cent entitled to it. The customer's always right. Always.' She forced a brave smile, then turned on her heel.

'Even when the customer screws up,' he said, 'because he's attracted to the lady in charge?'

She turned back, her jaw hanging. 'What did you say?'

He gripped both sides of the door jamb and admitted what must be obvious. 'I'm attracted to you.'

She shook her head, puzzled. 'So you don't want to contact me again?'

She was right. His reasoning was flawed, particularly now she was back, with her lips so near and his elevated testosterone levels demanding to know what the hell he was waiting for.

He held his breath.

What *was* he waiting for?

His hands left the jamb and found her upper arms. Drawing her close—with that maddening logo pressed against his chest—he dropped his mouth over hers.

Her body stiffened and her fists came up, two small rocks pushing against his collarbone. But he didn't release her…truth tell, he couldn't. The heat combusting between their bodies had fused them together; she was glued to him as much as he was to her.

As his mouth opened, her lips parted and the kiss evolved and deepened, growing beyond spur-of-the-moment into something-special. His hold on her arms eased; as if a crutch were removed, she leant against his length. Taking the cue, his tongue performed a lazy sweep against hers, and again. Her relaxed fists began kneading his shirt.

When a compliant mew vibrated in her throat, he imagined slipping that T-shirt over her head and running his hands over the sweetest heaven on earth. His blood felt on fire. Every red-hot ion ready to ignite. God help him, he didn't want to stop.

The kiss broke gradually, reluctantly, the caress growing strong again before, hot lava flowing through his veins, he finally eased off.

Her eyes were closed, her breathing ragged. Out of breath himself, he murmured against her warm soft lips, 'Now do you see?'

Her eyelids flickered and her focus sharpened. 'You wanted to *kiss* me?'

'Very much.'

'And you thought I wouldn't want you to?'

Wincing, he pulled slightly back. 'That's not quite it.'

Her shoulders sank. 'Is it another woman?'

He groaned to himself. 'Not just one.'

When she unravelled herself from what remained of his grasp, he rubbed his brow. How could he explain that he didn't need any more ties?

'What I mean is, sexual attraction is one thing, but compatibility should be built on—' He stopped, then started again. 'When two people get together, they should be on the same page as far as—' No, that wasn't right. He took a breath. 'Well, the thing is—'

'That water should meet its own level?' She darted a wounded glance towards his spacious living room and, beyond that, the priceless view. 'Is that what you're trying to say?'

He exhaled. 'I'm saying we don't know each other very well.'

'But you know enough.'

'Vanessa—'

As he stepped forward, she stepped back and held up a hand. 'Please don't be embarrassed. I'm a pragmatist, Mr Stuart. I know the way the world works.' She reached around and took her torn card from the hallstand. 'In case you're tempted.'

With infuriating good grace, she shut the door behind her. It took all his willpower not to call out and drag her back against him where she seemed to belong. He *had* wanted to kiss her, hold her… Damn it, in that moment of insanity, he'd wanted to peel the clothes from her body and make love to her, thoroughly and all night long.

But, as he'd said, he barely knew this woman and his rescuing-damsels-in-distress plate was full. He shouldn't get involved. In fact, he should thank his lucky stars it was over before it had begun.

He strode to the wet bar and poured himself a fresh Scotch. He swallowed a gulp, swallowed another. Frustration winning out, he smashed the glass down on the counter.

Like it or not, he was *already* involved. He wanted to see Vanessa Craig again. He wanted to listen to her stories. Taste her sweet lips. Damn it, he wanted to *help*.

The six million dollar question was…

CHAPTER TWO

How do I get myself out of this mess?

The following afternoon, Vanessa sat on the top tier of the Opera House steps. Squawking seagulls wheeled overhead while chattering tourists and other visitors swirled all around, many gazing up to marvel at the giant shells.

The construction of the Opera House had taken seventeen years to build. The end result was extraordinary in aesthetic, acoustic as well as patriotic terms. Whenever Vanessa needed to find strength and inspiration, she came here to appreciate what could be accomplished if one only tried.

Now she looked out over the water, busy with Sydney's commuter ferries, past the bridge's magnificent glinting steel arch and into the haze of her unknown future.

From the age of ten—the year she'd realised her parents really weren't coming back to collect her from Aunt McKenzie's—her heart had been set on finding homes for others. That was what made her happy. What kept her connected. Without her store—her *purpose*—she'd feel…

She gazed at the seagulls.

Adrift.

Her cellphone vibrated in her trouser suit pocket. The darkening line of the horizon smudged as she put the phone to her ear. 'Great and Small. Vanessa speaking.'

'Oh, I'm *tho* glad to have caught you.'

Vanessa flipped through her mental PDA. An elderly woman, enthusiastic, with a slight lisp didn't ring a bell. Another creditor after a payment?

She suppressed a worn-down sigh. 'Yes, this is she. How can I help?'

'My son, Mitchell, gave me your number. He said you were the lady I needed to see.' Her voice lowered. 'He altho mentioned you do house calls.'

Vanessa straightened from her slouch. Mitchell Stuart, aka Mr Goldfish?

At one stage, when she and Mitch Stuart had spoken about sirens, she'd felt increasingly drawn to him. He'd looked at her with those startling blue eyes and her nerve-endings had reached out and tingled. Then his expression had dropped from simmering to a degree below tepid and she'd known why.

She'd shared personal information regarding her financial situation with a veritable stranger. She'd come across as needy…perhaps even soliciting. Her upbringing had been humble and she'd been raised to value tenacity and dignity; she should've known better.

God, she should never have returned to get the smaller tank. Worse, she shouldn't have allowed him to kiss her as she'd never been kissed before. Though it was clear they'd both enjoyed the interaction, that wasn't enough. She'd read him right when he'd first walked into her shop.

Water meets its own level. Guys like him—guys with money and family and the world at their feet—didn't end up with girls like her. But she couldn't very well hang up on his mother.

She quietly released that pent-up breath. 'What can I do for you, Mrs Stuart?'

'Cockapoos.'

'Also known as spoodles,' she confirmed. Cocker spaniels mixed with poodles.

'In the past I've always purchased toy poodles.'

Vanessa remembered. The little yappy ones. Was Mrs Stuart in the market for a puppy? 'I don't have any cockapoos in store at the moment.'

'My son regards your expertise highly. He said you'd be able to help. I'm after four as soon as possible. I'm willing to pay for the best.'

Vanessa's toes curled as she squeezed the phone tight. The bank representative she'd spoken with late this afternoon had turned her application for a loan down flat. His exact words: *it's best to face reality, cut your losses and find a paying job.* But pedigree cockapoos sold for a great deal. If she tracked down and sold four, the extra funds could keep the wolf from the door, perhaps long enough to find a way to keep Great and Small alive and in its current location.

If there was any way, she wanted to stay where she was. The shop was set up exactly how she'd always envisaged. It was far more than a business.

It was her home.

'Miss Craig? Are you there?'

Vanessa pushed to her feet. 'How soon do you want them?'

'The sooner the better.'

She was already jogging down the steps, phone still pressed to her ear. 'I'll make some enquiries and call you back.'

'I'd prefer if you'd drop by.'

To pass on a few details? She didn't see the point. But Mrs Stuart did indeed sound pampered and Vanessa wasn't in a position to argue.

The customer was always right, particularly one with a few thousand to spend. She should be grateful Mitch Stuart was man enough to let bygones be bygones. He'd forgiven—and most likely forgotten—their embarrassing moment and had put his mother's needs before any hard feelings. She, in turn, would be professional and do her best to track down those dogs.

Thirty minutes and three phone calls later, Vanessa turned her Honda CRV into the address Mrs Stuart had provided. A mansion greeted her, its stately sandstone walls surrounded by immaculate mint-green lawns. A Union Jack and Southern Cross flag, perched atop a mast that touched the sky, flapped in the cool early evening breeze.

She'd thought Mitch's stylish contemporary abode was something special, but this place might have belonged to royalty. She remembered her own single bedroom granny flat and mismatched furniture and sighed. His world and hers were not only miles apart—they were light years.

After parking on the paved circular drive, she swallowed her jangle of nerves, ascended the stone steps and rang the bell that droned a sombre tune behind the imposing ten-foot-high oak door. A uniformed maid, with a severe overbite that reminded Vanessa of Mr Cheese, answered the door. Before either of them could speak, Mrs Stuart scurried across the polished timber floor and into view.

'Come in, come in.' Mrs Stuart waved Vanessa in, then called over her butter-yellow blouse shoulder, 'Cynthia! The dog lady's here.'

Vanessa cringed. Had Mitch suggested she call her that?

Mrs Stuart addressed the maid. 'Thank you, Wendle. I'll take care of our guest.'

Wendle left them and Mrs Stuart linked her arm through Vanessa's, guiding her down a wide hall trimmed in ornate dark timber, into an elaborately furnished living room—decorative high ceiling, polished brass and crystal fittings, baroque couches and window seats pulled from the pages of *Celebrity House and Garden*.

On the far couch, a woman around Vanessa's age lifted her reddened nose from a lace handkerchief. She was finely boned and, although unwashed, her hair looked blonde like her mother's. However, rather than hazel, her eyes were ocean-blue like her brother's, and rimmed with red.

Cynthia found the strength to mutter, 'Nice to meet you.'

Mrs Stuart clasped her bejewelled hands under her chin. Diamonds and rubies flashed in the dying sunlight slanting in through a tall arched window. 'Our Cynthia has had a bad time of it. Day before yesterday she was engaged. Today, sadly, she is not.'

Vanessa cocked a brow. These people mightn't mind laying open their private lives in the parlour but, after yesterday's blabbermouth experience with Mitch Stuart, she'd learned her lesson. She wouldn't divulge the fact that she'd once lived through a similar ordeal.

She'd once dated a good-looking man of some means. He'd been charming, but something beyond mysterious about him had sent up a red flag. When, after two months, she'd suggested they have a break, he'd vowed he couldn't give her up, then he'd popped the question. She'd been flattered but unconvinced. Good thing she hadn't made a fool of herself and accepted, because the following day she'd received a call: apparently he was already engaged to someone more befitting his station. The ruffled female caller with the superior tone had said Vanessa was his 'fluff on the side'.

At least animals didn't omit the truth or flat out lie. What you saw was what you got.

'I'm sorry about your news,' Vanessa said sincerely. Then, squaring her shoulders, she moved forward with business. 'You were interested in acquiring four cockapoos?'

Mrs Stuart sat beside her daughter and patted her hand. 'Cynthia looked into purchasing one before…well, before this terrible affair. I thought going ahead and finding her a little friend would help. Then I got to thinking. My darling Sheba passed away six months ago.'

The calculation wasn't difficult. 'That's only two puppies.'

'Two each makes four,' Mrs Stuart corrected. 'It's nice for them to have company. Cynthia and an older sister live in the cottage on the adjoining lot, so it'd be a real little family.'

Vanessa's heart warmed. She would've loved to have had a brother or sister growing up…Christmases, birthdays, boisterous family Sunday dinners. Maybe one day—if she was lucky.

'I've made a couple of phone calls,' she said, happy to proceed. Dogs were great company at any time, particularly when someone needed a friend who didn't judge and always listened. And more than instinct said any puppy sold to these women would certainly be cared for. 'A litter sired by a world champion should be available this week. Is that too soon?'

Mrs Stuart squeezed her daughter's free hand. 'I

should think the sooner the better.' The older woman's gaze drifted to the left and her face lit up. 'Mitch, darling. Your friend's arrived.'

Vanessa's blood pressure dropped and the room tilted forty-five degrees.

Good Lord, she hadn't known *he'd* be here.

She wheeled around to see Mitch Stuart sauntering into the room. His languid yet purposeful gait was that of a man effortlessly in charge. His smile was just as sexy, even if the slant of his lips was a little contrite. Vanessa's stomach muscles tugged. She wanted to run—from this house or straight into those strong arms? She wasn't certain which.

Warning herself not to, Vanessa nonetheless breathed in the subtle male scent as he stopped beside her. He was taller than she remembered, his shoulders in that crisp white Oxford shirt, sleeves rolled below the elbows, seemed far broader. His eyes were so blue and filled with light, she imagined she saw herself in their reflection.

He spoke to his mother but kept his eyes on their guest. 'Miss Craig and I are acquaintances, Mother.'

'Then your *acquaintance* is helping us no end,' Mrs Stuart replied. 'Vanessa thinks we can have our puppies by the end of the week.'

His chest inflated as that smile grew and simmered in his eyes. 'That's great news.'

Vanessa wondered…

He'd ripped up her business card, had kissed her passionately, then as good as admitted he didn't want to get involved, which was far nobler than stringing her along. Was this meeting about salving his conscience as much as helping his mother and sister? If that were the case, she would be wise to accept his peace offering graciously. Aunt McKenzie had often warned against false pride.

She'd be grateful but, foremost, businesslike.

Vanessa allowed a crisp smile. 'Thanks for the referral.'

'Least I could do.'

Had he stepped closer or was it that seductive rich tone pulling at her again?

Determined to ignore the rapid heartbeat thudding in her ears, Vanessa tucked in her chin. She needed to move this along. They'd already established that, whatever it was bubbling between herself and Mitch Stuart, it was going nowhere fast.

She faced Mrs Stuart. 'Would you mind if I had a look at the dogs' accommodation?'

She'd like to pass on any positive information to the breeders. Plus her enquiry would get her out of the room and away from the temptation of Mitch Stuart's hypnotic presence. She was human, after all.

Preoccupied, Cynthia sniffed, dropped the handkerchief to her lap and shuddered. Her mother clucked comfortingly and looked to her son. 'Mitch, can you show Vanessa Sheba's housing for me?'

Vanessa felt her eyes widen. She hadn't meant for Mitch to take her on a tour. She should've kept quiet.

Of course, he could always decline.

But his smile was dazzling. 'My pleasure. Follow me.' He tipped his head towards the ornate arch through which he'd entered the room.

Vanessa found her calm centre and braced herself. She could handle this. She was a mature, intelligent woman with a goal. She could spend a few moments alone with Mitch Man-god Stuart. She was hardly in danger of him kissing her again, particularly here, in his mother's home. They'd established he didn't want to get involved—they weren't 'compatible'.

It was her imagination, then, that something almost predatory gleaming in his eyes whispered otherwise.

He matched his stride with hers and they passed a sitting room, what looked like a study, then a massive library, boasting book spines to the ceiling. The very walls seemed to breathe an extended family history of privilege.

He swung a left. Given the increasingly delicious aroma, she guessed they were approaching the kitchen.

He surprised her with his question. 'How did your bank meeting go today?'

She took a moment to find a casual tone. 'No need to try to make conversation, Mr Stuart.'

'No good, huh?'

She pressed her lips together and looked straight ahead.

'I'd like to help.'

She sent him a questioning look. 'By sending more business my way?'

Did he have a swag of friends after companions? Not that that would be a long-term solution.

'I was thinking more along the lines of a loan.'

Vanessa stopped dead and measured the earnest expression in his eyes. Well, that was out of the blue. Just what was behind that offer? Surely he wasn't in the habit of gifting money to women he barely knew. Just what did he expect in exchange?

She set off walking again and they entered a huge kitchen. 'Thanks, but I don't take money from strangers.'

'Acquaintance, remember? And I run an investment and lending organisation. Helping with finance is what I do.'

She digested the information and slid him a jaded smile. 'You've suddenly decided to throw me a line?' Odd that he'd neglected to mention his profession last night, and he'd certainly had the ideal opportunity.

'We'd known each other five minutes. I've had time to think it over.'

'Think over being charitable or kissing me and wishing you hadn't?'

When his brows shot up, she walked a little faster.

She hadn't meant to be that blunt, but she wasn't in the mood for games, not where her beloved shop was concerned. And all these shining pans hanging from their gleaming hooks, the sparkling sinks set in glistening granite benches... This environment was so overly advantaged, goose bumps were erupting up and down her limbs. She'd see the dogs' housing, then get out of here fast, back to her own safe little world where she belonged.

He scratched his temple. 'You're not going to make this easy for me, are you?'

A perfect retort burned on the tip of her tongue. But she thought again and swallowed the words.

Annoying thing was that she had nothing to lose and everything to gain by putting their sizzling mistake of an embrace behind her, as he had clearly done. She needed a loan. He'd offered professional help. So he'd kissed her and didn't want to go there again. So what? She'd lived through worse and survived.

She pulled up by the million-dollar coffee machine and folded her arms. 'What would you like to know?'

Long legs braced shoulder-width apart, he mimicked her no-nonsense pose. 'Firstly, what are you seeking to gain out of your business?'

Puzzled, she shook her head. 'What do you mean?'

'Do you envisage yourself as a multimillionaire? Is it a living you fell into? Something to keep you out of trouble or a passion? Today's business world is more competitive than ever, as you've no doubt found out. A person can lose everything. The veritable shirt off his back.'

Wow. What an optimist.

If she'd clung to every negative piece of advice she'd been handed in her life, she mightn't get out of bed in the morning.

'I'm aware of life's knocks. Doesn't mean I don't

deserve my chance to provide the community with a service which I believe in, heart and soul.'

He studied her eyes for a calculating moment, then a grin kicked up a corner of his mouth and his arms unravelled. 'All right, then. Let's go through the figures, work on a business plan and we can take it from there.'

'I already have a business plan.'

'Obviously not a good one.'

Guess she had to give him that. She liked to consider herself independent; she'd done everything on her own, making mistakes and learning along the way. Not quickly enough, it seemed.

He set off again and she followed him into an adjoining room that might have been set up for infants— pastel pinks and blues, pint-sized cushiony beds, a playground with colourful balls and squeezy toys. Lucky dogs. But, before she commented on the quality accommodation, she wanted to push home a point.

'I appreciate your interest in my situation. But I want to make it clear that I'm not a charity case.' In other words, 'I don't want you to consider approving a loan simply because…' *Say it, Vanessa. Just say it.* 'Because you feel bad about last night.'

A muscle in his shadowed jaw flexed as he faced her. His subtle scent and aura of strength soaked into her skin, ambushing a good measure of her bravado and turning it to mush.

'While we're on the subject of getting things straight…I don't regret kissing you, Vanessa. Quite the contrary.' That curious gleam flared up and swam again in his eyes. 'Would it surprise you to hear I'd like to do it again?'

A hot jet of arousal flashed through her veins. For a moment, she was so shaken she couldn't respond. She wet her suddenly dry lips, then wished she hadn't. She didn't want to give him the wrong idea.

Her voice was a croak. 'That wouldn't be wise.'

The line between his brows gradually deepened. 'You're right. Of course. Not wise at all.'

'Clearly you have misgivings about me...*you* and me. *Us*. If we're going to be associated in a business sense, it wouldn't be appropriate to be...involved.'

Yet she melted as his head tipped, he focused on her lips and stepped closer. 'I agree. Totally.'

Her face grew tellingly warm, her legs frighteningly weak. 'It could cause problems.'

His fingertip lightly curved her cheek, around her chin, sending wondrous warmth unfurling through her system. 'I don't need any more problems.'

He gently pinched her chin, tipping her face a fraction higher, and a lightning bolt zapped and sizzled from her crown down to her toes. 'Me either.' Definitely not.

With his gaze scalding her lips, he moved unbearably close, until his hard lean hips met hers. 'So it's settled.'

She sighed and murmured, 'Absolutely.'

His lips touched hers and gently lingered, tasting, enjoying, until her fluttering soul grew wings and carried her away. When he carefully drew back, her senses were reeling and her feet no longer touched the ground.

She gazed up dreamily, lost in the entrancing mirrors of his eyes. 'So was that just part of the service?'

His jaw tightened. 'No. That was unforgivable. It won't happen again.'

'You're certain?'

The pad of his thumb grazed her lips before his mouth descended once more. 'Absolutely.'

CHAPTER THREE

As THEY came up for air, Vanessa sensed something at her back. A prickling. A stare. Then Mitch's smouldering eyes left hers, he straightened and cleared his throat.

'Mother. We didn't hear you come in.'

Vanessa swung around. Mrs Stuart's smile was easy. Almost too easy.

'I don't mean to interrupt,' the older woman apologised.

Vanessa absently finger combed her hair and shot a glance over her surroundings. For a moment, she'd forgotten where she was, which happened to be *way out of her depth*.

'We were just…er…looking around,' Vanessa mumbled.

Mrs Stuart moved forward. 'And you're happy with the accommodation?'

'I'm sure your dogs won't want for a thing.'

Delighted, Mrs Stuart clasped her hands and her smile grew. 'Then we'd best get this arrangement underway. Mitch, I've written a cheque for a goodwill deposit. It's on the credenza in the living room. Vanessa and I will be right behind you. I want to ask her something…about the puppies.'

Mitch gave a hesitant half grin, but he inhaled and nodded as if it wasn't worth the argument. 'I'll see you both soon.'

Before Mitch left the room, he sent Vanessa a secret wink. Heartbeat skipping, she winked back. Her return gesture was almost involuntary, like accepting his kiss a moment ago. Before Mitch, she hadn't come close to understanding the true meaning of the word *magnetism*.

Both women's gazes followed his retreat, Vanessa's sculpting over the wide rolling shoulders, trim waist, lean hips and long, strong legs.

'My son's a good-looking man.'

Vanessa acknowledged the obvious. 'He is that.'

They began to walk, Mrs Stuart's hands still clasped at her waist. 'He'll be a wonderful catch for any woman.'

Vanessa's step faltered and she slid a curious gaze Mrs Stuart's way. 'I don't want to leave you with the wrong idea. Mitch and I have only just met.' A kiss or two was hardly death us do part.

'Ah, but the seeds are quickly blossoming into romance.' Mrs Stuart's laugh was light. 'My dear, a blind man could see.'

Vanessa's cheeks toasted. How could she deny it? 'There are…certain feelings.'

They moved through the kitchen, Mrs Stuart

nodding at Wendle, who was busy rotating roast potatoes. When they were out of household staff earshot, Mrs Stuart stated, 'You're not a virgin, are you, dear.'

Vanessa choked out a strangled cough. 'I beg your pardon?' Mrs Stuart might like to be open, but this was taking freedom of information way too far.

'It's no secret my son is drawn to women of... well...*experience*.'

Even if it were broadcast on *Entertainment Tonight*, Vanessa didn't feel right discussing Mitch's love life with his mother, of all people. Although now, truth tell, she was a smidgeon curious.

And what, precisely, constituted *experience*? She'd had more than one lover; last time she heard that didn't translate into promiscuous.

As they passed the solemn library, the musty air seemed to wind out and smother her as Mrs Stuart's heels on the timber clacked and echoed dully through the hall.

'Please don't take advantage of him.'

Vanessa lost her breath at the same time her back went up. 'How on earth would I do that?'

Mrs Stuart raised a brow. 'A woman from your quarter has her means.'

As they moved into the living room, Mitch joined them. Her brain stuck on freeze-frame, Vanessa automatically accepted the cheque he offered. She barely registered the generous amount penned above Mrs Stuart's neat signature.

Mrs Stuart's smile was staid. 'I'm sure it'll be very pleasant doing business with you.'

Business, sure. But Mrs Stuart wasn't about to dance at Vanessa's wedding, particularly if it was to her son. Which wasn't on the cards. Not even close. Stock from different pots rarely blended. It might be the twenty-first century but, at its deepest level, class structure was still alive and well. If the torn card last night had been an indication, Mrs Stuart's performance today proved it.

So what did all that mean for today's kiss? And Mitch's let's-take-this-further wink?

Mitch's rich tone seeped in through the fog. 'We'll leave you and Cynthia to your meal, Mother.'

Mrs Stuart's face fell. 'Oh, Mitch. Won't you stay for dinner?'

'Not tonight.' He stooped and brushed a kiss on her cheek.

Mrs Stuart pouted. 'I'm disappointed.'

'Next time.' He took Vanessa's elbow. 'Vanessa and I have some things to discuss.'

Mrs Stuart's mouth pinched before a flawless smile covered it. 'Then I'll say goodnight.'

The lady of the house didn't accompany them out. As the door closed and they descended the stone steps into the twilight, Vanessa shivered at the chill creeping up her spine.

Mitch stopped, concerned. 'What's wrong?'

She bit her lip. Should she tell him about her conversation with Mrs Stuart? She had no hands-on experience with mothers; her aunt had been a good provider and wonderfully supportive when crunch time rolled around. Were mothers supposed to wedge themselves into their children's lives this way under the guise of protectiveness? She suspected not.

She stole a glance at the imposing front door. Still shut. A ruffle of the curtain was no doubt her imagination.

She'd left that house with Mrs Stuart holding the upper hand. But she couldn't take another step without being honest with Mitch.

'I think your mother just warned me not to seduce you.'

To say it aloud sounded absurd. But Mitch merely grinned.

Vanessa narrowed her eyes. 'You're not surprised?'

They continued to walk to her car. 'My mother doesn't approve of any woman I see. They're either too vain, too thin, too haughty, too extrovert.' He gave a wry grin. 'I could go on.'

How about too poor?

Although Mrs Stuart's observations weren't personal, her comments were no less hurtful. 'She sounds difficult to please.'

'On that level, impossible. My mother's a widow's widow, with a stake in maintaining the status quo.'

As he opened her car door, Vanessa put the pieces together. 'You're single. She and her daughters are your only family.'

'She misses my father a great deal.' He left the obvious unsaid: his mother relied on him far too much.

She'd taken umbrage at Mrs Stuart's questioning, but now Vanessa succumbed to a twinge of sympathy. It was horrible to lose those you loved and depended on; she couldn't remember her parents but she missed them every day and to the deepest level of her being. What if she were to find the love of her life, only to have him taken away? She wouldn't be able to bear it.

Forearm resting on the open door rim, he peered in. 'Now, what say we get this plan underway?'

Vanessa's mind flew back to the critical here and now. 'Our business plan?' She checked her watch. 'But it's getting late.'

He frowned. 'Vanessa, we need to dive into this as soon as possible. How about we meet at your shop?'

Josie had looked after the shop this afternoon so Vanessa could keep her appointment with the bank. She shook her head. 'The animals will be settled for the night.' The dogs and kittens were bedded down at the local vet each night, but Vanessa didn't like to disturb the others.

'Your house, then.'

After seeing the pristine existence Mitch had grown up in, God, no! He'd liken her granny flat to a slum.

She made a flippant excuse. 'It's a mess.'

One big shoulder pushed to his ear. 'Then it has to be my place.'

Still no good. After that last kiss, there was only

one place 'close proximity' could lead and it wasn't to Grandma's house.

She may not be anywhere near as experienced as Mrs Stuart would like to believe. However, she was in tune with her sexuality: she was attracted to Mitch and, as he'd made clear again a moment ago, he was attracted to her. But, as they'd both already stated—none too convincingly—it wasn't wise to mix rags with riches, or business with pleasure.

Last year, Josie had bowed to temptation and slept with her boss at the accounting firm she'd worked for. When his superior had found out, he'd assigned Josie to a different branch. It'd taken boss man three weeks to start up an affair with his new assistant.

And there was another concern. If she and Mitch did end up acting on this sexual buzz and sleeping together, wouldn't that make any acceptance of a loan feel more like some kind of payment? What if 'good times' turned bad and he decided to wield his power and pull the loan? Then she *would* be screwed. Vanessa liked to be optimistic, not careless.

'Do you like Chinese food?' he asked.

She blinked and answered instinctively. 'I do.' Chow mein was her favourite.

'I'll order in.' He flashed that killer smile. 'You know the address. I'll see you in, say, an hour.'

As he moved to close the door, panic hit Vanessa like a medicine ball to the stomach. This was happening too fast. She just wasn't sure.

'Wait.'

He swung the door back open. His expression was accommodating, but with a sultry hint of *I'm hungry in more ways than one.*

Her hands wrung the steering wheel as she nibbled her lip.

In or out. Yes or no. Chicken or go-for-it.

Finally she released a breath and offered a yielding smile. 'Don't forget the fortune cookies.'

He pulled up straight, unintentionally emphasizing that dynamite chest. 'Will do.'

He closed the door and walked towards the black sports car parked to the side of the drive. Vanessa watched his retreat in the side mirror, her mouth becoming progressively drier.

So commanding and refined; he couldn't guess that she talked to rodents and reptiles and sometimes wondered if they talked back. Or that her favourite dessert was pink jellybean smiley faces on caramel swirl ice cream. That should be enough to put anyone off, particularly when they were routinely served crème brûlée with a solid-gold spoon.

Setting her jaw, she fired the ignition and pumped the pedal. This—*them*—whatever the combustible emotion she was feeling—wasn't meant to be. Not even for one unforgettable, orgasm-filled night. There was too much that didn't fit.

Too much at stake.

When she got home she'd call; she had his number listed on the receipt info. She'd explain that she'd developed a headache and it would be best she made a time to see him at his office. Should he deem her little enterprise worthy of the chance, she'd say thank you for the loan, then leave well enough alone.

No way, no how would she go through with tonight.

'You're late.'

Vanessa swept some hair behind her ear and, despite her stomach skipping rope, tried to look as casual as her outfit. 'Am I?'

When Mitch gestured her through into his home's foyer, she heard his smooth intake of air as she passed. 'My, you smell nice.'

'Thank you. Dog shampoo is so versatile.' She laughed at his raised brows. 'That was a joke.'

His mouth flattened. 'I'm a banker, Vanessa. We don't do jokes.'

Her heart stopped beating. 'Oh. I'm sorry. I thought—'

'Gotcha.'

His face broke into a gorgeous grin and she held off play-slapping his beautiful big arm.

He looked better than edible in jeans, a shade lighter than hers, and a worn T-shirt. The musculature of his chest through the soft grey fabric sent her heartbeat on a mile-a-minute sprint. As he turned away to usher her in, her gaze dropped to the languid motion of his easy stride. God help her, she wanted to slip her hands into those back pockets and *squeeze*.

She'd decided not to come tonight. She'd had every intention of calling this business meeting-cum-rendezvous off. They were from two different worlds, and she wasn't forgetting his mother on the war path. Her business difficulties must take priority… Coming here alone equated to courting trouble.

But curiosity had got the better of her and she'd crumpled. Excitement wasn't a big feature in her life. The idea of having a wealthy, handsome, eligible bachelor, who today had given off all the right vibes, was too intoxicating to resist. Didn't mean she had to go the whole nine yards and *sleep* with the guy.

As he'd said, they had work to do. Great and Small was her main concern. She wouldn't let anything— not even the temptation of dissolving into the magic of another mega-superb kiss—come before her number-one goal: saving her shop.

'I bet Kami's looking forward to seeing you again,' he said over his shoulder, waiting for her to catch up.

'You haven't heard the theory?'

'What theory?'

That fish had a five second memory span.

She waved a hand. 'Forget it.'

They crossed into the family room. The tank was on its own special polished wood unit. Kamikaze stilled before shooting back and forth and around his trident, an animated streak of shimmering gold.

Mitch laughed. 'Told you he'd be glad to see you.'

Vanessa smiled. Yep, one day he'd make a terrific dog owner—when he was ready to settle down.

'Did you bring your financials?'

Focused again, she held up a satchel. 'I brought

everything my bank manager asked for today—lease details, utility receipts, account numbers…'

She pulled up a stool at the kitchen counter, desperate to bite her nails while he flicked through the sheets.

'You're stuck in the red,' he noted after a quick perusal, 'and it appears you've already done what you can to cut costs and fend off creditors, which has artificially buoyed your cash flow.' His eyes met hers. 'Unfortunately, it's a tough time for small businesses.'

She swung her mouth to one side. 'Good thing I'm tough.'

Only she didn't feel so tough around him. She felt delectably weak and wonderfully female. There was something about a physically powerful, capable man that made a woman want to let go and melt right there against him. Not that she'd experienced this quality brand of euphoria before. Certainly not with her ex.

These heightened feelings were new. And nice.

Very nice.

He set the papers down. 'We should eat first.'

Her gaze jumped up from the pulse beating at the side of his tanned neck. *Get with the program, Vanessa.*

'Eat, then work.' She pulled up straight. 'Great idea.'

He brought four takeaway containers from the adjacent bench and laid out them out on a cutting board. Next, he retrieved plates, cutlery, linen napkins—his efficiency was impressive. How many 'clients' had he entertained here?

He flipped off the lids and she inhaled the mouthwatering bouquet of oriental spices and sauces. Chow mein, special fried rice, a Mongolian dish and sautéed vegetables. She would've chosen the same menu.

He reached for some goblets, visible behind a glass display door. 'Care for wine?'

'Alcohol and I don't mix.'

On her twenty-first, she'd been talked into knocking back a Tequila Slammer. She hadn't thought she'd be able to swallow it or, if she did, that it might come straight back up.

'Freshly squeezed juice, then.' He crossed to the giant stainless-steel fridge and found a glass pitcher.

After dragging up a stool beside her, he nodded at the feast. 'Dig in.'

'Do you have chopsticks?'

'Sorry. You're a fan?' He didn't sound surprised.

'One day, I'm going to take a vacation through Asia. Vietnam, Tibet. Enjoy the real deal.'

Then it was on to France, Italy and, finally, Greece!

He scooped some steaming rice onto her plate. 'You'll have a ball.'

'Do you travel a lot?' She dished out the vegetables.

'Some. I got a taste for it when I was young.'

'Family vacations abroad?'

Geez. Imagine that.

'When Dad could spare the time,' he stipulated. 'Before opening the door on the family business, he was an insurance executive, back in the days when premiums weren't through the roof and the small print was legible.'

As they ate, he topped up her juice and she considered the solid connection he obviously shared with the remaining members of his family. She could well imagine that Mrs Stuart leaned on him, and she was equally certain he would never turn his back and let any of them fall. He had *hero* written all over him.

She watched his jaw work as he set down his fork and reached for his glass.

'It's nice you're all still close,' she said.

His mouth twitched. 'Sometimes too close.'

Probably best to acknowledge Cynthia's plight. 'Your sister looked pretty washed out today.'

He frowned, then set down his glass. 'It's best. The guy's a chronic gambler. I can't see him lasting in the medical profession. I'm only happy he cut her loose.'

Nevertheless, Vanessa's heart ached for poor Cynthia. 'It's hard to be brave when you feel as if your world is folding in around you.'

Holding your chin high didn't mean you weren't still vulnerable inside.

He chewed, swallowed. 'Better to be hurt now than annihilated later.'

She forked around some bok choy. He was the family protector. The one the women relied on to know—and to do—what was best. Guess he had to be strong. Maybe a little too strong.

A horrible sensation whistled through her. She studied him as he finished his broccoli. 'Mitch, you didn't have anything to do with her fiancé's change of heart, did you?'

Had he paid the gambler off?

His scowl was deliberate but amused. '*No*. Although I'd like to send him a thank-you note.'

She sat back. 'You're one tough cookie.'

'Not too tough, I hope.'

Their eyes held, a glimmer of something more than understanding running hot between them. Overwhelmed by the intensity of his gaze—compelling yet at the same time almost cool—she dropped her eyes and forked around her fried rice.

Had he had a bad experience long ago? With an 'experienced' woman, perchance? Was that why his mother was so nosey now? Still, a man of thirty or so was free to make his own decisions, his own mistakes. How many long-term relationships had he had?

She set her fork down.

Talk about getting ahead of herself. She should escape while there was still time. She already knew what was on Mitch's more primitive mind, but far too many questions were whirling through hers to think straight; this minute only the quicksilver coursing through her veins whenever he looked at her seemed to make sense.

His BlackBerry beeped. He checked the screen and apologised. 'Do you mind if I get this?'

She blew her long fringe off her forehead. 'Not at all.'

Some distance would be good. It was getting a little hot in here.

While he took the call, she eased off her stool and rinsed her plate. He was engrossed in a conversation

about signing papers, two week deadlines, everything being in order, no need to worry…

She drifted over to say hi to Kami and gave him
a sprinkling of food. Then she spotted an open
door. Looked as if Mr Stuart was the owner of a
full-blown gym.

She glanced at Mitch, turned slightly away from
her now, nodding as he concentrated on his call. No
telling how much longer he'd be. He wouldn't mind
if she had a quick look.

She wandered in.

The darkened room was spacious and featured a
full-length glass wall, which presented a masterpiece of the harbour at night—colourful city lights
hugging the dark velvet bays, the bridge twinkling
magically in the distance. There was enough light
from the hall to make out, directly in front of her,
a rowing machine, a speed ball and a massive
weight station.

A thrill rippled through her stomach. Muscles
bulging, testosterone surging. She'd kill to see him
hard at work on that.

A shadow passed over her, blocking out the light.

'Here you are.'

Her breath catching, she spun around. Mitch's sil-
houette all but filled the doorway—ominous, masterful. As a stir of apprehension weaved up her spine;
she cleared the thickness from her throat and offered
a shaky smile. 'I thought you might like some privacy,
so I showed myself around. Hope you don't mind.'

He snapped on the switch and the room lit up. 'Make yourself at home.'

His eyes glistened with a not-so-secret smile. If she'd turned left instead of right, she might have come across his bedroom.

He joined her, picking up a dumb-bell from a nearby rack.

She smirked. 'You like to work out, or is all this to impress the girls?'

He didn't blink. 'Health is a priority. A little each day—'

'Keeps the doctor away.'

He laughed. 'Right. How about you?'

'I spend all day on my feet. I'm usually too bushed by the time I get home to think of anything other than a warm shower and curling up with a good book.'

Plus, however fashionable, she wasn't a fan of exercise. Never had been.

'You'd have more energy if you put aside even twenty minutes a day.' He handed over a weight.

Taking it, her overburdened arm flew down. 'You mean somewhere between sunrise and when I leave for the shop thirty minutes later?'

She rubbed her shoulder and he took the dumb-bell back. 'The kids are up early?'

She laughed. Her animals *were* her kids. She might only provide them with a temporary home but she loved and would remember every one who passed through.

He moved to the weight station bench. Looking up

the stack, he pulled to test a cable. 'Are the Rotties still there?' he asked offhandedly.

She didn't miss the deepened note in his voice.

'One of the females sold this morning.' But his buddy—the male—was still waiting for his perfect match.

Without further comment, Mitch collected two hand weights. 'Here. Try these.'

Against her better judgement, she accepted and curled her right arm at the elbow, then her left. Doable. But preferably not.

He knocked both fists against his pecs, *me Tarzan* style. 'Feel the oxygen breathing life through your blood?'

She surreptitiously scanned the length of his braced legs, his stellar athletic frame. 'I sure can. What's this for?' she asked guilelessly, indicating the mechanism at the end of the workout bench.

His eyes lit. 'Ah, this one's great for building the quadriceps.'

Quadriceps. She liked the sound of that.

To demonstrate, he reclined back on the bench, got comfortable, looped his legs around the two pairs of black padded cylinders and straightened his bent knees. As the denim around his thighs stretched, the cords in his neck strained, and Vanessa fought the urge to fan herself.

After a few more levitations, he unwound his legs and sprang up. 'You try it.'

She gaped. 'Who, me?'

Not only was she tragically uncoordinated, she was terrified she wouldn't be able to lift an inch.

As if reading her mind, he moved to the weight column and repositioned a pin. 'I've adjusted the weight. Now you have no excuse.'

She batted her lashes. 'Did I mention that in my final year I broke the coach's nose with a mutant hockey stick swing? After my javelin try out, the teachers unanimously voted to ban me from sport.'

He playfully crowded her back. 'Not listening.'

Beaten, she huffed and reclined while he hovered over her, checking those cables again. Her attention gravitated to the sinew and rock working beneath that T-shirt. His every movement proclaimed absolute power, Olympian authority. His mere presence took her breath away.

'Hook your legs between the cylinders,' he said, and she let him manipulate her lower limbs. Happy with her positioning, he stepped back. 'Now use your thighs and lift.'

Hands bracing her weight on the bench either side, she surrendered to her fate and lifted once, twice, three times!

Close to spent, she flopped back. 'And you do this for how long each morning?'

He rubbed the corner of his eye. 'Right after dinner isn't the best time for a workout,' he admitted.

She struggled to get up. 'I'll remember that.'

His hand grasped hers, warm and big. Maybe it was the rush of adrenaline from the impromptu exercise, but he overdid the tug. She flew to her feet, her nose landing inches from the beating hollow of his clean-shaven, exquisite-smelling throat. As her heart crashed against her ribs, her fingers begged to reach up and trail a sensual line around his shadowed jaw, then compare the rough to the soft kissable line of his lips.

Keeping her eyes straight ahead, she felt the burn of his gaze as his voice rumbled in his chest. 'You okay?'

She swallowed against a rush of raw physical need. 'A little out of breath is all.'

'Exercise'll do that.'

She dared to look up. His smile was sinful.

His arm came out to draw her near; she found the wherewithal to dodge and head towards the window.

Business and pleasure—gods and mere mortals— do not mix. She was certain Mrs Stuart would agree. Mitch was tempting with a capital *Take me now*. But she was here to save her shop. Rescue the one tangible that had ever truly meant something in her life.

And then there was Mitch…

She stopped inches from the glass and its amazing twinkling view, wondering whether Kami, living out his existence in that tank, might feel a little like she did now. Restless…reckless…wanting something, yet not certain of the consequences should she suck in a big breath and go for it.

She could open her arms now and call to him. She was certain he would come. She could already feel the incomparable, never-to-be-forgotten hours ahead.

But if anyone ended up getting hurt in the end, hands down it'd be her.

Behind her, his natural heat radiated out, fanning new life on the kindling smouldering low in her stomach. His words stirred the hair at her ear. 'Guess we should go do some work.'

She couldn't quieten the pulse pounding in her throat. 'Work.' *Yes*. She nodded. 'Good idea.'

'I'd like to go through your P and Ls for the last twelve months.'

'And then?' She edged around and made the mistake of looking into his eyes. They were bright. Hot.

No doubt reading the yearning and indecision in hers, he tested, his hand skimming—barely a whisper—down her side. 'I'd like to look at your rent,' he said. 'Your location.'

The tips of her breasts grew to burning beads as his palm slid around to measure the rise of her hip. She fought to keep the pleasure from spreading lower and her eyes from drifting shut. 'Location's important.'

'If something you want is there right in front of you, it's hard to resist.'

His hot fingertips pressed into the small of her back, and her pelvis arced against him, melting wax against timeless stone. As if in slow motion, his head bowed over hers and his lips oh so lightly brushed hers, back and forth, up and down.

His warm wet tongue flicked the side of her mouth. 'Remember what I said about hard to resist?'

She succumbed to a sigh and admitted, 'Right this minute I can't remember my own name.'

She felt his wicked grin on her cheek. 'This is up to you.' His hands found hers as he walked her back till her shoulders touched the cool windowpane. He slid her arms out in a seductive arc against the glass so they came to rest either side of her head.

'If you're not sure,' he murmured against her temple, his body burning so close to hers, 'I won't push.'

The kindling in her belly leapt and sparked. 'Not even a little?'

His growing smile slid an erotic promise up around her jaw, leaving a wake of sizzling pleasure. His teeth found her earlobe, tugged, and the fire below burned more.

'Vanessa, I want you in my bed.' As her knees buckled, he caught her waist and held her hips against his—hard, insistent, irresistible. His voice lowered. 'What's the verdict?'

She took a deep, brave breath and dived in.

How could she deny it? 'I feel good about this.'

His blue eyes darkened. 'So do I.'

CHAPTER FOUR

As MITCH's eyes held hers, his burning fingers splayed down, winding around the hem of her T-shirt. Entranced, Vanessa lifted her arms and let the fabric glide up over her tummy, her bra, her head. No sooner had her shirt hit the floor than she returned the favour and his T-shirt joined hers by their feet.

In the stark artificial light, they both stilled, acknowledging the moment of no return. With his chest expanding fully on each breath, his head angled, then his gaze lowered to her lips. He leaned forward and their mouths lightly touched, touched again, and with each caress her need to have more went deeper.

Got stronger.

When he flicked her bra's clasp and slid the straps from her shoulders, the fabric of time warped and her surroundings dissolved. As each kiss grew less controlled and more fun, she surrendered to instinct, letting her palms fan over the delicious rock of a chest before searching out and fumbling with his jeans's button while he unzipped her fly. Hearing his soft groans, feeling his smile, aware that his hunger matched hers…

When had she thought she could stop this force from driving them together?

After they'd each kicked off their denim, his fingers twined with hers and he pinned her against the enormous back window. He first tasted a seductive path down her neck, progressed to her cleavage and around the aching peak of her right breast, then, with deliberate lack of speed, her left. His hands released hers to sculpt over her shoulders, over her ticklish ribs. She smiled as his palms moved lower, followed by his searching mouth.

Flexing her fingers through his hair, she revelled in the slide of his teeth as she burned white-hot inside. Delectable flames licked beneath her skin… oxygen evaporated before hitting her lungs…the connective cells in her body melted and all she wanted was to give herself to him, then happily die.

Crouching now, his knees either side of her shins, he peeled her panties down her thighs, his warm, skilful mouth trailing a thumping heartbeat behind. When she stepped out of the last of her clothing, he ground up against her, familiarising her with a sensory slide of his strength and furnace heat until they stood nose to nose.

The glass at her back no longer felt cool but rather *safe*—a transparent anchor to hold her against the torrent of giddy sensations casting her high. He cupped her cheek and kissed her again while his chest hair teased the points of her breasts and the room temperature jackknifed again.

She was light-headed—floating—when his lips eventually left hers. His heavy-lidded eyes gazed into hers, reaching so deeply she heard their souls whisper.

'I've thought a lot about this,' he murmured.

She sighed out a smile. 'That's nice to know.'

'I'd imagined going slow—' he grazed his lips back and forth over hers '—imagined making it last.'

She swallowed the groan of need pushing up her throat. *Make it last?* How much longer could she stand this sweet torture?

As if hearing her prayer, he scooped and hooked his pelvis under hers. Having peeled off his briefs when he'd ditched his jeans, his unrestrained erection gave a friendly nudge and the movement persuaded her thighs to part. She heard a hiss—his sharp intake of air—as his every muscle bunched and steamed.

Then he laughed, a low laboured sound. 'Know what I said about going slow…?'

As he spoke, he massaged her behind, manoeuvring her expertly until his tip pressed inside. The gasp of delight caught in her throat.

With a double grip, she clutched his jaw. 'Fast, slow. I'm not going anywhere—unless it's to your bedroom.'

He growled. 'Now we've started, don't think I want to wait that long.'

When he moved again and his engorged length filled her more, her mind went blank but for one simple glimpse at the truth. She only needed this feeling, this wild crazy spiral. Before now—before Mitch—she hadn't lived.

Without warning, he bounced her up and her legs automatically scissored around his hips. Now given the access they both craved, he took her mouth again and drove harder, plunged deeper, until the friction lit a candle so blindingly bright, a flurry of colour-filled sparks shot through her blood.

As her orgasm hit, intensified, multiplied—squeezing a mind-blowing beat—she clung to his neck and, over and over, murmured his name. In those few wonder-filled moments in time, nothing else existed.

Nothing else mattered.

All too soon the heady rhythm fell away. As the stars in her head faded, the visceral tension eased and she became aware of the fierce energy holding her close. His body trembled as the tendons between his shoulder blades locked, hard and slick.

Groggy, she drew slightly away. His eyes were shut tight. Did her warrior have a cramp?

'Mitch, what's wrong?'

He ground out, 'Forgot…condom.'

The light in the room suddenly got brighter. Protection was one thing no one wanted to neglect.

His eyes opened a crack. 'There's one problem. I don't want to let you go.'

That went double for her.

She had an idea to minimise the separation. 'How far's the bedroom?' If he had condoms, she guessed they'd be there.

He didn't answer but rather, understanding, turned up a wicked smile and proceeded to carry her through to his room, her legs still wrapped around his hips, his head buried in the grateful curve of her neck.

In the darkened bedroom, he carefully eased her back onto the cool quilt. She watched, awe-struck, as he retrieved a wrap from the nearby drawer, his superbly built frame working in the moonlight streaking in through the window as he prepared. She felt half sorry when the delectable show ended, but any disappointment vanished when he joined her again, seamlessly picking up where they'd left off.

Sinful yet also in some way sweet—his long full strokes rekindled those internal embers still aglow. She'd thought she'd been satisfied and he'd been on the brink, yet now he took the time to skilfully coax and love her, until soon she was leaping off that same mountain, freefalling into unsurpassed bliss with him close behind.

The drop was higher, the sensations clearer, and as the tingling ripples lessened and her spirit floated back, she knew no experience would ever top this, not if she lived a hundred years.

Afterwards he suggested a shower, where the water was warm, his kisses warmer and she learned that near nothing was forbidden between lovers.

Was it because he was a master of the game or because she'd been so attracted from the first? His strong arms felt as if they'd been created purely for her need and comfort. The way he adoringly soaped her back, the curve of her bottom, then up and down her thighs felt strangely familiar and yet all so new.

In the spacious black marble bathroom, they painstakingly dried each other with huge fluffy towels, then returned to the bedroom and burrowed beneath the fresh lavender-smelling sheets, gloriously naked and content. Yet already she wondered about next time.

About tomorrow.

At a twinge of guilt—they were from different worlds…she'd vowed not to succumb—she drew slightly away from the hard but comforting curve of his arm. Despite the hypnotic yellow glow of a corner lamp, she needed to push sexual compatibility aside and force her focus back upon the real reason she'd come to Mitch Stuart's home. She had a business, her home, to save.

'We should probably get up and go through those figures.'

His growl rumbled through her palm resting on the crisp hairs of his chest. 'I have a better idea.'

'What?'

'Let me hold you while you sleep.' His mouth twitched. 'Then again…' He rolled so that she lay beneath him, the tip of his nose touching hers. 'Who can sleep?'

When he'd finished kissing her thoroughly, his head kicked back as if he were coming to terms with a not unpleasant thought. 'I just had this amazing vision of you on my rowing machine.'

A laugh slipped out. She liked his adventurous

spirit but that was *so* not happening. 'You weren't listening to my school anecdotes, were you?'

She and sport were as compatible as oil and water.

His tongue drew a loving line around the shell of her ear. 'You're naked.'

She tingled and hummed as her fingertips weaved over his big shoulder, down the indentation of his muscled back. 'Of course I'm naked, silly.'

'I meant in my vision.'

He nibbled her chin. She closed her eyes and slipped back into nirvana. 'Mitch, I don't exercise, remember?'

His hot hand slid over her hip and between them. 'I think you do.'

Despite the drugging effects of his touch, weaving its spellbinding magic, she managed to tease. 'I far prefer intellectual pastimes.'

'I prefer you.'

When he kissed her, she kissed him back, again… and again…and again.

By 4:00 a.m., they'd made love twice more and Vanessa lay wide-awake on her side, watching her lover's darkly handsome face as he slept.

She would happily study him for ever—the faint scar below his left eye, the smooth bronzed rocks of his shoulders, the aura of animal magnetism that defined him even in his sleep.

Stopping herself from kissing his bristled cheek one last time, she eased back the sheets and slipped quietly out of bed. Through the smoky pre-dawn light, she stood, naked, willing herself to end the evening of her life and steal away.

Fresh wonder washed through her as, still asleep, a corner of his mouth curved and his arm moved from his side, his hand splaying out over the sheet as if searching for her warmth in his dreams.

She hugged herself. Lord, she wanted to snuggle back in. But she had to duck home and change before heading off to the shop. Chances were he'd want to see her tonight. But common sense and past experience said, as wonderful as it had been, this affair wouldn't last.

Water met its own level…no matter how great the temptation was to slip in and sleep with Mitch again, ending this now and protecting her heart was far wiser than facing the prospect of enduring poor Cynthia's acute strain of pain.

Mitch Stuart would be all too easy to love.

And lose.

She slipped into the gym, found her clothes and dressed, then made a detour to the kitchen. She collected her bag and, seeing the leftovers on the counter, remembered their first meal together; it seemed like someone else's lifetime ago. In the lightening shadows, she noticed a brown paper bag.

Fortune cookies.

Slipping her hand in, she selected just one. Then she tiptoed through to the living room, and Kami came to life. She bent and pressed her fingertip to the glass. 'Be good.'

Sliding the cookie in her jeans' back pocket, she stepped out and quietly clicked the door shut.

When would Mitch wake and realise she'd gone?

CHAPTER FIVE

LATER that morning, Mitch sat at the large, orderly oak desk, which had once been his father's, whistling as he organised his files for next week's board meeting, his last as Vice-President.

Not that his mind was on promotion today. His brain was stuck on a delicious groove that brought him back time after time to Vanessa's laugh, Vanessa's curves, Vanessa's moans and cries of pleasure as their lovemaking pitched them both farther out of orbit.

Either it had been way too long, or she indeed possessed powers that drew him in like the tide on full moon. His blood had ignited whenever she'd moved beneath him, or placed her lips on his skin—dear Lord, especially *there*.

When he'd woken, far later than usual, he'd been surprised and disappointed not to find her in his bed. He'd wanted to phone but instead he'd skipped his regular workout to spend time on the info in her business folder and put together a best fit financial rescue strategy. Within an hour of docking at the office, he'd had her loan in the pipeline. Tomorrow the money would be in her bank account. But tonight…

He twirled his pen and whistled again.

Tonight's agenda was pleasure only.

The office door flew open, threatening to fly off its hinges when the heavy wood slammed against the wall. As his father's solemn portrait rattled on its hook, Mitch lowered his pen and Garret Jeffson, acting President of Stuart Investments and Loans, stormed in.

The older man flung a set of papers on Mitch's desk. 'What the hell's wrong with you today?'

He'd spent a sensational evening with a woman in a million and this morning the sun had never shone brighter.

Mitch sat back. 'Nothing's wrong, Garret. I feel great.'

'Great or delirious? How do you explain this?'

Mitch recognised the papers, his signature. Vanessa Craig's loan application. He wouldn't ask how Garret had zeroed in on it so quickly. 'Honest Garret Jeffson' was straight as a die and possessed uncanny business instinct, reason enough for Mitch's father to entrust Garret the job, in the event of his death, of grooming his son for the top position. But Mitch had proven his competence, loyalty and commitment to Stuart Investments and Loans time and again; he did not appreciate having his authority questioned now.

Elbows on armrests, Mitch steepled his fingers under his chin. 'I've processed big loans before.'

Too many to count and way bigger than this.

'The applicant has no money, no assets, no guarantor. She's in debt up to her eyeballs. What the hell's supposed to be securing the loan—' Garret stopped, sharpened his gaze on Mitch's, then swiped his hand down his mortified face. 'My God, you're *sleeping* with this woman.'

Mitch's hands and expression tightened. He knew this job backwards. He'd lived and breathed this place for as long as he could remember. Day in, day out, and every minute in between. He didn't take kindly to being questioned now.

'That's really none of your business.'

Garret's fierce expression softened to fatherly understanding. He hooked a leg over the side of Mitch's desk and thatched his fingers on a thigh. 'Son, buy her a diamond necklace. Take her on a weekend trip to Paris. Don't put your reputation on the line—' his nostrils flared '—or this company's.'

'Garret, take it easy.' Mitch tried a wry grin. 'Just think, in less than two weeks you'll retire and won't need to worry about me or any of this ever again.'

Jowls turning as crimson as the carpet, Garret slowly pushed to his feet. 'Your father entrusted me to make the call on whether to promote you to top chair. I won't betray his memory or our investors' trust by going against my conscience if it tells me it's not time.'

Mitch studied his mentor's steely gaze. He'd learned so much from Garret. He trusted and genuinely admired this man above any other living. But

Garret hadn't interfered with his work in too long to remember. Mitch didn't like having what amounted to veiled blackmail held over his head now—and for no good reason.

However, he was also smart enough to know he had no alternative but to live to fight another day. After his thirtieth birthday, he would answer to no one. He couldn't wait to be free.

He grabbed his pen, swept the necessary instructions over the application's front page, then tossed the pen aside. 'There. I'm guarantor. No risk.'

Despite his earlier knee-jerk assumption about her financial dilemma, he believed Vanessa Craig had what it took. What was more, he intended to stand by and make certain that her troubled venture pulled through. Now he'd given her this loan, he'd steer her in the right direction. Relocation, of course, was a must.

With a knowing, almost smug look, Garret headed for the door. 'So it's true.'

'What's true?'

'Love truly is blind.'

Mitch felt the smack like a belt to the jaw.

He wasn't in *love*. He'd known Vanessa two days! He felt deeply about her, in a way that couldn't be explained to those who hadn't experienced the same roller coaster of emotions with someone of the opposite sex. What Vanessa and he enjoyed wasn't love—it was sublime pleasure.

He leaned back in his chair. 'I know what I'm doing.'

Hand on the door handle, Garret nodded as if he'd got what he wanted. 'Invite me to the wedding.'

When the door closed, Mitch cleared his throat.

Garret had it wrong. Marriage wasn't for him; he had enough family responsibility. What he wanted was a little fun. Hell, he'd almost forgotten what it was like to simply let go. And Vanessa was sexy and witty; better yet, she was independent, or had the potential to be. Which was a far cry from *dangerous*, which seemed to be Garret's implication. His mother's too, though that was no surprise.

When he was with Vanessa, his world felt…*enhanced*. So much so, he was counting the minutes until he held her again.

His gaze fell upon an invitation to a charity cocktail party this Saturday night. He'd already RSVPed, but he'd have his secretary call again and accept for two. In the meantime…

Picking up the phone, he pressed in a number and waited for the tinkle of her voice.

'Great and Small. How can I help you?'

A wave of endorphins burst through his blood. 'I can think of several ways.'

Mitch caught sight of his father's portrait looking down his long nose with a judgemental glare. He spun the chair away towards the city harbour view.

'Mitch?'

She sounded hesitant but also lawlessly sexy. He imagined her standing in her shop in her jeans and her T-shirt and his blood began to heat. 'How's the cockapoo adoption plans going?'

'They've had their shots and the breeder is sending some photos via email today. They sound gorgeous.'

He remembered the magic of her kiss. 'You're gorgeous.'

She made a modest noise that pumped his want for her that much higher.

'I take from that you're not annoyed I left without saying goodbye.'

'I forgive you,' he growled. 'Don't let it happen again.'

He expected her to laugh and was surprised when she didn't.

'Are you tired?' she asked instead.

He pitched his heels up on the desk and crossed his ankles. 'Never felt better. What about you?'

'I think I'll sleep tonight.'

'As long as it's with me.'

Her voice changed. 'Is that an invitation or an ultimatum?'

He grinned. 'Whatever works. How about we eat out tonight?'

He waited out two unexpected beats of silence. 'Actually, I'm expecting someone late this afternoon. I'm not sure what time I'll be free.'

Disappointment dropped through him like a giant lead weight. He blinked several times and came up with a solution—one that would have him seeing her as soon as possible.

'I'll drop in after closing time and see how you're doing.' A light on his phone lit—Garret's extension. His first instinct was to ignore it. Which was ludicrous.

Less than two weeks.

He threw his legs down and sat forward. 'Vanessa, I have to go. I'll see you around six.' Wondering who her visiting 'someone' might be, he frowned, running a palm over the approved application on his desk. 'I won't be late.'

'Aunt McKenzie!' Vanessa flung her arms out and pulled her aunt near. 'How wonderful to see you, but I was surprised when you rang this morning and wanted to visit. You hate the city.'

McKenzie gave her another quick hug, then stepped back and glared towards the broad front windows of her niece's pet store. 'Smog and traffic and too many folk. I haven't been off my property since—well, can't quite remember when.'

Vanessa walked with McKenzie through to the back of the premises, which she'd decked out with photos, favourite plants and a comfortable couch. It was near closing time; if someone entered the shop—including Mitch—she'd hear the bell.

All day she'd mulled over her decision to put the brakes on their intimate relationship. Again and again she'd reminded herself she wasn't in Mitch Stuart's league. Although she'd rather deny it, when push came to shove, chances were the downtown girl with next to no family and definitely no money would be little more than an entertaining interlude.

That didn't mean her heartbeat didn't skip whenever she thought of seeing him again.

Forcing her mind away from sexy Mr Stuart, Vanessa stopped with McKenzie in the centre of the back room. 'So, what's happened? Why the sudden visit?'

McKenzie set down her vinyl handbag and slid off her pristine white gloves. 'A dear friend called last month. We haven't seen each other since—' She all but sighed, then smiled softly. 'Since before you came to live with me. He's ill. I'm going to visit.'

Vanessa felt her expression open with surprise. 'Mac, that's so thoughtful. He'll be so glad to see you.'

McKenzie playfully snapped both her gloves over her left palm. 'So he should be. Flying all the way to Los Angeles.'

Vanessa's jaw unhinged. 'As in *California* Los Angeles?'

A smile danced in her eyes. 'My plane leaves later tonight.'

'I thought you were afraid of flying.'

That was what McKenzie had always said, and Vanessa knew why. Her parents had been killed in a light plane crash. Vanessa, not much more than a baby at the time, had miraculously survived, buckled securely in her child seat. McKenzie had kept her niece wrapped in cotton wool ever since.

Vanessa had loved her for it, but she'd also longed to spread her wings and experience life. To date, the ordinary girl from an ordinary town hadn't made it past Pitt Street. She wasn't discontented. As long as she could keep her shop, she shouldn't, and wouldn't, complain.

McKenzie dug into her bag. 'This is a super-quick stop. My cab's waiting but, before I go…' She withdrew an envelope. 'I want you to have this.'

Wondering, Vanessa took the envelope. Her birthday wasn't for months.

At first the large envelope appeared to be empty. She ferreted around and extracted, 'A cheque?' She ran an eye over the signature, then the amount and a hot chill dropped over her face and through her body. She swallowed. 'For a *million dollars*.' Had Aunt McKenzie robbed a bank? Done away with someone for insurance? 'Please tell me you're not running from the law.'

McKenzie laughed, a throaty chuckle Vanessa had missed very much. 'Remember your great-grandfather's painting he brought back from Europe?'

'You said it was an original.'

Obviously proud, McKenzie offhandedly toyed with one decades-old opal eardrop. 'I had an art dealer offer me a cool mill for it. I've sold the property too for round the same money, so half goes to you, half to me.'

Stunned, Vanessa pushed the cheque towards her aunt. 'You don't have to give me this. I can't accept.'

Aunt McKenzie's work-worn hands folded over hers. 'Nessy, I have no one in the world but you. I've never been flash. I prefer to be careful. And I've taught you to be careful too. So—' She thrust back her thin shoulders. 'Like Jim said, you can't take it with you when you go.'

'Jim's your friend?'

'The best.' McKenzie's pale green eyes glistened. 'We were engaged once.'

Vanessa dropped into the chair behind her. 'I had no idea.'

Her aunt was the classic spinster. She'd never spoken of former loves, had never seemed interested in men and now Vanessa knew why. She'd lost her heart to this man.

Mac's eyes searched Vanessa's, then she nodded as if it were time. 'After the accident and you came to live with me, I didn't have any room in my head or my heart for anyone's needs but yours. Jim was patient. For a long while he was. But I kept him waiting too long.'

Vanessa's hands went to her warm cheeks. McKenzie had given up her chance at real romance for love of her niece? No one could make a bigger sacrifice.

With a lump in her throat, she eased up and wound her arms around her aunt, the only mother she'd ever known. McKenzie smelled like the inexpensive powder she'd bought her every Mother's Day. McKenzie had insisted it was her favourite and didn't want anything else.

Vanessa bit her lip. 'Oh, Auntie, I'm sorry.'

Holding her niece, McKenzie patted her back like

she had when Vanessa's best ever friend had left in sixth grade. Vanessa had thought her life was over and McKenzie hadn't told her to grow up; she'd simply held her while she'd cried.

'You have nothing to be sorry for, sweetie. You've always been good. You've always made me proud.' She hugged her tight and murmured, 'There were times, so many times, I forgot that you weren't really mine.'

'Hello. Anyone in?'

Pulling back, Vanessa wiped her hot wet cheeks and focused through her tears on the doorway. She hadn't heard the front doorbell ring, yet Mitch was here, one foot pegged back, clearly worried he'd intruded.

She was letting her fantasies run away with her, but he looked so impossibly perfect, he gave her the most incredible butterflies, and when they were together…

Vanessa squared her shoulders.

She was a realist. But she was also an optimist. Was she being too hard on the possibility of *them*? Was it time she put past mistakes and insecurities aside and became optimistic about love? Aunt McKenzie's visit seemed to be a sign she shouldn't ignore. If someone hesitated and didn't grab for their chance, the man of their dreams could simply pass them by.

Moving forward, she took his hand and immediately felt reconnected—a key for her matching lock. 'Mitchell Stuart, this is my Aunt McKenzie.'

He tipped his head. 'Good to meet you.' He sent Vanessa a puzzled smile. 'I was under the impression you didn't have family nearby.'

'She doesn't.' McKenzie collected her bag from the table. 'My property was inland a ways.'

'Aunt McKenzie's on her way to the States.'

'In fact, I must get my saddle on.' McKenzie snatched a kiss and another hug. 'Have fun, kids.'

Vanessa laughed. 'You too.' It was high time.

'I'll see myself out,' her aunt said, slipping through the doorway that connected to the front of the shop. 'I'll visit when I get back.'

Vanessa remembered the envelope she held but Mitch's arms were already gathering her close. Misgivings about being left with that cheque and any lingering doubts about their relationship were replaced with sumptuous, explicit memories of the night before.

As his mouth dropped over hers, his warm palm cupped the back of her head, adjusting the angle enough to work a kiss that left her legs slightly shaky. When he reluctantly drew away, she was so dreamy, she barely heard his husky words.

'I missed you, Ms Craig.'

Her palm drifted up, fanning over the heat searing through the white shirt visible beneath his custom-made jacket. 'I like the sound of that.'

'I thought about you all day.'

She melted. 'Tell me more.'

The corners of his eyes crinkled. 'To save water and time, we're going back to my place first.'

'To shower before dinner, you mean?' She tingled head to toe and feigned a thoughtful look. 'That could work.'

'I'll tell you what else will work.' His hands slid

into her back jeans pockets. 'It involves post-dinner strawberries and warm chocolate dip.'

'Let me guess. In bed?'

He pretended offence at the same time that he shunted her hips closer to his. 'I don't like to be predictable.'

Surrendering to the sublimely inevitable, she snaked her fingers up through his strong dark hair. 'I'm willing to be surprised.'

Willing to be proven wrong.

His mouth had almost met hers again when Aunt McKenzie's frantic voice broke in.

'Lord above, Ness, there's someone outside who needs your help.'

The marrow in Vanessa's bones froze before she jolted into action. Mitch was already charging out.

'What's the problem?' he asked McKenzie, striding ahead through the store.

McKenzie didn't have time to reply. Mitch was already out of the door and coming to an abrupt halt as he stared down at a large tatty wicker basket. He swung a glance around at the inner suburban street and its busy pedestrians, moving patchwork shadows in the lights of passing cars.

'Anyone could've left them here.'

Her heart going out, Vanessa knelt on the hard concrete beside the basket. The mother cat, a tabby with frightened round eyes, growled to warn anyone thinking of harming or taking her five precious kittens. Half enthralled, half broken-hearted, Vanessa touched her fingers to her mouth. 'You poor darlings.'

McKenzie's tone was grim. 'Those kittens don't look more than a couple of weeks.'

Mitch squatted down. 'I'll take them in.'

As Mitch and his basket moved inside, McKenzie finished wiggling on her gloves. 'Seems like a nice fella.'

Handsome, strong, amazing in the bedroom. Vanessa nodded. 'Nice fits too.'

McKenzie stroked her niece's cheek. 'You deserve nice.' Then she sucked in a quick breath. 'And I need to catch that flight.'

Vanessa waved her aunt off in the cab, then scooted in after Mitch, locking the door behind her.

Mitch stood in the centre of the room, between curious Mr Cheese and the latest guinea pig family. He held the basket a little away, a look of mild discomfort stamped on his brow.

'Where do I drop them?'

She sent him a half serious scowl. He wasn't a cat person, but now was not the time for jokes. 'You can *place* them out back.'

He followed her through and settled the basket in a quiet, warm corner of the room next to her DVD player and stack of romantic comedies. They watched as the mother busily tended to each, making sure her clan was safe and well and clean.

Mitch absently looped an arm around her waist. 'Will you have the vet check them tomorrow?'

She instinctively leant her head against his shoulder. 'They all look healthy enough. I'll keep an eye on them overnight.'

'Meaning we're not going out to dinner?' She looked at him with an apologetic face and one corner of his mouth kicked up. 'I'll order takeout. How's Italian?'

She beamed. 'I *love* Italian.'

A loud mew shot her attention back to the basket. Releasing his hold around her waist, Mitch took a step closer. 'That little grey tabby…he looks thinner than the rest. Think he's hungry?'

'Maybe we should give him a bottle.'

He looked at her. 'Cats have bottles?'

She smiled. He had so much to learn. 'I have some kitten formula. But I might leave it a while and see. He does look smaller than the rest, but if she hasn't rejected him yet, there's not much chance of it now.'

The kitten continued to mew, then nudge at the mother's tummy, padding and searching out a nipple.

Mitch's frown eased. 'Damn. Never thought I'd be concerned over a basket of strays.'

The warmth in her chest transformed into a heart-felt smile. 'You don't like to be predictable, remember.'

He dropped a kiss on her brow, then gazed again at the basket and rubbed the back of his neck. 'So, are we going to sit up in a chair all night keeping watch?'

Floored, she stared at him. 'You want to stay and help babysit?'

He turned her in the circle of his arms. 'Lady, neither sleet nor hail nor howling cats could keep me away from you tonight.'

Longing spread exhilarating warmth through her body as she slid her palms over his shoulders.

'In that case, I'm willing to share my sleeping bag. It's a double.'

He smiled and drew her closer. 'That sounds ideal.'

CHAPTER SIX

Two hours later she and Mitch lay atop her pale pink sleeping bag, anticipating the rest of their evening alone—just them, the cats, Mr Cheese, the guinea pigs and a few hundred fish.

Mitch had gone home, showered, changed, and returned with penne and linguini dishes, as well as Italian salad with extra olives. After showering in the shop bathroom, she'd slipped into a change of clothes too—track pants and an *I Love Sydney* singlet.

They'd devoured the food and with full bellies now lay on their sides, snuggling spoon style, his front to her back, sipping soda water and quietly watching the mother cat and her babies sleep. Or she was. Mitch was more interested in finding new and fabulous ways for his mouth to caress her neck.

High on a cloud, her cheek on a palm, Vanessa reached back and wound his arm more securely over her waist.

'Wonder how long they'd have been out there if Aunt McKenzie hadn't noticed?'

Mitch lifted his head and chuckled. 'She's quite a character, your aunt.'

Vanessa smiled. 'She's difficult to describe. Strong on the outside, soft and sweet in the centre.' Like a cream-filled brandy snap.

Vanessa thought of the cheque and telling Mitch she didn't need to go ahead with applying for a loan with his firm. But all she'd known of life with McKenzie had been, of necessity, frugal. To be presented with a cheque for a million dollars out of the blue was mind-boggling.

Her aunt wasn't a liar. Still, Vanessa had the hardest time believing such a figure could be true. Before she said a word to anyone, she needed to be sure.

Besides, she didn't want to talk shop now. This moment—with Mitch's warmth so near and the atmosphere just right—was far too special to spoil with talk of money. Last time she'd confided in him about her financial state, he'd ripped up her card. She didn't want to think about that now.

'Aunt McKenzie gave me a home when I didn't have one,' she said instead.

His tone deepened. 'Did your parents kick you out?'

'They died when I was six months old.'

She felt his body tense. 'Ness, I'm sorry.' No one but McKenzie called her Ness. She liked the sound of it coming from his lips. 'I can't imagine never having known my parents.'

She pressed her lips together. 'I compensate.'

'By finding homes for others?' He grazed a tender

kiss over her temple. 'I'm betting one day you'll do even greater things.'

A beautiful sensation seeped through her chest. She'd never envisaged herself as a 'doer of great things'.

She looked over her shoulder at him. 'Really? How?'

He narrowed his eyes, half playful, half serious. 'Not sure, but I bet you'll find the perfect way.'

Did he mean it? For a moment, she was lost for words. 'Such blind faith.'

His eyes grew distant before his lips twitched. 'Maybe you've cast a spell.'

'Like the siren over her sailor?'

His smile held although his brow pinched almost imperceptibly. 'Should I watch out for rocks?'

A tiny mew came from the basket. They both pushed up on an arm, but all five kittens were curled around each other in a fluffy multicoloured ball.

Vanessa relaxed. 'One of them must've had a dream.'

He slid his lips along the receptive arc of her shoulder. 'Now the kids are all asleep, must be adult time.'

When she looked over her shoulder again, his mouth captured hers. The caress was slow and meaningful, making the blood in her veins thicken and heat. She would never tire of his mouth on hers. Never tire of having him near.

Lord, she really ought to rein in her emotions.

Shouldn't she?

When the kiss dissolved, she couldn't smother a blissful sigh. 'That's your thing, isn't it?'

He rubbed her nose with his. 'Kissing you is *definitely* my thing.'

'I'm talking about you racing to the rescue.' The protector. Her warrior.

'You mean the kittens?' He laughed. 'You make it sound so noble.'

'It *is*.' If she didn't know better, she'd guess he was a firefighter, or a doctor. Instead he was a highly successful banker.

Rolling completely over onto her other side, she faced him. 'You must love your work.'

He shunted her hips closer to his; his body language said he wasn't inclined to talk right now. 'I take over as President in less than two weeks,' he said, nipping her earlobe.

'That's *great*. Congratulations.'

'It's not final yet. One man can still veto the promotion.'

He stilled as if he were checking himself. Was she guessing right: that he didn't speak so openly with other women he'd only begun to date? That the super-highway conduit she felt buzzing and feeding between them wasn't imagination?

'This man,' she asked, 'he's some kind of enemy?'

'A friend of my father's, actually. Garret Jeffson.'

'Then what's the problem?'

'There hasn't been one…'

She carried the sentence through. 'Until recently?'

Pushing up on an elbow, he cradled his head in his palm. 'My father entrusted me to take care of the business and family. He went so far as to include as a condition of his will my performance at the firm. Only if I pass Garret's ultimate test do I win the chair.'

She remembered. 'Tough love. And you've rattled this friend's cage lately?'

'Yeah, for daring to have a personal life.' Thinking more deeply, he combed his palm over her hair. 'I live and breathe my work. Tonight I want to forget about responsibility.' His smile changed. 'Tonight I only want you.'

The backs of her eyes prickled. But, rather than gush, she tried to make light. 'The dog lady.'

When a brief shadow flickered over his eyes, she wondered.

Was he thinking about that Rottie pup? Wondering if he might have room in his life after all? She wouldn't tell him that a man had come in late today interested in the male for his son's tenth birthday.

But then Mitch's eyes sparkled. 'I have a function on Saturday night—a charity event. Come with me.'

She bit the inside of her cheek. 'Are we talking black tie?'

'Exclusively.'

'This might come as a surprise, but my wardrobe's a little light on Chanel.'

'Then we should shop.'

She theatrically clutched her heart. 'A man who *shops*?'

He grazed his sandpaper chin along the sweep of her neck. 'First time for everything.' He nipped a sensitive spot. 'Speaking of which…'

He slid his hand beneath her track pants' elastic and began to explore her in a way he'd never done before. As his warm fingers delved lower, she reflexively arched in, clutching and kneading his hard shoulder. 'Honestly, you don't have to do that.'

He looked up from nuzzling. 'I hope you're talking about shopping.'

When he resumed his attentions, his tongue trailing up her arched throat, her eyes drifted closed and she rolled onto her back. 'Shopping…yes… mmm…right.'

'Buying you a gown would make me happy.'

'You're easy to please.'

'I have a suspicion that I'm not. You just make it seem that way.'

He'd said it playfully, but when she opened her eyes she saw a glimmer of self-awareness in his.

As if a dimmer switch had been turned on high, her every sense seemed suddenly heightened. The sensation of his touch, the clock ticking on the wall, the clean musky scent of his skin.

His hand stopped moving. 'Is something wrong?'

She blinked and came to. 'I was just having a moment.'

His brows fell together. 'A moment?'

'You know. A special moment you want to lock in time and remember for ever.'

His chin went up in understanding. 'Oh, one of *those* moments. In that case—' he brought the top of the sleeping bag over their heads '—let's both remember this.'

The kittens woke her at dawn.

Dead tired, Vanessa rubbed her eyes, then saw Mitch gazing down at her, his weight resting on an elbow, his head in his palm, a lazy grin on his face.

He flicked a glance at the basket and deadpanned. 'I hate these early morning feeds.'

Remembering the glorious hours before, she stretched long and hard then, looping her arms around the broad column of his neck, brought his mouth down to hers. If the sound of mother cat licking and the baby cats clawing at the wicker hadn't been so intrusive, heaven knew how the embrace might have ended.

She let his lips leave hers and then shrugged. 'Looks like the world's awake.' Even if she'd rather not be. What time had they eventually got to sleep?

He pretended to frown. 'Do I have to go to school today?'

She wanted to laugh but covered a yawn instead. 'Unfortunately I really think it's best.'

Particularly given what he'd said last night about that 'friend' at his work and the coming promotion. She understood Mitch's reluctance; she too would love nothing more than to spend a decadent day in bed with him, but she had things to do. Most importantly, depositing that cheque.

He pushed back the cover and rocked up onto his feet. He seemed to have read her mind. 'So what's on your agenda today?'

As he sauntered to the kettle, checked the water and flicked the switch, she couldn't keep her eyes from the way the sinew in his back and butt and legs worked together, like a well-oiled, well-loved machine. Whatever he did on those regular morning workouts, she approved.

When he looked around and found his jeans, she knocked her dreamy self into gear and slipped on her trackies and singlet.

'I have a rather eventful day planned,' she replied with a secret smile.

'Well, find time to check your bank balance after 9:00 a.m.'

Yawning again, she rubbed an eye. What was he talking about? Did he know something about McKenzie's cheque? And that was only if she could believe it. But *she* hadn't even deposited it yet. 'What's up with my bank balance?'

His pecs bunched tight as he zipped his fly. 'I approved your loan application yesterday. The money would've been wired overnight.'

The shock struck, numbing her all the way through. 'I don't think I heard right.'

'We can clear your debts and start afresh with a healthy overdraft to play with.'

Her mouth didn't want to work. 'But I haven't signed any paperwork.'

'All fixed.'

'Is that legal?'

He hesitated, slotting his arms through his button-down's sleeves. 'I thought you'd be happy.'

'I *am* happy. I'm just…stunned. I wasn't expecting anything so soon.'

'We'll go over everything tonight and have you sitting high and dry by Monday.'

'I…' *Oh, Lord. Oh, no.* 'I don't know what to say.'

Chuckling, he slipped on a loafer. 'You say *thank you*. I say *you're welcome*.'

She held her spinning head. She had to sit down. 'Sorry. I'm still half asleep.'

Before she had time to blink, he was there, steadying her.

'I kept you up late again.' Bringing her close, he gave her a soothing hug, kissed her crown for a long moment, then moved away. 'I'll leave and you can catch another hour or so.' He jabbed a thumb at the basket. 'Tell that brood to behave till I get back.' He hesitated before leaving, coming back to steal another kiss that got stronger before he grudgingly let her go. 'I'll ring.'

When he left, Vanessa dragged herself over to make an extra-strong coffee. He'd gone to all that trouble, had processed the forms in extra-quick time. Who could've guessed that a miracle would take place: she had a cheque for a million dollars in her bag.

But it was so hard to believe. Her aunt wore the same Sunday best dress year in and year out. And the cheque wasn't a bank cheque but a *personal* cheque—it could very well bounce.

Mitch was a banker. If she showed him, he'd be sceptical too. He'd probably look at her as if she were, at the very least, gullible. At worst, nuts. So maybe she shouldn't tell Mitch right away that she no longer needed his loan. First, she would wait to be certain that the cheque truly represented what it stated.

A million dollars.

A mewing drifted out from the basket and she crossed to investigate. The runt, the grey tabby with a white-tipped tail, was clinging to the side of the wicker, trying to escape.

Setting her cup down, she gently collected the kitten in two hands, then held the ball of fluff to her chest. She stroked its wee head and it instantly settled. Another kitten was crawling up too. She squatted, her heart warming at the sight of the healthy little family.

'Any one of you guys want to tell me what I should do?'

All the kittens had shared a cuddle before she finally arrived at an answer. She hoped it was the right one.

CHAPTER SEVEN

LIFE just kept getting better.

After jumping in the car and visiting a couple of real estate mates with regard to better choice locations to re-establish Great and Small, Mitch strolled into his office some time past eleven.

He'd had a win as far as sourcing out sites that would offer improved expenditure without sacrificing on prime location. The couple he'd narrowed down to were in an upper-class neighbourhood, with affluent passing trade. The space was on the small side; Vanessa would have to cut her stock by at least half, and there was no back room. But the trendy, slick operation he had planned—dealing more in boutique and corporate pets—needed a minimum of floor space.

Tonight he would explain the pros and cons; he was sure she'd be excited. But, for now, he had some administrative catching up to do.

Inside his office door, Mitch whistled as he shrugged out of his jacket. Turning to drop it over the coat stand, his buoyant mood dipped when he noticed Garret Jeffson sitting behind his desk.

In his chair.

Checking his cufflinks, Mitch assembled his thoughts and moved forward. 'Morning, Garret.'

The older man rapped his fingers on the solid timber desk. 'Where have you been?'

Disagreeable heat surged in his gut but Mitch found a temperate smile. 'Clearly I've been out.'

'You missed the meeting with Vanmir Strivers.'

'I briefed Vanmir yesterday on my opinion regarding our groundwork interest in expansion into Australasia. I let him know I'd be out this morning. I also left a message with your secretary in case you were looking for me.'

'Then you turned off your phone.' Garret exhaled and shook his head. 'This was an important meeting. I'm not interested in excuses.'

Mitch's right eye twitched and he crossed his arms. 'Why do you think I'd feel a need to make excuses?'

'You're avoiding my question.'

Mitch kept his voice low and calm. 'Where I've been is none of your business.'

'You're wrong.'

Mitch dropped his arms. 'And you're sitting in my chair.'

Garret's stern expression eased. 'Your record is exemplary. I'm willing to overlook these last couple of days, but, Lord above, Mitch, I was young once too. I know the signs. You've picked the worst time to go fall in love.'

Amused, Mitch hacked out a laugh. He was *not* in love. And, 'I'm not a teenager. I'm an accomplished businessman who's earned a track record of running this corporation beyond successfully.'

'Be that as it may, you're not home and hosed yet. I must have a clear conscience when I hand over the chair.'

Setting his knuckles on the timber, Mitch leant over the desk.

'What's that, Garret? A threat? You're going to hold that miserable clause in my father's will over my head now?'

He was conscientious like Garret, honourable like Garret, but, *hell*, he deserved a life! He made decisions for everyone else. Surely he could make his own.

Garrett patted down the air. 'Son, I understand the pressure—'

Not wanting to listen, Mitch shut his eyes and concentrated on summoning his usual cool self. When he had it together, he straightened, exhaled and walked around his desk. 'I have work to do.'

Garret evaluated him before pushing to his feet. 'My wife took ill last night. She's in hospital. The doctors believe she's had a series of mini strokes. I need to cancel my meeting in the Melbourne branch this week. I'd like you to go in my stead.'

Mitch blinked several times, absorbing each section of news. Feeling like a prize heel, his shoulders slumped. *Damn.*

'Garret, I'm sorry.' He rubbed his forehead. 'Go be with your wife. I'll look after Melbourne.'

Garret's mouth moved, perhaps to say thanks. Instead, he put a hand on Mitch's shoulder. 'Don't ever forget, I believe in you, son. I know you'll do what you have to and come through.'

He shut the door behind him.

For ten minutes, Mitch strode up and down the length of his office. Garret meant well. And of course he'd go to Melbourne; Garret needed to be near his wife. But Garret had to understand Mitch Stuart was no longer a kid, hadn't been for too long. If for the first time in his life he wasn't acting himself, so *what*.

He'd been an adult since he was fifteen, tied down to 'head of the house and family and business'. Now, damn it, he deserved a little freedom.

The portrait on the wall caught his eye. His hands bunched and flexed before he strode over and unhinged his father's portrait from the wall.

'Sorry, Dad. Time to do things my way.'

'Wow.'

That Saturday night, standing before an obviously appreciative Mitch Stuart, Vanessa proudly swirled the skirt of her one and only, real life evening gown. Not having seen Mitch since Tuesday, she'd spent the afternoon at a beauty salon and felt as though she ought to be on the cover of *Harper's Bazaar.*

She hitched up a shoulder, cheeky but also coy. 'So, do I get a pass?'

'I like you in jeans but…' He rubbed the back of his neck. *'Wow.'*

Her laughter bubbled up.

Even standing here, at the doorway of her lacklustre granny flat, she felt like a princess. She'd never owned a dress anything like this divine creation. Shoestring straps looped from the outer edges of a soft bodice that resembled an open clam shell. The airy skirt, which drifted down from high on the waist, fell close to her body…until she moved. Then the aqua jewelled silk floated out, as the shop assistant had noted, like glistening waves on the sea.

It had cost way too much, and she didn't regret a penny of it.

Her smile faltered, however, when Mitch glanced past her shoulder. Her flat was small, lacking personality, really quite drab. But she'd always viewed it as temporary, a place to lay her head. She spent most of her time where she most felt comfortable—her shop. The place she preferred to call home.

'No need to come in,' she said quickly. 'I'll get my things and we'll go.' She swung back to grab her bag from the hall stand.

'Don't rush. My driver can wait.'

Driver? 'Does that mean I get to ride in a limo?'

She turned back. With more distance between them, the full effect of his extraordinary presence took her breath away. His tuxedo was classic, cut to fit his superior masculine frame to a perfect T. Black tie suited him. Well, of course it would. He was born to wear Armani with an air of entitlement, yet he did it with such effortless style.

She studied his hair. Was it combed differently, or had it merely grown? Dark licks touched his collar the barest amount. She couldn't wait to run her fingers through and muss it up a little.

She grinned.

Actually, a *lot*.

This unexpected five-day, four-night separation had been agony. She'd been so disappointed when he'd rung to say he needed to fly to Melbourne straight away. Looking back, how austere life had been before him.

With a sultry grin, Mitch reached for her arm. Crossing the threshold, she happily joined him and went to descend the two unpainted steps. But he held her back, winding his arms around her waist and tugging her close for a pulse-racing kiss hello.

Her senses buzzed and swirled and ultimately became one with his.

Oh, yes, she remembered this feeling…

With his eyes still closed, he released her, groaned and then pretended to shake himself awake from his trance. His satisfied smile roamed her face. 'What were we saying?'

Feeling lighter than air, she took his arm. 'Your driver.'

'Ah, yes. We do, indeed, have a stretch limo tonight,' he replied, heading down the steps. 'My friend appreciates if his guests put on a bit of a show.'

'It's a charity event, yes?' He nodded. 'What does your friend raise money for?'

'The annual cocktail party raises funds to support fledging entrepreneurs.' He arched at brow at her. 'A timely event for you.'

As he escorted her down the cracked cement drive, Vanessa spotted overweight Mrs Micheljon and her hair rollers peeping through a bent kitchen blind. At her landlord's curiosity, a moment of doubt hit—Little Ness Craig from the country in fancy dress. Who was she fooling?

But then she remembered how special she felt in her evening gown, walking beside this incredible man. She lifted her chin and held onto his arm all the tighter.

'I make a sizable donation each year,' Mitch was saying as they headed towards a gleaming black stretch; a fully uniformed driver stood by the passenger back door. 'But all the organisation and distribution of funds is Thomas's baby.'

The driver's salt-and-pepper moustache twitched as he smiled at Vanessa and opened the door. Feeling like Cinderella—had the driver of the pumpkin coach been a horse or a dog?—she sat back and soaked up the otherworld luxury of polished wood grain, softest leather, even a mirror-shine champagne bucket, complete with two sparkling flutes.

Lowering himself beside her, Mitch reached for the bucket. She was waving her hand *no* when he pulled out the bottle—her favourite label lemonade.

She laughed as her heartbeat fluttered.

He'd thought of everything.

Before the limo pulled out from the kerb, he poured and raised his flute to hers. 'Here's to my beautiful companion.'

She *tinged* her flute with his. 'And to my handsome escort.'

Sipping the sweet bubbles, she remembered McKenzie's cheque had been cleared yesterday. Now was the right time to let Mitch in on her news. She didn't know if she'd ever felt more excited. More proud. More *nervous*. How would he take the fact that she was a millionairess?

Lowering her glass, she cleared her throat. 'Mitch, there's something I need to tell you.'

'Let me guess. You overspent on the gown. Don't worry.' His blue eyes flashed over the rim of his glass. 'I'm disappointed I didn't get to go on that shopping trip, but let me know how much I owe you for the dress. Whatever the cost, it's worth it.'

She dropped her gaze and slid a palm over the jewelled silk. She knew he was only keeping his word—he meant well—but something about his offer now made her almost uncomfortable. 'I'm glad you like it, but I don't want your money.'

He set down his glass. 'If it's about your shop,' he went on, 'I researched some properties earlier in the week.'

'Properties?'

Now she had her own funds, she intended to stay where she was. The biggest drain on her finances was rent. If she *bought* the premises, earnings could be funnelled directly back into the store. She'd even indulged in a wild dream about eventually buying the whole street. But, realistically, it would be more than enough to keep the place that she'd built a thousand happy memories around. Thanks to Aunt McKenzie, it actually seemed possible.

'The properties are a bit smaller,' he said.

Her question was automatic. 'How much smaller?'

'Not much less than half of what you have now. And no back room facilities,' he said quietly but firmly. 'That's hardly a necessity anyway.'

She was gobsmacked.

His knee hooked onto the seat as he angled more toward her. 'The two spaces I've narrowed it down to are in a great neighbourhood. Lots of people with lots of money to spend on the very best.'

She pushed against the hollow ache in her stomach. She liked where she was.

Although she didn't want to sound ungrateful for all his time and thoughts, her disappointment came out sounding like irony. 'Mitch, if I'm meant to be responsible for a loan, shouldn't I get some say?'

Concentrating on the limo slowing and pulling up, Mitch only half heard her question. Vanessa peered out of a tinted window. Were they there already?

The door swung open and a tall, attractive man, with a straight nose and liquid brown eyes leant into the car. 'Mitchell Stuart Esquire, how the dickens are you?'

Mitch moved across and they bear hugged on the pavement before he turned to help Vanessa out.

'Thomas, this is Vanessa Craig.'

'Your exquisite date for this evening.' Thomas made a performance of kissing her hand. 'Pleasure's entirely mine. Your gown is delicious.'

Mitch sent her a wink.

Thomas gestured at the wide tier of steps behind them that led to an opulent function room—Grecian columns, giant marble pots and strategic falls of colourful landscaping framing the building like a picture.

'Go through and mingle,' Thomas said. 'Champagne's going round. Canapés too. Dancing's to come. Hope you're staying for the fireworks.' Another limo pulled up and Thomas waved at the occupants. 'I do love these nights.'

As Thomas strode off, Mitch linked his arm through Vanessa's and escorted her up the steps.

'Yes,' he offered, 'Thomas is gay.'

She inclined her head. 'He's charming.'

'And a great business brain. If I weren't so tied up with the bank I'd like to work on something more with him.'

Once inside, a couple swept up to them—a business associate of Mitch's from a legal firm and his wife. A leading computer analyst, then a controversial politician came next. Soon several others had joined their circle.

What she caught of the conversation was stimulating, but when asked her opinion on the new trend in Parisian fashion, then the decline in world economic stability, she didn't know quite how to reply. Mitch kept her close and must have thought she was enjoying herself. But it seemed everyone knew each other so well and were speaking a language only those in the clique understood.

After a couple of hours, her smile began to ache. Stupid, but she was homesick, wondering about her kittens, particularly Roger, her little grey tabby.

When she shifted her weight and her shoes pinched her toes so much that she flinched, she tugged Mitch's sleeve. 'Would you excuse me for a minute?'

He frowned. 'Something wrong?'

'Not at all,' she fibbed. 'I want to go powder my nose.'

He dropped a lingering kiss on her cheek, close to her mouth, then returned to the conversation.

Feeling outside the bubble—*adrift*—Vanessa wandered out onto the balcony. She needed air. More than that, she needed to get out of these five-inch heels!

At times she felt so right with Mitch and yet here, in his world, she felt…alien. The feeling had been the same at his mother's house. Out of her depth. A tolerated intruder.

On the balcony, she gazed out over the glistening black harbour, which danced with colours reflecting off the surrounding city lights. Bending, she slipped off one shoe, then the other and groaned as she wiggled her freed toes.

She'd hoped—had very nearly *convinced* herself, in fact—but who was she kidding? Mitch enjoyed her company, and he'd gladly made a concession tonight.

But shouldn't he be with a woman who knew and loved this language—the nuances of *glitz and glamour*?

He'd confirmed as much that first night when he'd torn her business card in two. He hadn't wanted her kind—ordinary folk who lived from pay packet to pay packet—infringing on his world. But then, at his mother's house, he'd kissed her again and she'd found herself swept away…willing to believe…

When a warm hand settled on her shoulder, she jumped, spun around and held her racing heart.

'*Mitch*. It's you.'

His eyes glowed darkest blue as he smiled. 'So this is where you got to.'

Letting out a guilty breath, she didn't bother to hide the shoes in her hand. 'The view's just so beautiful.'

He kept his eyes on hers. 'Yes, it is.'

Her stomach muscles clenched. Oh, God, this must be—*he* must be a dream. The moment she dared think otherwise, she would wake and know handsome millionaires didn't inhabit her world. Not on a long-term intimate level, anyway.

He ran his warm palms down her arms. 'You're shaking.' He claimed her hand and turned towards the connecting French windows. 'We'll go inside.'

She bit her lip, but then said it anyway.

'Can we stay out here a little longer?'

He edged back around and searched her eyes. 'Then I'll warm you up.'

He wound his tuxedo-clad arms around her, tucked her in and began to sway to the music filtering out from the ballroom. Vanessa could have swooned. Their first dance.

His cheek resting against her temple, he breathed in and melded her closer to his heat. 'Mmm, that dog shampoo really works for me.'

A laugh slipped out. 'See. You're just too easy to please.' But her voice didn't carry true conviction when she said it this time.

He brushed his lips over her crown. 'You want to leave?'

She inwardly groaned. Darn it, no matter how out of sorts she might feel, she had to go back inside. She couldn't ruin his night.

'No, no,' she assured him. 'I'm fine.'

He tugged her away, looked into her eyes, then said more firmly, 'We'll go.'

She hesitated but finally conceded. She'd been told she should never play poker.

They said goodbye to Thomas and a few other guests then resumed their seats in the back of the limousine. As the vehicle pulled out, Mitch gave her his full attention. 'Now, we were interrupted earlier. What did you want to tell me?'

She sat up straight and ploughed right in. The sooner it was out, the better. 'You know my Aunt McKenzie?'

His expression twisted. 'Don't tell me she's found more cats.'

Her laugh was edgy. 'No. She sold her property as well as a painting that belonged to her grandfather. She got quite a sum for it.'

His teeth flashed as he smiled. 'That's great.'

'She wanted me to have it.'

'All the money?'

'Only from the painting.'

He nodded carefully. 'I see. How much are you talking about?'

'Four times the amount your firm loaned me.'

After a moment, his jaw shifted. 'When did you learn about this?'

'The night you met McKenzie.'

He looked as if he didn't quite believe her. 'And you said nothing?'

Her explanation tumbled out. 'I didn't quite believe it at first. It was a personal cheque. I wondered if it'd go through. Then you told me about the loan approval when I was still half asleep and left the state that day. The cheque only cleared yesterday and I wanted to tell you in person, so… well…' Out of breath, she shrugged. 'I'm telling you now.'

When he merely nodded again, she went on. 'I want to pay out the loan.' His nostrils flared. 'I know there'll be fees attached,' she acknowledged quickly. 'I'm happy to pay whatever's involved.'

His face hardened. 'You think that bothers me?'

His eyes shifted from hers as if he were thinking something through.

She frowned. 'So what *is* bothering you?'

'Nothing.' His lips pressed together.

'Mitch…what aren't you telling me?'

'Nothing serious. Nothing that makes a difference.'

She had a bad feeling. She wouldn't rest until she knew. 'Please…'

A pulse in his neck throbbed before he rolled back one shoulder and admitted, 'I went guarantor for you.'

The statement sank in like a stone plummeting to the bottom of a well. The loan had been processed in the blink of an eye, without even a signature, when three other institutions had turned her down flat. But never in her wildest dreams had she thought he would as good as put up the money for her. At that time they'd known each other only two days.

It was lovely.

It also made her feel naive. Duped. Possibly even bought.

Hadn't she told him at the outset that she didn't want to be treated like a charity case? She'd never wanted to feel patronised or paid for. Was she right to feel hurt? Embarrassed?

Her neck and face began to burn. 'I was a bad risk—I knew that—and yet you let me believe something different.'

He exhaled, almost wearily. 'I went guarantor because you believed in your future.'

Which he'd thought malleable enough to steer towards a tiny space in upmarket Snobsville. He didn't understand what that modest pet store meant to her and that she would do everything in her power to stay. But then why should he understand? They might have slept together but in reality they were little more than strangers. Two people with different values from totally different worlds.

Still stinging, she murmured, 'You should have told me.'

His expression was less than amused. 'And you should've told me.'

As a withering feeling leached from her middle, she looked away and sat back. So, here it was: the first crack…the first indication Cinderella was back from the ball.

She'd fumbled her way through tonight, but Mitch would fit better with someone who was clued up. Who laughed at highbrow jokes. Who knew the best wine. Who didn't live in a tumble-down house, but rather habitually flew to Hong Kong to shop. Someone he truly respected, not inadvertently patronised.

She was just another flighty female who had the potential to be a drain on his time. The million dollars she now had in the bank couldn't change that.

She fought the urge to hold her pounding head. She needed to get home before her gown turned to rags.

Long moments of silence dragged out before the limo parked outside the house attached to her granny flat.

Mitch swung open the door. 'I'll come in.'

She put her hand on his thigh and fought the urge to react to the steely warmth. She wouldn't meet his eyes or the tears edging hers just might fall.

'Please, Mitch. Don't.'

She was aware of his chest rising, falling, then his hand scrubbing his jaw.

Finally, he nodded. 'I'll call tomorrow.'

He let her pass and alight onto the pavement. She heard him rap on the window, which separated passengers from the driver, then listened to the door shut.

As the limo purred off, she clutched her bag to her bodice, willing away the sensation of her heart breaking in two.

Would he call tomorrow?

Should she have let him in?

If he didn't call, if he was so damn easy to put off, wasn't it better that this was over now?

Feeling as lifeless as the unwatered daisies in the garden, she slipped off her shoes, picked up her hem and trudged down the path. She ignored Mrs Micheljon spying through the window. She only wished she could ignore the crushing pain beneath her ribs, the tears building in her throat.

She'd reached the steps when, in the still night, she heard an approaching noise—the purr of a car.

Her grip tightened on her bag and she spun back in time to see the stretch limo reversing up. Before it stopped, the door fanned open and Mitch leapt onto the footpath. He strode down the drive until they stood a foot apart, then he swept her up into his arms. Without a word, he headed back to the road.

Overwhelmed, near speechless, she struggled to find her voice. 'What on earth are you doing?'

His tone was deep and determined. 'Consider yourself kidnapped. You're coming home with me.'

'But Mitch—'

He stopped and his hot kiss swallowed her words.

When her bones had liquefied and delicious hope pumped again through her veins, his mouth gradually released hers.

He held his unswerving gaze on hers. 'You were saying?'

She pressed her tingling lips together as a pitifully relieved tear slid down her cheek. 'I don't have a change of clothes.'

He continued to walk. 'You won't need one.'

Arriving home, Mitch sank into a plush living-room chair and impatiently wrenched his bow tie to release the knot. Vanessa stood before him in her shimmering gown, looking unsure, like a wide-eyed vision only the most privileged of men got to see.

He snapped open his collar stud.

Did she have *any* idea?

She'd been quiet on the drive here—as had he—both mulling over the relationship-altering events of the night. Each had been taken aback. In hindsight, they should have shared what they'd learned tonight earlier. When the wall had gone up, he'd knocked it down quick before a molehill of misunderstanding had the chance to grow into a mountain.

But Vanessa appeared so fragile standing before him now, he had to ask.

'Do you want to be here?'

In the soft down light, her eyes glistened, a reflection of her exquisite gown. 'If I didn't, I would've said so.'

'Maybe I wouldn't have listened.'

It was said in jest, yet the deepest primal part of him laughed and said it was true. Every day he'd spent in Melbourne had seemed like one more day lost. He'd managed to keep his mind on business nine to five, but when night had fallen he'd been sorely tempted to jump on the earliest jet and fly home.

And that was crazy.

She was a woman—a tempting, beautiful, enthralling woman. But nothing and no one had ever had a detrimental effect on his job performance. As he'd told Garret, he wasn't a teenager. He might be taken with her, but work had to remain his priority.

He'd got through the time away by looking forward to tonight. Some ruffled feathers over a loan wouldn't upset this time now.

He pushed to his feet. Before he uttered the words, he imagined the result of his unashamed request.

'Ness…take off your gown.'

Her lips parted and her eyes widened more before her lids grew tellingly heavy. The movement of her breasts—her breathing—quickened. Then she crossed her arms high and eased the silk strings off her shoulders. She reached behind and he heard the murmur of the gown's zip easing down. The silk slipped, exposing her firm, rose-tipped breasts, before the dress fell in a rush, a soft layered bundle at her feet.

With his heart banging in his chest, Mitch drank in the heavenly symmetry—her perfect breasts, the hand-span waist and, lower, a V of aqua silk that covered that most feminine sacred part of her.

He shrugged out of his jacket, tossed it on the chair, and went to her. He let her sweet scent fill him, savoured the heightened anticipation, then he took her hand and led her to his room.

Her hand in his, Vanessa was surprised when Mitch stopped before reaching his bed. In his room, they stood before decorative strips of floor-to-ceiling mirror. Naked, but for her panties, Vanessa allowed herself to be turned in his arms until she faced her reflection, her fully clothed lover, his black bow tie hanging, standing behind.

His unhurried gaze wound up her legs, her hips, lovingly caressed her breasts and finally, in the mirror, found her eyes. She held her breath and trembled as his expression intensified and his hot hands moulded around the column of her neck. His fingers tightened slightly, then fanned out, sculpting over her shoulders, her arms, making every inch of her flesh burn and catch light.

His touch roamed across her abdomen before his hands climbed to measure and weigh her heavy breasts. Her heartbeat pounded as he drew a teasing circle around each areola then gently rolled the hyper-sensitive peaks. She tried to maintain their eye contact in the mirror but, when he rolled harder, she surrendered to the overwhelming thrill and let her neck arch back.

She moaned in her throat as his lips moved against her hair. 'Say my name.'

Arching into his touch, she swallowed and tried to think straight.

'Mitch,' she breathed.

His right hand slid down to clutch the V of her panties and drag them to one side. With deliberate lack of speed, one finger spliced between her folds, curling deep inside her before slipping up again. Pressing her against him, he circled that pulsing spot while his other hand rolled and pinched and she went up in flames.

His hot breath warmed her cheek. 'Say it again.'

The words spilled out. 'Mitch…oh, God, Mitch… you're driving me mad.'

'Like you drove me mad last week.'

Through her building delirium, she grinned. 'So, this is your payback.'

'This is our reward.'

He whirled her around and, kissing her as if it were the first time, walked her back towards the bed. When she lay upon the sheets, he pulled her panties off, then undid his shirt, one agonising button at a time.

Not soon enough, he joined her.

She coiled her legs around his thick thighs, urging him to a powerful pace until every plane in his body gripped tight and shuddered with release. When his breathing steadied, he rolled on his side. Taking what

he knew of her body and her mind, he rocked her—
loved her—until she, too, shot deliciously high and
over the edge.

CHAPTER EIGHT

THE next morning, in a red silk suit, Mrs Stuart descended the stately steps of her home and greeted her son with a possessive hug.

'You look as handsome as ever,' she declared before shifting her attention to Vanessa, who already itched with prickles of discomfort.

Mrs Stuart extended her hand. But, before Vanessa had time to accept the token gesture, the older woman whipped her hand away to hold her cheeks in delight.

'Do I hear the baby barks of my cockapoos?' Mrs Stuart cried.

Vanessa closed her eyes and wished herself away.

After the cocktail party and her fantasy kidnapping last night, she'd woken in the tangled sheets of Mitch's bed. This morning, neither of them had needed to rush off.

Following another luxurious hour of 'Mitch magic', he'd tried to coax her into the gym to participate in his morning workout. When she'd protested, he'd instead shown her the indoor pool. There, amidst the echoing quiet and smell of salt and chlorine, he'd coached her in the art of water play—minus swimsuits, of course.

Later, at Great and Small, she'd introduced Mitch to the new junior she'd hired during the week, after she'd been sure her shop would survive. He'd pretended not to be too interested in the Rotties while she'd checked on the kittens—Roger mewed the loudest—and the cockapoo breeder had arrived.

All four pups were silky pale red in colour, but each was unique in temperament. Nicknamed Sleepy, Sneezy, Dopey and More Dopey—MD for short—the littlest was just a hopeless bundle of fun and energy.

Although everything seemed fine and wonderful on the outside, and Vanessa was relieved they'd got over their hiccup regarding the loan he'd organised and her confession about Aunt McKenzie's money, the connection between herself and Mitch seemed to have changed. The way he'd looked at her when she'd brushed her hair this morning. How he'd studied her hand, rubbing her thumb with his, moments after they'd made love.

The difference was almost imperceptible, except to say that the purest essence of what they'd shared had been altered.

She felt closer and yet…

Well, must be she was still coming to terms with this past week: accepting she might lose her shop, meeting Mitch, being gifted that money from McKenzie and, last night, discovering Mitch had withheld the fact he'd taken personal responsibility for the loan he'd organised.

Little wonder she'd felt overwhelmed and over-sensitive.

Now, delivering the cockapoos to Mrs Stuart didn't help. Vanessa was happy for the pups; they'd be loved and well cared for. But, man, she couldn't wait to leave. Being here, amidst this overt grandeur and Mrs Stuart's haughtiness only scratched at those feelings of inadequacy and not fitting in that, last night, Mitch had managed to caress and kiss away.

Striding back towards the vehicle, Mitch answered his mother. 'The pups are in the back.'

Mrs Stuart clasped her hands under her chin as Mitch opened the tailgate of Vanessa's CRV. 'Let's each carry one in, shall we?' She turned towards the house and called, 'Cynthia, the dog lady's here!'

Vanessa sniffed.

A coincidence? She thought not.

In a casual lemon dress, Cynthia appeared and hurried down the steps. Unlike the last time they'd met, she greeted Vanessa with a sincere smile. Her blonde hair looked and smelled freshly washed and there wasn't a handkerchief in sight.

'I'm looking forward to meeting the new family members.'

Vanessa returned Cynthia's good vibes. 'They're looking forward to meeting you too.'

They each collected an excited parcel from the carrier; the puppies were wiggling bundles of joy.

This was what Vanessa most loved about her job. Every time she found a great home for one of her pets, a tiny piece of her found a home too.

Not that she could see this place ever taking on that meaning for her, the knowledge of which only served to stir up those nagging insecurities again—the deeper understanding that Mitch's world and hers couldn't be more different.

Vanessa mounted the stairs with MD in her arms, wishing she weren't counting the minutes till her escape. As they traipsed through the house, Wendle and her mousey overbite were drawn from her polishing by Cynthia's laugh: Sneezy was scrambling up Cynthia's bodice, desperate to lick her nose.

Out back in their room, Mitch closed the door. The four lowered their puppies, then stood back while they sniffed and scampered around their beds and balls and bowls, a different colour for each.

Cynthia sighed. 'Thank you, Vanessa. They're just gorgeous. I feel a thousand times better already.'

As Cynthia moved away to play with Dopey and Sleepy, Mrs Stuart slipped up beside Vanessa and said, for her ears only, 'It's wonderful to see Cynthia smiling again. Sometimes it's difficult to let go, but when relationships are damaging…' She gave a resigned shrug.

While Vanessa bristled, for herself as well as Cynthia, insensitive Mrs Stuart flicked her a glance.

'We have some settling up to do. Would you follow me?'

Vanessa looked for Mitch. He was playing with

Dopey and a tug toy so, with her next belt of oxygen, she sucked down some courage too. She didn't need Mitch to face this woman. She'd provided a service. If Mrs Stuart didn't approve of her personally, frankly, too bad.

Except, if she and Mitch continued to see each other…

She shuddered.

The idea of a mother-in-law like Beatrice Stuart curdled her blood.

When she and Mrs Stuart reached the living room, the slant of Mrs Stuart's lips aptly conveyed her sense of superiority. 'I was right.'

Although her heart *ka-thumped* wildly, Vanessa kept her face a mask. 'About what?'

'You *are* experienced.' She moved to a credenza to collect what looked like a cheque. 'We're very happy with the puppies.'

Vanessa didn't allow her gaze to waver. 'Mrs Stuart, is there something you want to say to me?'

The older woman's smile spread. 'You're direct.' She nodded. 'Good.' Cheque in hand, she bent to smell the credenza's vase of scarlet roses. 'I had a visit yesterday from Garret Jeffson, my husband's closest friend and interim President of his bank. Mitch is scheduled to take over the lead reins at the end of the week. Unfortunately, after some uncharacteristic behaviour these past days, Garret's concerned Mitch isn't in a sound place mentally to assume such a responsible position.'

As Mrs Stuart collected a pair of mini secateurs from a hidden drawer to prune some thorns, Vanessa let the information sink in. When she continued to prune, Vanessa pushed.

'I take it you're blaming our relationship for Mitch's...mental state.'

Mrs Stuart turned her acid smile on her guest. 'When do you suggest we have the puppies spayed? I don't want strays chasing my precious babies. I'm sure the breeder would agree.'

Vanessa's throat clogged. Where did this woman get off? 'Mitch wouldn't appreciate this conversation,' she said with remarkable restraint.

'Perhaps not today. Just as Cynthia didn't appreciate her broken heart last week.' She waved the secateurs towards the back room. 'But you see she's feeling so much better. It was the right thing to do.'

As realisation dawned, slow and vivid, Vanessa's head tingled with the truth. Mrs Stuart had thought Cynthia's fiancé wasn't truly good enough, just as *she* wasn't good enough for Mitch.

Her face twisted in disgust.

'You paid Cynthia's fiancé off, didn't you?'

Mrs Stuart set down the pruners and joined her. 'I want you to look inside, Vanessa. I want you to put Mitch's well-being before your own...ambitions.' Vanessa opened her mouth, but Mrs Stuart hurried on. 'And, before you tell me you aren't ambitious— my dear, any woman worth her coiffure wants to better herself. I understand that. I'm merely concerned that you're trying to conquer Everest when you should, perhaps, be content tackling territory closer to home.'

Vanessa coughed out a humourless laugh. 'You're unbelievable.'

Any scrap of pity she'd felt over this woman's loss of her husband was, sadly, well and truly gone.

'You care about my son,' Mrs Stuart went on, a beseeching note to her voice now. 'I can see that. So do I. I would sacrifice myself to see him achieve his best. That's the truest measure of love.' Her mouth pursed. 'He needs to get his mind back on business or risk losing the reward he's worked towards and deserves after fifteen long years. My dear, you don't want him to resent you later for getting in the way. And, let's be honest, that resentment *could* surface as soon as next week.'

Vanessa closed her mouth. She hated that Mrs Stuart had touched a nerve—*two* nerves, in fact. Aunt McKenzie had shown the truest measure of her love when she'd sacrificed Jim to devote herself to her newly orphaned niece.

On top of that, secretly, Vanessa was waiting to wake up and have Mitch realise that her vastly different history and circumstances might make her an interesting interlude but cancelled her out of competing in any long-term stakes. One day—maybe as soon as next week?—she expected Mitch to have had his fill and say goodbye.

Like a hound scenting blood, Mrs Stuart went on.

'Please, take the time to consider it. To acknowledge that Mitch needs someone beside him who under-stands the establishment. Who can help with the social aspects, who went to the right schools and talks to the right people.'

Vanessa's thoughts wound back to how out of place she'd felt among the ridiculously rich and famous last night, then to how her affluent ex had considered her 'fluff on the side'.

Mrs Stuart was nodding as if she had a direct line to Vanessa's unspoken doubts. She handed over the cheque.

Feeling like that poor country orphan all over again, Vanessa looked down at the cheque. And tried to shake the disbelief from her head.

Her gaze snapped up. 'This is far too much.'

Mrs Stuart's soft hand settled over hers. 'Call it a bonus for a job well done. I don't believe we'll be needing you again.'

Mitch's deep voice broke into the nightmare.

'Formalities over, ladies?'

Mrs Stuart's face lit up. 'I think so, yes.'

Mitch moved to Vanessa and, smiling, threaded some hair behind her ear. 'Do you want to say goodbye to the pups?'

Vanessa's tongue felt swollen and useless in her mouth. She swallowed twice, then pushed out the words. 'No, no. I'm sure they'll be fine.'

'In that case—' Mitch moved to brush a kiss on

his mother's cheek '—we'll see you later. Go join Cynthia. I've never heard her laugh so much.'

'You won't stay for lunch?' his mother asked.

'Not today.'

Mrs Stuart didn't look concerned. 'Next week then.'

With Vanessa's new assistant minding the shop, on the way back from his mother's house, Mitch suggested they stop for lunch at Manly Beach.

Vanessa's appetite was non-existent, but they'd skipped breakfast so she knew Mitch must be starved. With burgers, chips and colas in hand, they found a bench and table on the fringe of the white sand. Vanessa donated most of her lunch to the gulls, who waddled and flapped in a noisy, ever-growing mob. But the food she did manage to get down, combined with the fresh, salty air and tranquil blue sky, helped to regenerate her spirits.

Aunt McKenzie's fondest saying was: believe in yourself and surround yourself with others who believe too.

After last night she'd been willing to give Mitch the benefit of the doubt—that his intentions towards her went deeper than merely *here and now*. Mrs Stuart's poisonous words had eroded a good measure of that belief. Sitting beside Mitch now, Vanessa was certain of only one thing.

No matter how long she and Mitch dated, she never wanted to see his mother again. It was a long way from cowardice or stubbornness. It was self-

preservation. Some people—and their prejudices—
she simply didn't need in her life.

And yet a voice inside her persisted in pointing
out that at least *some* of Beatrice Stuart's argument
made sense. Vanessa did care for Mitch. She did
want what was best. But wasn't she—*this*—best for
him now?

Or was she merely an untimely distraction who
might jeopardise his future?

Vanessa pushed against her pounding temple. Oh,
she was sick of thinking and rethinking. And if she
spoke with Mitch about this second private conversation with his mother, she'd come off sounding like
a whiner. Or maybe even being manipulative herself.
Mitch didn't need the aggravation.

Mrs Stuart might consider her a would-be-if-she-
could-be. She didn't need to dignify that insult by
giving it another voice and sharing it with Mitch.

She was here with her handsome, vibrant lover
on a glorious spring day. She was damn well going
to enjoy it.

Throwing the last chip to a squawking gull, she
inhaled deeply. 'Doesn't the ocean look wonderful?'

Mitch finished his can of cola. 'I was thinking the
same.' He nudged her. 'Wanna go for a dip?'

She gave him a wry smile. 'We don't have
swimsuits.'

'Didn't stop us this morning.'

'Except now we're in public.'

'You're right.' His hand slid up her leg, beneath

her dress. 'Let's go back to my house and I'll teach you how to bomb dive.'

She caught his hand, but then inched it higher. 'Sounds a little energetic—' her mouth twitched '—but fun.'

'The fun comes when we're both underwater.' He shunted closer and his cola-cool mouth lowered and found her breastbone. 'How long can you hold your breath?'

'How fast can you run?' Vanessa jumped up. 'Let's go down to the beach.'

She wanted to sprint as fast as she could, which didn't happen often. In fact, had never happened before. She had an overwhelming urge to run free!

Looking pleasantly surprised, he bent and slid off his loafers. She kicked off her sandals and bolted off ahead, down onto the warm, soft sand.

'Hey!' he called out. 'Wait for me.'

Turning around, she jogged backwards and sing-songed, 'You can't catch me.'

He picked up speed. 'The heck I can't.'

She squealed as he hurtled towards her, kicking up sand as his legs pumped across the clean stretch of beach. When he was almost upon her, she dodged, swerving towards the giant curls of teal water.

She found enough breath to laugh. 'Sorry, but I thought you were fit.'

His big chest heaved as his eyes narrowed. 'Know what I think?'

'What do you think?'

'I think you want to get wet.'

He edged towards her, a menacing glint in his eye.

On a flash of panic, she held up her hands and tried to reason. 'Mitch, listen to me. We don't have a change of clothes.'

His grin was unconcerned and fatally sexy. 'You're always on about clothes.'

She looked down. Lacy scallops of cool water swirled around her ankles. 'It's cold in here.'

'It'll be invigorating.'

She raised her hands higher. 'I give up.'

'Too late.'

'I'll make it worth your while.'

He lunged towards her. 'I know you will.'

Laughing, they fell at the same time a wave crashed and tumbled over them. How he found her lips in the powerful foamy rush she couldn't guess. She only knew he was right. It *was* invigorating.

And she was in love.

When they arrived back at the shop, thanks to some towels in the back of the CRV, she and Mitch were more damp than wringing wet. And Vanessa was still alight with optimism. She wouldn't think about nasty mothers. She would concentrate instead on the coming days, hours and minutes she'd spend with the man she adored.

Would it be too hopelessly absurd to think—to hope—that he might fall in love too?

He was a grown man; he could and should make

his own decisions, as should she. And they'd decided to be together. They wanted to enjoy the ocean, and the laughter, and the—

'…last of the Rotties sold, Miss Craig.'

Halfway to the counter, Vanessa stopped dead. She studied her new assistant's bright expression as her greeting sank in.

'Lucy, you can call me Vanessa, remember.' She glanced back to see Mitch squelching in through the entrance of the shop, his chinos dark in patches and his black hair drying in wisps. He stopped by the glass pen holding the last Rottie.

Vanessa turned back to Lucy and lowered her voice. 'But the male's still there.'

Lucy and her nose ring leant forward and innocently mimicked her boss's conspiratorial tone. 'A man came in and left a deposit. Said he'd be back week after next to pick the puppy up on his son's birthday.'

Having caught up, Mitch set his hands on Vanessa's shoulders. Behind her, none the wiser, he asked, 'What's up?'

Vanessa was about to say *nothing* when Lucy announced, 'I was just saying the last Rottweiler's gone. Or will be. The man who left the holding fee had such kind eyes. The puppy wanted to leave with him there and then. He said he'd spoken with you before, Miss Craig.'

Her back still to Mitch, Vanessa closed her eyes as her stomach dipped and looped.

'Oh. Yes. I remember now.'

Mitch's hands left her shoulders. 'Well, guess the little guy found the right home.'

Dreading to see his expression, she edged around. They'd known each other a week; did she have any right to believe he'd changed so much so soon? That he'd been contemplating—even looking forward to—bother and fuss and noise.

That he was ready for more.

She squeezed his hand. 'I'm sorry, Mitch.'

He dismissed it. 'I'm fine. I'm good.' But his easy smile didn't quite reach his eyes.

Efficient Lucy wasn't finished. 'And a lady called.' Her long purple nails collected a message from next to the cash register. 'A Beatrice Stuart. She said the cockapoos are doing fine.'

Vanessa wanted to block her ears, not to news of those pups but the sound of that name. 'Thanks, Lucy.'

'She also left a message for someone called Mitchell.' Lucy turned her hazel eyes on Mitch. 'That's you, right?'

Mitch held that unconvincing smile. 'I'll call her tomorrow.'

Lucy rattled the note. 'But this is *about* tomorrow. The lady said,' Lucy read carefully, '*Mr Jeffson has called a meeting regarding Australasia and the chair. He hasn't been able to get you today. You need to be in the office by 7:00 a.m. sharp—*'

Mitch interjected. 'Got it. Great. Thanks.' His face was tight when he gestured towards the back room and said to Vanessa, 'I'm dying for a coffee. How about you?'

Out back, Vanessa peeled off her dress while, preoccupied, Mitch flicked on the kettle, then stared blankly out of the window at the alley's brick wall. She retrieved two towels and handed him one. Absently fluffing her hair, she moved to the single-door wardrobe to fish out a change of clothes.

She found the jeans she'd left there earlier in the week, as well as fresh underwear and a T-shirt. Moving to the small adjoining bathroom, she spoke to him through the open door.

'Your mother's message sounds serious.'

She imagined that he shrugged as he grunted. Then came the tinkle of a teaspoon as he prepared instant coffee.

She slipped on the new underwear and T-shirt, then, curious, ducked her head around the corner and saw him staring out of the window again, dripping teaspoon poised above one of two cups.

'You're going to that meeting, aren't you?'

Thrusting back his shoulders, he inhaled. 'I've been in touch with Garret more than a few times last week. He's just edgy…trying to make a point.'

'About you having a personal life?' she ventured, knowing Mrs Stuart would love the fact she felt responsible.

He grunted. 'As for my mother, leaving that message, here of all places—' He threw the spoon in the sink. 'I'm too old for Simon Says.' He sipped his coffee, frowned and poured the rest down the drain. 'God, I hate instant.'

Remembering the million-dollar coffee machine in his mother's mansion, Vanessa's stomach knotted as she blindly found her jeans and slipped one leg in. 'It's only another week. Maybe you should—'

She stopped when his eyes caught hers. They weren't smiling.

'Vanessa, I can handle this. I've known this man all my life.' She slipped in her other leg as he came to her and set his big hands on her hips. His tone softened. 'Don't worry. This has nothing to do with you.'

The blood rushed to her feet.

How wrong he was.

He caught a kiss that didn't linger beyond a few seconds. 'You finish getting changed. I need to get out of these trousers.' He set his forehead to hers and held her gaze. 'Come over later. I'll look after dinner.' He smiled. 'It's getting to be a tradition. What do you feel like?'

She smiled weakly. 'Maybe Thai?'

He wiggled her hips. 'Extra-hot.'

As he left, Mrs Stuart's words reverberated through Vanessa's mind…

He needs to get his mind back on business or risk losing the reward he's worked towards and deserves after fifteen long years. My dear, you don't want him to resent you later for getting in the way.

Turned inside out, Vanessa sank onto the chair

behind her. Her pocket crunched. Wearily, she reached behind and found the shards of that fortune cookie she'd forgotten about.

She pulled out the squashed cookie, along with its words of wisdom, and read:

When you see another with a contrary character, look inward and examine yourself.

Terrific. Why couldn't it have said, *Remember to brush your teeth after meals*?

She wandered over to the kittens and collected baby Roger.

As much as she didn't like Beatrice Stuart, they had one thing in common. They both wanted the best for Mitch. But, although she believed she and Mitch were entitled to this time, it was as flattering as it was obvious…

She *was* a distraction.

A potentially dangerous one.

For years, Garret Jeffson had wielded a cane over Mitch's head, its full length inscribed *tough love*. Last week, she'd apparently unleashed a streak of pent-up rebellion in Mitch that wouldn't be silenced, even when he knew there could be consequences.

But she had the power to stop this battle of wills from getting worse. If Mitch stuck to his guns and refused to play the game as his mother and Garret Jeffson directed, what was to stop Garret from withholding the Presidency of the bank from Mitch indefinitely? Maybe Mitch would end up telling them all to go jump. If she had indeed been the catalyst, how would she live with that?

Burrowing her cheek against Roger's little head, she looked inward and knew what to do.

CHAPTER NINE

'WELL, now, this is a surprise.'

Feeling the rapt smile stretch across his face, Mitch stood back as, an hour later, Vanessa crossed the threshold. Jeans, T-shirt, blonde hair loose and shining, face clean of anything other than its natural glow. He was taken back to that first night—was it only a week ago? A life-altering, unforgettable week he couldn't have anticipated when they'd first met. She'd been so different from any woman he'd ever dated. This evening she looked fresher and more tempting than ever.

He tugged his ear.

Even if that particular pair of jeans was ready for the rag bag. And looked *sensational* on her because of it.

If that new girl, Lucy, was in the shop tomorrow, perhaps they could get to sleep in.

Mitch flinched.

Except for that meeting. If Garret's wife hadn't been ill, he'd have no hesitation believing tomorrow had purely been devised to see if he'd jump. And the harder Garret turned the rope, the less inclined he was to play.

Some people might call that pig-headed. Mitch called it finally making a stand, even if, yes, the timing was inopportune.

'I bought some supplies.' Vanessa held up a green carrier bag.

He gave her a playful scowl. 'You don't have to bring groceries here. Anyway, we're having Thai.'

'Guess again. I'm going to cook.' His brows shot up as she brushed past. 'Hope you like soy burgers.'

Was she serious?

He shut the door. 'Actually, I prefer mine with ketchup.'

He chuckled but she spun around and tapped his nose. 'Wrong answer.'

Feeling a little off balance, he followed her into the kitchen and, succumbing to the hot pulsing tug in his gut, wrapped his arms around her slender waist, nuzzling her neck as she prepared to unpack the carrier bag. She'd been on fire down at the beach today. Sexy and reckless and teasing beyond reason. Good thing they *had* been in public or she'd have been in real trouble.

He ground against her.

Then there was tonight…

Waiting for the moment she'd melt against him and turn around, he stopped tickling her lobe with his tongue when he spotted a foreign object on his counter.

He broke away and took a step back.

'Lentils?'

She frowned over her shoulder at him. 'You like to keep healthy, right?'

He edged forward and tugged open the bag. 'What else have you got in here?'

She smacked his hand and wiggled her brows. 'Magic ingredients.'

As she busied herself unpacking again, understanding dawned. He spun her around and crushed her against him until she must have known how strongly she'd been missed.

'Ness,' he growled, 'you don't need to impress me. Deep down, I'm a man of simple tastes. Three veg and a big steak more than does it for me.'

She looked disappointed. 'No steak, I'm afraid. But I do have carob rice-cake tarts for dessert.'

Horror dropped through him. What was this? Cravings? She couldn't be pregnant. Either way, no matter how much he wanted to please her, cardboard smeared with fake chocolate was not up for discussion.

Anyway, who was hungry?

Getting back on track, consciously stoking the kindling that smouldered down below, he steered his hands down her sides while he tasted her temple, her cheek.

'We can cook tomorrow night if you want,' he murmured. 'I've already ordered. This restaurant has the best Pad Thai in town.' He lowered his head to sample her sweet mouth. 'Hot and spicy.'

When he felt her teeth tug her lip, he drew back

to see she looked more sulky than worried. 'Can I say I'm a little tired of takeout?'

His head snapped back and he blinked several times. All he could think to say was, 'I see.'

The doorbell rang at the same time that off-balance feeling pushed the back of his knees in again. He drove a hand through his hair and headed for the door. 'Guess the delivery guy's early too.'

They ate at the dining table, Kami blowing bubbles and looking on. Mitch only opened his mouth to eat, mainly because Vanessa wouldn't keep quiet.

Halfway through the meal, he had the absurd feeling she might be pulling a joke. Was he being filmed for *Punked*? But, hell, basically he was happy to listen to her voice, all night long if she wanted.

He got his wish.

Long after dinner, the chatter kept coming. Some time around eleven he decided she could continue her dialogue in a different part of the house.

He pushed to his feet and held out his hand. She took it, looking uncertain. 'What are you doing?'

'Going for a walk.'

As he pulled her up she caught the time on her watch and exclaimed, 'Oh, gosh, look at that. No wonder I'm bushed. We've both got big days to-morrow. Perhaps we should…'

He slanted his head over hers and kissed the words away. When she surrendered and relaxed, he swept her up in his arms and didn't let go his silencing lip-lock until he'd moved through the gym and reached the edge of his indoor pool.

Their mouths softly parted. Her eyes were drowsy with longing as she sighed, 'Where are we?' She frowned and sniffed. 'I smell chlorine.'

'Remember that bomb-dive lesson I promised?'

Her lidded eyes opened wide. 'Mitch…no. You *wouldn't.*'

Her last word came out a howl as he pitched her into the drink. He waited for the splash, then bomb dived in too.

Geronimo!

Mitch slept like a log and jumped out of his skin when Vanessa woke him at dawn, shaking his shoulder, then leaping out of bed to go brush her teeth.

Scrambling up on an elbow, he scrubbed his sleepy face.

After their skinny dip last night, they'd climbed into bed some time after one. Was she on steroids? And, if she was, how about coming back and sharing some more of that energy around? He daydreamed about the limitless joys of their morning sex…the first rays edging in through the blinds, the curlew crying from afar while they pleasured each other front to front, head to toe and, his favourite of favourites, Ness on top.

But something in Vanessa's frantic brushing in the bathroom told him that wasn't on the cards today.

A moment later, she breezed out and proceeded to

choose a shirt and tie from his wardrobe. Frowning and scratching his chest, he pushed up higher.

Okay. This was weird.

His laugh was short and he wished he hadn't forced it. 'Ness, settle down. You're not my mother.'

Already dressed, she turned from the tallboy, a pair of socks in each hand. 'Oh, I know that.'

He patted the mattress three times. 'Stop flitting around and come back to bed.'

Still on her sock mission, she didn't seem to hear.

This was getting beyond weird.

His voice lowered. 'Ness, what's going on?'

When she turned to him, she looked almost offended.

But, come on. She was acting like… Like a *wife*. He didn't *want* a wife. Or a cook. Or even a chatterbox. He wanted a lover.

He wanted his Ness.

She dumped his socks atop the tallboy. 'I have to leave really soon,' she said. 'I have some new Rotties coming in today.'

Mitch ground his back teeth. She knew he had a thing for that Rottie pup. Why mention a new lot now?

'I wonder if you could come to the shop?' she went on. 'Say, around nine and help me bundle up a couple for an important customer who lives a little out of town. You were such a help yesterday with the cockapoos.'

Air turned to icicles in his lungs. All he could think was, *Was I so wrong about her?*

His words grated out. 'Yesterday was Sunday. Today's a work day.'

When he flung back the covers, her clasped hands flew to her chin. 'Mitch, God, I'm sorry. That was so dumb of me.'

Her eyes were so big and green and beautiful. Without grabbing his robe, he went to her, unable to help wishing that she was still naked too. Irritation forgotten, he curled a knuckle around her cheek. 'Don't worry.'

She smiled, pleased that he'd forgiven her. 'Maybe you could come over later in the afternoon, then. Four would be fine. Three would be better.'

His right eye twitched, he dropped his hand and headed for the bathroom. 'I have meetings today.'

From behind, he heard, 'Oops. Of course.'

Brushing his teeth, he caught the time on his watch. If she was heading off, he'd have time for a workout before getting to the office at seven.

He rinsed, then splashed his face.

God, he wished this week was over.

When he returned to the bedroom, a towel lashed around his hips, Vanessa stood by the bedroom doorway, her eyes uncertain. She looked cornered… or guilty.

Mitch's heart twisted.

Hell, maybe this was just a bad morning. Maybe he needed to wake up. Maybe he should get this week done with—get his priorities straight—before switching his attention to other things.

He went over, cupped her face and his mouth met hers. She coughed a little and drew back. 'Sorry.'

Smiling, he went to kiss her again, but she barked out another one. He stepped back and frowned. 'You ought to watch that cough.'

She held her throat. 'I do feel a little scratchy. Tea's supposed to be good for colds. I'll get one at the shop.'

In a blink, she was gone, leaving him standing there with that weird off-balance feeling happening again, as if he were standing on the slippery deck and the ship was listing.

About to go under.

Mitch got to the office five minutes before seven. Garret was waiting. The meeting went smoothly—no surprises, no hiccups. The Australasian expansion plans were discussed and the chair handover was set to go ahead Friday. But, for the entire two hours, Mitch was sidetracked, thinking about Vanessa.

That afternoon around three, Mitch picked up and fast-dialled Great and Small.

Lucy answered. 'Vanessa's out the back with a lemon tea. I'll tell her you're on the phone.'

A full five minutes later, Vanessa croaked down the line, 'Hey, Mitch.'

He shuddered. 'You sound awful.'

'I'm coming down with something bad. Do you mind if we don't see each other tonight?'

He drew a circle on his day pad and cocked a brow. 'I could bring over some lozenges. Massage oil with eucalypt is said to work wonders on the respiratory system too.'

She coughed so loudly, he pulled the receiver away from his ear. 'I feel like rolling into bed and sleeping for a week. In fact, I was about to pack up now, go home and die.'

He slashed a cross through the circle. 'Do you want me to drive you home?'

'You're busy.' Those words sounded livelier, firmer, but then she coughed again. 'I'm fine to drive.'

'I'll call tomorrow, then.'

But the following day it was the same story, only she didn't make it to her shop. Over the phone, she sounded as if she were talking past needles stuck in her throat. He pushed back his office chair. 'I'm coming over.'

She wheezed, then sneezed. 'I look terrible. *Feel* terrible. I just need to hide away in my cave until I'm well.'

He hated to give in. He had to do *something*. A big bunch of spring flowers seemed a good plan.

The next day she told him, 'I'm getting better but I don't want to infect you.'

He drew three straight lines on his day pad. She didn't sound any better.

He sent a bigger bunch, roses this time. When Thursday came and went, the doubt monsters began to bite. She could have TB or some deadly strain of bird flu. Then another voice whispered, *And she could be avoiding you.* He hadn't forgotten her odd behaviour last Sunday night and the following morning. Was this all connected?

By Friday, Vanessa wasn't answering her phone and Mitch was unstoppable. He wanted answers. Was she truly sick? Or was his gut feeling right: she was putting on the voice and the symptoms in order to avoid him? If she no longer wanted to see him, he would deal with that. But he wasn't living in this limbo any longer. Not knowing was doing his head in.

Garret stopped him in the hall on his way out. 'Mitch, do you have a moment?'

Mitch silently cursed before manufacturing a smile. 'Not right now. Sorry.'

Garret set his hands on his hips. 'Have you forgotten what today is? I've called the meeting for midday.'

'I haven't forgotten.' It was handover day. The day he'd slogged towards for years. The day all the hard work was supposed to pay off. But…

He held up an index finger. 'I'll be back in an hour.'

Garret's scowl deepened, then he grunted, 'Perhaps you shouldn't bother.'

On his way past, Mitch slowed up. 'What are you talking about—?'

'I'm talking about being worse than distracted in the board meeting this week. I'm talking about managers phoning or filing in to my office wondering what the hell's gotten into you. I'm talking about important clients who've claimed that you're preoccupied. One was so concerned, I had to talk him down from taking his business elsewhere.'

Mitch ploughed his hands into his pockets. 'Jasper Target?' Garret nodded. 'You know if Target's not complaining, he's not happy.'

'*I'm* not happy.'

He wouldn't admit it aloud, but Garret had a point; he *had* been distracted. And that was what he intended to sort out. 'I'll be back by midday.'

Shaking his head, Garret returned to his office and shut the door.

Mitch strode for the lift and half an hour later he was storming down Vanessa's drive. As luck would have it, she'd just come out of her flat and was walking towards him. On seeing her unexpected visitor, her face drained of colour.

Her mouth opened, then shut before she got out, 'What are you doing here?'

Feeling the connection—the immediate sizzle in his blood whenever she was near—he stopped before her. It had felt like a year since he'd held her, not a few days. 'I needed to see you.'

Her gaze dropping to her sandalled feet, she mumbled something unintelligible, then said more clearly, 'I'm going for more antibiotics. I'm still not well.'

His face hardened. She was lying.

Ignoring the ache low in his throat, he told her, 'Try again.'

With guilty eyes, she glanced over at a window; in his peripheral vision he saw a blind snap shut.

Then she looked him dead on and must have

known he meant business. Giving in, she expelled a worn-down sigh. 'I guess you need to know…'

He bit down against the pulse beating in his jaw. 'Guess I do.'

'I thought it was better we didn't see each other for a while.'

He counted to three—to ten—then raised his chin. 'Want to give me a reason?'

'You were having such an important time at work.'

His head kicked back. *Sorry?* 'And what does that have to do with anything?'

'I didn't want to get in the way of—' She dropped her gaze. 'Don't ask me, Mitch.'

Damn right he'd ask! 'What's going on, Vanessa?'

'I need to go.' She stepped around him.

But he caught her arm. 'The avoidance game's over. And, in case you're considering skimping, I want to know it all.'

She slumped and closed her eyes, as if she couldn't bear to see his face when she came clean.

'Your mother filled me in on your problems at work. She said you were in danger of losing the chair if…'

'If *what*?'

Her throat bobbed as she swallowed. 'If you continued to see me. Apparently I'm bad for your mental health.'

He didn't suppress his growl. He'd have it out with his mother later; this time she'd gone too far. But was he reading the rest of this story right?

He released his grip on her sleeve and tried to control some of his agitation by crossing his arms. 'Go on.'

'I decided it would be best if we didn't see each other until after your promotion was settled.'

'So you tried to be a pain in the butt last Sunday night to put me off?' She nibbled her lip and nodded. 'And to make sure I wouldn't be tempted, you pretended to be contagious.'

'I wanted you to be able to concentrate fully on your work. I didn't want to get in the way.'

'And lying and worrying me sick was the plan you came up with?'

She flinched. 'It doesn't sound very bright now.'

No, it really didn't. She'd had his best interests at heart—with her background, she wouldn't have had any experience with the scheming likes of his mother. But, *sweet blazes*, acting in a mature, logical manner and talking to him would've made far more sense, as well as saving a lot of angst. He cringed to think how she'd act in a real crisis.

Speaking of which…

He caught the time on his watch. He needed to get back and placate Garret. Garret wasn't to blame for being peeved over his protégé's recent preoccupations. Jasper Target was an extremely important client. Mitch had acted less than professionally.

It wouldn't happen again.

Vanessa touched his arm. 'I'm sorry. I didn't mean to make things worse.'

'It's not your fault.' He squeezed her hand then lowered it away. 'It's mine.'

'Because you should've trusted your instincts?' she ventured in a quiet voice.

He fought the urge to say, *Perhaps*.

Instead, he straightened his tie. 'I only know the most important meeting of my life is in fifteen minutes and I don't have any more time to waste. So—' he managed a tip of his head before turning away '—I'll let you go.'

'That sounds like goodbye.'

He stopped. Turned back.

He was annoyed. Angry. If he spoke now, chances were he'd make this mess worse. He'd rather let it slide.

And slide a little more.

When his BlackBerry beeped, he growled and headed off. 'I have to go.' He had to go *now*.

'Mitch, you didn't answer me.'

He wheeled back again. Counting his heartbeats, he held her glistening gaze with his. People relied on him. After today, the buck stopped with him. He couldn't afford to lose his head. On top of that, Ness wasn't comfortable in his world. Her discomfit at the charity cocktail party the other night had made that clear enough. They were good together—on one level. But on every other…

He held his breath.

Maybe it was kinder…

Maybe it was better…

To be tough.

He set his jaw and looked her in the eye while his heart dropped in his chest. 'Goodbye, Ness.'

Her pupils dilated before she exhaled and a wan,

close to accepting smile appeared. She nodded slowly. 'Bye, Mitch. Be sure to watch the rocks on your way out.'

When Mitch arrived back at the office and burst into the boardroom, a sombre Garret Jeffson glanced up from the end of the long table.

With bigger than usual bags under his eyes, the older man indicated the chair on his right. Then he sat back, tapping his pen on the notepad before him. 'Glad you could make it.'

Finger-combing his hair—he'd driven back with the top down—Mitch lowered into the chair. 'It's been a crazy couple of weeks.'

'Indeed. Do you anticipate the following weeks being as crazy?'

With his heartbeat pounding in his ears, Mitch held his breath, then shook his head. 'As of now, things are back to normal.'

Garret measured Mitch's expression for a long moment, as if looking for cracks, then retrieved a set of papers from his briefcase. 'It's all here, ready for your signature. Put your *X* on the dotted line and the chair's all yours.'

His hand slightly shaky, Mitch casually extracted the gold pen from the breast pocket of his jacket. After a token perusal of the document—he trusted Garret to have everything in perfect order—he initialled each page, then swept his signature over a final line and sat back.

Done.

After Garret witnessed the signature, he pushed back his chair. Mitch rose too, taking the older man's hand.

For the first time in weeks, Garret's smile looked sincere. 'Let me know how it goes.'

Waiting for the high to kick in, Mitch shook hands heartily. 'Will do.'

Garret nodded, collected his briefcase and headed for the door.

Mitch blinked. 'You're leaving now? I thought you might hang around and crack open a bottle of champagne to help celebrate.'

'Trudy's coming home from the hospital today. I promised—' Garret stopped himself and rephrased. 'I want to be there for her now.'

Mitch evaluated the man who'd taught him so much—hard lessons in life and business he would never forget. He shrugged. 'Guess that's it, then.'

'Good luck, son. Not that you'll need it. I was wrong to worry. This institution's your life. I should've known you wouldn't let the team down.' He lifted a brow. 'Doesn't mean you can't have a balance.'

As the door shut, Mitch thought over Garret's parting words, but then quickly pulled himself back. He might have finally reached the top, but that merely meant, more than ever, he needed to keep his eye on the game. Needed to keep his mind on the task. Balance was a luxury other people could afford.

Sweeping up the document, he strode down the hall and into his office. He shrugged off his jacket, swung it on the coat stand. But his determined expression slid as he peered around his massive penthouse office suite…the space on the wall where his portrait as President would hang…the piles of paperwork on his desk he would look through tonight.

He'd thought he'd feel different.

And he did.

He felt hollow.

CHAPTER TEN

THE following day, Vanessa sat cross-legged on the worn carpet in her shop's back room, her chin in her hand, her heart bleeding on the floor.

She'd tried to put Mitch out of her mind; she'd tried till three in the morning. But she simply couldn't do it. Their last conversation kept going round in her head. What he'd said, his expression, her replies, how she'd persisted, then she'd replay it all over again.

The repetition drove her mad, but she knew why she persisted. She was hoping that somehow the outcome would be different and, rather than goodbye, Mitch would declare his love. She'd imagined it. Her soul had *cried* for it.

Sad thing was, she didn't blame him. She hadn't wanted to deceive him, but she hadn't felt she'd had a choice. Staying out of his life had seemed the best bet; if she'd been upfront and told him about his mother's pointed chat, given his black mood towards Mr Jeffson on Sunday after receiving his message, she shuddered to think how the following days would have played out. She'd figured once he had Garret Jeffson off his back and the promotion in the bag, they could resume their relationship.

But she'd been caught out. Her absence from his life last week had caused more harm than good. He no longer trusted her.

No longer wanted her.

Knocking aside the tear falling down her cheek, Vanessa sucked in a breath and focused.

The fairy tale was over. She'd known it couldn't last. Too much had been against them. Now she was back to where and what she knew. These animals were her family. This was her home. Maybe one day a more realistic Prince Charming would come along.

But, after having Mitch, she honestly didn't see herself ever loving again.

She was playing with Roger, dangling a thread of orange wool which he pawed and chased, when Lucy interrupted.

'Miss Craig—' She amended, 'I mean Ness, a man's here. Says he's the landlord. He's with a lady.' Lucy hugged herself as if a chill had swept through the door. 'He doesn't look happy.'

Vanessa rose to her feet and put Roger back in his big corner pen with the others.

She'd left messages for her landlord and had asked him to return her calls; she wanted to speak with him about buying the shop. She was willing to pay more than the market price and, incorporated in the contract, they could tidy up the matter of outstanding rent.

Seemed they would start negotiations face to face.

Slipping on her shoes, she moved into the shop proper and held out her hand to her male guest. 'Hello, Mr Hodges.'

'Miss Craig.' Mr Hodges' bright red mop of hair wobbled on a curt nod. 'This is Mrs Ordiele. She's interested in taking over the lease.'

Mrs Ordiele forced herself away from running an approving eye over the clean, bright interior and popped out her hand. 'Great place. Absolutely ideal.'

Vanessa was still getting over Mr Hodges' statement; had he said this woman wanted to take over her lease?

'Thank you,' she replied to Mrs Ordiele's compliment. Then, to Mr Hodges, 'But something needs to be cleared up. I don't need to leave. Mr Hodges, I've left several messages—'

'But no money in the bank.' He looked slightly embarrassed for Mrs Ordiele's sake, but the willowy brunette was checking out the Lhasa Apsos.

Vanessa rubbed her palms down the outside of her jeans. 'About the rent...I actually wanted to speak with you about that.'

'Time for talk is over.' He sucked down a settling breath and his ruddy cheeks dropped a shade. 'Let's do this amicably, shall we? Without the bother of eviction notices and solicitors.'

'You don't understand.' Relishing the moment,

Vanessa squared her shoulders. 'I want to *buy* this shop.'

His expression froze before he laughed. 'I doubt you have that kind of money, Miss Craig.' He cocked a brow. 'Unless you've inherited a small fortune.'

'Name a price.'

He did—an amount she knew was too high.

'I'll put another twenty thousand on top of that,' she said, willing to go higher.

His tawny eyes sparkled, then narrowed. 'Thirty and it's yours.'

She stuck out her hand. 'Done.'

A delighted Mr Hodges crossed over to Mrs Ordiele. Vanessa saw the older woman's face drop when he spoke quietly and slid a glance back over his shoulder at the proud new owner.

Vanessa found a smile.

Me.

Lucy tapped her shoulder. 'There's a call for you, Ness.'

Vanessa wanted this moment to last. She might not have Mitch, but she'd achieved her earliest dream; soon she would own her own home. No one would ever take that away.

She threw a glance to Lucy. 'I'll call back.'

'It's about your aunt. The man sounded real upset.'

Vanessa studied Lucy's alarmed gaze, then rushed to grab the back extension.

Her heart was drumming in her throat when she asked of the receiver, 'Who is this?'

'Miss Craig? The name's Ernie Curtis. I purchased a painting from your aunt a few weeks ago. I believe she's left the country.'

Vanessa pulled the hair back from her damp brow and sat down. 'That's right.'

The man cleared his throat. 'This is a little embarrassing. I know she had no idea.'

Vanessa squeezed the receiver. 'What is it, Mr Curtis?'

'The painting…it's a replica. An incredibly good fake. I have no intention of bringing in the law. I know your aunt is a reputable woman.' He paused. 'I merely want my money back.'

The receiver slipped from her hand as every ounce of energy deserted her. She couldn't get her mouth to work and her fingers felt like rubber.

After a dazed moment, she bent and collected the phone.

'Miss Craig? Are you there?'

She moistened her lips but was unable to stop the spots from dancing before her eyes. 'I'm… sorry.'

'Sorry?'

He'd misunderstood. 'I mean—' her stomach wrenched '—of course you'll have your money back.'

She heard his expulsion of air. Relief. 'How can I contact your aunt?'

Vanessa pictured McKenzie—by the sink, loading washing, helping with homework, smiling proudly at birthdays. Last week had been the first time Vanessa had known McKenzie to put herself first, and even that was to see a sick friend.

The decision was unbearably painful but also explicitly clear.

She consciously released the tension locking her muscles. 'There's no need to contact my aunt. Give me your details and I'll wire your money through.'

Five minutes later, she found the strength to drag herself back out to her landlord, who was looking rather anxious and minus the chirpy Mrs Ordiele.

Vanessa stopped to look around.

Everything was hushed. Each animal, bird and fish seemed to be looking at her, waiting for the verdict. She'd already paid back Mitch's loan. She'd kept the correct amount from the cockapoos but had mailed back a cheque to Mrs Stuart for the surplus amount—the money Mrs Stuart had hoped she'd take to leave her son alone. Now she needed to pay back McKenzie's money.

Her guardian angel must have sent a saviour in Mrs Ordiele; she'd take over the care of this place and its boarders.

The pain of full understanding hit so strongly, she almost doubled over.

Oh, God, I have to leave.

After a few deep breaths, she joined the puzzled Mr Hodges to explain her changed circumstances. He could tell Mrs Ordiele the good news…

She was going to love it here.

CHAPTER ELEVEN

A WEEK later, Vanessa somehow found the strength to say farewell to Great and Small.

With her possessions removed, she said goodbye to her pets, to the male Rottie waiting to be collected, to Lucy, and finally to her kittens, who would soon be old enough to find their own homes.

Leaving Roger broke her heart. Had her landlord permitted cats, she'd have taken him with her. Instead she took solace in the knowledge that he was bound to lead a pampered fat cat life. She only wished it could've been with her.

When she walked out of the front door for the last time, feeling bedrock empty inside, she found herself heading to the steps of the Opera House.

Looking out over the silky blue water now, peering up at the wheeling gulls, she breathed in the briny air and wondered, *what next?* She'd had a couple of ideas, but she couldn't find enthusiasm for any of them. In fact, she dreaded nightfall because she worried she didn't have the wherewithal to even lift her butt off this step.

As if her memories weren't enough, the distant yap of a puppy caught her ear and the backs of her eyes prickled with fresh tears. Everywhere she looked—everything she saw or smelled or heard—kept bringing her back.

To what she'd lost.

To Mitch. Her home.

Where did she belong? Certainly not in his world; he'd made that choice for her. But today she felt utterly lost. As if she had no world of her own. No one at all.

Something wet bumped her elbow. She blinked and saw it was that excited puppy she must have heard barking before. A Rottweiler…

Heartbeat booming, she grabbed his panting face and looked into those happy chocolate-brown eyes. *Good grief.* 'Is that you, boy? You shouldn't be here.'

'He wanted to come visit.'

Vanessa's startled gaze shot up.

Mitch!

At his gorgeous crooked smile, she caught her runaway breath and a portion of her deep sadness slipped away, replaced by confusion. 'How did you find me? I don't understand.' She didn't understand any of it.

Had he heard about her misfortune and wanted to offer her another loan? If that was the case, thanks, but no thanks. That wasn't the answer.

Wearing that black wool-blend shirt she adored,

he sat down and lifted the dog onto his lap. 'I went to see you. Lucy filled me in on what happened. She told me that customer rang and said he no longer wanted this little guy. Then she mentioned you'd come here a few times this past week.' With next to no space between them and the pull of his magnetism so near, her skin began to heat. 'What'll you do?'

Although her head swam and her fingers itched to reach out and touch, she tried her best to digest what he'd told her and sound casual in her reply. 'I haven't decided. I might travel. Maybe Asia. More likely Greece.'

A dark brow jumped up. 'Plan to eat goat cheese and drink lemonade on a pebbled beach?'

After all the outstanding bills had been settled, thanks to the cockapoos, she'd had a little money left over. If she didn't make herself go now, perhaps she never would.

She deadpanned back, 'I don't see why not.'

'Me either.' His expression intensified. 'As long as I'm there too.'

Her pulse started to hammer and her cheeks began to burn. 'We've already said goodbye.' She didn't need to go through that again. Having her heart wrenched from her chest. Feeling as if tomorrow no longer mattered. She'd made a choice, perhaps a bad choice, to avoid his company that week; she was paying for it now. But she didn't need to hang around and suffer this added torture.

She pushed to her feet. 'I really have to go.'

He set the puppy down on his lead and stood too. 'Home?'

Outwardly cool, she shrugged. 'Probably.'

'We'll come too.'

She frowned. 'My landlord doesn't allow animals.'

'I'm talking about your shop.'

She obviously hadn't heard right. Or he'd misunderstood something. But then the sparkle in his eyes had her wondering.

Hoping.

'I heard your place was on the market for the right price,' he said.

'And you bought it?'

'I did.'

Tears filled her eyes, blurring her vision. The question she had to ask came out a squeak. 'But why?'

He smiled. 'Why do you think?'

She covered her mouth to block the emotion. This was too much. 'I can't do this right now.'

His face pinched as if he'd been slapped. 'Don't run away from me, Ness.'

She shut her eyes tight as desperate longing fisted in her chest. She didn't want to see his face or hear the words. It would only confuse her. And she didn't want to be confused again.

When she opened her eyes, he was still standing there, looking almost amused now.

'I suppose I could always kidnap you again,' he said.

She thought of that incredible night in his bed. How he'd held her. How he'd loved her.

Unwilling to be blinded again, she pointed out, 'That was a short-term solution.'

'And you want long-term.'

Her throat clogged up. 'What I *don't* want is to be toyed with. You got it right that first night, when you wanted to kiss me but decided to rip up my card instead.'

'Because I made an assumption,' he finished for her.

She tried to swallow the hurt. 'Yes.'

'Like I made another assumption last week.'

'No assumption. You and I had fun together. That's it.'

'I know.'

Taken aback, she looked at him harder. 'You do?'

'You like stories. Let me tell you one. After I left you the other day, I signed a paper and assumed control of an entity I thought would make me happy. It didn't. Instead, I felt angry. Unfulfilled. Frustrated. I needed to cool down, so I went back to our beach. I started to jog, to run, and then I was diving into the waves, swimming out. Way out. When the shoreline was a smudge, I realised what I was doing.'

She waited, breathless.

'Looking for sharks?'

'I was looking for my siren.'

She bit her inside cheek as a tear slipped down her face. 'You realise that the sailor in my story didn't succumb to the siren's call. His mates on the ship kept him tied up and he was saved.'

'Or damned?' His warm, strong hands found hers.

'I'd rather go on swimming and searching for ever than make a choice to go on living without you.' His voice lowered. 'I don't want to be married to my job. I want to be married to you. I want to have fun. I want to be your family. I'm ready. So are you.' As another salty trail ran into the corner of her mouth, his smile changed. 'I hurt you. I was wrong. Ness, I'm so sorry.'

She battled the raw emotion pushing up her throat. She was sorry too.

'Mitch...' She confessed, 'I couldn't bear to lose you again.'

'You won't have to.' His arms went around her and brought her close. 'From this moment on, I promise I'll be here. You don't have to worry about anyone else.'

'Your mother—'

'Knows she's beaten. Once she lowers her defences, she'll fall right in love with you. Just like I did.'

Her voice was a thready whisper. 'How do you know?'

'Know that I love you?' She nodded and his lips tugged. 'That's the easy part. I miss you. I laugh with you. I adore you. You're fabulous underwater.' She laughed and his smile widened. 'I could go on.'

Heck, he almost had her believing.

He cupped her face again and his essence swam out to embrace hers. 'I'm bewitched by you, Ness. Be my wife.' His expression sobered to an earnestness she'd never seen before. 'I love you with everything I've been or will ever be. Will we give us a go? What do you say?'

After that heartfelt affirmation, there was only one thing she *could* say.

She filled her lungs and dived in. 'I love you too. Seems like I always have.'

By the smile glowing in his eyes, she might have given him the only prize worth having.

He set his forehead on hers. 'You can be you. I'll be me, and we'll invent our own world. The very *best* world.'

When his mouth dropped over hers, and his promise-filled heat held her close, Vanessa knew to her soul it was true. Theirs would not only be the best.

Theirs would be for ever.

EPILOGUE

'It's settled. We're having moussaka for dinner.'

With eyes closed and one cheek resting on her crossed forearms, Vanessa roused herself at the rich, deep tones of her husband's voice. Giving a lazy stretch and rolling over, she blinked sleepily as a flock of sparrows darted and swooped across the endless azure sky.

The scent of orange blossom and wild oregano drifted in on a warm breeze, and if Mitch hadn't been standing above her—hands low on his hips, his sexy smile electrifyingly real—she'd have known that lying on the deck of a private yacht, moored in the cool blue waters off a popular Greek island, must be a dream.

Blissfully content, she reached out her arms to him. 'Perhaps we should stay on board tonight.'

She was still more than satisfied by the charcoal fire barbecue, baklava and strong Greek coffee they'd enjoyed early this afternoon at that gorgeous taverna. Hidden within a labyrinth of narrow cobblestone lanes laced with pink bougainvillea, she'd felt as if she'd entered another world. A world she'd longed to experience and was now enjoying on her honeymoon.

In chinos, rolled to his shins, and no shirt, Mitch made himself comfortable, lying beside her on the plush double towel. Warmed right the way through, she snuggled into his hard, bronzed chest and sighed as his strong arm drew her near.

He growled playfully as his lips grazed her temple and his natural scent joined with the other delights awakening her senses, feeding her soul.

'I'm more than happy staying put,' he said. 'All I need is some cheese, fresh bread—' he nuzzled her neck '—and a whole pile of you.'

His lips drifted over her jaw, sparking a trail of desire, which ignited and blew flames through her blood when his mouth covered hers. The roughness of his chin working languidly near her cheek…the rhythm of his breathing speeding up along with hers…

The kiss was deep and lasting—the kind of kiss poets wrote about and lonely people pined for.

She was lonely no more.

After a six-month engagement, they'd married two weeks ago in a ceremony that celebrated both tradition and individuality. The giant fairy-tale marquee had held over two hundred guests and offered a smorgasbord of cuisines from around the world. All of Mitch's family had been happy for them—including his mother. It had seemed good timing that, a week after Mitch's marriage proposal, Mrs Stuart had begun seeing a reclusive multimillionaire, who had instantly fallen for her 'frailty' and charm, and now doted on her every whim.

Josie and Tia had made beautiful bridesmaids, and Vanessa was thrilled that their guests had included Aunt McKenzie and her now fiancé, Jim, who had recovered enough from his respiratory illness to fly from L.A. to Australia. Around 10:00 p.m., the bride had kicked off her shoes; the dancing had lasted till long past midnight.

Now, as their lips softly parted, Vanessa enjoyed the high of her giddy heartbeat as she remembered their special day—the day she'd become Mitch Stuart's wife. But as the whitewashed houses dotting the craggy hillside in the distance caught her eye, she felt a twinge.

Homesickness.

Mitch's brow pinched before his fingertip weaved up her thigh. 'Let me guess. You're missing the shop?'

Her mouth swung to one side. 'Silly, huh.'

'No, not silly. But remember that Lucy was beside herself that you entrusted her with its running while we were gone.' He tickled her ribs. 'And we still have another couple of weeks before finding out whether our tender to buy the rest of that block is successful.'

A couple of weeks before the wedding, she'd mentioned her fantasy of expanding the store—but *her* way, with her own vet, grooming facilities and heaps more pets who needed good homes. Mitch hadn't hesitated in putting a bid for the entire string of shops into motion.

She stole a quick kiss and stayed close. 'You certainly know how to make a girl's dreams come true.'

He chuckled. 'Absolutely my pleasure.'

It seemed as if they had it all. The balance. The best of both worlds.

Well, almost.

She'd never allowed herself to think too deeply about the possibility of becoming a mother. Guess there'd been a part of her that had been afraid of a commitment she would take more seriously, and cherish more dearly, than any other. But now…

She sat up, then, cheeks heating, lowered her gaze. 'Mitch, I want to run something by you.'

'Another business venture?'

'This is strictly personal.'

His mouth caressed the sensitive inside crease of her arm. 'Tell me more.'

Her heartbeat raced as she voiced an idea that had grown so strong, she could no longer contain it. 'What would you say to an adoption?'

His eyebrows jumped. 'Not another cat.'

'Mitch…I mean a *baby*.'

His head kicked back. His startling blue eyes had never looked wider.

'There are so many who need a good home,' she hurried on, 'and two loving parents who can give so much. I haven't changed my mind about having our own children, like we talked about. But I didn't think that should cancel out an adoption…or two.'

At his frozen expression, her spirits dropped and she hugged onto her knees. 'It was just an idea.'

His eyes began to sparkle, as mesmerising as the

surrounding sequinned blue sea. 'And possibly the best idea you've ever had.'

She let his words sink in. 'You think so? You *really* do?'

When he nodded, she threw her arms around his neck. Her heart felt so full, she wondered if it might burst. Now her secret wish was out and he'd agreed, she felt as if this moment of immeasurable joy had always been her destiny. A natural progression. The smiley-face icing on her cake.

With happy tears edging her eyes, she finally released him. 'We'll look into it as soon as we get back?' she asked.

'The very minute we get back,' he replied.

She melted as his hot fingers curved around her nape to draw her mouth to his. But when, over his shoulder, she saw something jump in the water, she pulled back and shielded her eyes against the glare. 'Did you see that?'

As a donkey brayed in the distance, he sat up taller too and glanced around. 'See what?'

'I think it's a dolphin.'

'Or possibly a mermaid?' He shrugged at her dry look. 'Hey, you never know.'

But she did know one thing. When they'd met, she'd wanted a home; Mitch had wanted fun. Now they had both, wrapped up in the beautiful big ribbon of their everlasting love.

Leaning in, she rubbed the tip of her nose with his.

'Guess what?' she murmured.

'What?' He smiled back.

'I feel happier—more in love—every day.'

The commitment in his eyes held her still before he gathered her close again.

'Oh, baby, so do I.'

* * * * *

BIG-SHOT
BACHELOR

BY
NICOLA MARSH

Nicola Marsh has always had a passion for writing and reading. As a youngster, she devoured books when she should have been sleeping, and later kept a diary whose content could be an epic in itself! These days, when she's not enjoying life with her husband and son in her home city of Melbourne, she's at her computer, creating the romances she loves, in her dream job. Visit Nicola's website at www.nicolamarsh.com for the latest news of her books.

For my editor, Maddie,
who is fabulous to work with!

CHAPTER ONE

'COME in and take off all your clothes.'

Ariel Wallace grimaced at how forward that sounded and tried another tack.

'Make your way out the back. You'll find pegs to hang all your clothes on.'

Uh-uh. Worse.

'You've probably done this a thousand times before so head through that door, disrobe and let's get started.'

No hope!

Shaking her head, Ariel covered her face with her hands, not surprised to feel heat scorching her cheeks and deriving little comfort from the familiar smell of turpentine on her paint-splotched skin.

She couldn't do this.

Being an artist involved spontaneous bursts of creativity, fabulous blending of colours and frantic slashes of brushes, not inviting some guy she didn't know to get his gear off so she could paint him.

Whopping big commission or not.

She'd find some other way to keep Colour by Dreams afloat. She had to. She'd promised Aunt Barb, the founder of this amazing gallery and the woman who had practically raised her, that her legacy would live on.

And she'd do anything to make that happen.

The soft tinkle of wind chimes signalled a visitor entering the gallery and Ariel stiffened, her hands dropping from her face as she braced for an awkward confrontation. She knew how much uni students needed money and giving some poor guy the brush-off, no pun intended, didn't sit well with her.

If anyone knew about being poor, she did.

Which was exactly why she had to paint her first life portrait since art school. She had no choice.

'Hello? Anyone here?'

'Be there in a sec,' she called out, casting a final longing look at the back door, wishing she could make a quick dash for it.

Instead, she smoothed her favourite ochre peasant skirt, retied the Paisley bandanna under her unruly curls and pasted an I'm-in-charge-and-not-in-the-mood-for-nonsense look before stepping through the beaded curtain that separated her work area from the gallery out front.

'Miss Wallace? I'm Cooper—'

'Hi, Cooper. My studio's out the back so if you head out there, I'll lock up in here and be with you shortly.'

The words tumbled out in a rush, a combination of nerves, embarrassment and shock. She'd expected a lean, young, scruffy guy to come slinking into the gallery looking half as embarrassed as she felt.

Instead, she struggled not to stare at Cooper. She had no interest in his surname; she didn't want to get too personal considering she'd soon be seeing him in the buff.

Buff…

Naked…

In the raw…

She swallowed, unable to link those words with the guy standing in front of her. If she'd been mortified at painting some dishevelled, half-starved student without his clothes on, the thought of Cooper—all six-three, broad shoulders, long legs, killer smile, too-blue eyes and dark hair—sitting for her without a stitch on made her positively light-headed.

Though that could just be the oil-paint fumes.

'I wasn't sure you'd want to do this,' he said, amusement lighting his eyes, making them sparkle in the muted lights and sending an unexpected bolt of awareness through her.

'No choice.'

She stared, stunned by his easy confidence, his cool poise.

Wasn't this guy the teensiest bit embarrassed about getting naked before a stranger?

Judging by his confident smile and casual stance, obviously not.

'We always have a choice, Miss Wallace,' he said, his deep voice resounding in the high-ceilinged room, as sexy as the rest of him.

Darn it, and that was with his clothes on!

'Actually, I don't have a choice. If I can't capture you on canvas and sell the painting for the fortune I've been promised, I lose this place to some slime-ball developers who've been buying up the rest of this street.'

Confusion clouded his steady stare for a second before a tiny frown creased his brow and his smile vanished.

Great, she was scaring off prime model material before she'd even started.

Blowing a stray curl out of her eyes, she said, 'Look, I'm sorry to dump all that on you. I tend to babble when I'm nervous and, to be honest, I haven't done nudes in quite a while. Guess I'm a bit bashful.'

She averted her eyes and crossed the room, her beaded flip-flops slapping noisily against the polished Tasmanian oak boards, not wanting to see him staring at her as if she had two heads. Or, worse, laughing at her.

'You think I'm here to model?'

Flicking the door switch to locked and flipping the

sign to 'closed', she swung back to face him, wishing she didn't need the money so desperately. Nothing was worth this awkward tenseness, even if he was the first guy to catch her attention in a long while.

'Well, aren't you?'

She flicked her gaze over him, starting at his almost-black hair worn a tad too long and curling at the collar of his navy polo shirt, over the snug way the shirt's cotton moulded his impressive chest and downwards, where faded denim encased long, lean legs.

No doubt about it. He was perfect model material, would be incredible to paint if those muscles hinted at beneath his clothes were as impressive as she thought. But there was something about him…something off-putting, as if he didn't belong here.

He paused, staring at her way too intently as if making up his mind about something.

Well, she would just have to make it up for him. She didn't have all night, and as much as she didn't want to do this, the sooner they made a start, the better.

'Look, I know this is probably awkward for both of us. Why don't I make us both a nice cup of honey and ginger tea? It'll help us relax and you can get changed behind that screen over there. I'll be back in a jiff.'

Ariel whirled around and headed into her studio, unable to fathom the stunned look in Cooper's blue eyes. She expected to hear his footsteps following her and when he didn't move, it suddenly hit her.

His confusion, his reticence: this had to be his first time doing this.

And she thought she was nervous!

Pausing in the doorway, she turned back to him, hoping to allay some of his discomfort.

'Cooper, if it makes you feel any better, you can keep your underwear on for this sitting,' she said, sending him her best smile, much cheerier now that she knew someone else in the room felt a lot more embarrassed about this whole fiasco than she did.

Cooper didn't move.

He couldn't.

He tried but both feet seemed firmly rooted to the spot as he watched the gypsy float through a curtain of shimmering purple glass beads after sending him the kind of bewitching smile that could make a guy seriously rethink his career.

After all, look at the way his mind was working at the moment. He'd gone from Melbourne's number one property developer to artist's model—nude model!—in less than a flash of pearly whites set against a luscious rosebud mouth.

He must be losing it.

All those extra hours at Vance Corporation trying to make a name for himself must've fried his brain.

This was obviously a silly case of mistaken identity and, the sooner he cleared it up, stated his business, secured what he'd come here for and headed back to the office, the sooner he could launch his own dreams.

'Cooper? Tea's ready. Come and get it.'

Squaring his shoulders, he pushed through the ridiculous dangling beads in the doorway, getting caught up in the process.

'Here you go.'

After disentangling himself, he finally looked up and stepped into Aladdin's cave.

At least, that was what it sure felt like to him: in each corner of the large room, swatches of gossamer-thin gold fabric hung from hooks on the ceiling and fell to the floor in cascading waves. Two ruby sofas sat at opposing ends of the room, covered in royal blue and purple cushions. There were unlit candles of all sizes, shapes and colours covering every available surface, both floor and glass-topped tables alike, while oil paintings of every description covered the walls.

The overall effect was bright, stunning and welcoming. Though that might have more to do with the gorgeous woman standing in the middle of the eclectic room with a strangely vulnerable smile flickering around her lush mouth.

'Drink some of this. It'll make you feel better.'

He took the chipped pottery cup, mentally searching for the right words. Maybe he should take a leaf out of her book and opt for brutal honesty? Something

to the effect that he was the 'slime ball property developer buying out the street'?

Yeah, that would go down a treat.

Taking a tentative sip of the pungent brew—a
brave move, considering he was a five espressos a
day kind of guy and hated the herbal stuff—he tried
not to stare at the woman standing between him and
his own corporation.

'Good?'

'Mmm,' he said, surprised he didn't have to lie as the
warm honey and spicy ginger slid across his tongue,
giving his taste buds a pleasant jolt in the process.

'Drink up, then we can get started.'

He tried not to stare, he really did, but there was
something about Ariel Wallace that drew his gaze like
a connoisseur to a masterpiece.

She wasn't a beauty in the classic sense of the
word, what with the crazy flowery bandanna
covering her blonde curls, the heart-shaped face
devoid of make-up, the pert nose and wary green
eyes that looked as if she'd seen more than her fair
share of trouble. As for her body, what little he could
see of it beneath a voluminous ruffled skirt that
matched her bandanna and loose white cotton top
that hid more than it revealed, he couldn't pass
judgement.

Okay, he couldn't see a lot of Ariel beyond her un-
usually striking face and bizarre dress sense, but,

somehow, the exotic combination and her unique style had captured his attention. Go figure. He found it particularly strange when he usually admired elegantly dressed women, the bulk of his female acquaintances preferring black and expensive jewellery.

'Right. If you pop behind the screen and get ready, I'll get set up over there.'

Her brisk, no-nonsense tone had him hiding a smile behind his mug. She could be instructing him to take out the garbage rather than get naked.

Time to set the record straight.

'Miss Wallace, I don't think this is going to work. In fact, there's been a mistake—'

'No!'

She crossed the room in two seconds flat, standing toe to toe with him before he could blink. 'There's no mistake. I haven't got time to find another model. I need this painting done ASAP and that means you're staying, nerves or not. Got it?'

If she'd jabbed him in the chest, he wouldn't have been surprised.

'And call me Ariel.'

She stared at him, so close he could see the tiny gold flecks flickering in the green depths of her striking eyes, issuing a challenge he had no intention of taking up.

'I'm not nervous.'

Though with this crazy woman looking ready to

deck him if he refused to get his gear off, maybe he should be.

'It's just that I'm not who you think I am.'

She quirked an eyebrow, a sassy elevation that drew his attention to her eyes again, their unusual crystal-clear green distracting him from the task at hand: set the record straight, seal this deal and get away from the office, his father and the memories.

'Look, Cooper, I don't care who you are. You could be the Crown Prince of Transylvania for all I care. Right now, I need you sitting on that stool, without any clothes on, staring out that window and holding the pose till I say move. Okay?'

'This is insane,' he muttered, admiring her sass and wondering if she'd deck him when he told her the truth.

She was close enough to do it. Way too close. Her intoxicating scent, the faintest hint of flowers and oranges, had to be playing havoc with his brain because for one, tiny, infinitesimal second, he almost considered doing what she said.

'No, you're insane if you think you're leaving here tonight before I get your form sketched. Now, shelve the shy act and let's get to it.'

She cast him one last challenging look before strutting to an easel about five feet away, busying herself with charcoals and paper to give him time to disrobe.

He must be mad.

Nuts, crazy, totally loco.

But then, considering how desperate he was to obtain this gallery, the last bit of prime real estate in Brunswick Street and his ticket out of Vance Corporation, maybe taking off his clothes for the crazy lady wouldn't be so bad.

'You ready yet?' she said without turning around.

'Almost.'

With a wry grin, Cooper headed for the ornate Japanese screen, pulling his T-shirt off along the way.

As a method to inveigle his way into a client's confidence, he'd never imagined getting naked.

Then again, this wasn't his fault. He'd tried to tell her the truth and she wouldn't listen. Ariel Wallace wanted a model and it looked as if he was it.

He just hoped she wouldn't spear him with the nearest paintbrush when she discovered he was here to pull the easel out from under her.

CHAPTER TWO

'DON'T move!'

Ariel picked up her third charcoal nub, tilted her head to get a better view of Cooper's impressive pecs and let her fingers fly across the paper, hoping to capture some of her model's essence before her aching hand gave out completely.

Easier said than done considering she'd never seen a guy's body like this before: all hard lines, delineated muscles and large expanses of smooth, tanned skin.

Wow.

'You've been sketching for an hour and I'm cramping. I've got to stretch my legs.'

'Oh, no, you don't.'

She fixed him with a glare, determined to get as much from this first sitting as possible. The less she saw of Cooper's toned body, the better. The thought of having to sit through more than a few evenings of seeing his muscles in all their glory made her break out in a cold sweat.

She really needed to get out more.

'You're a hard woman,' he muttered, shifting slightly to the left as light fell across his right shoulder, creating intriguing shadows with his upper torso.

Magnificent.

If Sofia Montessori, Melbourne's society matriarch, wasn't happy with this commission, nothing would do.

'I'm a businesswoman. I guess being hard goes with the territory.'

She stared at his right clavicle, hoping she could capture the exact angle, not surprised she'd focussed all her attention on his upper body and virtually ignored his bottom half.

Even with boxer shorts—brief, black, poured-on boxer shorts—and his leg bent, heat flooded her cheeks at the thought of sketching Cooper in his entirety. Having such an impressive model had startled her enough for one night and she couldn't quite face drawing the whole 'life' bit in one setting.

'So you own this place?'

Happy to answer his question—anything to deflect her wandering attention away from those skimpy boxers—she said, 'Technically, yes. My aunt opened this gallery years ago and she left it to me when she died. But what with the recent fire in the storeroom, the sky-rocketing insurance premiums and the increasing overheads, it's getting tougher to keep the place open.'

Not that she'd contemplate closing for one second. She owed Barb, her surrogate aunt, more than she could hope to repay.

'Sorry to hear about your aunt.'

Concern flickered across his face and he glanced away, not quite able to meet her eye as a ripple of unease slid down her spine.

Cooper looked almost…guilty? Couldn't be. What did some guy who didn't know her have to be guilty about? Must be her exhausted mind playing tricks on her. That, and the shock of his gorgeous bod sending her wow-factor off the scale.

'Thanks. Barb was amazing. Just ask anyone in the street.'

'How's that?'

'She fostered local talent and more. Barb rarely made a profit, donating huge chunks of money to charities and doing a lot with the street kids in the area.'

Such as taking in a runaway eight-year-old and giving her a home, something Ariel had never had before. 'She was a Brunswick Street icon.'

'Sounds like quite a lady.'

Touched by the admiration she heard in Cooper's voice, Ariel continued babbling about a subject close to her heart. 'That's why this particular portrait is so important to me. I need the cash to keep the gallery going and I need it yesterday. So if I seemed a bit pushy earlier on, I'm sorry.'

'Chalk it up to the temperamental artist, huh?'

'You got it.'

Ariel lifted her gaze from Cooper's shoulder to his face, hearing the gentle teasing in his voice and liking it way too much.

She didn't date much; she didn't socialise a lot. Keeping the gallery open and viable took up all her time and she liked it that way. Work she could rely on, people rarely.

Then what was it about this guy that had her wishing for something more? Wishing for an easy-going companion at the end of a hard day to listen to her rambling, to send her an encouraging smile when she needed it, to tease her?

'We're done,' she said all-too-briskly, snapping shut her box of charcoals and running a weary hand over her eyes, more to block out the sight of Cooper's body than anything else.

Now that she'd stopped working, seeing him almost naked took on an intimate connotation. The last thing she wanted or needed was to associate the words 'naked' and 'intimate' with him.

After all, she had at least another four sittings till the painting was complete.

'Great.'

He slid off the stool and she quickly averted her gaze, not wanting to see any more than she had to.

'So is it finished?'

'What?'

She sank back onto her ergonomic seat, blowing on the annoying curl that consistently fell across her eyes no matter how much she moussed, gelled or waxed it, relieved he'd popped behind the screen in record time.

'The painting. I take it I'm all done here?'

His voice drifted over the screen and she closed her eyes to savour the rich timber.

Great. Apart from needing to get out more, maybe she should air the studio a bit better. The paint and turpentine fumes were definitely affecting her.

'You really haven't done this before, have you?'

'Uh…no.'

He emerged from behind the screen and his presence struck her anew, his appeal not diminished in the slightest by clothes. Especially now she knew exactly what lay beneath.

'Well, let me clue you in. You sit, I sketch, draw, paint, whatever it takes to get this baby done. Tonight, I sketched your basic form but there's a lot more to be done.'

Like sketch his *whole* form. But she wouldn't think about that right now.

'I don't think—'

'You're not paid to think, you're paid to sit. So, how does tomorrow evening suit you?'

By the pained expression on his handsome face, it looked as if he equated having a wisdom tooth pulled without anaesthetic to posing for her again and she rushed on, not giving him an opportunity to refuse.

'No problems? Good. See you here at seven. You know the way out.'

Ariel bolted up the stairs to her apartment, waiting for the front door to shut before sidling down again.

After the inane chatter and light banter she'd exchanged with Cooper, the gallery's silence seemed almost oppressive.

Sighing, she flicked off the light switches, secured the front door and headed for the stairs.

However, the lure of seeing what she'd achieved pulled her towards her easel. Usually, she preferred to leave her work overnight and appraise it with a fresh eye in the morning, but not this time.

Maybe it was the unusual subject she'd worked with, maybe it was professional curiosity, but, whatever drew her to the myriad sketches she'd done of Cooper, the minute she laid eyes on what she'd drawn she wished she hadn't looked.

Though usually modest about her work, she'd captured the curve of his jaw, his high cheekbones, the breadth of his chest and his strong arms perfectly.

She inhaled sharply, half expecting the sketch to

come to life and step off the paper and into her empty life.

It wasn't so much the thought of a guy like Cooper entering her life that scared her as much as the thought she might like it.

'How did things go with the Wallace woman? Get anywhere?'

Cooper nodded and handed his father a strong black, sugarless coffee just the way Eric Vance liked it. 'We met. I'm making inroads.'

Cooper hid a cynical grin behind his coffee mug, still not quite believing what had happened last night.

'What's that supposed to mean? Is she ready to sell? Because that's all I'm interested in, the bottom line here. That woman's been the bane of my existence for the last twelve months and if you're not up to the job, I'll find someone who is.'

His father glowered for extra effect, drank the scalding coffee in one go, yanked his leather chair out from behind his desk and plopped into it, his scowl deepening by the second.

'Rather than scare her off by barging in there, I'm taking a softer approach.' Unlike you, Cooper thought, but wisely kept that gem to himself.

Thankfully, he was nothing like his dad in the business arena, which was precisely why he had to get out of the company, the sooner the better.

'Waste of time,' Eric snapped, grabbing the nearest object, which happened to be a gold pen, and tapping it relentlessly against the edge of his blackwood desk. 'Damn woman is stringing us along, hoping to get more cash out of us.'

Cooper stiffened. Though he hardly knew Ariel, she was nothing like the mercenary vulture his dad had made her out to be. From the top of her mussed curls to the bottom of her pale blue painted toenails, she'd appeared genuine, an artiste doing it tough but with a pretty clear goal: keep her gallery open in memory of its original owner, a family member.

Honourable enough, but then where did that leave him?

He couldn't weaken over this, no matter how much he'd admired Ariel and her convictions.

He had dreams of his own to build, starting with obtaining the very property she was trying to save.

'I'm handling it,' Cooper said, avoiding his father's assessing stare by striding to the huge glass windows overlooking Flinders Street Station and the Art Centre Spire behind it.

He loved Melbourne, really loved the hip, cosmopolitan feel of the city, the multicultural restaurants, the architecture. He'd acquired and developed many buildings since completing his MBA and each completed deal had brought him immense satisfaction.

Then why the slight niggle that obtaining the last prime bit of real estate in trendy Brunswick Street, Fitzroy, wouldn't be the be-all and end-all he'd first thought?

His father's sinister chuckle didn't reassure him. 'You're handling it, huh? Well, take as long as you like. I'm not the one who proposed some stupid deal in the first place.'

Cooper slowly clenched and unclenched his fists, hating how his father baited him on a daily basis, hating how it had come to this.

'We've talked about this. It's way past time I branched out on my own.'

'Fool idea! We can be a team here, and when I retire this whole company is yours.'

With Eric being a fit fifty-five, retirement was a long way off. Besides, Cooper was through working with dear old Dad.

'It's time I left and we both know it.'

Eric's eyes narrowed to cold, hard slits, his mutinous expression reminiscent of every time Cooper had disagreed with him since he'd turned ten. 'You signed a two-year contract when you first started. You've been here less than a year. I could make things tough for you.'

Cooper controlled his voice, hating the urge to shout. They'd had this same conversation every day for the last week, ever since his dad had failed to buy the gallery for the umpteenth time and Cooper had seized on the idea as his way out.

'Cut the empty threats. I seal the Brunswick deal, I'm out of my contract and on my own. You agreed, remember?'

'Of course I remember. You seem to think I'm stupid. Now, I've had enough of your *brilliant* ideas. Sit down and bring me up to speed with the Docklands deal.'

Shaking his head, Cooper turned away from the window and took a seat opposite his dad, who glared at him with angry blue eyes and a perpetual frown.

They'd been so close once: him and Dad. Laurel and Hardy, bouncing jokes off each other, getting a kick out of the same stuff: football, old western films, sailing. The Vance guys on top of their game.

His dad used to laugh a lot then, thriving on the thrill of an acquisition, sharing his success with him, enjoying a quiet celebratory beer together after work. Fishing holidays, blokes' weekends-away.

Then Cooper had joined the firm and started to make his own success in the business arena and his dad had changed. For the worse.

'The Docklands deal is almost completed. Contracts are in the legal department as we speak. So once I've got Ariel Wallace's go ahead and I wrap up the Brunswick deal, that's it. I'm done.'

For a second, something close to anguish flashed

in his father's eyes. Before Cooper could fathom it, Eric blinked and his latent anger quickly replaced any other expression Cooper might've imagined.

'You'll never make it on your own.'

Cooper stood abruptly, keeping a tight leash on any number of fiery retorts and headed for the door and the sanctity of his own office.

'We'll see, Dad. We'll see,' he said, more determined than ever to get the deal done with Ariel Wallace.

CHAPTER THREE

'*CIAO, bella*. How's my favourite artist today?'

Sofia Montessori breezed into Colour by Dreams, her plump figure swathed in head to toe crimson, making her look like a ripe tomato. Ariel loved colour and Sofia's vibrant wardrobe never failed to brighten her day.

'I'm fine. How's life in the fast lane?'

'I can't complain. You know how it is. Places to go, people to meet, men to impress.'

'Actually, I don't know,' Ariel said, bracing for the onslaught of Sofia's suffocating hugs and smacking kisses on both cheeks, smiling when she saw the usual matchmaking gleam in Sofia's dark eyes. 'And I like it that way!'

Sofia threw her hands up in the air and looked towards the heavens. '*Santa Maria!* You are young, you are beautiful. You should be partying, meeting men your own age, dancing the night away—'

'I'd rather paint the night away.' Ariel quickly cut in, knowing that once Sofia got on a roll, she'd be here all day. 'Speaking of which, I started on your commission last night. Want to take a look?'

'*Sí.* I want to see this life portrait that my sister is so keen on hanging in her house. Can you imagine, a naked man in the dining room? Ha! Enough to put me off my ravioli. But it's Maria's fortieth birthday and it's all she's talked about since she visited the National Art Gallery and what my baby sister wants she shall get.'

Sofia rolled her eyes and puffed out her cheeks in disgust and Ariel chuckled at her theatrics, knowing full well the rich Italian woman had a reputation as a connoisseur of younger men. Sofia was excited about this portrait and would probably order one for herself once she got a good look at Ariel's subject.

'I've only done a few preliminary sketches but you'll get the general idea,' Ariel said, pushing through the bead curtain leading to her studio and holding it up for Sofia to pass through, slightly nervous about the woman's reaction.

She rarely showed anyone her work before the final canvas but this was different. Sofia was paying her a small fortune and she didn't want anything to go wrong. She desperately needed the money. Like yesterday.

'They're over here.'

Ariel needn't have pointed. She knew the exact moment Sofia laid eyes on the sketches of Cooper.

'*Mamma mia!* Who is that?'

'That is the gift you're giving Maria.'

Ariel's casual wave of her hand didn't fool Sofia for a second.

'*Bella,* I know what *that* is. I want to know *who* that is.'

Ariel laughed at the predatory gleam in Sofia's eyes, which were round as pasta bowls.

'The model's name is Cooper. That's all I know.'

Actually, that was a lie.

She knew a heck of a lot more than that. Such as the way his blue eyes hid some sort of secret, as if he were ashamed of modelling.

And the way his muscles rippled when he moved.

And the way his deep voice had made her feel: like a woman who didn't have responsibilities, like a woman who could forget everything for the glimpse of his smile.

Sheesh! She really needed to start wearing a face mask to block the studio fumes from frying her brain.

'*Bellissimo!* This Cooper is gorgeous, no?'

'No. Yes. Oh, you know what I mean,' Ariel said, turning away from her sketches before her cheeks flushed crimson like Sofia's.

She didn't like admitting Cooper was gorgeous

even if it was a fact. To her, the guy was work. A means to an end.

She just hoped she remembered it tonight when she had to sketch his bottom half.

'Is there more?'

Sofia's plucked eyebrows wiggled suggestively and Ariel knew exactly how much 'more' the older woman wanted to see.

'No, I haven't got to that part yet.'

And despite her earlier intentions not to blush, heat surged into her cheeks.

Sofia's ear-splitting grin didn't help. 'Ah…but I'm sure you're looking forward to it. If that part is as impressive as the rest, we're all in for a treat, no?'

'No!'

Sofia cackled and slipped an arm around her shoulders, the heady combination of expensive floral perfume and hairspray tickling Ariel's nose.

'You are a sweet girl, *bambina*. Why won't you accept money from me rather than paint men's bits?'

'We've been through this,' Ariel said, slipping from Sofia's claustrophobic embrace and crossing to an open window. 'You're a wonderful, kind woman but I can't accept your charity. I need to do this on my own.'

Sofia clucked and shook her head, sending mushrooms of hair product into the air while her bouffant didn't move a millimetre. 'Barb wouldn't have wanted you running yourself into the ground to keep the gallery open. She loved you too much.'

'And that's exactly why I have to continue her work. I've got Chelsea Lynch's first show coming up next week and Chelsea's exactly the type of local talent Barb would've busted a gut for. Chelsea's had a tough life, brought up on the streets around here, making good, finally doing something with her life. I need to be there for her, for all of them.'

Just as Aunt Barb had been there for her.

What the kind-hearted woman had ever seen in a rebellious eight-year-old street urchin Ariel would never know. From the first minute Barb had found her sleeping out the back of the gallery, wrapped in a paint-splattered canvas, Ariel had known nothing but patience and understanding and love.

She'd been one of the lucky ones and now it was her turn to give something back.

'You are a saint,' Sofia said, kissing her fingertips and blowing the kiss towards her.

'At the price I'm charging you for this commission, you think?'

Ariel's gaze drifted towards the sketches of Cooper, wondering if her luck had finally changed when he'd walked in the door last night.

For her, art was about beauty, and though life portraits came in many shapes and forms, she knew that working with a perfect subject like Cooper would do a lot more for her inspiration than painting some recalcitrant, skinny guy.

And who knew? With a portrait of a great looking subject like Cooper hanging in the house of one of Melbourne's richest women, she might get inundated with commissions, meaning she could teach more classes, support more shows and do more for the local charities.

She'd make sure this was her best work, bits or not, if it killed her.

'Your work is beautiful, *bambina*. You don't charge nearly enough. Uh-uh!' Sofia held up a hand when Ariel opened her mouth to refute this. 'I will not hear another word. You do this painting for me, we talk some more then. Now, I must go. Antonio is taking me to a divine new trattoria in Lygon Street.'

'And who's Antonio?'

'A very sweet boy.' Sofia batted her long, mascara'd eyelashes and Ariel laughed, knowing Antonio would be young, handsome and pliable. '*Ciao, bella.* You have fun with your model, no?'

'No,' Ariel muttered, returning Sofia's continental kiss-on-each-cheek and hoping she could complete this portrait in record time.

Having fun with the model was the furthest thing from her mind.

At least, it should be.

* * *

Cooper stood outside the gallery, admiring the wide windows, cream rendered walls and green fretwork. He'd been past this site a thousand times over the last few months—even when his dad had been handling the acquisition through the local council. Each time, he'd been more intent on assessing the gallery's street position and how the space could be developed than aesthetics.

Colour by Dreams.

A nice name.

A name of hope and imagination and creativity.

Shame he had to tear it all down.

He'd never had qualms about business before, no point starting now, even if the gallery's owner had piqued his interest.

Pushing through the front door, he dodged the ridiculous wind chimes signalling his entry and hoped Ariel was in a receptive mood.

He had to tell her the truth before this farce went any further. Lying didn't sit well with him and he'd always been scrupulously honest in past deals.

Though where had that got him? Bound to his dad with the same ironclad contract all Vance employees signed, trying to be the best he could and now determined to get out.

'Hi, you're right on time.'

Ariel strolled into the gallery from the back, having little trouble with the silly beads dividing the rooms and he faltered, staggered by the power of her smile and the glint in her sparkling eyes.

Tonight, she wore a white ruffled shirt, a plum crushed velvet vest, black pleated shorts and pink wedges that made her legs look impossibly long. A crazy ensemble, which would've looked ridiculous on any other woman but on Ariel it looked like haute couture. She wore her clothes with aplomb and he smiled, thinking an eye patch wouldn't have looked out of place with her rakish pirate get-up.

'Something funny?'

'No, just admiring your outfit.'

To his amazement, she blushed, the hint of pink accentuating the green of her eyes and the rich gold of her hair, which she wore in a high pony-tail.

With her straightforward manner and sassy mouth, he hadn't thought she'd be prone to blushing.

'You like my taste in clothes? I find that hard to believe. Anyway, enough of the chit-chat. Let's get started.'

Hell. This was going to be harder than he'd thought.

He cleared his throat. 'Actually, that's what I want to talk to you about.'

'Oh, brother!' She rolled her eyes, plopped onto a stool behind the counter and rested her chin in her hands. 'Don't you think we moved past the whole virginal act last night?'

Cooper stared at her, torn between wanting to

laugh out loud and call her bluff. Every time he tried to tell her the truth, she either interrupted him or came at him with some smart-ass remark.

He'd give it one more shot.

If she wouldn't listen, he'd shelve his good intentions and use tonight as one last opportunity to get some inside information on the opposition before approaching her with his plans for the gallery.

And when the time came, he wouldn't take no for an answer, however cute the word sounded coming out of her sweet mouth.

'I think you should know more about me, listen to what I have to say—'

'Nope. Sorry. No can do.'

She jumped up from her stool, her ponytail bouncing like a jaunty flag amidships. 'Please don't take this the wrong way but I'm not interested in getting to know you. I'm not interested in you, period. You're here in a work capacity and that's it. You sit, I paint. End of story.'

She flounced past him, the same weird, intoxicating scent of flowers and oranges wafting over him, as enticing as the rest of her, and locked the front door.

End of story, huh?

Fine.

If Miss Bossy-Boots wouldn't give him a chance

to explain, he'd take what he could from tonight and try the professional approach in the morning.

'On the contrary, the story is just beginning,' he murmured, following her into the studio with an extra spring to his step.

The man was a menace.

The harder she tried to concentrate on drawing the more he'd smile. Or fidget. Or want to chat.

She could strangle him with her bare hands.

Though she didn't want to get that close considering he wasn't wearing any clothes—bar the requisite boxers, which she'd insisted on again.

Chicken…

'So tell me more about this painting. Where's it going to hang?'

She silently cursed as her charcoal slewed off the paper. He'd spoken just as she'd captured the curve of his hip—and butt, but she didn't want to dwell on that piece of anatomy just yet. Time enough to study it, next sitting. Or the one after that…

'This is a private commission, a gift for a friend's sister, so it will hang in her home.'

'This isn't the fabled friend-of-a-friend thing, is it, and it's actually for your private collection?'

Ariel gritted her teeth, wondering if the use of duct tape over a model's mouth would be frowned upon by any worker's union.

'Sorry to disappoint, but this sort of art doesn't do it for me.'

'Then what does?'

Darn it, she'd been the queen of quick comebacks all her life. She'd had to be, living on the streets. But this guy fired back with a skill to be envied.

'None of your business, Mr Shy-and-retiring-before-whipping-off-your-clothes-in-record-time.'

'Hey, that's not fair. You practically shoved me behind that screen. I was terrified you'd actually rip them off me if I didn't get a move on.'

His smile did crazy things to her insides where her tummy flip-flopped and somersaulted and reminded her she hadn't eaten dinner. She'd tried before Cooper arrived but the thought of seeing all that gorgeous expanse of bare, tanned skin again had taken care of her appetite well and truly.

'You wish,' she said, aiming for a frown but failing miserably when their gazes locked over her easel and something zinged between them, an unspoken link, a zap of invisible electricity that made her heart join her tummy in the gymnastic stakes.

'Don't you ever shut up?'

Ariel's question sounded short and sharp in the loaded silence and she ducked behind the easel, buying valuable time to gather her wits and get her breathing under control. Alongside her pounding heart, her lungs had joined in the party and deprived her of much-needed oxygen.

Must be more of those nasty fumes affecting her again…

'It's pretty boring sitting here. A little conversation breaks the monotony.'

He sounded reasonable enough and she sneaked a peek, wondering if he was being serious or teasing her again.

To her mortification, he caught her furtive glance and winked, exacerbating her embarrassment no end.

She'd strangle him.

Once she'd captured his exquisite body—on canvas, that was.

'Have you always been an artist?'

She picked up a charcoal nub, determined to ignore him, but his question seemed innocuous enough and his voice had lost its teasing lilt.

'I loved drawing as a kid. I graduated from a blackboard to chalk drawings on sidewalks. When other kids were playing hopscotch, I'd be sketching their faces. Later, I did a bachelor of arts to help on the teaching side of things but, basically, I worked alongside Barb here. We loved doing it…'

Her fingers stilled as she wondered what had possessed her to reveal so much to a guy she didn't know, a guy she didn't even particularly like all that much.

The cosy ambience of the studio at night seemed conducive to shared confidences but Cooper wasn't a friend and she'd be smarter remembering it.

'Anyway, that's it for now. I think I've done all I'm going to do tonight. Long day.'

She didn't look at him as she wiped her hands on a dusty rag, wishing he'd hurry up and get dressed so she could shove him out the door.

For a guy she hardly knew—and didn't want to know—Cooper had her in a spin, answering questions she'd usually ignore, deriving some comfort from confiding in another human being when she had so little social contact with anyone.

What a sad case.

'Ariel?'

'Yeah?'

She looked up, grateful he'd slipped into jeans and a white T-shirt quickly, obviously sensing her need to get rid of him without delay.

'Whatever happens, you should be proud of what you've done with this place.'

'Thanks,' she said, surprised by his serious expression and somewhat confused by what he'd said.

But she was too tired to think about it, let alone ask him to explain and she hurried him to the door, flicking the lock and all but wrenching it off its hinges in her haste to see the back of him.

As the door swung open and a chilly gust of

wind blew it out of her hands several things happened at once.

Chelsea Lynch, her protégée, rushed into the gallery in a flurry of turquoise denim, red pashmina, emerald scarf and floppy fuchsia beanie.

Cooper took a polite step back, nodded at Chelsea and turned to Ariel. 'I'll see you tomorrow. We really need to talk.'

Ariel flashed him a tight smile, thinking her talking days with the too good-looking model were over if she had to finish his portrait with her sanity intact.

Chelsea's head swung between the two of them, her eyes wide with shock, her mouth hanging open before pointing an accusing finger at Cooper and shouting, 'What's he doing here?'

'Cooper's a model.'

'Like hell he is.'

Chelsea unwound her scarf in furious swirls, not taking her flashing hazel eyes off Cooper for a second. 'He's the scumbag who's been buying up the street and I bet he has his sights set on this place next.'

Ariel's protest died on her lips as she saw Cooper's stricken, guilty expression one second before her hand reached out, landed squarely in the middle of his broad chest and shoved him out the door.

Hard.

CHAPTER FOUR

ARIEL tried to slam the door in Cooper's face but took a second too long. The lying cretin stuck one of his shoes in the doorway and, as tempted as she was to amputate it, she couldn't afford a lawsuit on top of everything else at the minute.

'Get out!'

Ariel jiggled the door, hoping he'd get the hint, what with the way she'd shoved him out the door and now threatened to wedge his foot with it.

'Let me explain—'

'Explain what?'

She planted her hands on her hips, fury surging through her body at being taken for a fool.

When she'd been living on the streets as a youngster, people had always thought she was stupid, equating a dowdy appearance with nil intelligence, and she'd hated it.

She'd shown everyone and then some.

Exactly how she was going to show Cooper whatever-his-name-was—after giving him a verbal flaying he'd never forget, that was.

'I tried to tell you the truth a few times but you always shot me down, talked over me or didn't want to know,' said Cooper.

Ariel rolled her eyes. 'Give me a break! Guys like you can talk with a mouth full of marbles for business and you reckon you couldn't get the message across because I wouldn't let you? What a load of rubbish. You kept your big trap shut because you wanted to sleaze your way into my good graces. Isn't that right?'

'That's telling him,' Chelsea murmured, and Ariel sent her a quelling look to keep out of it.

Though she was grateful to her star pupil for outing the rat, she could fight her own battles. Always had, always would.

'Can we talk in private?' Cooper's steady gaze locked on hers, urgent, compelling, willing her to listen.

Too bad for him, she'd listened to enough of his lies already.

She shook her head. 'I'm not interested in anything you have to say. Now, if you don't mind removing your big foot from my door and shoving it back into your mouth, I have work to do.'

'This isn't the end,' Cooper said, sending her a look that meant business as he stepped out of the doorway.

'That's what you think.'

Ariel slammed the door, grateful for the double re-inforced glass: it saved her from shattering the windows and afforded a fantastic view of the price-less look on Cooper's face.

If she didn't know any better, she'd say he looked ashamed.

But that couldn't be right. Guys like him didn't have a conscience and they never took no for an answer. They wheeled and dealed their way to the top regardless of the little people trampled in the process.

Well, she had news for him. This little person wouldn't let him near the place again, let alone buy it and ruin her plans for the future.

Cooper the marauding model could develop some other property, preferably in Timbuktu.

'Wow, that was awesome,' Chelsea said, slapping her on the back. 'You sure showed him who was boss.'

Suddenly fatigued, Ariel watched Cooper march up the street past the organic fruiterers, the vegan take-out and the Nepalese home-wares and turn the corner where he'd probably hidden some fancy sports car.

Lying louse.

Lying louse who had gotten under her skin in two short meetings.

And to make matters worse she had to work from memory to finish the portrait. The last thing she felt like doing was resurrecting memories of the louse's body and how great it would look on canvas.

'You okay?' Chelsea passed a hand in front of her eyes and Ariel focussed on the young girl.

'Yeah. How did you know who he was?'

'I've seen him around the Fitzroy area over the last few months. Mr Fancy-Schmancy works for a company that is responsible for ousting the Ngs from the corner grocer's, the Bortellis from their café and closing down the old Irish pub. All in the name of "development".' Chelsea held up her index fingers on both hands and made inverted comma signs. 'I hate guys like him. They've never done it tough. They don't know the first thing about the area or locals like me who live in it. They bulldoze their way in and rip lives apart. Tell me you won't let them get the gallery.'

Chelsea threw her arms wide and did a three-sixty. 'I love this place. All the local kids do. Barb made it more welcoming than any halfway house and you've continued the tradition. You can't let those blood-suckers take it.'

Ariel managed a weary smile, buoyed by Chelsea's enthusiasm but more afraid than she'd ever been. She'd known about the property developers buying up every last piece of prime Brunswick Street land, but to hear Chelsea verbalise it somehow made the threat all the more real.

'Don't worry. I have no intention of letting them anywhere near Colour by Dreams.'

Chelsea clapped her hands like an excited child.

'Good, because my first showing is here in a week and I want the world to see my brilliance.'

'And your modesty,' Ariel said, trying to banish from her mind the threatening image of Cooper's final glower before he'd marched away and what it could mean for the gallery. 'Now, how about some tea and you tell me why you dropped by?'

Chelsea led the way out the back, bouncing with vitality, her pashmina trailing in her wake like a bright flag while Ariel followed, knowing it would take more than herbal tea to dispel her anxiety at the moment.

'Oh, wow!'

The minute Chelsea laid eyes on the preliminary portrait sketches Ariel had done of Cooper, she stopped dead in front of the easel.

'I'll take that as a compliment to my artistic skills and not the subject in question,' Ariel said, busying herself making tea and hoping to God she had enough sketches for a final portrait.

Chelsea grinned, tearing her gaze from the sketches for a second. 'Don't get me wrong, I think you're the best artist this side of the Louvre, but wow-ee! That guy might be a slime-ball but he is one hot slime-ball.'

'I should've known he was too good to be true,' Ariel muttered, trying not to scald herself as she poured the boiling water into mugs, her hands shaking in anger at how Cooper had taken her in. 'Model, my butt.'

'Doesn't look like you got to that bit, worse luck.'

Chelsea winked as Ariel handed her a mug of steaming raspberry, the young woman's favourite. Ariel tentatively sipped at her peppermint brew, the steam heating her cheeks.

'Shouldn't be a problem. I can improvise.'

Sadly, Ariel knew her imagination wasn't *that* good.

'Whatever.'

Chelsea shrugged and took a seat on one of the ruby sofas, curling her long, legging-clad legs beneath her while she cradled her mug.

'Okay, Chelsea, what's up with you?'

Ariel didn't need any more problems right now. She had enough of her own to keep her busy into the next century.

'Do you really think I'm any good at all this art stuff?'

Chelsea's large hazel eyes radiated doubt and Ariel smiled, confident she could solve this easily.

Taking a seat next to the nineteen-year-old, she said, 'Do you trust my judgement?'

'Yeah.'

'And you know how tough it is to get a showing in Melbourne?'

The corners of Chelsea's mouth turned upwards. 'Yeah.'

'Plus you know how busy I am, right?'

Chelsea sat up straighter. 'Right.'

'Okay, you're a smart girl. Do you think I'd waste my time if I didn't think you're talented and inspired and are going to be the next big thing?'

'When you put it that way…' Chelsea plucked Ariel's mug out of her hand, deposited it next to her own on the floor and flung her arms around her. 'You're the best! Barb was so lucky to have someone like you take over for her.'

'I'm the lucky one,' Ariel murmured, blinking back sudden tears.

If only she could keep the likes of Cooper from taking away the only place she'd ever known as home, she'd be very lucky indeed.

'So where are we at with acquiring that gallery?'

Cooper refrained from glaring at his father, especially with a conference table full of developers, wishing his dad didn't keep pushing so hard. He'd said he'd handle it.

Yeah, like you handled it last night?

Silently cursing, he shuffled the papers in front of him and faced the curious looks of the men who'd invested millions into the project so far.

He'd give them what they wanted to hear before settling the deal one way or another.

'As you all know, Ariel Wallace isn't keen on selling. However, I've met with her the last two days and I'm optimistic she'll change her mind.'

She'd better. He needed to get out from this company and his dad's overbearing presence.

'What makes you think you'll succeed where I didn't?'

This time, Cooper couldn't stop his swift glare of condemnation at his dad. Sure, he knew Eric had taken professional jealousy to extremes, but did he have to air his feelings in this forum?

Quelling his anger, Cooper addressed the table at large. 'Eric, everyone here knows you're a top negotiator but I've established a rapport with Miss Wallace.'

Yeah, they'd grown real close if her shoving him out the door constituted camaraderie. 'I'm confident that, with a few more meetings, she'll come to the party.'

His farewell party, that was.

The day she signed on the dotted line was the day he would be free: free of his contract, free of Vance Corp, free of seeing the edge in his dad's eyes every time he walked into the room.

'Good.' Eric barely inclined his head in Cooper's direction before continuing. 'I've sealed the deal on several properties around the block from the gallery and we need that piece of land.'

Eric stabbed at a remote and a screen lit up with a PowerPoint presentation behind him. 'These are the preliminary plans, but once we secure the gallery we can demolish it along with the old houses behind it and create a six-storey apartment block. With

property prices at an all-time high in suburbs surrounding the Central Business District, that's a
killing for us.'

Eric stared at Cooper with contempt, as if saying,
And you want to leave all this behind? You think you
can match me? Beat me at my own game?

'Any questions?'

Cooper met his father's gaze directly.

He settled for keeping the peace just as he had
every day for the last ten months since he'd graduated and signed on the dotted line with his father's
company. He'd been full of ideals, full of enthusiasm
and his father's attitude had whittled it away to this:
a ridiculous trade so he could back out of his legally
binding contract.

'The plans look good. I'm just as eager to get this
deal done as all of you so perhaps we can reconvene
next week?'

That should give him enough time to talk sense
into the bohemian harridan who'd tossed him out
like yesterday's garbage. He'd make sure of it.

'Fine. Meeting adjourned.' Eric headed straight
for the built-in bar in the corner of the conference
room where Cooper knew he'd swap shop talk with
his cronies over a bourbon or two.

Not for him.

He had more important things to do with his time,
such as getting Ariel to listen to his pitch.

If he were a betting man, he'd place a hundred on the nose that she wouldn't open her door to him again, let alone hear what he had to say.

Well, he planned to change all that.

Starting now.

CHAPTER FIVE

'YOU despicable low-life!'

Ariel slashed at the canvas with her brush, streaking across the blank expanse while glaring at the sketch of Cooper propped next to it.

She'd been trying to capture his likeness on canvas all morning and had tense shoulders, a tight neck and three ruined canvases—all recycled, thank goodness—for her trouble.

Her muse had deserted her.

Unfortunately, she had a sneaking suspicion her muse had hitched a ride on the despicable low-life's broad shoulders and cruised straight out the door.

She'd tried everything: burning her lime and tangerine candles for concentration, dabbing neroli—her favourite scent—on her pulse points for inspiration and to calm her mind, wearing her lucky holly garland on her head and a five-minute meditation which usually worked wonders if her imagination clogged.

The result?

Nothing.

And to make matters worse, Sofia had rung, gushing about some fancy charity do at her sister's place where everyone who was anyone would see the portrait and inundate her with work—she wished—and imploring her to finish it a week early.

Which gave her exactly six days to get the portrait finished.

Would've been a cinch if she'd had a normal model and not some delusional businessman happy to whip off his clothes to get what he wanted, the lunatic.

Staring at the sketches of Cooper, she could've happily drawn devil's horns and pointy fangs all over his smug face, but they were all she had…and that wasn't much.

Sighing, she closed her eyes, trying to conjure up the memory of his form, hoping to translate it to canvas. Deep blue eyes, too long dark hair, strong jaw, broad chest, great pecs, tapered waist, long legs…magnificent…

The wind chimes over the front door tinkled and her eyes flew open. To her annoyance, a stupid little smile had snuck up on her and she wiped it, along with her too real—and too hot—images of Cooper's amazing body out of her mind.

'Can I help you…?' The rest of her words trailed into insignificance as the object of her vivid imagination a second earlier strutted into the gallery, the epitome of the slick businessman she now knew him to be: fancy suit, white shirt, duck-egg blue tie that matched his striking eyes. He looked amazing, but she preferred him in jeans and T-shirt.

Are you insane?

That was right, she didn't prefer him at all. Or was that in nothing at all?

'Go away,' she said, planting both hands on the counter and glaring at him with as much disdain as she could muster.

'No can do.'

He stopped exactly opposite and Ariel suddenly wished the too-thin glass-topped counter were wider.

He was too close, too masculine, too everything.

'I have a proposal for you.'

'After two nights? Gee, you must be really desperate to get this place but, sorry, I wouldn't marry you if you gargled a litre of turpentine and painted the street red.'

He gave her an arrogant smile that screamed 'bring it on'.

'You know I'm not here with a marriage proposal. You strike me as a smart woman and in the interests of your business I thought you should hear me out.'

'You thought wrong,' she blurted, not ready to hear anything he had to say.

She was too angry with him: angry he'd lied,

angry he'd ruined a project so vital to the viability of the gallery, but most of all, angry with herself for the slight, inane leap of joy she'd experienced when she'd walked through the beaded curtain and seen he'd come back.

He ignored her petulant outburst. 'This will only take five minutes of your time. Believe me, it's important.'

She wouldn't believe him if he were the last man on earth. Still, something about his steady gaze and intense expression had her shrugging her shoulders and leading him out the back.

'Five minutes,' she said, propping herself on her ergonomic stool, not caring if he stood or sat. He wouldn't be around that long if she had anything to do with it.

'What's that on your head?'

Hmm...not exactly what Cooper had in mind as a stunning opening to his pitch, but he couldn't talk sense to a woman wearing a Christmas wreath on her head, even if she wore it with the aplomb of a queen sporting a priceless tiara.

Ariel frowned and patted her head, the frown disappearing when she touched the weird crown.

'This is my lucky garland. I often paint in it.'

'It looks like a Christmas tree gone wrong.'

Rather than taking it off her head in embarrassment as he expected, she adjusted the angle till it sat like a crazy halo perched at odds with her curls.

'I made it years ago during my first Christmas with Aunt Barb.'

Cooper wished he hadn't seen the vulnerability behind her eyes.

He was here on business. To present a clear plan to benefit them both. He didn't want to hear about this woman Barb whom Ariel held in such high esteem or feel the slightest twinge of guilt that in following his own dreams he'd probably have to tear hers down.

She was young. She'd get over it. Take the money, start a new gallery somewhere else.

'Your five minutes started about thirty seconds ago so whatever you have to say, make it snappy.' Ariel's expression had hardened, her green eyes flinty, her mouth compressed in a thin line.

Squaring his shoulders, confident a softer approach would work rather than railroading her as he usually did the rest of his clients, Cooper met her cool gaze head on. 'Firstly, I'd like to apologise for not telling you the truth earlier. You were right, I had plenty of opportunity and could've let you in on my identity sooner.'

'Why didn't you?'

'Honestly? You intrigued me. I had my spiel all worked out when I first walked in here, but before I knew what was happening you'd bustled me out the back and told me to take off my clothes. Guess the Neanderthal male in me took over and I kind of liked it. The whole situation was extraordinary and once we started talking, I couldn't leave.'

He opted for honesty, hoping the truth would convince her he was on the up and up now. By her unchanging expression, it didn't look as if it had worked.

'More like you didn't want to leave because you thought you could weasel inside info out of me before homing in for the kill.'

'That too. Pretty despicable but I was going to tell you the truth even if that girl hadn't outed me.'

She rolled her eyes before tapping her watch. 'Three minutes left.'

'Okay, my idea is this. I have a business proposal to present to you. It will probably take a few hours all up to do it justice and I was hoping you'd give me the time.'

'No.'

Short and sharp, without the slightest hint of thawing towards him in sight, and he pushed on, hoping she understood how things worked in the business world and wouldn't be offended by his next offer.

'I'll pay you for your time.'

'What?'

If her eyebrows shot any higher, they'd tangle in the wreath still perched on her wayward curls.

'In the world I come from, everyone charges by the hour, from lawyers to architects. I see your time as being no different and I'm willing to compensate you for the few hours it takes to deliver my pitch.'

'You're willing to compensate me…how *generous*.'

By her strange, high-pitched fake voice and the clenched hands twisting the cuffs of her crushed velvet shorts, he knew she didn't think his offer was that generous.

'The point I'm trying to make is that this place is your business, your time is just as valuable as everyone else's and I want to recognise that.'

Better, much better, and by the softening of her ramrod-straight posture, she thought so too.

'I don't want your money.'

'You'll still listen to my pitch?'

He held his breath, wishing this bohemian beauty didn't hold his future in the palm of her paint-stained hand.

She had to listen to his pitch and she had to go for it.

He couldn't contemplate any other outcome.

Starting out on his own after a lengthy legal battle to escape the contract would drive an irreversible wedge between him and his father.

Suddenly, Ariel's face cleared. Her brow smoothed, her lips tilted up at the corners and her green eyes sparkled with excitement.

Oh-oh. This couldn't be good.

He'd seen that same look when she'd all but pushed him into her studio the first night and told him to get his gear off.

'I won't accept your money but how about we do a fair trade for time?'

'Sounds feasible,' he said, not liking the smug expression spreading across her beautiful, unmade-up face.

He liked the tense, uncertain Ariel a lot more than her cheeky counterpart who made him want to drop his business ideals at the door and get creative with her in a variety of imaginative ways.

'What did you have in mind?'

To his surprise, Ariel slid off her stool and crossed the space between them, placing a finger under his chin and tilting his head this way and that.

'Yes, yes, yes!'

She dropped her hand and stepped back, continuing to study him like a prized masterpiece.

'This is perfect!'

She clapped her hands and smiled at him, the type of mega watt smile that could melt a guy's hardened heart if he wasn't careful. 'You pose for me till I finish the portrait and I'll listen to your boring proposal. How's that for fair trade? A few hours' modelling for a few hours of hearing you run off at the mouth?'

Cooper stared at her, unwillingly admiring her glowing eyes, her wide, confident smile. He bit back his first gut response of 'no way' knowing that a smart businessman would take every opportunity that came his way and turn it into something big.

In this case, it might be the only chance he got.

She'd let him in the door, she'd heard him out and she'd agreed to listen to his plans for this place.

Sitting in the near-buff, albeit on a damn hard stool, for a few hours would be nothing if he pulled this off.

'You've got a deal.'

He held out his hand, managing a genuine smile when she placed her tiny hand in his despite the jolt physical contact brought.

By the slight widening of her eyes, she felt it too but pulled away before he could analyse it further.

Not that he wanted to. She wasn't his type.

He preferred cool, aloof women who were happy with the occasional date and had no expectations.

A warm, vibrant, creative woman like Ariel would be nothing but trouble for a level-headed guy like him and he'd make sure he concentrated on business around her.

He didn't have room in his life for anything else.

'Herbal tea is better for you,' Ariel said, trying to subdue her triumphant grin and failing as she bustled about the tiny kitchen off her studio.

Twisting Cooper's proposal to suit her own ends had come to her in a flash of brilliance and the way she saw it, she had it made. She'd get to finish the portrait and collect the much needed money for it and, in exchange, she'd spend a few boring hours listen to him prattle on about his plans for her gallery, plans that would never see the light of day if she had anything to do with it.

Easy.

'I'll stick with coffee, thanks.'

'Suit yourself,' she said, handing him the steaming mug of decaf he'd requested, knowing he'd find it lacking. He looked like a double espresso hold-the-milk-and-sugar type of guy to her. 'Speaking of which, you're looking a lot more uptight in that get-up than the other night. What were you trying to do then—con the crazy artist in your slumming clothes?'

His mouth twitched. 'I happen to live in jeans and T-shirts outside the office.'

'And?'

'And I thought you wouldn't be as intimidated if I turned up dressed casual.'

Ariel smiled. The guy was sneaky. And sexy, way too sexy.

'Wow, you better be careful, Mr Big-Shot. That's the second time in half an hour you've sounded honest. Didn't think your type had it in you.'

'If you're trying to bait me, forget it. I've got a thick skin. Comes with taking off my clothes for twisted women posing as artists.'

Okay, so the guy had a sense of humour. Lucky for him. He'd need it when she knocked his business proposal for the gallery on its head.

'The human body is a work of art. I can't help it if your head's filled with taking over buildings and ruining people's lives rather than appreciating the finer things in life in the way I do.'

She kept her tone light, enjoying trading banter with someone who could match her, even though her quip had a barb of truth to it.

She would never understand how he could barge into people's lives and turn them upside down with scant regard for the little people. Sure, he probably justified his actions with money but then that was all a successful guy like him understood.

'Have you ever considered I improve people's lives rather than ruin them?'

He took a sip of coffee and grimaced, hiding his distaste behind a discreet cough.

'Whatever lets you sleep at night.'

She drained her cup of peppermint tea and peered into the bottom, a silly old habit considering she'd switched to bags and didn't use loose leaves any more. Too bad—she could use a bit of forecasting right about now: such as how the portrait would turn out, would she keep the gallery, would she be able to keep her interest in the model purely professional?

'Would you like a refill before we get down to the nitty gritties and establish a few ground rules?'

'No, thanks.'

He beat a hasty path to the kitchen where he rinsed his mug in record time as Ariel followed at a slower pace, chuckling softly. He thought she'd assume he was being super helpful but she knew better; she'd seen his three-quarters-full mug and what better way to surreptitiously tip the whole lot down the sink than pretend to wash?

'What's this about ground rules?'

He dwarfed her kitchenette and she waited till he moved away from the sink before rinsing her own mug. She'd jokingly called him Mr Big-Shot but Cooper was just that, big in every way. It was more than a size thing, though; it was something about his supreme confidence, his imposing aura, the way he carried himself.

Usually, guys like him intimidated her, but Cooper had an innate kindness she sensed, an indefinable quality that drew her to him even if she kicked and screamed all the way.

Drying her hands on a tea towel, she resisted the urge to flick it at him as he turned away and walked out of the kitchenette. What was it about this guy that brought out her impish side?

The funny thing was, now they'd established where things were going and she'd got her way with the portrait, she couldn't stop teasing him and trying to get him to loosen up.

'Would you like to take a seat and we can discuss this?'

He shook his head and glanced at his watch. 'Can we make this snappy? I've already been here longer than anticipated.'

So much for teasing and lightening up.

'Fine. I just wanted to make sure we both understand the time involved in our trade. I probably need you to sit for another four sessions, about an hour each. How long will your pitch take?'

'Around two, but that's fine. When I make a deal, I stick to it.'

He folded his arms, the fingers on his right hand drumming ever so slightly against his left bicep. If he'd started tapping his feet, whistling and staring at the ceiling in impatience, she wouldn't have been surprised.

Talk about Jekyll and Hyde. The guy switched from light banter to cold indifference in a flash. The decaf must've really irked.

'Good. As for the posing part, you know it's a life portrait?'

She couldn't resist pushing his buttons.

'So you've told me.'

He didn't obviously look embarrassed, but a faint pink definitely stained his tanned cheeks.

'Just to put your mind at ease, you won't have to get completely naked. What you've been doing so far is great, with your leg covering, uh…'

Great, now it was her turn to blush. 'Anyway, I just

have to do the bottom half, then get some really detailed sketches of your hands, feet and face and transfer the whole lot onto canvas. Once I've finished, I'll hear your pitch.' *And see the back of you, literally.* 'You okay with all that?'

'Fine. Can we get started tonight?'

He hadn't lost his antsy look. If anything, it had intensified. Boy, he must really want her to hear his proposal.

'See you back here at seven.'

'Good. See you then.'

With a mock half-salute, he all but ran out of the studio, through the gallery and towards the front door.

'Cooper, I forgot something.'

He paused with his hand on the doorknob. 'What's that?'

'Bring a fig leaf. It might come in handy for camouflage.'

She tried to keep a straight face and couldn't, her laughter following him out the door as his exasperated expression told her exactly what he thought of her sense of humour.

CHAPTER SIX

'CAN I take a look?'

Cooper wiggled his fingers and toes in an effort to restore circulation to his extremities, grateful that this modelling gig would be over soon.

Not that he didn't enjoy spending one-on-one time with Ariel, who surprised him at every turn, but he needed to seal the deal before next Friday. He had a feeling the investors wouldn't be too impressed if he stalled again.

As for his dad, he'd been close to up and leaving, contract or not, several times this week. They didn't just not see eye to eye any more, they seemed to be on a different plane altogether.

'Stop moving! I need to capture the arch of your right foot tonight and I'm done.'

She glared at him over the easel, dabbing her brush in the paints on a worn palette next to her before returning her attention to the canvas.

Even with a smudge of paint on her cheek, her curls escaping their customary bandanna—zebra stripes tonight—and falling across her forehead, and dark circles under her eyes courtesy of how hard she was pushing to finish this portrait in record time, she was the most beautiful woman he'd ever seen.

From the bottom of her pink raffia ballet shoes to her broderie-anglaise bolero worn over a chartreuse ribbed singlet, she looked adorable, a bright spark in his otherwise dull day.

As for those shorts she wore…for the last three nights, tonight included, he'd been subjected to long, gorgeous legs poking out from truly ugly shorts. Vintage tartan checks, awful blue flowers against mustard backgrounds and purple polka dots against turquoise. Thankfully, her eccentric taste in clothes hadn't blinded him to the beauty of her luscious legs and he'd done a fair bit of his own looking while she'd been studying him.

'When you say you're done, is that done as in finished completely?'

'You wish,' she said, absentmindedly twisting a curl around a finger while dabbing at the canvas.

Actually, he didn't.

The logical, business side of his brain was yelling 'woo-hoo' but the emotional side he'd deliberately shut down wished they could stay ensconced in her cosy studio for ever.

'How much longer?'

Exhaling loudly, she stabbed her brush into a glass jar of water, rolled her neck a few times, stood up and arched her back. 'Anyone ever tell you you talk too much?'

'Anyone ever tell you you're great at avoiding answering questions?'

After another catlike stretch, which had him averting his eyes in record time when she finally looked at him, she said, 'If you must know, I'm pretty much done. I just need to get a few details of your face completed and that's it.'

'Tonight?'

His heart sank. As much as he liked being here, he'd had a long day at the office and needed to finalise a report for a presentation first thing Monday morning.

She laughed, a genuine loud, throaty chuckle that made him want to join in. 'With you sounding so enthusiastic, I guess not. Why don't you get dressed and I'll make us a hot drink?'

Cooper tried not to screw up his face. If he had to endure one more cup of her foul-tasting herbal brews or equally horrid coffee, he'd happily walk away from this deal here and now.

'I've got a better idea. Why don't we grab a coffee at the café across the street? The place looks new; they could probably do with the business.'

'Before you tear it down, you mean?'

Her smile had vanished and he couldn't tell if she was serious or joking. Either way, he was too tired to argue.

'Whatever you decide to do, I'm heading over there for the largest strong black they've got. I have a long night ahead of me.'

A flicker of remorse crossed her face and she disguised it by tidying up her work space. 'Hot date, huh?'

'Yeah, the hottest,' he said, sliding his oldest cotton T-shirt over his head and slipping into faded denim. 'Just my slinky little laptop and me.'

'Do you enjoy what you do?'

He stepped out from behind the screen to find her perched on the stool he'd just vacated, a curious look on her paint-smudged face and her spectacular legs tucked up on the rung underneath.

'It's challenging. I like seeing things develop and take shape from the infant stages right through to the finished product. You can identify with that, surely?'

He expected a vehement rebuttal, but to his surprise she nodded, a tiny frown between her brows as if she was pondering what he'd said.

'Yeah, I can. Apart from the whole creative side of art, I love seeing something develop before my eyes. It's often hard work but the reward is worth it.'

'Exactly.'

They locked stares, his challenging, hers curious. However, before she could chastise him any more for being a developer or tease him about his uptight ways, he turned away and shrugged into his leather jacket.

'Right, I have a mega-strong black with my name all over it. I'm out of here.'

He sent her a casual wave, a major part of him wishing she'd join him. Sure, they'd chatted a fair bit while she'd worked but he still didn't know what made her tick. She'd deliberately kept things light between them and he hadn't pushed, despite hoping to get more of an idea behind her absolute refusal to sell the gallery.

There had to be more to it, more than a promise to a dead aunt.

He'd bide his time, knowing the pitch he'd prepared to deliver would convince her. If there was one thing he had learned, the gorgeous woman with the kooky dress sense had a brain in her head, and hopefully, she'd see his proposal for what it was: good business, smart business and a win-win solution for them all.

He'd barely taken a step when she slid off the stool, picked up a giant straw holdall that looked like it could easily contain the proverbial sink and then some, and smoothed her wrinkled shorts.

'I think I'll come with you. I've been cooped up in this place working every night for a week straight. A change of scene will do me good.'

'So it's not my scintillating company that enticed you to join me?'

'Honestly? No.'

She matched his sardonic expression, tilting her chin up to meet his gaze head-on.

The minute he reached out to touch her cheek, he knew it was a mistake.

'You have a paint smudge right here.'

But then, he'd hardly been his usual rational, conventional self since setting foot in this place.

He slid his finger down her cheek, slowly, gently, her velvety smooth skin a magnet to his touch.

He should've pulled away the second her luminous green eyes widened and her lush mouth formed a small O, but instead he lingered, savouring the close contact, the intimacy enveloping them as surely as the heady perfume she wore.

'Th-thanks,' she said, stepping away to rub at her cheek, her eyes not leaving his. 'Just give me a second to get cleaned up and I'll be right with you.'

'No problems.'

However, he lied.

His reaction to the beautiful artist was definitely a problem, a major one.

He had no qualms about her focussing on the business side of the deal he proposed, but the million dollar question was, could he?

Ariel snuggled into the comfy lounge-style chair, loving the homely ambience of The Cypress Tree.

The new owners had done wonders with the place and she wasn't surprised to see it packed on a Friday night.

'What'll you have?'

'I'll have a decaf skinny soy latte, please.'

Cooper stared at her in disbelief. 'You're kidding, right? Tell me that's not a real drink.'

Ariel chuckled. 'To a boring, caffeine-swilling, strong black coffee hick like you, I guess not.'

Shaking his head, he placed their order with a waitress sporting a magenta Mohawk and enough facial piercings to keep the local silversmiths in business for the next decade. Though the punk hair-style didn't do much for her, Ariel admired the teenager's gold lamé hot-pants and wanted to ask her which boutique she frequented.

'At the risk of sounding like the hick you just accused me of being, is it fancy-dress night at this place?'

Ariel smiled, knowing exactly what he meant but wanting to tease him a little. 'Why would you say that?'

Cooper's gaze traversed the cosy café, his eyes growing wider by the minute. 'For starters, there's a guy over there wearing cow-print leather pants and a red vest with nothing underneath. Then there's another guy wearing orange leather chaps over denim shorts. Throw in the overabundance of black spandex, gold sequins and silver metallic objects protruding from every body part imaginable, and do you blame me for asking?'

Ariel shrugged, suddenly saddened by the huge gulf between them. They really were from opposite ends of the planet in every way: their tastes, their occupations, their thinking.

Yet she still found him attractive. Go figure?

Darn hormones!

'I don't blame you for asking. I'm not surprised a man like you wouldn't know about a cultural hub like Brunswick Street. Take another look around.'

She swept her hand wide in an all-encompassing gesture. 'This place is where it's at. Hip, funky, brimming with life. If you took a walk up the street and actually looked into the buildings rather than dreaming about tearing them down, you'd see a hundred places like this. Jazz bars, tapas bars, Latin American clubs, comedy clubs and restaurants from all around the world. It's a hub of incredible contrasts and I love it.'

'You really think I'm some sort of ruthless cretin, don't you?'

He spoke softly and she had to lean forward to hear him over the din of chattering patrons and Spanish guitar music.

Thankfully, the waitress arrived at that moment and deposited two enormous steaming mugs in front of them, giving her time to phrase her answer carefully. She wanted to be honest but something about his watchful, brooding expression told her that now wasn't the time to be too brutal.

'Look, I have this habit of shooting off at the mouth. You know, honesty is the best policy and all that. Guess I just realised exactly how different we are.'

Ariel made a mad grab at her latte and took a huge sip, scalding or not. There was *honesty* and there was honesty and from what she'd just said, he might take it she was interested in him. If she burned her tongue on the hot coffee, it mightn't be a bad thing. She might actually shut up for two seconds.

'You got that right,' he said, a speculative gleam in his eyes.

Great. The guy wasn't stupid and he'd picked up on her interest just as she'd suspected.

'One more session should see us done,' she said, gratefully hiding behind her latte mug.

'Make that two sessions.'

'Pardon?'

'One for you, one for me. My business proposal? Remember, that one tiny detail you seem to have forgotten?'

'Oh, *that*. You're right, minor details.' She smiled, showing she intended no malice. 'Maybe I'll be too exhausted after finishing the portrait to hear what you've got to say.'

'And maybe I'll spread nasty rumours about the artist getting up close and personal with her model.'

'You wouldn't dare!'

'Try me.'

By his challenging smile, she knew he was kidding but somehow, she didn't want to test him. Besides, the thought of what he'd suggested sounded way too good.

'Do you always get the final word?'

She could've backed down but then, where was the fun in that? If there was one thing guaranteed to get her fired up it was a challenge, particularly from a guy who probably always got what he wanted.

Rather than answering her mild dig, he changed the subject altogether.

'You mentioned earlier that all you need to finish is some facial details?'

'Uh-huh.'

'Do we have to do that in the studio?'

He finally reached for his coffee and drained the mug in one go, when what she really wanted to see was his entire face and read where a strange question like that was leading.

'The studio is where I do my portrait work.'

Though that wasn't entirely true. She'd often taken a sketch pad down to the St Kilda foreshore or Albert Park Lake, capturing whatever scene took her fancy whether it be a person, animal or view. New surroundings inspired her and she loved it.

But, somehow, the thought of sketching Cooper outside her studio seemed way too personal.

Like this.

One-on-one time in a cosy café, sitting across from his sexy smiles and piercing blue eyes, definitely entered the realm of too personal and made her forget one very important point.

This guy was the enemy.

No matter how charming, how glib, how sexy, he was here for one reason and one reason only: to tear her world apart. And she'd be a darn sight smarter to concentrate on that salient fact rather than the intense colour of his eyes.

'Too bad. Seeing as tomorrow is the weekend and it promises to be a perfect one, I thought it would be good to get a change of scenery. Don't know about you but I need to shake off my moon tan and catch some sun.'

He held his chin and turned his face from side to side, a half-smile on his face. 'It would be a good opportunity for you to study my exceptional profile in some real light. You know, to put the finishing touches on the masterpiece and all.'

She shouldn't encourage him, she really shouldn't.

But who could resist a man with a smart mouth like that?

'Where did you have in mind?'

Cooper winked and tapped the side of his nose in true conspirator fashion. 'Why don't you leave that up to me? Who knows, this boring hick might surprise you yet. Pick you up on Sunday around ten.'

With that he stood up, took a final glance around the café, sent her a sexy smile and headed out the door, leaving her wondering if she'd taken leave of her senses.

Painting Cooper was one thing.

Spending Sunday morning with the infuriating man, another.

Think of the finished portrait...think of the money...

Instead, all she could think about was how denim did incredible things to his butt and how stupid she was for noticing.

Worse yet, how in just under a week she liked this guy more than she'd liked any guy before.

Not good.

And she had a feeling that by spending her precious Sunday morning with him, things were about to get a whole lot worse.

CHAPTER SEVEN

'WELL, aren't you just full of original ideas this morning?'

Cooper smiled at Ariel and held open the door to Hideout, the funkiest café he could find in Brunswick Street. 'Hey, you were the one who said I needed to check out what this precinct has to offer, so here we are.'

'Wise guy,' she said, her smile warming him better than the sun's rays had for the last hour while he'd sat on Brighton Beach, more relaxed than he'd been in a long while as she'd studied his face, her fingers flying over her sketch-pad to capture his likeness.

He'd loved the ocean once, had made a weekly trek to some of Victoria's best surf beaches all within an hour's drive from the Central Business District. However, since starting work at Vance Corp he'd been too busy proving himself, putting in the hours, to chill out. He wanted to be the best and it came at a price: limited down time and alienating the one guy who should've been cheering him on rather than hating him for it.

'We don't have to do the brunch thing if you don't want to,' Ariel said, a tiny frown puckering her forehead as she searched his face for reassurance. 'I've got what I needed to finish the portrait so you're obligation-free now.'

'Let's eat.'

It wasn't her fault his mood had soured courtesy of thoughts of his dad's hang-ups. Besides, he wanted to make sure this final session ended on a happy note considering the next time they met he'd be pitching his plans for the gallery.

'As long as it's not my head you're biting off,' she said, sending him a knowing glance that said she hadn't bought his abrupt brush-off for a second.

'I promise to be nice.'

He led the way to the closest table, which happened to be a purple, kidney-shaped one boasting lemon vinyl chairs and a cartoon-like backdrop. Like everything else in this street, the Hideout café was bright, out there and eclectic.

Ariel fit right in with her denim shorts, indigo silk camisole top and rope espadrilles, whereas he stuck out like a beacon in his conservative navy cargo pants and white T-shirt.

Then again, he'd never fit in around here. Orange leather chaps just weren't his thing.

'See anything you fancy?'

To his amazement, Ariel blushed and toyed with a long blonde curl that persistently bounced in the vicinity of her right ear.

'I'll have the mushroom omelette.'

'And let me guess. A skinny decaf soy latte chaser?'

She tilted her nose in the air and sent him an imperious look. 'Ha! You don't know me at all. I'll have a wheatgrass, orange and ginger juice, please.'

The thought of all those ingredients blended together made him want to forgo the big fry-up he was about to order. 'Anyone ever tell you you're a health freak?'

Rather than bristling as he'd expected, she leaned back against the vinyl booth and chuckled. 'I'd rather be a health freak than any other kind of freak.'

'You are one interesting woman, Ariel Wallace,' he said, locking eyes with her over his menu, wondering if she noticed the growing attraction sizzling between them or it had just been too damn long since he'd dated.

He'd been so busy lately trying to get out of Vance Corporation that he'd neglected his social life. Once this deal went through, he'd make sure he remedied that. Though somehow, he had a feeling he'd need quite a few dates with women the antithesis of Ariel to make him forget her.

'Oh, yeah, that's me and I know exactly what you find so interesting about me.'

She quirked an eyebrow, full of sass and challenge and he wondered if he was slipping. Surely his interest in her beauty, her feisty nature, her sharp wit and her stunning body wasn't that transparent?

He settled for a safe 'What's that?' rather than make a complete fool of himself.

More than he had already, that was.

She snapped her fingers. 'My gallery, of course. We both know there's no other reason why a guy like you is hanging around a girl like me.'

She spoke calmly, without rancour, as if stating an obvious fact. The intriguing part was, even though he agreed with her, it still rankled.

'You're really into the whole stereotyping thing, aren't you?'

She shrugged. 'I'm just being honest. No use pretending when we're both grown up and we know what this is all about.'

Her hand waved between them, a smooth, flowing, graceful movement demonstrating her artistic side.

He loved watching her hands, so full of life and energy and creativity.

'You and I have a business arrangement, Cooper. You've fulfilled your part of the bargain and I'll follow through with mine. So let's just call it what it is and you can save the sweet talk. I'm going to stick to my end of the bargain whether you find me "interesting" or not.'

'You don't get compliments very often, do you?'

Which he found incredibly hard to believe considering she was a knockout.

Her green eyes narrowed, as if trying to ascertain if he was serious or toying with her.

'Dressed like this and with hair like this?' She plucked at her trendily creased top and loose curls, which hung halfway down her back in a frizzy curtain. 'What do you think?'

In response, he leaned forward and captured one of those lively, bouncy curls between his thumb and forefinger, rubbing the silky softness between them. 'I think you underestimate yourself. I also think you're beautiful.'

For one long, loaded moment she stared at him, her eyes glowing with gratitude and something more, something akin to desire, with a small, secretive smile dancing across her lips.

He tugged gently on her curl, leaning forward, knowing what he wanted to do was crazy but unable to stop the gravitational pull towards her.

He wanted to drag her across the table, wrap his arms around her and kiss her senseless, to taste her rosy lips, to silence her sassy mouth for two seconds and see if his spiralling desire was a figment of his imagination or not.

He didn't think about business or what kissing her could do to his chances for a fair hearing.

He didn't think about tomorrow.

Instead, caught up in the moment, he leaned forward till their faces almost touched, which was exactly when Ariel placed her hand square in the middle of his chest and shoved hard, just as she'd pushed him out the door when she'd first learned his true identity.

'That isn't going to win you any Brownie points. I said I'll hear you out and I will.'

Ariel acted cool but her fiddling hands told him otherwise as they moved from pushing back her hair to adjusting her top to rearranging the cutlery.

Trying to get his ragged breathing under control, he schooled his face into a polite mask, thankful that one of them had kept their cool and furious it hadn't been him.

He needed to wrap this up and fast.

He had no room in his life for emotions.

Yet the more time he spent in Ariel's intoxicating company, he floundered and, worse, found himself re-evaluating his vows not to get close to anyone.

He had to focus on business.

It was the only way.

'I don't need to score Brownie points. My proposal will speak for itself.'

He folded his arms and determinedly avoided looking at her mouth, the very same sexy mouth he'd almost kissed a second ago.

'We'll see, Mr Big-Shot. We'll see.'

With an enigmatic smile, she called the waitress over and left him mulling over the wisdom of consorting with the enemy.

Even an enemy as delightful as Ariel.

Ariel's heart sank as she caught sight of Sofia peering through the gallery's front windows. If the verbose woman caught sight of her with Cooper, goodness knew what might pop out of her gargantuan mouth.

'Who's that?' Cooper said, his long strides making her wish she'd worn flat shoes rather than wedge-heeled espadrilles today. She felt like a munchkin running on triple speed to keep up with a giant.

'Sofia Montessori. She's the one who commissioned the portrait.'

'I thought she looked familiar. I've seen her in passing at several events.'

That'd be right. She should've known a man like Cooper would move in the same moneyed circles as Sofia.

Her feet dragged, walking at a snail's pace as they neared the front of the gallery, not wanting to get caught up in any name-dropping, name-swapping game that might take place. She hated that sort of thing, which was why she hid out in her studio and produced art for people like Sofia and Cooper rather than attend their hob-nob parties and exhibitions.

She'd been to the occasional party in her early days and hated every minute of it: the yawning cultural and social gap between her and other people, the patronising, condescending attitudes when they discovered she was the artist.

'Hurry up. She looks ready to break your door down,' Cooper said, sending her a quizzical look.

'Thanks for walking me back to the gallery but I'm fine, I'll take it from here,' she blurted, anxious to get rid of him, knowing that any second Sofia would turn her beady gaze their way and have them halfway up the aisle before she could say, 'In your dreams'.

That stopped him dead in his tracks.

'Don't you want me to meet your friend? Are you that ashamed to be seen with me?'

If Cooper's warm, friendly persona had scared her, the icy contempt she now heard in his voice terrified her more.

'It's not that. I just want to finish the portrait ASAP and if Sofia lays eyes on you, believe me she won't leave in a hurry.'

He must've been satisfied with her answer for the cold gleam in his eyes softened. 'I won't stay. Besides, I've handled worse than Sofia in the business arena and come out unscathed. Trust me.'

Shaking her head, she fell into step beside him again. The guy was seriously delusional if he thought she'd trust him with anything. He was here to tear her life apart and all the sexy smiles and almost-kisses in the world wouldn't change that.

'Sofia, what are you doing here?'

Ariel injected warmth into her voice, knowing she would've been glad to see the lovely Italian woman if Cooper's large, looming presence weren't at her side.

Sofia stopped peering through the gallery windows and turned, and Ariel knew the exact moment she spotted them. The woman's eyes fairly bulged out of her immaculately coiffed head.

'*Ciao, bella.*' Sofia kissed both her cheeks briefly before pulling away to study Cooper with blatant curiosity, a hungry look on her expertly made-up face. 'And who is your friend? He looks awfully familiar.'

Ariel took a deep breath to perform the introductions, wishing everyone would go away and leave her alone so she could get on with the business of finishing the portrait, obtaining the money and securing the gallery for another month or so.

'Sofia, this is Cooper Vance. Cooper, my friend Sofia Montessori.'

'A pleasure, Ms Montessori.'

Cooper captured Sofia's hand and bowed over it in an antiquated gesture from years gone by. The old smoothie…

He must've known exactly how a woman like Sofia would react. She preened and simpered and practically fell in a swooning heap at his feet.

'Ditto, Mr Vance,' Sofia tittered, smiling and gushing like a teenager. 'Have we met before? I'm positive I've seen you before.'

Ariel rolled her eyes, resisting the urge to stick two fingers down her throat and make gagging noises.

'Your reputation in Melbourne society precedes you. Perhaps we've seen each other in passing at a function?'

Sofia's eyes narrowed, her gaze speculative. 'No, I don't think so. It's somewhere more recent…'

'Would you like a cup of coffee, Sofia? Cooper was just leaving and I really have lots of work to do.'

Ariel didn't want Sofia connecting Cooper to the portrait right now. If that happened…

'That's it! You're the model in my portrait.' Sofia's hungry gaze travelled the length of Cooper's body while Ariel's heart sank.

Great, just great.

'*Bello*,' Sofia murmured, obviously liking what she saw.

Not that Ariel could blame her. Sofia was a red-blooded woman after all and if she'd admired Ariel's sketches of the man, they were nothing on the real, live model in the flesh. So to speak.

Cooper smiled, a brash, unaffected smile that made Ariel want to throttle him for being so blasé about the whole situation. 'Yes, I'm sitting for Ariel. She's a very talented artist. I think you'll be very pleased with the final result.'

'And a nice boy, too,' Sofia said, sending Ariel a pointed look as if to say, Are you crazy to let this guy get away? Why aren't you married by now and expecting his *bambino*?

'Speaking of which, I better finish the portrait if you want it by Tuesday—'

'You must come too, Mr Vance!' Sofia's loud voice drowned out a passing tram as she waved her hands about in excitement. 'Ariel is coming to the little soirée I'm having for my sister's birthday where the portrait will be unveiled and it is only natural that you should attend also.'

'No!' Ariel blurted out before she could stop herself, blushing furiously when two sets of eyes turned on her, Sofia's knowing brown eyes and Cooper's dazzling blue. 'I mean, I'm sure Cooper has better things to do with his time. Besides, he'd probably be mortified if people recognise him as the model. He's a businessman and it wouldn't look good at all.'

Ariel babbled on and on, sending Cooper the evil eye, silently praying he'd back her up on this.

She didn't want him anywhere near that party. They'd spent enough 'social' time together, what with coffee on Friday night and brunch today. The longer she spent with him, the more befuddled she became and she needed her wits about her to fob him off after listening to his stupid proposal.

Liking someone, enjoying their company, wasn't

conducive to kicking them out the door, and that was exactly what she'd have to do after hearing his pitch.

So no more social stuff.

Starting now.

'What do you think, Mr Vance?'

Sofia frowned at Ariel before turning on a charming smile for Cooper.

'I think it's a great idea. Thanks for the invitation.'

'*Bene*! That's all settled. Now, why don't we go in and I can give you all the details?'

Ignoring Sofia's triumphant expression and Cooper's smug smile, Ariel sighed in resignation and unlocked the front door.

Two against one wasn't fair.

But then, since when had anything in her life been fair?

CHAPTER EIGHT

'I SHOULD never have agreed to this,' Ariel muttered at her reflection, wishing she could wield a mascara wand with the same expertise as a paintbrush.

She'd never gone in for the whole make up thing. She much preferred painting canvases to painting her face. Then again, tonight called for a confidence mask and if the barest foundation, sheer blue eye-shadow, a quick lashing of mascara and pale pink lip gloss would help quell the butterflies dancing a tango in her belly, she'd use it.

Seeing Cooper at Sofia's charity event was one thing, but agreeing to go with him?

Madness.

Right on cue, a sharp knock at the front door had her casting one last regretful look at her reflection in the mirror before she picked up her embroidered silver evening purse and flicked off the lights.

Though how hard could tonight be?

She'd wait around till the portrait was unveiled, make polite small talk with a bunch of rich phoneys then bolt back here in a taxi, leaving Cooper with his cronies.

Easy.

However, the minute she opened the door and saw Cooper standing there wearing a designer tux and a sexy smile, she knew nothing about this evening would be easy.

In fact, the way her pulse accelerated and her heart flip-flopped, nothing could be further from the truth.

'Wow, you look beautiful.'

He stepped into the doorway, blocking out the night sounds of a busy Brunswick Street, and took hold of her hand. His voice was soft, almost reverent, like a gentle caress and she shivered with delight that she could evoke a reaction like that from a guy like him.

'It's vintage,' she said, a totally inane remark. She stood frozen to the spot, her hand captured in his, enjoying the physical contact way too much.

As if he was interested in her dress.

'It suits you.'

Finally, after the hand-holding had gone on too long, he released her hand only to skim his palm over the sheer chiffon cascading in handkerchief layers from her waist to the floor.

'You look like a beautiful waterfall. Fresh, vibrant, invigorating.'

'And you need to move into the twenty-first century. With lines like that, I'm not surprised you spend all your time with your head buried behind a computer.'

She didn't mean to sound so cutting but she didn't handle compliments well. Especially compliments from a guy standing way too close and smelling like a dream come true.

To her surprise, he laughed rather than rebuke her. 'You're not going to spoil tonight with that smart mouth of yours. Insult me all you like but I'm not biting.'

More's the pity.

He raised an eyebrow as if reading her mind and she propelled him out the door, anything to put some much needed distance between them. Even seated in his car would be better than having him invade her personal space. Not that she minded exactly but if they didn't get a move on she'd be tempted to rush back into the gallery, slip back into shorts and a poncho and have a TV dinner while watching her favourite DIY house-renovation show.

Boring but safe.

The complete antithesis of allowing Cooper to drape her hand in the crook of his elbow and lead her to his low-slung sports car parked around the corner.

Exciting and dangerous.

Yeah, that was Cooper through and through. For

a girl who liked being dull and safe she sure was tempted by the prospect of living a little for once.

'Flash wheels,' she said, sliding into the plush leather interior as he held the passenger door open for her.

'It was a present.'

She looked at him in surprise, his abrupt tone implying he didn't like it. Or maybe didn't like the person who had given it to him?

As he slid behind the wheel, started the engine and pulled away from the kerb, she couldn't resist probing further. 'Let me guess. Daddy bought it for you as a bonus last year?'

'Close,' he said, his voice tight, his hands clenched around the steering wheel.

She could've left it there but she didn't. After being virtually ignored for the first eight years of her life as she'd flitted from orphanage to foster home and back again, living with Barb had opened a whole new world to her. Barb had encouraged her natural curiosity, had answered her endless questions with the patience of a saint.

Ariel loved mystery novels for that very reason, always wanting questions answered, the unsolvable unravelled and, right now, she had a doozy of a puzzle laid out before her and there was no way she could back down.

'Pretty generous gift. You two must be close.'

'We were.'

Okay, maybe now was the time to keep her mouth shut. Cooper's use of past tense could only mean two things; they'd fallen out or, worse, his father was dead.

'We don't get along these days,' Cooper said, his icy tone sending chills down her spine.

'I'm sorry.'

And she was, for ever thinking she could make tonight work. Even when she was trying to fit in, she made a mess of things. Rather than keeping the conversation light, she'd had to push, nosing around where she didn't belong.

Great.

'So am I.'

Cooper didn't say any more and this time she didn't push, clamping her glossed lips tightly shut and staring out the window at the glittering lights of Melbourne as they wound their way to Toorak, one of the city's richest suburbs.

However, after five minutes passed and the uncomfortable silence yawned between them, she said, 'Do you have any music?'

'Sure.'

He fiddled with a few chrome buttons that looked as if they could launch the space shuttle until muted jazz filled the car.

'How's that?'

'Not bad,' she said, hoping for something more upbeat. Anything to lighten the mood.

'What sort of music do you like?'

'Latin American. Flamenco. Anything with a bit of oomph.'

And the exact opposite of his choice, but she wisely kept that tidbit to herself.

However, he zoned in on her thoughts with unerring accuracy once again.

'You think I'm some kind of business-oriented bore, don't you?'

Got it in one, Coop!

However, in the interests of making the rest of the drive and the hour or so of torture she had ahead of her at the party bearable, she chose her words carefully.

'We're different, that's all.'

'Like opposites attract and all that?'

'Who said anything about attraction?'

She kept her tone deliberately light, knowing she'd successfully stepped through one verbal minefield only to plough straight into another.

A more dangerous minefield this time, one with the potential to detonate and leave her heart in tiny, shattered fragments if she acknowledged her growing attraction to this guy.

'Come on, you can tell me the truth. I've seen how you look at me when you're painting.'

'What a load of—'

His laughter drowned out the rest of her response

and she reluctantly joined in, recognising she'd been had and how he'd effectively lightened the mood.

'Okay, now I can add enormous ego to the list of your faults, you better quit while you're behind.'

'Ah…so you're fixated on my behind too, huh?'

Sending him a glare that could melt wax, she was unprepared for the swift, scorching glance he fired right back at her.

Thankfully, they were stopped at traffic lights otherwise the heat they created with that one locked stare would've made the engine seize or made him ram a light pole, whichever came first.

Tilting her nose in the air and sending him a superior smile, she said, 'The way I observed your body was purely professional. Anything else you imagine you saw is pure speculation on your part. Incorrect speculation I might add.'

He chuckled and refocussed on the road as the lights changed to green, his deep, rich laughter rolling over her like low-lying clouds on a sultry summer's day. 'Come on, Ariel, admit it. You want my body.'

'I want your head on a platter, preferably with an apple stuffed in that big mouth of yours.'

To her annoyance, heat crawled under her skin, setting her nerve endings alight with longing.

He was right, darn it.

She did want his body.

The whole look-but-don't-touch thing had driven

her slowly but surely mad over the last week or so and the more time they spent together, the more quips they traded, the more they laughed, she knew it wasn't just his magnificent body she wanted.

She was attracted to his mind too.

The same mind that is busily hatching plots to snatch the gallery and your life away from you.

How gullible could she be?

'On that note, we're here,' he said, pulling into a long, tree-lined driveway boasting enough fancy cars to keep thieves rolling in wealth till the next century.

Men in prim black uniforms rushed about like hyperactive penguins, opening car doors, taking keys and keeping the long line of vehicles moving at a steady pace past the imposing double doors at the front of the house, thrown open to let light from a crystal chandelier spill onto the marble-tiled entry porch.

Ariel unconsciously reached for a curl to twist around her finger, forgetting she'd piled most of them on top of her head in a poor imitation of a posh up-do.

This place wasn't her.

From the ostentatious cream-rendered, double-storey house that sprawled across the large block, the flood-lit tennis court she glimpsed behind the house to the right and the hand-trimmed topiary trees that looked like a real, live zoo leading up to the entrance, every self-preserving instinct told Ariel to make a run for it now.

People who lived in places like this, who drove cars like the ones lining the drive, who attended parties like this, meant one thing to her.

Trouble.

She'd battled the prejudices of rich people her entire life and, despite how far she'd come, she hated the feelings they evoked as they looked down their aristocratic noses at the scruffy, weird artist as if she hadn't risen far enough out of the gutter.

She didn't think she had a hang-up about her past, but whenever she got within two feet of a patronising snob all her old insecurities rushed back and left her feeling inadequate.

'What's wrong?'

Cooper had put the car into park mode and turned to face her, a frown lining his forehead.

'This isn't my scene.'

Her hand fluttered to her face again, searching for that elusive curl to twirl in comfort and coming up empty again.

Great, the one time that lousy curl behaved itself and actually stayed tucked up and off her face she had the urge to rip it down and twist it around and around her finger.

'Consider it part of your job,' he said, his voice soft and soothing. 'This is networking at its best, where you get to scope out potential customers, feed them what they want to hear, promote your business. And if all else fails, fall back on the old standard.'

'What's that?'

'Picture the lot of them naked.'

She managed a tight smile, suddenly grateful for his presence and the support he was offering. It would've been so much harder to walk in there alone. With Cooper, one of their own, she could blend into the background without too much difficulty.

'Anyone ever tell you you've got a fixation on the naked human form?'

'That's you, sweetheart, not me.'

He reached out and squeezed her hand, a brief, impersonal touch but supportive nonetheless and she could've kissed him for it.

Though she wouldn't go there...not if she knew what was good for her.

'Ready to go in?'

'Ready as I'll ever be,' she muttered, tugging on her tight bodice and patting the top of her head tentatively to see if her thick, unmanageable mop was still in place.

'Remember, think naked,' he said, giving her a heart-stopping smile before releasing her hand and stepping out of the car.

'It's show-time,' she murmured, feeling more like a bit actress than the star attraction and hoping she wouldn't fluff her lines.

Ironically, it wasn't only the hoity-toity crowd who had her stomach rolling with nerves but the thought she might make a fool of herself with Cooper, whose opinion she'd come to care way too much about.

Silly, irrational, absurd, and the sooner tonight was over, he delivered his pitch and he exited her life, the better off she'd be.

Then why the scary, empty feeling at the thought?

Cooper stuck to Ariel's side for several reasons: she looked stunning and he wanted to protect her from every man in the room, she'd seemed scared and vulnerable in the car and, lastly but most importantly, he wanted her next to him for the purely selfish reason that he liked having her there.

The quirky, sassy woman had him laughing more than he had in ages and he enjoyed firing right back at her. Not to mention the way her unique green eyes sparkled with glee when she scored a direct hit with her teasing barbs.

However, spending time with Ariel had one major drawback: he had to keep reminding himself of the real reason, the only reason, he was with her.

Business.

He'd never lost sight of the ultimate goal in any deal and he wouldn't start now. Not when leaving Vance Corporation was so important. Correction, when it was vital.

He'd had it with his dad. Time to get away, start up a little healthy competition and see if that made the old man sit up and take notice.

'Oh-oh, look at all these people.'

Ariel gripped his arm tighter and all but yanked him behind a marble pillar as they stepped into an elaborate foyer.

'Hey, wasn't my pep talk in the car worth anything?' He refrained from patting her hand, knowing she'd probably sock him straight in the nose for it.

She shook her head vigorously and the pile of curls on top wobbled, enveloping him in a bizarre fruity-floral scent he'd yet to identify and was too embarrassed to ask her about. The same scent that haunted him, enticed him and beckoned him to get closer to her.

'Sorry, the whole naked visualisation thing doesn't do it for me.'

'Even after seeing me with my clothes off?'

She rolled her eyes but at least he saw a glimmer of a smile.

'Especially after that!'

'Ouch, you sure know how to wound a guy's ego.'

He clutched his heart in mock pain, eliciting more of a smile from her enticing mouth coated in a shiny gloss.

He'd never seen her wear make up before. Her subtle use of cosmetics tonight just highlighted her exquisite features.

'With an ego the size of yours, Mr Big-Shot, I seriously doubt that.'

Shaking his head and exceedingly pleased his distraction technique had worked, he said, 'I take it the whole Mr Big-Shot isn't a term of endearment?'

Her smile faded. 'It's a fact. You're a big shot, I'm an artist. You want something I have, which is the only reason you're here tonight and being so darn nice to me. So let's go in, do the obligatory social thing and get out of here before this Cinderella turns into a pumpkin.'

'Fine,' he muttered, not sure if he was more annoyed by how little she thought of him or by the element of truth behind her brutal honesty.

'Fine,' she said, tilting her head up like a queen and marching away, leaving him with a tantalising view of a straight, bare back courtesy of her daring dress. The rest of it cascaded from her waist to the floor in shimmery shades of aquamarine, turquoise and emerald, the exact colour of the Great Barrier Reef on a clear day.

The woman was a burr in his side.

He tried to be nice and what did he get for his trouble? An earful.

He tried to be rational about this whole business deal between them and what did he get? Angst.

And she hadn't even heard his pitch yet.

Okay, so maybe he was the heartless tycoon she thought he was. He'd never pretended otherwise.

Business meant everything to him.

It was all he knew.

He'd blitzed his degrees, waltzed into a job and proceeded to set the business world alight. He deserved to be confident. Failure wasn't in his vocabulary. Never had been, never would be.

And no matter how stubborn the eccentric Miss Wallace wanted to be, he'd make sure he wouldn't fail this time.

He couldn't. There was too much at stake.

'You are enjoying yourself, *bella*, yes?'

Ariel took a sip of her sparkling mineral water, not wanting to lie to Sofia and needing a few seconds to compose an honest but graceful answer.

'Everyone seems to be having a wonderful time,' Ariel said, knowing it sounded lame and the astute Sofia would pick up on it in a second.

She did.

'I do not care for everyone else, *bella*. What about you? Is everything all right?'

Ariel nodded and forced a smile, hoping it didn't look like a grimace. 'Guess I'm just tired after rushing the portrait.'

Sofia's expertly made up face beamed. 'Ah…yes, the portrait. It is *magnifico*! Maria loves it.'

'And seems to be infatuated with the model.'

Ariel inclined her head towards Sofia's sister, who

for a woman of forty looked fifteen years younger in a siren-red poured-on dress, luscious dark hair that hung in perfect waves to her shoulders and huge, expressive brown eyes that were firmly fixed on Cooper, along with her talon-like hands gripping his arm as she stared up at him.

'So that's it…' Sofia waved her hand towards Maria in an abrupt, dismissive gesture. 'Don't be jealous, *bella;* she is no competition to you.'

Ariel stiffened, not liking Sofia's implication. She wasn't jealous. She'd have to care to be jealous and she didn't. Caring about Cooper would be like skipping into the dentist with a big, goofy grin on her face and clapping her hands with glee: pure and utter madness.

'I'm not interested in Cooper so you can get that maniacal matchmaking gleam out of your eyes,' Ariel said, sending Sofia a forceful look that meant business.

Predictably, the Italian woman ignored her. 'How can you not be interested? The man is beautiful, successful, charming, cultured—'

'And out to ruin me.'

Ariel glared at Cooper through narrow eyes, wondering why he let himself be pawed. Didn't the guy have any dignity?

Considering how fast he'd whipped off his clothes to insinuate his way into her good books, probably not.

'Maybe you should listen to him, see what he has to say about the gallery before jumping to conclusions?'

Sofia's tone had softened and Ariel knew that, though she meant well, in this case her friend didn't have a clue.

'That so-called charming man probably wants to kick me out of the gallery, tear it down and erect some awful monstrosity that won't fit in with Brunswick Street. I've been fobbing off his kind ever since Aunt Barb died. He's not the first and he won't be the last. The one thing I'm sure of, I'm not leaving. I promised Aunt Barb.'

Sofia laid a comforting hand on her arm, patting it gently. 'Babs would've wanted you to be happy. She was one of my closest friends and I know how much she loved you, how much joy you brought to her life. She would want the same for you. Instead, you're working too hard, battling too hard to keep the place open. You won't accept help from anyone and you bristle like some feral cat whenever anyone offers. Perhaps it is time to reconsider, *bella*?'

'No!'

Sofia jumped, the concern in her dark eyes hardening Ariel's resolve.

She didn't want to reconsider anything.

She'd made a promise to Aunt Barb and she'd do her best to keep it. She had to.

All she'd had to offer Aunt Barb in return for years of unswerving love and support was her word and there was no way she would break this promise even if it meant taking on ten extra jobs. Or doing ten more life portraits—as much as she hated them.

Though if all the models looked like Cooper...

Mentally slapping herself for going there, she enveloped Sofia in a hug. 'I'm sorry for biting your head off. I know you mean well, but I have to do this my own way.'

Sofia pulled back and patted her cheek. 'In that case, why don't you go and mingle? Several people have expressed interest in getting portraits done by the fabulous artist who painted Maria's birthday present. And, of course, the men are all dying to meet the gorgeous creature in the stunning green dress.'

Ariel glanced down at the fitted bodice, spaghetti straps and pointy-panelled, flowing chiffon of her vintage dress. With all the couture in this room, they thought this dress was stunning? Just proved her point about what a bunch of phoneys this rich crowd was.

However, obtaining a few more commissions could mean the difference between staying open for another year or not and, though she hated the patronising, condescending atmosphere in the room, she'd swallow her pride and think of Colour by Dreams.

'You're not pushing them in my direction, I hope?'

Sofia threw her hands up in theatrical despair. '*Bella*, how could you think such a thing?'

She winked and gave Ariel a none-too-gentle shove towards the main throng gathered at the floor-to-ceiling French doors opening out onto a sand-stone-paved patio. 'Now go!'

'I'm going, I'm going,' Ariel muttered, downing the rest of her mineral water and suddenly wishing she liked the taste of champagne. A little false courage wouldn't have gone astray at this point considering she hated marketing, particularly self-promotion.

Not surprising, when she'd spent the first eight years of her life trying to fade into the background at the various orphanages, foster homes and during that interminable week-long stint on the streets.

Falling asleep in an old canvas in Barb's backyard had been the luckiest break of her life. Now, if only her luck could hold…like for the next twenty years or so.

'Going somewhere?'

A hand clamped on her arm out of nowhere and she stopped, shrugging off Cooper's grip before speaking.

'I'm off to do some networking, just as some business guru advised me on the way over here.'

Cooper smiled and she wished her heart wouldn't do that weird little tango whenever he did. 'You mean you're actually listening to me? And, better yet, taking my advice?'

'Yeah, go figure? I must be drunk.'

'On that clear sparkling stuff you've been drinking for the last hour? I doubt it.'

A small part of Ariel was flattered that he'd managed to tear his gaze away from fawning Maria for more than a second to notice what she'd been drinking while a larger part—the logical part—told her she was crazy for caring.

'Look, why don't you head back to your friends and let me continue doing what I have to do?' *And the only reason why I came here in the first place.* 'In fact, once I finish chatting to a few people I'll never see again if I'm lucky, I'm heading home, so thanks for the lift.'

His smile vanished and his eyes darkened to a stormy midnight. 'Firstly, these people aren't my friends. They're acquaintances and the main reason I'm here is to support you, not party with people I barely know. Secondly, I'm not some immature little boy you can give the brush-off to when it suits you. I brought you, I'll take you home. And lastly, in case you didn't know, this whole "woe-is-me" act of yours is wearing a little thin. You're out of your depth here? Well, listen up, sweetheart. Everyone gets that feeling, from the Prime Minister to garbage collectors. You're a big girl, deal with it. Now off you go, show these people half the spunk you show me, and when you're ready I'll meet you outside.'

Ariel stared at Cooper in stunned disbelief as he strode through the open French doors without looking back, torn between wanting to run after him and give him a clip around the ears for speaking to her like that and doing exactly as he said: going out there and making this crowd notice her, make some contacts, promoting her business, no matter how much she hated it and how far out of her depth she felt.

Woe-is-me?

'I'll show him,' she muttered, glaring daggers in the general direction of the patio and squaring her shoulders to do what she had to do.

'You do know the only reason I let you drive me home was because I couldn't get a taxi for over an hour?'

Ariel flounced ahead of Cooper into the studio, not bothering to turn on more lights than the two corner elephant lamps she'd picked up for a song at a local car-boot sale.

He wouldn't be here long enough. Once she'd set a time for him to deliver his almighty proposal, she'd kick him out the door and concentrate on sorting through the business cards that had been discreetly palmed her way this evening.

Sofia had been right. People were interested in her work. Though, realistically, even if she worked night and day for the next few months, the commissions wouldn't stave off the inevitable.

She needed money, a lot of it, to keep the gallery running and, right now, with Cooper staring at her with a speculative gleam in his too-blue eyes, reminding her exactly why he was here, she knew she was fast running out of options.

'Well, I didn't think it was for my scintillating company, considering you didn't speak and pouted the whole way.'

'I didn't pout!'

'No? Then what's that pursing-up thing you're doing with your lips right now?'

Before she could blink, Cooper leaned forward, his thumb gently brushing across her lips and setting up a delicious tingle that spread throughout her body, lingering in places that hadn't tingled in a long while.

'Nothing to say? That's a first.'

Ariel couldn't have spoken if she'd wanted to. Her tongue was glued to the roof of her mouth at the sheer shock of being touched by Cooper like this, as if he wanted her, as if she were more than the enemy to him.

Besides, she was too scared to speak. If she opened her mouth, there was no telling what she might do with his thumb in the vicinity of her mouth, when her main impulse was to nibble it.

His thumb skidded across her bottom lip and drifted lower, tracing a slow, leisurely path along her jaw and back, making her knees wobble and her body sway towards him with a will of its own.

'Guess I better go before you ply me with any of your herbal concoctions, huh?'

He cupped her cheek, his hypnotic stare mesmerising, as if the last thing he wanted to do was leave.

Or was that her interpretation of it?

Was she wishing for something that wasn't there, considering he made her feel like *this*?

Like a desirable woman, like an equal, like someone he admired?

When he touched her like this, looked at her like this, she could almost forget the huge, yawning gap between them, a gap that attending the party tonight only reinforced.

Cooper belonged in the rich, uppity crowd she would've shunned given half a chance; she didn't. Never had, never would and that was just fine by her. He knew it, she knew it, then what was this tender act about?

Suddenly, it hit her.

The proposal.

The type of guy he was: a cold, arrogant businessman, who would probably do anything to get what he wanted.

However, before she could shove him away, he dropped his hand and stepped back, regret etched across his striking face.

'Mind telling me what that was all about?'

She tilted her head back to stare him in the eye, challenging, needing an answer and knowing it was futile to hope it wasn't what she suspected.

'I think you know,' he said, his gaze travelling over her from head to foot, slowly, lingering, and making her body shudder with need as if his hands had skimmed a similar trail. 'But until you're willing to admit it even exists, I'm not going to do anything about this attraction between us. And, no, it has nothing to do with business and everything to do with you and me and the way you drive me crazy.'

And for the second time that night, she allowed Cooper to walk away from her, leaving her gobsmacked.

CHAPTER NINE

COOPER finished reading the last page of the proposal, returned it to the stack of papers in front of him and tidied up the lot before slipping the copy into a presentation folder.

This was it.

D-day.

Developer day, when he convinced Ariel to sign over the gallery, guaranteeing him a new start away from his cantankerous old man.

The documentation was flawless and he'd planned for every contingency.

Apart from the one where she said no to his immaculately laid-out plans.

Though that wouldn't happen if she knew what was good for her. After getting to know the bohemian beauty, he knew for a fact that Ariel's brain was as impressive as the rest of her.

Something his father would've recognised if he

hadn't barged into this deal with all the finesse of a wounded rhino. Then again, his dad hadn't even rated Ariel, preferring to deal through the council that held her lease.

A small part of Cooper wished his dad had sealed this deal because that would've given him free rein to pursue Ariel, to explore the sizzling attraction between them, to kiss her…

Damn, he'd been so tempted last night, so close to throwing his ideals to the wind, hauling her into his arms and making every fantasy he'd ever had about her come true. Thankfully, his befuddled brain had kicked into gear at the last minute and he'd averted a mini disaster.

As much as he wanted Ariel, he wanted to get out of Vance Corporation more and make his stubborn old coot of a dad wake up.

'Got a minute?'

Speak of the devil…

Eric strode into the office without waiting for an invite and stood over Cooper's desk.

'Sure, what's up?'

It irked Cooper that he couldn't call Eric 'Dad' in the office. In fact, they'd both dropped the 'dad and son' act as soon as he'd joined the company. Sad but true.

He'd tried damn hard, putting in long hours, nailing big deals, doing more for Vance Corporation than any other employee in history.

No more.

'What's the deal with the Wallace woman? You signed her yet? We're due to meet with the investors in a few days.'

Cooper tapped the document folder in front of him. 'I'm meeting with her in an hour.'

An ugly sneer creased Eric's face. 'Well, that's just dandy but is she going to sign on the dotted line?'

'I'm confident.'

Cooper kept his answers short, non-confrontational, just as he'd learned to do in view of his dad's ever-increasing short temper.

'What then?'

Cooper stared at his dad in confusion. They'd never talked beyond the deal. Cooper knew the day he delivered the signed documentation was the day he walked out of here with his contract in tatters but his dad had never asked about his future plans. He just wasn't interested.

'Do you really want to know?'

To his surprise, Eric slumped into the chair opposite and lost the surly expression.

'Yeah, I do. You've worked here ever since uni; guess I'm entitled to know your plans.'

'As my ex-employer or as my father?'

Cooper almost spat the words even though he knew now wasn't the time or place to have the whole in-depth father/son chat he'd wanted for the last year.

He had more important things to focus on—like convincing a crazy artist to hand over her studio.

'I deserved that.'

If Cooper had been surprised by his dad's question, Eric's concerned expression floored him.

For a moment, it almost looked as if his dad cared.

'Look, Coop, things have been pretty full-on around here for the last year. Maybe I've taken you for granted. You're a good worker. You'll go places. Seems a shame to throw it all away on a whim.'

Cooper's tiny flicker of hope was extinguished in that second.

His dad wasn't interested in re-establishing a father/son bond. His dad was only concerned about his precious business.

He should've known.

Cooper stood up abruptly, shrugged into his suit jacket and picked up the presentation folder. 'Thanks for the vote of confidence, but this isn't a whim. Striking out on my own is something I have to do. You'd understand that if you knew me.'

Cooper ignored the stricken look in his father's eyes and walked out the door, his attention already focussed on the meeting ahead and its importance for his future.

Ariel fussed around the studio, lighting her lime and tangerine candles, plumping the sequinned purple cushions on the ruby sofas and tidying up the evidence of her nerves.

She'd drunk about a dozen cups of chamomile tea since ringing Cooper this morning and telling him today was as good a time as any to hear his pitch and now, as she stacked the cups in the dishwasher and made her umpteenth bolt for the loo, she wondered if she'd done the right thing.

'Keep your friends close and your enemies closer' had been one of Barb's favourite sayings so Ariel had taken the plunge and rung him, despite her tummy still churning since their almost-kiss last night.

If she'd had her way, she would've never laid eyes on the too-gorgeous guy again but they'd made a deal, he'd upheld his end of the bargain and now it was her turn.

As she glanced around the studio her heart swelled with pride. Sunlight streamed through the soaring windows, filtered through the colourful gauze swaths of chiffon she'd hung from curtain hooks, casting a warm, rainbow-like feel over the room. Combined with the refreshing tang of citrus from the aroma-therapy candles and the bright ruby and amethyst colour combination of the furniture against the polished oak boards, the place looked inviting: warm, welcoming, a haven.

And it was her haven. Had been from the minute she'd set foot into this room, a scared and starving eight-year-old who'd thought she'd stepped into Aladdin's treasure cave.

She wanted Cooper to see the studio how she saw it, to feel its ambience, to recognise how much it meant to her.

This wasn't just about her fervent promise to Aunt Barb. This was her home, the only home she'd ever had and she would fight with everything she had to hold onto it.

The wind chimes over the gallery front door tinkled and Ariel took a deep breath, wondering if she was more nervous about rejecting Cooper's pitch or seeing the guy so soon after he'd almost made her swoon like the women of her past whose vintage styles she favoured.

'Ariel?'

'Be right there,' she called out, casting one last frantic gaze around the studio and wondering if it was too late to wear her lucky garland.

Though it would clash terribly with her flowing, flower-child dress cinched at the waist with a cro-cheted macramé belt, and pink flip-flops. Not that she usually cared, revelling in combining colours, patterns, fabrics and shoes with creative abandon, but she'd already told Cooper about the garland's signifi-cance and she didn't want him prying any further.

Crossing her fingers behind her back that after hearing Cooper's pitch she wouldn't want to tear his eyes out, she pushed through the beaded curtain. 'Right on time. This business meeting must be important to you.'

'It is.'

Her tone had been light and flippant, his was anything but. Combined with his charcoal designer suit, white shirt and burgundy tie, and an expression that could've frozen ice in Antarctica, he looked ready for business. Serious business.

Ironic, considering she could've sworn he'd had monkey business on his mind when last here.

'Go through and I'll flip the lunch sign. How long is this going to take?'

'Not long if you're sensible about it.'

Ariel's narrow-eyed glare was lost as Cooper strode past her and into the studio.

She waited for some recognition of her efforts, some small comment that he appreciated the beauty of the room, but, after locking the door, flipping the sign and heading back into the studio, one look at the grim expression on his handsome face told her she'd prettied up the place for nothing.

He didn't get it.

Not that she should be surprised. Despite the cute chats, the traded barbs, the light-hearted banter they'd exchanged, Cooper was basically the cold-hearted businessman she'd labelled him as soon as as she'd learned his identity.

So he'd dulled her senses with his nice act? Looked as if he was here to well and truly pull the blinkers off today.

'Have a seat. Would you like a drink?'

'No, thanks.'

He barely looked at her, rifling through some huge, scary black folder in his hands before pulling out an equally scary huge wad of paper.

'If you're going to bamboozle me with a whole lot of facts and figures about projections and land values, forget it. Just give me the basics.'

She plopped onto one of the sofas, kicked off her flip-flops and curled her feet under her. Though her insides churned with dread, she needed to present a cool, calm façade and making herself comfortable was part of that. Maybe she should invite this new, uptight version of Cooper to slip out of his shoes and take a load off too?

She smothered a giggle at the thought.

'I'm glad to see you in such a good mood,' he said, sending her a quizzical look as he perched on the opposite end of the sofa, as far away from her physically as he could get without sliding onto the floor in an undignified heap.

'Let's keep it that way,' she said, pasting a confident smile on her face when in fact she desperately needed to make another mad dash to the loo.

He didn't return her smile.

In fact, he didn't do much of anything.

His face appeared carved out of granite, his blue eyes cold and flat like Port Phillip Bay on a frigid winter's day.

Darn it, she'd known he had this side to him. In fact, this was probably the real Cooper and the nice side he'd been showing her had been part of his elaborate plan to loosen her up in preparation for this day.

She'd been a fool.

But then again, what had she lost apart from a few nights' sleep? She'd had the most amazing, erotic dreams of her life about a model with a body to die for and an artist who'd turned to sculpting and therefore had to have her hands all over him.

'You want the basics?'

'Uh-huh.'

'Okay.'

He laid down his hefty sheaf of papers on the coffee-table in front of them and turned to face her, those chilly, lifeless eyes scaring her more than the words she knew would pour out of his mouth. 'Here's how it is. This gallery is on land that is leased and that lease is coming up for renewal very shortly. Apparently, Barbara Kane, who signed the original lease, signed it for twenty-five years and in doing so effectively gave you control after she passed away. You have refused previous offers to vacate the property but, in effect, it will be in your interest to consider accepting the offer I've set out in the documentation. Otherwise, once the lease runs out, you may find you have no option but to leave with nothing as the council can re-lease or sell to anyone they please.'

Ariel stared at Cooper in growing horror, hearing every cold, callous word he uttered, wishing she didn't understand.

However, she did, all too well.

She'd known about the lease being up for renewal shortly but she'd assumed the council would be happy to renegotiate with her. After all, she was a good tenant.

She paid her rent on time—mostly.

She didn't cause trouble at all—apart from that one, tiny fire in the storeroom, which hadn't been technically her fault.

Besides, the council always supported local ventures, encouraging the alternative, hip vibe that made Brunswick Street unique. Mr Big-Shot was just trying to scare her into giving him what he wanted and she wouldn't budge.

She would continue to make Colour by Dreams one of Melbourne's most prominent galleries—if she scraped up enough money over the next few months to pay her sky-rocketing overheads—and face the lease renewal when it came up.

'By that horrified look on your face, I'm guessing you're not too keen on the idea.'

Ariel tucked her legs tighter and folded her arms, inadequate defence mechanisms against the on-slaught of trouble she was facing.

'Your powers of deduction are amazing. I'm not surprised you're such a great businessman.'

'Don't!'

Cooper stood abruptly and strode to a window, his gaze fixed on some faraway spot, though what he found so intriguing about the run-down fence, the back neighbour's rusted chimney flue or the pile of old easels she'd never know.

'Don't what? Call it how it is? Throw in a little sarcasm to lighten the mood? Come on, you've had your fun, let me have mine.'

She unfolded her legs in one smooth movement and stood, joining him at the window to gaze out at the tiny square patch of backyard, the same patch she'd curled up in eighteen years earlier on that freezing winter's night when she'd been so famished, so light-headed, she hadn't been able to take another step.

'This is a business proposal. It's nothing per-sonal,' he said, not turning to acknowledge her, not moving a muscle.

Not personal?

She could quite happily sock him in the nose for that one. Everything about this low-down deal was personal.

Taking away her home? Personal.

Ruining her dreams? Personal.

Making her break a promise to the one woman who had ever taken a chance on her? Personal.

Destroying her plans to continue Barb's work in fostering local talent and helping street kids as she'd once been? Personal, personal, personal!

Whirling to face him, she grabbed hold of his arm, forcing him to look at her. 'You just don't get it, do you? Look around. Tell me what you see.'

At least she finally got a reaction out of him, a tiny frown indenting his forehead.

'Do it!' she said, tugging on his arm when he didn't move. 'Go on, describe what you see.'

After a long pause, he turned to face the studio and she dropped her hand, determinedly ignoring the heat scorching her palm.

'Big room. Polished boards. Two red sofas. Sparkly cushions. Heap of art stuff. Fancy material which could be curtains.' His flat, deadpan voice suited his flat, deadpan description perfectly and her heart sank further.

She'd known they were worlds apart with little common ground but she'd hoped he might've developed some aesthetic sense over the last few weeks, some idea of what she was about and where she was at.

She'd been wrong.

About everything.

Including her warped, messed-up feelings that she might actually like this guy. She'd thought once she knocked back his stupid business proposal they might actually have a chance at being more than friends.

Right now even friends seemed out of the question and it hurt more than it should.

'What else do you see?' she urged, giving him one last chance to show her he understood where she was coming from, where she was going.

'Tiny kitchenette, elephant lamps, candles, art magazines.'

He turned back to her, an expectant look on his face like a pupil expecting praise from a teacher.

Praise? In his case, he'd just scored a big, fat F.

'You would see that,' she muttered, turning away from him and crossing the room so he wouldn't see the sudden tears filling her eyes.

She never cried, yet the harder she blinked them away, the more tears swelled in her eyes till they soon overflowed and ran down her cheeks in pitiful rivulets.

'I'm not sure I understand.'

Thankfully, Cooper's voice came from near the windows, indicating he hadn't moved.

She didn't want him to see her like this.

She wouldn't give him the satisfaction.

'I didn't think you would,' she murmured, holding back the sobs that threatened to join the tears. 'Just go. Leave the proposal. I'll consider it and get back to you.'

'But I need an answer—'

'I don't care what you need! Please leave and lock the door behind you.'

Her voice shook and she bit down on her bottom lip to stop the quivering, hating him for making her feel this vulnerable, this weak.

'I'll call you,' he said, his footsteps echoing on the polished boards as he left the studio, the soft tinkling of the wind chimes an eerie signal to his departure.

'Don't bother,' she muttered, dashing an angry hand across her eyes only to find the tears falling faster than before.

Furious at Cooper, furious at her impotent tears and furious at her inability to see a clear way out of this mess, she marched into the kitchen and flicked on the kettle.

A cup of chamomile tea mightn't soothe her seething soul but it would go a long way to erasing the awful chill that had seeped into her bones at the thought she might lose this place.

And that Cooper didn't give a damn.

CHAPTER TEN

COOPER strode up Brunswick Street in desperate need of a caffeine fix, entering the first café he came to which happened to bear the interesting name The Red Tongue.

Was there anything about this suburb that wasn't way-out or different or designed to throw him into a spin?

From the minute he'd first set foot here he'd been slightly off-kilter and out of his depth, both foreign feelings that didn't sit well with him. He liked control, order, planning, and forward thinking. Instead, since he'd set his sights on acquiring the gallery nothing had gone according to plan, particularly the conscience he'd suddenly grown.

The same conscience that now screamed he'd let Ariel down somehow, that he'd driven an irreversible wedge between them.

It hadn't been intentional. The proposal was

business and he'd hoped that once the deal was behind them she might be interested in catching up on a social level again.

Fat chance.

He could handle her teasing, her loaded barbs, and her occasional put down—but tears?

No way.

The sound of her choked-up voice and the glistening moisture on her cheeks had kicked him in the gut and sent him straight out of there, torn between wanting to comfort her and strangle her for making this deal more complicated than it had to be.

'What'll it be, mate?'

Cooper tried not to stare at the young guy taking his order, but it was pretty hard not to. The kid sported enough metal studded through his face to construct a bridge and had a white G-stripe through his gothic black hair.

'Strong espresso, please.'

'No worries. Coming right up.'

He watched the skunk guy saunter away, slashes in his denim jeans, a less-than-white cloth hanging out of his back pocket and a black T-shirt featuring the café's logo, feeling way older than his thirty years.

He'd never considered himself overly conservative but spending time in this suburb made him feel more ancient than Noah.

Though this place wasn't too bad in the displacement stakes: brown vinyl booths, chrome modern chairs, plain wooden tables. The only eye-catching things in the café were the fire-engine-red menus, those and the metal-favouring staff.

'Here you go.'

Skunk guy returned in record time and placed a steaming espresso in front of Cooper. He wanted to inhaled it, needing a jolt of caffeine to hotwire his brain into coming up with a solution to the Ariel problem.

'Thanks,' Cooper said, stirring two sugars into his coffee for added oomph and wondering why the waiter hadn't moved. 'Is there something else?'

Skunk guy looked nervous about something, the metal rod in his nose twitching. 'Actually, there is. You look like a guy who'd appreciate art. Here, take a look at this.'

He pulled a flyer from his back pocket—the opposite pocket to the one containing the dirty rag, thank goodness—and slapped it on the table. 'This artist is awesome! She's having her first showing tomorrow and you should go. Tell all your friends.'

Cooper glanced at the flyer as he took his first, welcome sip of coffee, almost snorting it out when he saw where the exhibition would be held.

'Colour by Dreams, featuring Chelsea Lynch.'

The artist's name rang a bell too but he couldn't quite place it immediately.

'It'd be cool if you brought a whole heap of people. The artist really needs support.'

'And who are you? Her PR manager?'

Cooper admired the young guy's push, wondering if he was a friend of Ariel's rather than the artist. It wouldn't surprise him in the least if she had a whole string of guys like this ready to promote and support her.

Look how she had him feeling.

Skunk guy grinned sheepishly. 'No, I'm her boyfriend. Chelsea is the best and I said I'd help her out by passing out some flyers to customers. Hope you don't mind?'

'After you brought me a coffee like this? No problems.'

'You're cool for a business dude,' skunk guy said, giving him some weird hand sign involving his index and little fingers pointing up with the rest of his fingers aiming down before slouching away to try his sales pitch on the next customer.

Cooper picked up the flyer and studied the short bio of Chelsea Lynch: local girl who had grown up in Fitzroy, won scholarship to study art, first showing sponsored by Colour by Dreams.

The last fact interested Cooper more than the rest. Why would Ariel sponsor another artist? Weren't gallery showings as rare as the last piece of prime developing land in this street?

From what he'd read, it took most artists years of hard slog and self-promotion to obtain a showing, yet here was a young artist starting out being sponsored by a gallery?

Cooper drained the rest of his coffee, folded the flyer and tucked it into his jacket pocket, hoping the old adage 'out of sight, out of mind' might work. For some inexplicable reason, he suddenly felt like a big, bad bully for pushing the gallery deal and, in the process, ruining the dreams of people like this new artist.

Not to mention ruining the dreams of another artist.

He had his own agendas, his own goals, but what if Ariel's dreams were just as important as his?

This is business...this is business...

The hard thing was, no matter how many times he told himself it was only business, seeing Ariel's vulnerability had delivered a kick in the guts to his cool, aloof act he'd donned for the presentation.

She'd found a chink in his impenetrable armour and he didn't like it.

Business was one thing, caring about the opposition another and, unfortunately, he'd actually grown to like the fiery artist with the zany dress sense.

Enough to forfeit your dream?

Shaking his head and wishing for a clear-cut solution to this new problematic development in his quest for success, he left payment for the coffee along with a hefty tip and headed for the door.

He didn't make it.

The fiery artist burst through the door and made a beeline straight for him, and by the murderous expression on her face it looked like her tears were a thing of the past and she'd rather skewer someone's head.

His.

'Tell me more about this lease business.'

Ariel resisted the urge to stab Cooper in the chest and settled for plopping into the booth opposite the chair he'd just vacated.

She preferred the soft, comfy vinyl to the hard-backed chairs. Not that his choice surprised her: hard chair for a hard ass.

'Drink?' he offered, sliding back into the chair with obvious reluctance. 'And how did you find me? Is stalking another of your hidden talents?'

Ariel toyed with the cutlery in front of her, particularly the knife, and contemplated all sorts of delightful ways she could use it on the infuriating man opposite her.

'Everyone in the street knows me and when I asked about a tall, uptight guy in a fancy suit the old man from the Nepalese shop pointed me straight here.' She smirked, seeing his frown at her uptight dig. 'And no, thanks, I don't want a drink, I want answers.'

To give him credit, Cooper's sombre expression didn't change. Most guys would've bawled her out for her outrageous behaviour, from sniffling tears to arrogant demands in less than ten minutes. He took it in his stride, leaning back in his chair and folding his arms, his blue-eyed gaze unwavering.

'All the answers are in the proposal you asked me to leave you.'

'I'd rather hear about it from you. Besides, I don't have time to read a whole lot of legalese that you've probably peppered through that doorstopper of a document you prepared.'

Okay, so she sounded ruder by the minute but she couldn't help it. When she was nervous, she got defensive and obnoxious and pushy.

So, he could sue her. Wouldn't be much different from what he was trying to do to her at the moment anyway, ripping out her home and livelihood from under her.

'You could've heard more if you hadn't booted me out of the gallery.'

A challenging gleam glittered in the intelligent blue depths focussed on her and a tiny thrill went through her that here was a guy she could match wits with, who could give as good as he got.

She tilted her chin up and glared him down. 'Could've, should've, would've but didn't. How about you tell me everything you know about that lease now?'

So she could high-tail it straight to the council offices and see if she had an easel to stand on.

He folded his arms, a cool, casual gesture of a confident guy rather than a defence mechanism, and met her stare straight on. 'The council has had a ninety-nine-year lease on the land twice. The original owners, when the land was pastoral, leased it to the council who later bought the lease once the owners offered it to them for a hefty price. As I told you before, your Barb signed a twenty-five year lease with the council, which was extremely generous, and that's up for renewal. However, I've spoken to several people within the council who are ready to negotiate a sale for the right price. If that happens, you get nothing, which is why it's in your best interests to vacate now, take what's on offer and lease elsewhere. That about cover it?'

Ariel listened to every damning word, her heart sinking lower than Cooper's lousy offer.

Could he be right about the council selling or was he toying with her as he had from the start?

Only one way to find out and that was push him.

'The council won't sell. You're bluffing.'

He leaned forwards, placing his forearms on the table and drawing her attention to his long fingers which she'd noticed when painting him. Long fingers that she'd fantasised about, skimming her body, bringing her pleasure...

'I'm telling you how it is.'

She grabbed for a curl and wound it around her finger, meeting his unflinching stare while her insides quaked. He had to be wrong. She couldn't contemplate any other option.

She'd made a promise to Barb, she had a legend to keep up, to continue the work Barb had started in the local community. She'd be a monkey's aunt if she let a guy like Cooper railroad her into making a decision out of fear.

'You've seen enough of this street to know the type of image the council wants to portray and the gallery is a vital part of the local colour. Besides, we do a lot for local talent, not to mention the street kids in the area.'

'Street kids? What's your involvement with them?'

If his upper-class lip had curled in derision, she wouldn't have been surprised. His incredulous tone said it all.

Heat surged into her cheeks, a potent combination of anger and resentment that a guy like him wouldn't understand the first thing about what it was like to be starving, cold and desperate, and that he'd dare question her about it.

'Never mind—it's not relevant to your *business proposal*, is it?'

By the sharp flare of awareness in his eyes, he registered her venom-loaded barb.

Shaking his head, he pushed back from the table. 'Look, this is getting us nowhere. I've answered your question about the lease, I've tried to lay out the offer as plainly as I can. The figures are in the document so once you have a chance to think it over, I'm sure you'll make the right decision. I'll call by later for your decision.'

'Don't bother!'

She leaped to her feet as he stood up, knowing she should shut up and get out before she said something she'd regret but her defensive hackles were well and truly bristling and her thoughts became words faster than she could stop them.

'I'm not interested in anything you have to offer, now or ever. I know you've been hanging around me, acting nice to soften me up, but it hasn't worked. So you storm into the gallery today doing your intimidation act. Which, I hate to tell you, hasn't been successful either. So why don't you quit while you're behind and leave me alone?'

To her amazement, he laughed. 'Does this mean you won't have dinner with me tonight so I can get your final answer?'

She clenched her hands.

'It means I don't want to ever see you again.'

She turned on her heel, hoping her worn flip-flops wouldn't send her sprawling and spoil her attempt at a dignified exit.

'That's going to be hard, considering I've been invited to Chelsea Lynch's showing tomorrow and I'm all for supporting new talent.'

She stiffened as he brushed past her, waving a flyer in her face with a smug smile of his own as he held open the door.

She didn't respond.

She couldn't; it took all her concentration to walk past the guy who, while he couldn't take no for an answer and it annoyed her beyond all reason, stood up to her as no one ever had.

And a huge part of her admired him for it.

She liked this guy.

Against her better judgement, with every instinct screaming they were worlds apart and he spelled trouble with a capital T, she liked him.

Now what was she going to do about it, considering she didn't want to see his smug face ever again?

'Ariel, wait.'

If she'd had half a brain, she would've ignored him and kept going. Instead, there was something in his tone of voice, a softening, which made her halt in her tracks.

'What?'

He broached the short distance between them and took hold of her upper arms; she couldn't have bolted if she'd tried.

'Why did you follow me?'

'Because I'm insane,' she muttered, wriggling in his grip to get free.

It wasn't so much his probing question that had

her wanting to flee as much as his touch, his firm hands scorching her with his particular brand of heat. The type of heat that made her lose her mind. Having her arms tingling wasn't enough. She wanted that heat to spread through her body, to have his hands all over her, exploring, caressing, stroking. Every last inch…

'You listened to me in there where you wouldn't back at the gallery. What changed your mind?'

Darn him for being so observant, so persistent.

She stopped wriggling, fixing him with a glare that would've sent a lesser man heading for the hills.

'Fine, you want to hear the truth? I always keep a promise. Simple as that. I felt bad for reneging on my part of the deal when you'd been pretty good about the whole posing thing, so that's it. You happy?'

'I am now,' he murmured, his hands sliding around her waist, moulding her to him, sending her pulse into overdrive and her belly into freefall. 'I'm not the enemy, you know.'

'Says who?'

She tried to pull back but his arms tightened, pinning her against him. Logic told her to make a run for it, but desire flowed through her body and made her wish he'd drag her back to the gallery this second and make love to her. Maybe once they got rid of all this pent-up tension, she might be able to steel herself against him once and for all?

Or maybe she was making excuses for wanting to get naked with the hottest guy she'd ever known?

'I can prove it to you,' he said, tilting her chin up to gaze into her eyes, his blue eyes boring into her with an intense expression she couldn't fathom.

'Prove what?'

She'd lost track of the conversation the second her mind had put the two of them together naked.

'Prove I'm not the enemy.'

'And how are you going to do that? By schmoozing me?'

'Don't tempt me.' His gaze dropped to her lips and her breath hitched.

Kiss me, you fool!

Her lips parted and for an insane second, she wondered if she'd spoken aloud.

His head descended, blocking out the brilliant sunshine streaming down on them, and she held her breath, her hands splayed on his chest, craving the feel of bare skin rather than expensive cotton.

Her eyelids fluttered shut and she tilted her head a fraction, craving the touch of his lips more than she'd craved anything in her entire life.

'I'll call you,' he said against the corner of her mouth, his lips brushing hers in the briefest of almost-there kisses before pulling away.

What the—?

Her eyes snapped open and she reeled from the

disappointment of another missed kiss from the most infuriating guy she'd ever met.

He stepped away and she steadied her legs, knowing if she swayed towards him he'd know how truly pathetic she really was. One minute she was telling him to get lost, the next she was offering herself up like some virgin sacrifice to the Vikings.

'Whatever,' she said, brushing an errant curl out of her face, turning the gesture into a casual wave as he smiled, gave her a smart salute and walked away.

However, there was nothing remotely casual about the blood pounding through her body or how much she wanted the guy who had the potential to ruin her once and for all.

CHAPTER ELEVEN

'WHY the glum face, *bella*?'

Ariel summoned a smile for Sofia, knowing it fell well short of her usual beam when the Italian woman's dark eyes filled with concern.

'My muse is being stubborn,' Ariel said, fiddling with the dimmer switch on the gallery lights, wanting to get the ambience just right before opening the doors to the public in ten minutes for Chelsea's show.

Sofia tapped her upper lip with a manicured, crimson fingernail. 'Are you sure it's just your muse being stubborn?'

'What do you mean?'

Ariel stepped back and studied the vibrant oil landscape in front of her, pleased with the vivid colours dancing beneath a soft spotlight.

'Maybe that delicious man has you in a spin and you're holding out on him? *Santo cielo*, what a dish that one is!'

Sofia kissed her fingertips and waved them heavenward—holy sky indeed!—while Ariel smiled, a genuine, from-the-heart smile, her first since her confrontation with Mr Big-Shot yesterday.

'That kind of dish gives me indigestion so I'd rather not talk about him.'

She should've known not to deny anything too vehemently with Sofia. It only served to inflame her curiosity.

'A-h-h-h…a lover's quarrel, perhaps?' Sofia's eyes sparkled with intrigue. 'All great love affairs need drama and I think you have this with your young man, no?'

'No! And he's not my young man.'

Ariel moved onto her next task, making sure the cheese platters were arranged just right and interspersed with the exotic dips and crackers, wondering why a small, traitorous part of her soul wished he were.

'*Bella*, life does not have to be so tough all the time. What will be will be.'

Concern laced Sofia's words while Ariel mentally disagreed.

Life was tough. At least, hers always had been and she didn't know any better. Losing the gallery would be just another example of it. A sad, heartbreaking example as she lost the one thing that symbolised hope to her: hope for a better life, hope that good things could come out of bad, hope that she could be the type of person Barb would've wanted her to be.

The type of person she wanted to be: successful, proud and independent. Qualities guys like Cooper took for granted.

Well, she'd show him.

If she could rustle up a cool million or so, that was.

'If there is anything I can do to help...' Sofia trailed off, quirking a stencilled eyebrow while draping a plump arm across her shoulders.

'I'll be fine,' Ariel said, submitting to a quick hug before shrugging out of Sofia's embrace, wondering if the lie sounded as hollow to Sofia as it did to her.

She wouldn't be fine, considering the council had confirmed her greatest fear this morning: they were selling the land the gallery stood on.

Like most councils around Melbourne, they were strapped for cash and in desperate need of more schools and health-care facilities. So selling off the last piece of prime real estate in Brunswick Street was a no-brainer.

Of course, they'd given her an option. Come up with the cash herself or lose the gallery.

Some option.

For a person struggling to meet the monthly rent, they might as well have handed her a rope knotted into a noose.

'Hey, you guys. Do you think everything looks okay?' Chelsea bounded up to them, red hair gelled into fearsome spikes, a funky beige leather ensemble draping her lithe body.

Ariel pasted a smile on her face and sent Sofia a pointed look to change the subject. 'Relax. Your paintings look great and this showing is going to be a hit.'

Chelsea's confident grin waned. 'What if no one comes?'

'Pah! Do not worry, *bambina*. I have told the whole of Melbourne. Everyone will be here!' Sofia flung her arms wide and Chelsea straightened, her confidence restored.

Ariel sent Sofia a grateful glance, wishing her problems could be solved as easily. 'Chelsea, why don't you make sure the inventory list and red sale dots are in order while Sofia checks on the wine?'

While she scooted out the back to brace herself for Cooper's appearance.

Surely he wouldn't show?

He'd probably been trying to intimidate her again by saying he'd come to Chelsea's showing, wanting to up the pressure, turn the screws a little tighter.

Well, she had news for him.

If he did show his sorry face here tonight, she'd be the only one doing any screwing over.

She'd thought long and hard about her options all afternoon while preparing the gallery, and as much as Cooper's offer seemed her only chance at getting a fresh start elsewhere, she couldn't do it.

Taking his money would be selling out on her dream, selling out on her promise to Barb, and she wouldn't let that happen. She couldn't.

She would fight this with every weapon in her limited arsenal. Approaching the National Trust, the Arts Council, the Victorian Grants Committee. Whatever it took, she would do it.

People depended on her, people like Chelsea who would never have a chance at discovery if it weren't for the gallery and Barb's legacy. As she watched the young red-haired woman flit around the gallery one last time to ensure everything was in order she knew there was no other choice.

She could never sell out and if Cooper or the local council wanted this piece of land, they would have to drag her screaming from it after she'd exhausted every avenue.

'Ariel, there's a crowd outside. Shall I open the door?' Chelsea's hushed tone alerted Ariel to just how nervous the young woman was, for Chelsea never spoke in anything below a dull roar.

'Go ahead. It's your moment to shine,' Ariel said, giving Chelsea's arm a reassuring squeeze, fervently hoping this wouldn't be the girl's first and last showing at Colour by Dreams.

* * *

He came.

Ariel knew the exact moment Cooper set foot in the gallery because the hair on her nape stood to attention. So did most of the women in the room.

To give her credit, she averted her gaze after the first soul-wrenching moment when their eyes met and what could only be described as sizzling heat arced between them.

But that one, loaded moment was all it took for her to imprint his powerful image on her brain: black jeans, black T-shirt, black leather jacket, the bad-boy wardrobe looking way too good on uptight Mr Big-Shot.

Throw in the sardonic glint in his too-blue eyes and a natural confidence that turned heads and she knew she'd have trouble getting through the rest of the evening.

He could've played fair and avoided her.

Of course, he didn't.

'You can run but you can't hide,' Cooper said, sneaking up on her in the studio kitchenette while she hunted for extra plastic cups under the sink.

Ariel's head snapped up and she avoided clunking it on the rusty metal sink by a millimetre.

'Nice view, by the way.'

With heat flushing her cheeks, she wriggled backwards from her awkward position and hoped her butt didn't look big in the crushed velvet hot-pants before mentally slapping herself for caring.

'What are you doing here? I told you not to come.'

He leaned against the door jamb and raised an eyebrow, sending her pulse hammering. 'In answer to your first question, I'm here because I'm interested in art. As for you telling me not to come, surely you know that I love a challenge?'

She clenched the bag of cheap plastic cups in her hand till they crackled. 'That's what I am to you, isn't it? A challenge. "Let's see how much I can suck up to the flighty artist and watch her capitulate and hand me her gallery on a platter." Well, I've got news for you, boyo. It ain't going to happen!'

She expected him to frown, to glower, to get that stern business look on his face he'd had yesterday when he'd presented his lousy pitch.

Instead, his infuriating smile widened.

'You're stunning when you're angry.'

A tiny thrill of happiness shot through her—a girl had her pride, after all—before she fixed him with a glare designed to intimidate. 'And you're full of it. Now, if you don't mind, I have to get back out there.'

'Oh, but I do mind,' he murmured as she attempted to push past him and, short of plastering her body against his in the doorway, she stopped dead and waited for him to lower his arm.

He did.

Only as far as her waist.

'You can keep running from me all night but I'm not going anywhere. We need to talk and I'm not leaving till that happens.'

He spoke softly, his words dripping with gentle persuasion, but she barely registered them as the light touch of his hand resting on her waist sent her into a tailspin.

The warmth from his palm scorched through the snug velvet hugging her waist, branding her skin and enticing her to do all sorts of crazy things such as slide into his arms and get an all-over body experience of that seductive warmth.

She knew his touch didn't mean a thing.

She knew flirting was second nature to a successful guy like him.

And she knew without a shadow of a doubt that she should boot him out the door so quickly he wouldn't have time to register it.

Instead, she tilted her chin up, looked him straight in the eye and said, 'If you're sticking around, make yourself useful. I could do with a spare pair of hands.'

With that, she picked his hand off her waist, holding it a fraction too long before dropping it and walking away without a backward glance.

'What a night.'

Ariel flopped onto a sofa, slid her three-inch

cork wedges off and rubbed her aching feet, wishing a cup of tea would miraculously appear before her.

'Would you like something to drink? A nice hot cup of tea perhaps?'

Cooper squatted down in front of her, still looking bright-eyed and bushy-tailed while she felt like a washed-out rag. Darn him.

'I knew I let you stay for a reason,' she said, hating the way her heart lurched at the sweet expression on his face, at the way his lips curved up in a smile and at the way he read her mind and knew exactly what she needed at that precise moment. 'A cup of black-currant and apple tea would be great.'

He grimaced. 'That combo belongs in kiddies' fruit drinks.'

'It's delicious. Then again, a caffeine addict like you wouldn't have a clue.'

She softened her dig with a smile and his answering grin warmed her from the inside out and better than any cup of tea ever had.

'You sit tight and this clueless coffee connoisseur will bring you your poison in a jiffy.'

Ariel watched him straighten and stride away, admiring the way the black denim moulded his butt and his long, lean legs.

She shouldn't have let him stay.

She should've booted him out with the rest of the

stragglers, mainly an exuberant Chelsea and match-making Sofia, but she hadn't had the energy. Besides, there was nothing he could say that would change her mind about selling the gallery and she wanted to make that clear.

Once she outlined her plans for raising the necessary funds, she had no doubt that she'd see the back of Cooper Vance.

She should be rapt.

Instead, an empty feeling blossomed in the vicinity of her heart and spread outward, icy tentacles of loneliness creeping through her and making her wish for all sorts of futile things.

She wished Cooper weren't a take-all businessman.

She wished they'd met under different circumstances.

Scariest of all, she wished she didn't have a huge crush on a guy who had no interest in her other than as a means to an end.

'Here we are, one cup of hot fruit punch as requested. Gross.'

Cooper handed her a steaming cup of tea and she inhaled the irresistible fruity aroma, sighing with pleasure after her first sip.

'Thanks. This is heaven,' she said, tucking her feet under her and taking blissful sips while studying Cooper over the rim of her cup.

'You're easily pleased if that's your idea of

heaven,' he said, taking a seat next to her on the sofa, his proximity setting off warning bells in her head.

She could've scuttled away like a frightened mouse but lethargy infused her body. She simply didn't have the energy to move, or the inclination, if she were completely honest.

What did she expect to happen anyway? For the guy to kiss her senseless? As if.

You wish.

The stupid thing was, she did and she took several gulps of hot tea to wash away the thought.

'You're not having anything?'

He shook his head. 'I'm fine. Are you?'

Before she could decipher what he meant, he reached across the short space separating them and skimmed his fingertips across her cheek. 'You look worn out.'

'I haven't been sleeping well,' she muttered, glaring at the main cause of her insomnia and wishing he'd revert to uncaring business mode.

She could handle that guy.

This softer, astute version of Cooper had the power to undo her in a second.

'Guess that's partly my fault, huh?'

'There's no partly about it. It's all your fault.'

His eyes widened and for an embarrassing second she wondered if he knew exactly how he affected her.

'Having you breathing down my neck, trying to

oust me from this place, hasn't been pleasant,' she rushed on, focussing on the business side of things in the hope he wouldn't delve deeper and realise there was more to her sleepless nights than worrying about the gallery's future. 'It's stressful, and you're talking to a person who doesn't do stress. Yoga, yeah. Meditation, yeah. Stress, uh-uh.'

He pulled away from her, a tiny frown indenting his brow. 'It doesn't have to be stressful if you'd listen to reason.'

Anger shot through her and she placed her near empty cup on the floor. 'Reason being?'

'I'm not going to rehash old ground,' he said, leaning back in his corner of the sofa and spreading his arms across the top, looking way too confident. 'You know that my offer is fair, considering the council can oust you once the lease is up and you'll be left with nothing.'

'How about I throw you out of here right now?'

She leaned closer, refraining from jabbing him in the chest at the last second. 'Or, better yet, you finally get the message that I'm not interested in anything you have to offer, ever, and walk on out of here of your own accord?'

His eyes darkened to midnight-blue as he sat forward and lowered his arms. 'You're lying. I think you're very interested in what I have to offer.'

Her heart thudded at his loaded response, at his

nearness. He smelt so good, an intoxicating blend of sandalwood and something lighter that evoked a powerful response in her. She loved scents: fresh flowers, aromatherapy oils, rain on freshly cut grass, but none of her favourite smells came close to Cooper's heady scent.

Damn the man, he knew how he affected her and he was rubbing her nose in it.

Well, she'd show him.

'You're delusional. And if you're trying to imply there's something behind the weird flirting thing we do occasionally, forget it. We both know you're slumming it for a while, getting to know how the other half live.'

His jaw clenched, his eyes narrowed and tension radiated off him in palpable waves.

She moved in for the kill. If this didn't get him out of her life once and for all, nothing would.

'Don't worry, I'm a big girl, I can take it. You spend time with the eccentric artist, flirt a little, soften her up, get her to buy into your crazy scheme. I get it. It's the way you do business. Take no prisoners, tell no lies and all that. Hey, no hard feelings.'

Though he was right; she was lying.

At least about the feelings part.

She had feelings and plenty of them. The problem was she couldn't do anything about them. Her life was complicated enough without letting her erratic emotions join the party.

'Are you finished?' he said, his tone low, menacing.

'Actually, I haven't. I also think you're snobby, condescending and—'

His lips crushed hers into silence and she gasped in shock, realising a second too late that opening her mouth might be construed as an invitation.

Cooper didn't hesitate, deepening the kiss, challenging her to meet him halfway, coercing her with a skilful precision that took her breath away.

Well, he wasn't the only one who liked a challenge and in the split second where reason warred with passion she threw caution to the wind and showed him exactly who he was messing with.

Her lips clung to his, frantic, desperate, meshing in a whirlpool of hot sensation that lit a fire deep within.

Her hands took on a life of their own, skimming the wall of his rock-hard chest before sliding higher, tangling in his hair to pull his head closer, to anchor herself in a world tilting crazily out of control.

Heat streaked through her body and she leaned into him, wanting more, needing more, and as his arms slid around her, hauling her across his body to lie on top of him, logic fled only to be replaced by a deep-seated yearning that this should go on for ever.

Cooper broke the kiss to stare into her eyes, his hands pushing the curls off her face in a gentle caress.

She couldn't fathom the expression in his eyes and reality hit as he shifted slightly beneath her. Here she was, lying on top of an extremely hot guy, a guy she could easily fall for in the blink of an eye if she completely lost her mind, a guy she'd been in the process of dismissing from her life a few moments ago, a guy who had just sent her spiralling out of control with a simple kiss.

What on earth was she doing?

Okay, so maybe the kiss hadn't been so simple. In fact, it had been downright amazing. But that wasn't the point. She still needed to get rid of him, and fast. No telling what her kick-started desire might do in the next ten seconds or so.

Disengaging his hands from her face, she slid onto the floor in an undignified heap before leaping to her feet like some bumbling clown act in a circus. 'Well, that was an interesting diversion but I hate to tell you, it didn't work. I still want you to get out of here.'

Cooper stood with a lot more grace than she had, his inscrutable expression annoying her. Couldn't the guy at least look the teensiest bit shaken by the cataclysmic kiss they'd shared? Then again, maybe it wasn't so extraordinary for him. He probably went around kissing half the female population in Melbourne like that.

And, no, that sharp stab of pain in the vicinity of her heart wasn't jealousy; it had to be all that cheese she'd consumed earlier mixing with the tea to give her heartburn.

'If you don't shut up, I'm going to kiss you again till you do.'

She opened her mouth with an instant rebuke, but shut it quickly as he took a threatening step towards her.

Then again, the thought of more of that sensational kissing wasn't so bad…

'Good, now that I've got your attention, I want you to listen up. Yes, I want this deal to go through and, yes, it's very important to me. In fact, it's more than important, it's imperative.'

He paused for a moment as if searching for the right words and she waited, prepared to give him a little leeway. After all, it was the least she could do before she booted him out the door permanently.

'As for what's happening between you and me, it's got nothing to do with business. Do I wish you were some shriveled-up old prune that wouldn't tempt me? Yeah. Do I wish I could completely separate business from everything about you that entices me? Yeah. Do I wish I could seal this deal and not look back without remembering the curve of your smile, the fire in your eyes, the passion of your kiss? You bet. But there's no use wishing for the impossible and, right now, pretending that something doesn't exist between us would be doing just that and I won't. I can't.'

Ariel's jaw hit the floor and her mind whirled as Cooper stared her down, the bad-boy businessman daring her to disagree.

Okay, so he was man enough to acknowledge the spark between them. Big deal.

That didn't mean she had to agree with him or encourage him, despite how her heart raced at the wonderful things he'd said about her and the fact he found her just as attractive as she found him.

He was still the enemy and would still tear her world apart given half a chance.

A chance she had no intention of giving him.

'Got nothing to say? Come on, give it your best shot,' he said, the grim look in his eyes at odds with the sardonic half-smile playing about his lips.

'What do you want me to say?'

Apart from the obvious: I like you, I desire you, I can easily lose my head and go crazy for you.

But then, she wasn't the type of girl to lose her head. She had too much at stake, too many responsibilities, starting with making the gallery a viable proposition for the next umpteen years just as Barb would've wanted.

'How about you start with the truth?'

Ariel compressed her lips, a simple, defensive gesture to prevent her from blurting a whole host of truths that Cooper wouldn't want to hear: the truth was, she was petrified the gallery would slip through her fingers despite how hard she'd worked to keep it afloat, she was petrified she'd let everyone down and, the biggie of them all, she was petrified of how this guy made her feel.

So, despite her usual trait for brutal honesty, she opted for the easy way out.

She lied.

'There isn't anything between us beyond the usual guy-girl chemistry. We're opposites in every way and you want something from me I can't give you, *imperative* or not.'

Avoiding his penetrating stare, she continued, 'I won't sell, you don't get what you want and we have no reason to keep meeting like this so let's call it quits while we're both still being civil to one another, okay?'

She expected him to bamboozle her with a whole lot of convoluted arguments, similar to the ones in his long-winded business proposal, to change her mind.

She expected him to pressure her, to ram home the reasons why obtaining *her* gallery was so darn *imperative* to him.

Instead, he surprised her yet again.

He took a step forward, invading her personal space with his overpowering presence, and she resisted the urge to lean into him, to experience the thrill of having his arms slide around her one last time and making her forget every single reason why they couldn't be together.

Placing a finger under her chin, he gently tipped it up and stared into her eyes. 'You know the interesting thing about chemistry? It can lead to explosive reactions and unexpected outcomes.'

She should look away.

She wanted to look away.

Instead, she stared at him like a hypnotised dummy while his thumb brushed her bottom lip with infinite tenderness and he smiled, a hot, loaded smile.

'Oh, and one more thing. Chemistry was my best subject.'

Before she could gather her wits and tell him exactly what he could do with his subjects, he pulled her into his arms and kissed her.

This was her last chance.

Push him away, and ignore all the great things he'd said about her.

He deepened the kiss, his hands winding through her curls, angling her head for better access, and the second his tongue touched hers she lost it.

The point of no return.

She pushed him back against the sofa, her hands everywhere, sliding under black cotton, stroking the hot skin of his tight abs beneath.

Someone moaned, a low, sexy sound, and in the passionate haze that had invaded her brain she had no idea if it was him or her. Nor did she care.

The scent of him, the feel of him, the taste of him, the sounds of ragged breathing and low moans set a spark to her latent libido.

'You sure about this?'

Cooper broke the kiss for a second, capturing her face in his hands, staring deep into her eyes.

'Shut up and kiss me,' she said, the blatant lust radiating from his too-blue gaze setting fire to any tiny residual doubt she might have harboured and sending it up in smoke.

'Your call.'

And he did exactly as she'd instructed, with one heck of a difference.

He didn't hold back.

Their mouths clashed in a heated frenzy of lips and tongues, challenging, duelling, an erotic game where there were no losers, only winners.

Ariel sighed as his lips slid down her throat and she arched against him, bringing her into direct contact with his erection, his very impressive erection if the size of his hardness against her belly was any indication.

'God, you're beautiful,' he said, his lips ceasing their leisurely exploration as he swiftly unbuttoned her top and peeled it open, the anticipatory gleam in his eyes like that of a man opening the best present ever.

The few times she'd had sex in the past, she'd hated the undressing bit. Inadequacies had plagued her growing up, and they manifested at the oddest of times, such as now when she hoped her boobs weren't a disappointment and he wouldn't find her too skinny.

'Stunning,' he breathed, unclipping her bra with a deft flick of his fingers and staring at her breasts as if he'd found treasure, before capturing a nipple in his mouth.

'That feels so good,' she murmured, writhing beneath him, wishing their clothes would disappear, burning up from the inside.

'You feel so good.'

And he set about proving it, drawing his tongue slowly across her chest, sucking one nipple then the other, feasting on her as if he hadn't eaten in a decade.

Ariel throbbed in so many places she didn't know whether she should shock the living daylights out of Cooper and devour him now or prolong the sweet agony and let him continue to lavish her with more of the exquisite licking and sucking that was sending her into meltdown.

'I need you,' she whispered, proving just how much by sliding a hand between them and cupping his erection.

Cooper tensed, muttered a very sexy curse and pulled away, staring at her in such a searing way that desire shot through her veins, her nipples pebbled and a heaviness settled in her core.

'Now.'

He hovered over her, a sexy smile playing around his mouth. 'You know you're bossy and sassy and thoroughly irresistible, don't you?'

'I'll show you bossy.'

She surged upwards, her hands against his chest, pushing him upright against the back of the sofa and straddling him.

He laughed, a low, rich, wicked sound that provoked her to show him just how bossy she could be.

She whipped his T-shirt over his head in a second, leaning forward to nuzzle his neck and drape her hair across his bare chest. He groaned and she smiled, a small, self-satisfied smile of a woman who knew she had the power to drive a guy crazy.

'Hmm…think you're in charge, huh?'

His hands spanned her waist, holding her in place while he shifted beneath her, leaving her in little doubt that the second their clothes vanished down below, she'd be in heaven.

'You ain't seen nothing yet,' she said, sliding off him to kneel at his feet, her fingers making short work of his zipper and button, easing the denim down his long legs with her gaze locked on his the entire time.

His low moan turned her on.

His glazed look empowered her.

His stirring erection beneath tight black boxers encouraged her to toy with the elastic, brush her fingertips against his penis and slowly, tantalisingly peel the cotton down his legs.

'Oh, wow,' she said, sitting on her heels and admiring the view. A very hard, very large erection was standing to attention, liquid heat pooling between her legs as she reached out to stroke it.

'Hell, Ariel,' Cooper gritted out, hanging onto what little self-control he had left when her hand wrapped around his shaft and started moving up and down in slow, rhythmic movements.

'Don't you mean heaven?'

Her sassy mouth curved into a knowing smile as she flicked her thumb over the hood, sending him into overdrive.

'You're a minx.'

He stilled her hand, sliding to the floor next to her, grateful for the soft, plush rug over the boards.

'Hey, what happened to me being in charge?'

'My turn,' he said, knowing he couldn't last much longer.

He'd been fantasising about Ariel for too long, wondering what she'd look like naked, wondering what colour her nipples would be, wondering how she'd sound when he took her.

Her breasts were gorgeous, a perfect handful, with dusky pink nipples that stood out at the slightest provocation. Considering his hands and mouth hadn't left them alone since he'd taken off her top, they were very provoked.

Now, he had to see the rest of her, taste the rest of her, feel her hot and tight around him before he lost it completely.

Sliding a slow, sensual kiss across her swollen lips, he had those sexy little hot-pants off her in one smooth tug. The red satin G-string beneath got tangled up at the same time and when he broke the kiss to stare down at her, his sigh bordered on reverence.

'You're stunning. Every exquisite inch.'

He kissed her again, softly this time, teasing, pleasing as his fingers delved in her moist heat, finding her nub and circling it with his thumb, loving the small, excited sounds she made in his mouth.

She broke off the kiss, her head falling back, her breathing ragged as he slid two fingers inside her, his thumb stroking her folds, her clitoris, with increasing pressure.

'Cooper.'

Their gazes locked as she convulsed around his fingers, her body arching upwards, her orgasm heating the gold flecks in her eyes till they glowed amber.

He had to have her, right at that precise second, with her soft and pliant and sated in his arms.

'More.'

He stared at her sassy mouth, knowing a woman like Ariel would be a never-ending source of surprises and hoping he'd get an opportunity to discover them all.

Though he wasn't a fool.

This was sex and she'd probably withdraw from him in a big way in the morning. Not if he had his way. This attraction had been simmering between them right from the very beginning and he had no intention of letting this be a one-night stand.

Besides, he had a feeling sex with the stunning artist could become addictive. Very addictive. And he didn't have too many vices.

'More, huh? Boy, there's no pleasing some women.'

'I'm pleased all right,' she said. 'You, on the other hand, could do with a bit of pleasuring yourself.'

She sent a pointed look at his groin, her fingers closing around his erection, and he groaned.

'Hold that…thought,' he said, fumbling through the back pocket of his jeans for his wallet, grabbing a condom and ripping open the little blue foil packet while Ariel continued to stroke him, her sexy laugh driving him as insane as her hand.

Ariel loved the silky hardness of Cooper's penis, loved the fact she turned him on. She reluctantly released him, watching him slide the condom on, her insides constricting at the thought that she'd soon be sheathing him just as effectively.

'Hurry,' she said, wondering when she'd become such a floozy and not particularly caring.

She wanted Cooper.

Inside her, pleasuring her, hard and hot and pounding, satisfying the ache that had begun the first time he'd taken off his clothes for her.

'Come here.'

Cooper opened his arms to her and Ariel didn't

hesitate, straddling him, kissing him, revelling in the tip of his penis nudging at her entrance as she sank down, almost passing out with sheer satisfaction as he stretched her, filled her.

'You feel…' he groaned, loudly, as she raised up and sank down again, taking him in deeper, relaxing her muscles around him, savouring the fullness, the heat.

'Good?'

'Sensational.'

She lost it after that. Thankfully, he did too. Her hands tangled in his hair, she bit into his shoulder as he thrust upwards so hard she almost hit the ceiling and he flipped her over, driving into her with a wild pounding that sent them both into orbit.

Her abandoned scream matched his noisy groan and as she floated back to her senses her first thought was, That was absolutely incredible.

Closely followed by, What the heck have I done?

CHAPTER TWELVE

PALE gold filtered through the tiny bathroom window, heralding the dawn of another perfect Melbourne day.

Though it wasn't just another day.

Ariel braced herself on the antique washbasin, staring at her tousled reflection in the bevelled mirror.

You had sex with Cooper Vance.

And not just ordinary sex. Scintillating, mind-blowing, burn-up-the-sheets sex, though they'd never quite made it to the bed till later. Much later.

She'd never be able to look at her favourite rug in the studio again without remembering the way he'd felt inside her, the way he'd touched her all over, the way he'd made her crave him with every turned-on cell in her body.

The man was a menace.

She'd known it from the first second he'd set foot in her studio and now she had proof. And how!

Closing her eyes, she leaned forward and rested her forehead against the cool glass. What had she done?

She'd been doing her level best to push him away, to ignore the sizzling attraction between them, to focus on saving her business—which meant getting as far from corporate Mr Big-Shot as possible.

Instead, she'd melted into a puddle of lust the minute he'd kissed her and nothing would ever be the same again.

At least, not for her.

She didn't do casual sex, never had. She could count her past encounters on one hand and each had been with guys she'd been dating for a while, boyfriends. The scary thing was, nothing about last night with Cooper felt casual. She felt as if she knew him and that was what scared her more than the way she'd been with him. Or how much she'd enjoyed it.

'You okay?'

Ariel jerked upright and her eyes flew open; she wished she'd kept them tightly shut. The sight of Cooper, a very naked Cooper, reflected all too clearly in the mirror and her heart flipped.

'Fine. Just a bit tired.'

'I'm not surprised.'

He smiled, a warm, intimate smile that notched up the temperature in the bathroom by a hundred degrees.

'I didn't mean to wake you,' she said, fiddling with the tie of her favourite kimono, wishing he'd stop staring at her as if he were starving and she were breakfast. 'I'm usually up pretty early.'

'No problems.'

Silence stretched between them, an awkward, tense silence she would've given anything to avoid. Why couldn't he get dressed and get the heck out of her life? Why couldn't he stop gawking at her?

'You're okay about what happened last night, right?'

To her annoyance, she blushed. 'Fine.'

'You sure about that?'

She stiffened as he came up behind her and slid his arms around her waist, leaving her no option but to lean back against him or jump up on the antique vanity.

'You're gorgeous,' he murmured, nuzzling her neck, sending shivers through her body, resurrecting erotic memories of the way he'd kissed every inch of her last night. Every inch...

'And you're crazy,' she said, taking in her blonde frizzy hair, her swollen lips, which looked as if they'd been ravaged all night—pretty darn close to it!—and her eyes, large and luminous and filled with fear.

Fear of where to now, fear of how much she'd miss him once he exited her life, fear of never finding a guy to make her feel half as good as he'd made her feel last night.

'Whose fault is that?' He kissed his way up her neck, turning her around slowly, staring deep into her eyes. 'You make me crazy. With your sexy smile, with your incredible eyes, with that mouth that makes me want to do everything I did with you last night and so much more.'

'You can cut the sweet talk. I'm a sure thing, remember?'

'Time for you to shut that sassy mouth of yours. Again,' he said, lowering his lips to hers in a slow, sensual kiss that would've curled her toes if she hadn't been standing on them to reach up, desperate for his kiss, hating her treacherous body for it.

'I thought you said you didn't have any more condoms?'

By the feel of his erection pressing against her stomach, she guessed he wasn't popping into the bathroom for a quick goodbye. More like a quickie something else.

'I don't.' His hands strummed her back through the silk of her kimono, the slow, steady rhythm making her arch like a cat. Next she'd be purring. 'Don't worry, we won't need them. I was only planning on taking a shower, that's it.'

But that wasn't it.

He tugged on the knotted tie and slid his hands under the front of her kimono, skimming her skin, teasing with his touch, brushing her nipples with his thumbs till they peaked in sweet agony.

Her breath hitched as he slid the silk from her body with infinite patience, one exquisite inch at a time till the kimono pooled at their feet in a slash of vibrant emerald-green against the white tiles.

'I don't think my shower's big enough for the both of us,' she said, eyeing the small glass cubicle with suspicion, considering Cooper took up most of the bathroom already.

'All the better for a nice close fit.'

With an arm firmly draped around her waist to prevent escape—great, the guy was a mind-reader too?—he turned on the hot and cold taps, tested the water temp and took the opportunity to turn the five-second wait into another scorching kiss.

She could've shrugged out of his grip.

She could've picked up her kimono and stalked from the bathroom with what little dignity she had left intact.

But then, where was the fun in that?

She'd spent a lifetime being serious, first surviving and later being the model niece for Barb. And more recently, worrying her head off about how to keep the gallery afloat. She never had time for fun.

For that was what this last taste of Cooper would be: pure, unadulterated fun.

'You coming in? The water's warm.'

He didn't force her, standing there wearing nothing but a sexy, persuasive smile, his arm loosely draped around her waist.

Now or never...

Sending him a coy glance from beneath her lashes, she said, 'You bet,' and stepped with him into the shower.

A staunch environmentalist, Ariel conserved water by taking minimal showers even though she loved the hot spray peppering her skin. Today, however, her ideals flew out the window along with her reservations as she leaned against Cooper, her back wedged against his front, while his hands travelled her body in long, slow strokes, soaping, circling, teasing, turning her legs to jelly before he delved between them and brought her to a screaming orgasm with a few deft flicks of his fingers.

'You're a dangerous woman,' he said, pulling her into a tight hug that squeezed the breath out of her. Or was it the intensity in his blue-eyed stare that robbed her of the normal function of air-in, air-out?

'Not really. But I can be.'

She sent him a smile designed to entice, a smile filled with promise.

He'd given her so much pleasure, it was time to return the favour. In spades.

Reaching between them, she captured his erection in her hand, stroking it till he groaned, loving the ecstasy etched on his face as she moved harder, faster, till he came in a hot rush.

His head had fallen back, exposing the strong column of his neck, and she placed a gentle kiss there, knowing they could never recapture this moment, shocked by how sad that made her feel.

Neither spoke.

Instead, Cooper opened his eyes, smiled and rested his forehead against hers, not moving, not saying a word.

And as the water sprayed down on them Ariel knew why.

They had nothing to say.

After all, what could you say when you'd just slept with the enemy?

Cooper knew the precise time his revamped proposal had been delivered to Ariel: ten o'clock. It was now ten twenty-five and it would've taken her exactly twenty-five minutes to high-tail it to Vance Corporation in the Central Business District of Melbourne, including the time she would've spent jumping up and down on the spot having a tantrum.

She wasn't going to like the amendments he'd made to the proposal.

In fact, if the ruckus outside his office door was any indication, she intended on making her feelings known to all and sundry before she even made it into his office.

As he pushed back from his desk and strode across his office the door flung open.

'You've got a nerve!' Ariel shouted, making a

beeline for him while Beryl, his secretary, gave an apologetic shrug and made crazy signs with her finger circling her temple.

'I'll take it from here, thanks, Beryl,' he said, walking straight past Ariel to shut the door.

Not that it would make much difference. Half of Flinders Street would've heard Ariel's indignant shriek as she whirled and advanced on him, her eyes filled with emerald fire and her curls bristling about her like a fuzzy halo.

Not that there was anything remotely angelic about the woman considering what they'd got up to last night and in the shower first thing this morning.

'Why don't you take a seat and we discuss the new developments like two rational adults?'

'Rational?'

She drew back her shoulders, drawing his attention to her breasts straining against the Paisley halter top that moulded her like a second skin, eliciting erotic memories of the way she'd felt lying on top of him last night, passionate, feverish, responsive, like a fantasy come to life.

'You expect me to be rational when you have a courier deliver me this?'

Reaching into a huge straw carryall, she flung a sheaf of papers onto his desk and planted her hands on her hips, looking like an avenging Amazon come to slay him. 'Tell me this isn't what it looks like.'

'What does it look like?'

He shouldn't antagonise her further, he really shouldn't, but a small part of him was enjoying their confrontation.

She'd had all the comebacks last night, shooting him down in flames when all he'd tried to do was lay the foundations for a possible future relationship.

She'd hadn't listened to him, she hadn't acknowledged his honesty and she sure as hell hadn't given them a chance even after the most mind-blowing sex. Several times.

If he were completely honest with himself, he didn't know if he wanted a future with this woman but he'd be damned if he walked away without exploring the fireworks that exploded whenever they were within two feet of each other.

She was confusing business with pleasure and the only way he knew to bring this to quick closure was to finish the business and move onto more of the pleasure. A lot more…of her soft lips clinging to his, her hands all over his body, her excited little moans as he licked her to orgasm…

'What is wrong with you?' She broached the short distance between them and snapped her fingers in front of his face. 'Cut the vague act and start explaining.'

Wrestling his raging libido into some semblance of control, he headed for the safety of his desk and away from Ariel's intoxicating scent. He'd never smelt anything like it and the weird perfume he could now label as neroli thanks to the tiny essential-oil vial he'd spied in her bag the other day had grown on him. A lot. He doubted he'd ever smell oranges again without remembering the blonde goddess with the eyes of green fire.

'Would you like a drink?'

'No! I would like an explanation. Now.'

She grudgingly plopped into the leather chair opposite his and folded her arms, looking like a recalcitrant schoolgirl waiting for punishment from the principal.

He sat down, straightening the messy papers scattered on his desk, hoping a few extra seconds would help calm her down.

When he caught her eye and saw the narrow green slits glowing with anger, he knew a few extra hours wouldn't help.

'If you've read the amendments, you don't need an explanation. It's pretty clear.'

'The part where you're threatening me or the part where you'll do anything to get your grubby hands on the gallery?'

She leaned forward, her fingers clenching his desk till the knuckles whitened. 'Oops, silly me. The gallery doesn't mean a thing to you, it's the land you're after. I really must learn to clarify my terms, just like you have in this pathetic excuse for a proposal.'

He let her vent. He'd expected the animosity, the antagonism, but it hurt nonetheless.

He cared about her.

And he hadn't realised how much till just now when she looked at him with loathing and contempt.

Damn it, what if his plan backfired?

What if, in attempting to finish the business side of things and move onto the personal, he finished them completely?

'I'm not threatening you; I'm giving you an opportunity to come out of this deal a winner.'

Her scornful look burned a hole straight through to his conscience. 'You're trying to buy me off to get what you want. And if I don't comply, you go ahead and offer the council twice what the land is worth by the end of today?'

She shook her head, golden curls rioting around her face and a perfect contrast for the faint pink staining her cheeks. 'Some "opportunity".'

'This deal has to go through. Today,' he said, feeling like a heel when the fire drained from her eyes only to be replaced by fear.

'I need some more time.'

Her whispered plea slammed into his soul, raising questions he'd rather ignore.

Was his dream more important than hers?

Did he care enough about her to turn his back on his own future?

If he cared, how much?

And what was he going to do about it?

'Time isn't going to help.'

Either of them. He needed to get out of Vance Corporation, she needed to start a new gallery elsewhere with the money he was determined she would have. And they needed to recreate the fire that had consumed them both last night, repeatedly.

'You don't know that. There's the National Trust, the Victorian Arts Council…' She trailed off, the truth finally dawning in her stricken eyes. 'You've already made the offer, haven't you?'

Cooper hesitated, knowing he couldn't lie to the woman he loved yet aware the truth would potentially ruin what little chance they had for a future.

The woman he loved?

He slumped in his chair, the words echoing through his head like a gunshot.

He loved her…he loved her…he loved her…

It couldn't be.

No way.

His mind must've slipped up under the strain, substituting the L word for caring.

Yeah, that sounded better. He cared for her.

Much better.

Yet when he met her defeated stare, unshed tears glistening green, his heart made a mockery of his head.

For a guy who thrived on cool, hard facts, who used

logic to sort through everything, an emotion he had little time for had snuck up and whacked him a beauty.

The longer Ariel stared at him, the worse his heart clenched till it took every ounce of will-power not to leap from his chair and cradle her in his arms.

'Tell me the truth.'

Cooper started, shocked to think she'd seen right through him in his moment of revelation before realising she meant the truth about his offer to the council. He could've sagged with relief if the thought that what he was about to say would probably rob him of any chance to express his newly discovered feelings ever.

Taking a deep breath, he selected his words carefully. 'I have approached the council and had discussions about the sale of land but nothing has been formalised.'

'But you've basically thrown more money at them than they know what to do with, right? So if I don't accept your offer now and sell out before the lease is up, they're going to jump at it pretty much straight away?'

He nodded, hating the defeated slump to her shoulders, the shaking hand that fiddled with a curl near her right ear, winding it furiously around and around till he thought it would snap off.

'So what was the extra time about? Giving me another twenty-four hours to stew before I finally capitulate to Mr Big-Shot and make his day?'

Scorn dripped from every word and she straightened, anger replacing defeat in her eyes.

That's my girl, he thought, admiring her fighting spirit yet wishing he weren't the one to instigate it.

'I want you to do this of your own accord, to make the decision yourself.'

She laughed, a harsh, hollow sound that had nothing to do with happiness. 'That's rich coming from you.' Tapping her temple, she looked heavenward as if deep in thought. 'Let me see. I get to make my own decision as long as it's by the end of today. Thanks so much.'

'We're going round in circles here. That's my final offer and, as a smart businesswoman, I think you should take it.'

Though it wasn't his final offer, not if he had any say. Once this whole mess got sorted and they could put business behind them, he had a whole host of other offers in mind, the main one being a relationship.

He didn't have a whole lot of experience with love.

He'd loved his mum; she'd died when he was too young.

He loved his dad; he might as well have died.

No, love wasn't a reliable emotion, but one thing was for certain; he loved Ariel and he'd make damn sure he gave it his best shot.

Her steady green-eyed gaze locked on his. 'Why is this deal so important to you? You've used words

like imperative. I just don't get why a ruthless businessman like you would fluff around for a couple of
weeks, posing almost naked, going out for coffees,
attending art shows and the like when you could've
shafted me right from the start. What's with that?'

Cooper bit back an ironic smile. Here was his big
chance to hint at his burgeoning feelings.

And get the same reaction he'd had last night
before they'd had sensational sex? No way. Making
a total ass of himself twice in less than twenty-four
hours wasn't his style.

He settled for semi-truth. It was the least he could
do considering she'd stood up to everything he'd
thrown at her and then some.

'This deal is my ticket out of here. It's something
I've been planning towards for a while now and I
really need to make it happen.'

Her lips twisted in a cynical smile. 'Why? Aren't
they paying you enough? Not enough perks? The
boss got you over a barrel? Though with a name like
Vance Corporation, I'm guessing you like to keep it
all in the family.'

All in the family.

Ironic, considering he'd lost the bulk of his family,
his dad, that fateful day almost a year ago when he'd
signed on the dotted line, blown away to be working
with someone of Eric's reputation.

'My father's the CEO,' Cooper said. And all his

dad cared about these days was making money, acquiring prime land, developing properties. And all at the expense of the things that used to matter to him, like fishing, four-wheel driving and hanging out with his son.

Despite Cooper's drive to leave Vance Corp behind, he knew he'd miss his dad. Cooper hadn't given up on him completely. Maybe his dad would remember the old saying 'absence makes the heart grow fonder' and make an effort to patch things up once he left?

He hoped so but he wouldn't hold his breath.

Ariel quirked an eyebrow, losing none of her sass despite the anger tightening her exquisite features. 'So it can't be the pay or the perks that's the problem if daddy holds the purse strings. What is it? The executive bathroom not up to scratch? You've lost your car park?'

'It's time for me to go it alone. You of all people should understand that.'

'Oh.'

Ariel blushed and practically squirmed in her seat, and he held up his hand to ward off whatever she was about to say when she opened her mouth.

'My motivation is irrelevant. What needs to be done right now is you placing your signature on the dotted line before five o'clock today. That's all that matters.'

He rustled papers and, along with his brisk tone,

hoped that gave her the message. He needed to concentrate on the business at hand, get away from the sensitive topic of his motivation. The momentary concern he'd glimpsed in her eyes had him wanting to blurt out the whole sorry tale just to get it off his chest.

But he couldn't. He was a guy, a tough Aussie bloke, a man's man. He would stifle his feelings and get on with things. His dad's mantra, not his.

And for the last year, he'd thought his dad's mantra sucked.

'All that matters?' she muttered, grabbing her bag and leaping from her chair as if she'd sat on hot coals. 'What matters is that you're a selfish, spoiled rich boy who always gets what he wants. You don't care about who gets trampled on the way or whose dreams your ruin. And to think I was actually feeling for you a few seconds ago, about the whole going-it-alone, doing-it-tough thing!'

'I don't need your pity.'

He shot to his feet, torn between wanting to blurt the truth and sending her packing for her damning character assessment. Though at that moment, he didn't know what rankled more: the fact she thought so poorly of him or the tiny niggle of truth in what she'd said.

He was selfish.

He did want this deal to go through, whatever the cost.

But what if it cost him the woman he loved?

'I guess not. A guy like you wouldn't need anything from a girl like me. Besides sex, of course, and now that you've got that it's back to business as usual.'

He was surprised it had taken her this long to mention what had happened at her place last night. He'd been grateful for it, preferring to keep this a business discussion and totally separate from the other important issue: them.

'That's not fair. We talked about what happened last night before I left this morning. It has nothing to do with this.'

'You would say that.'

Her scathing look of condemnation kicked him in the guts before she twirled on her heel and headed for the door.

'Last night was incredible, Ariel, and you know it. Don't spoil it by bringing business into it.'

She hesitated at the door but she didn't turn around.

Damn it, the sooner this deal went through, the sooner he could move on to more important things such as showing this stubborn, beautiful woman just how much she meant to him.

'This needs to be finalised, Ariel. Today.'

She ignored him and strutted out the door, slamming it in her wake, a hollow, empty sound that reverberated through his soul as he realised she'd probably just slammed the door on any chance of a future between them.

'What's all the ruckus about?'

Eric barged into Cooper's office, shirt sleeves rolled up to the elbows, tie-less and with a killer crease in his navy trousers, his usual work garb. His father never conformed, though he expected nothing less than perfection in his employees.

Cooper sank into his chair and gestured for his dad to take the seat Ariel had just vacated. 'Ariel Wallace was just in here.'

Cooper held up his hand to forestall his dad's usual interrogation. 'The deal will be done by the close of business today.'

'Good.'

Cooper struggled not to gape at his dad's one-word, one-syllable answer without a hint of emotion. He'd expected cartwheels from the man who had been after the last bit of prime land in Fitzroy since for ever.

However, what shocked him more was the uncomfortable, almost sad look on his dad's creased face. It resembled the expression he'd worn after his mum's funeral, the same devastated, lost look that came with realising you would never see that person again, would never talk to that person again or share a hug or a laugh with them again.

'What's up? You don't sound so thrilled.'

Cooper expected his dad to give him the brush-off, the usual 'back to business' gruff response he normally got.

His dad ran a hand through his thick thatch of peppery grey hair, his gaze darting around the room as if he wanted to look anywhere but at him.

'Guess I can't change your mind about leaving?'

'No, Dad. You can't,' Cooper said, deliberately keeping his voice devoid of emotion.

Close on the heels of his draining confrontation with Ariel—and the stunning realisation he loved her—he didn't need this.

He'd waited long enough, hoping his dad would broach the yawning gap between them. He'd given his all to Vance Corporation, playing the dutiful son, trying to prove his worth rather than live off the family name, but it looked as if his best efforts weren't good enough.

Nothing he could do or say would ever be good enough and he'd stuck around way too long already. Time to cut his losses and run. And hope to God that his dad would realise what he'd lost when he wasn't around every day.

'That's the first time you've called me that in a long time,' Eric said, his gaze finally coming to rest on his face, the wavering uncertainty Cooper glimpsed there surprising him.

His father was never uncertain about anything.

Ruthless, domineering and pushy, yes.

Uncertain and wavering? No way.

Probably the old man's last-ditch effort to make him stay on at Vance Corp.

'You haven't exactly encouraged familial bonds since I joined the company,' Cooper said, opting for blunt honesty to get this over and done with. No use rehashing the last year now.

Once again, his dad surprised him. Rather than blustering his way out of an unwelcome topic and changing the subject quick smart, his dad seemed to crumple before his eyes: slumped shoulders, head slouched forward, mouth slack with pain.

'Look, forget I said anything—'

'No.'

His dad's head snapped up and some of the familiar fire blazed in his dark eyes. 'You're right. I don't blame you for not calling me Dad. I've pushed you away. I've made a mess of everything.'

Cooper didn't respond, considering he agreed with everything his dad had just said. Besides, his dad had a look he hadn't seen in twelve months, a look that he genuinely cared about Cooper enough to want to talk to him about something other than business.

'I thought I'd never recover from losing your mother but having you got me through her death. You were my world. Then you started working here...' Eric drifted off, pain glazing his eyes and accentuating the multitude of lines fanning out from their corners.

'But that's what you wanted,' Cooper said, confusion lending a sharp edge to his words.

'I know.'

His dad raised pain-stricken eyes to his, his mouth twisted into a grimace.

'Then why?'

Cooper didn't have to add, Why ignore me? Why treat me like dirt? Why act like I didn't exist, like I wasn't your son any more?

'Because I'm an old fool. A gutless old fool who saw his life flash before his eyes the minute you sealed your first deal. I'm jealous, son. I've been so jealous I couldn't see straight. Throw in the fear that I'll soon be redundant, and the fact you keep negotiating deals I can't seem to seal these days, and there you have it.'

'You're jealous?' Cooper shook his head, knowing there had to be more to it. 'That's it?'

His dad sagged before his eyes. 'Age does stupid things to a man. I was bursting with pride when you first signed up then within two months I wanted to boot you straight out the door.'

'Then why the contract? Why not let me go months ago when I wanted to?'

Eric looked away. 'Because you're great for the company. You've brought more business in over the last year than I have in the last five years. I pushed you harder, knowing you wouldn't disappoint.'

'You took advantage of the fact your son wouldn't tell you to shove it,' Cooper said, stunned to discover the reason behind his dad's animosity, feeling as if he was still missing a major piece of the puzzle.

'There's something else.'

Cooper leaned forward, not sure if he'd heard Eric's whispered words.

'What?'

'A guilty conscience,' his dad said, shaking his head, sorrow ageing him ten years before his eyes. 'Masterson's approached me just after you started here. They were head-hunting you. Heard about the whizkid from uni, knew you were my son, wanted to throw a few spanners Vance Corp's way but wanted to do it right. They were fishing around, wanting to know if you'd signed a binding contract, that sort of thing. All over a friendly beer, of course. They were going to approach you directly after paying me the courtesy visit, but I lied, put them off.'

A light bulb went off in Cooper's mind. 'So that's why you made me sign a contract like everyone else the month after I started?'

Eric nodded, his mouth downturned. 'I told them you were legally bound to Vance Corporation and that was that.'

'Before I signed the contract?'

'Uh-huh.'

'Was their offer any good?'

'Unbelievable.' Eric hesitated, wringing his hands before continuing. 'I'm sorry, son. I was selfish, wanting you to carry on the family tradition, then when I had you where I wanted you, I couldn't handle your success. Stupid, irrational, call it what you like. I'm an idiot.'

Cooper digested the information, knowing he should feel more angry, more deceived. Instead, a strange feeling of relief seeped through him. He finally knew the truth and it had nothing to do with him.

'I know I've treated you like crap, but I want you to know that I'm damn proud of you, Coop.'

Finally, his dad met his gaze and, thankfully, the spark had returned. If anything, the dark eyes glowed with fervour as if daring him to disagree, to challenge. Instead, Cooper smiled.

'You know, for a smart guy, you've made some pretty dumb judgement calls, but I'm willing to forgive and forget if you'll do one thing.'

'What's that?' His dad glared at him with some of his characteristic suspicion and Cooper's smile widened.

'Go fishing with me this weekend. Have a beer or two, just like old times.'

'You're on, son.'

Eric's grin matched his and Cooper shook his head, wishing they'd had this conversation months ago.

'Does this mean you're staying?'

'Don't push your luck, old man.'

Though his dad had posed a valid question.

Today was the first time he'd really looked at his dad in a long time and he didn't like the changes. His dad looked older, more fragile than he had in ages and maybe now wasn't a great time to spread his wings and leave the Vance nest, particularly as it looked as if re-establishing bonds would be high on both their priority lists for a while.

Eric held up both hands as if warding him off. 'Fine, fine, no harm in trying. By the way, is there something going on between you and the Wallace woman?'

Cooper hesitated a second before answering. 'No, why do you ask?'

It wasn't a completely untruthful answer, considering Ariel would probably never speak to him again after today.

His dad shrugged. 'Just a hunch, by the doomsday look on your face when I first came in here and by the tears streaming down her face as she raced out of here after slamming your door.'

'A difference of opinion,' Cooper said, his heart stuttering at the thought of Ariel crying over what he'd done.

'Looked more like a lovers' tiff than a difference of opinion over a business deal to me.'

His dad paused, giving him ample opportunity to deny it. Cooper merely clamped his lips together.

'Then again, what do I know? I'm a stupid old fool and now we both know it.'

His dad rose to his feet, pushed his shirt sleeves higher and stuck out his hand, looking like the confident Eric of old. 'You know I'm proud of you, Son.'

'Thanks, Dad.'

Cooper shook hands with his dad and shared a smile, a smile filled with hope for their future, before his dad sent him a half-salute and strode out of the office, leaving Cooper to decide how big a mistake he'd made with Ariel and how he could rectify it.

CHAPTER THIRTEEN

ARIEL dabbed her paintbrush in the crimson daub on her palette and made great slashing movements across the canvas propped on the easel in front of her.

Red, the colour of anger and fury.

She followed up with a dab and slash of ebony.

Black, the colour of darkness and gloom.

Another slash, this time with sunshine yellow.

Yellow, the colour of that lily-livered, no-good Cooper Vance's belly, the coward.

She slashed away, combining the colours in a frightening free-for-all in a painting that would never see the light of day but was soothing to her battered soul nonetheless.

The colours summed up her mood perfectly. She'd never felt as angry, gloomy or scared as she did right now, the afternoon she would lose her dream. Not to mention renege on a promise that she'd vowed to keep till her dying day.

Cooper Vance was evil.

Pure, unadulterated evil.

He'd used her, schmoozing up to her, acting like a friend, playing on her emotions, initiating her into the best sex she'd ever had in her life, making her love him and all for what? To whip the gallery right out from under her nose anyway.

What Cooper wanted, Cooper got and she'd been justified in calling him a selfish, spoiled brat earlier. She just wished she'd had the guts to say more.

Slumping forward, she rested her forehead against the canvas, not caring about the instant oil-paint tattoo imprinted there.

She'd never felt so alone, so defeated…and in the midst of her absolute misery a thought so profound, so awful, pierced her gloom.

What had she thought a few seconds ago? Something about *making her love him*?

She loved him? Was she out of her mind?

Uh-uh.

No way.

No how.

Must be the stress sending her insane. She'd heard about people going crazy with post-traumatic stress disorder. Maybe her bout had set in early?

She couldn't love him.

He was obnoxious, self-centred and a know-it-all Mr Big-Shot.

He had insinuated his way into her life and got under her skin before flaying it off her with cold, calculated precision, all in the name of sealing his precious deal.

The very idea she could love a guy like that was preposterous.

But what if you do?

'Oh, heck,' she muttered, sitting bolt upright and staring blankly at the vivid canvas, wishing she could turn the clock back a few minutes and wipe out her thoughts.

For, once the question had been raised by her stupid inner self, she knew without a doubt what the answer was and it made her want to head-bang the canvas repeatedly in the hope it would knock some sense into her.

'*Bella*, you here?'

Ariel hadn't heard the chimes signalling Sofia's entrance to the gallery—probably all those insane inner voices whispering silly nothings in her head about loving Cooper Vance—and knew she wasn't in the mood for a chat.

Maybe if she pleaded a headache she could get rid of her friend, close up for the day and harass some poor courier to deliver a bomb along with the signed papers to Cooper?

The stupid proposal she had no option now but to sign thanks to the traitorous louse's deadline.

'Out the back, Sofia,' she called out, cleaning her brushes and palette out of habit rather than a driving necessity to do so.

Besides, she needed something to do with her hands other than put the finishing flourish on the document signalling her ultimate demise.

'Bella! How are you?'

Sofia bustled into the studio, dressed in head-to-toe fuchsia and sporting a hat that could take out a person's eye at twenty paces.

Ariel turned from the sink and rubbed her hands down the front of her smock. 'Actually, I have a headache.'

To her surprise, Sofia laughed rather than cooed in concern. 'Must be all that paint seeping into your brain,' she said, pointing to her forehead and beaming, her perfectly capped teeth in stark contrast to the bright pink of her dress.

Ariel managed a rueful smile as she picked up a nearby rag and swiped at her forehead. 'I forgot in all the excitement.'

'Excitement?'

Sofia's nose twitched at the faintest hint of gossip and right now, her nostrils fairly quivered.

'Yes, the excitement of trying out a new technique. I read about this tribe in Africa who only paint with their heads so thought I'd try it out. Want to see the results?'

Ariel's smile broadened at the confused expression on Sofia's exquisitely made-up face. In a way, Sofia's impromptu visit had achieved a miracle already. She'd smiled when a few minutes earlier it had felt as if she'd never smile again.

'*Mamma mia!*'

Sofia's hands flew to her mouth as she stared at the canvas, her shocked gaze darting between the painting and Ariel's face and back again.

'You don't like?'

'It's horrible, *bella*! Nasty. Angry. Ugly. No, no, no, this is not you at all.'

Ariel stood alongside Sofia and stared at the canvas, the vivid streaks of red, black and yellow telling an emotional story she couldn't hide.

'I take it you don't want to buy this one for your collection?'

Ariel stepped away from the painting, finding it suddenly depressing. Usually, painting was a way to express herself, a way to feel good about the world, a cathartic experience, but somehow seeing the angry slashes of vibrant paint saddened her and reminded her exactly why she'd picked up the brush on the return from Cooper's office.

She'd needed to debrief, to offload, to express one iota of the devastation wreaking havoc on her psyche, and painting had been her only option.

Sadly, it hadn't helped and now she had to allay

Sofia's qualms before she blabbed the whole sorry tale to her friend.

'What is it, *bella*? What is the problem?' Sofia grabbed both her hands and squeezed, her coal-black eyes beseeching, a frown creasing her brow.

'No problem,' Ariel said, using every ounce of self-control not to fall into Sofia's arms a babbling mess.

'Is it money? You need more than what the commission brought you? I can give it to you right now!' Sofia dropped her hands long enough to scramble in her handbag for the cheque book Ariel knew she always kept on her 'in case of a bargain'.

Ariel laid a hand on Sofia's arm, stilling the scrambling woman. 'I don't need money—' *I need a miracle* '—but thanks for offering.'

'You sure?' Sofia didn't seem reassured, her penetrating stare sweeping Ariel's face with the vigour of a bloodhound getting a sniff of a trail.

'I'm sure.'

Ariel could never ask Sofia for the money to buy out the lease on the gallery. She would never risk their precious friendship over a loan she had no way of repaying. Aunt Barb had taught her many things, one of them being never borrow more than you can repay, and she'd adhered to that policy her entire life, which explained why she didn't own a car, had no mortgage and paid her rent on time.

Until now.

'Okay. In that case, I dropped by to invite you over for dinner tomorrow night.'

Sofia paused, a sly grin spreading across her face. 'And I thought you might like to bring that delightful young man of yours? He likes lasagna, no?'

'No!'

Ariel knew her reaction was over the top but the mere thought of Cooper made her want to retch.

'No?'

Ariel calmed her voice with effort. 'What I mean is, Cooper isn't my young man. He's busy with work and I'm busy here so we won't be seeing much of each other any more.'

Try never. Which would be too soon for her.

Sofia's mouth drooped. 'Oh, no, what a shame. Such a nice boy. Such manners, such class, so handsome.'

Nice boy? Ariel tried not to choke on the lump of disgust suddenly lodged in her throat.

'Ah-h-h…now I understand.' Sofia pointed at the painting and grimaced. 'You are very sad about not seeing him any more. You love him and you are pining for him. It all makes sense now.'

'I don't love him!'

But the moment the denial left her lips, Ariel knew it wasn't just the thought of losing the gallery that made her want to weep into the next century but the thought of losing Cooper too that added to her pain.

For once, Sofia didn't push or probe or offer a ten-minute matchmaking lecture.

'Don't worry, *bella*. It will all work out in the end.'

However, as Sofia wrapped her in a smothering hug Ariel seriously doubted it.

Cooper paced outside the entrance to the National Gallery, oblivious to the stunning fountains, the impressive lead light windows and the natural beauty of the Royal Botanic Gardens opposite.

He had a lot on his mind, namely a stubborn, gorgeous artist and whether she'd give him a chance to explain.

It had all seemed so clear after he'd sorted things out with his dad and he hadn't wasted a second in putting his plan into action. He just hoped the wheels in motion wouldn't be derailed by the fiery blonde harridan who had captured his heart without trying.

At that moment, he saw Ariel alight from a tram on St Kilda Road and he exhaled in relief.

She came.

Then again, she would have considering she thought she was meeting a representative of the Victorian Arts Council rather than the selfish brat she'd accused him of being earlier today.

His pulse raced and his heart turned over as she waited at the traffic lights, a stunning figure in crazy striped knickerbockers, a flowing purple top and towering cork wedges that tied around her ankles with black satin ribbon. The mix would've looked silly on any other woman. On her, it looked amazing.

She had an inner grace, a special glow that made anything on her or around her take on special significance, and he'd been mad enough to almost let her slip through his fingers.

Thank God he'd come to his senses. Now, if only she'd give him a chance to prove exactly how much she meant to him.

Cooper waited in the lengthening shadows as early dusk fell over Melbourne, watching Ariel's every step with increasing impatience.

This had to work.

It had to.

Ariel glanced at her watch as she reached the entrance to the gallery, relieved to see she'd made it with a minute to spare.

This could be it, her one and only opportunity to save Colour by Dreams. And a golden opportunity to rip up the document burning a hole in her carryall; the signed document that she hadn't couriered to Cooper once the Arts Council's director's summons had arrived.

She hadn't questioned the timely request. Instead, she preferred to see it as a sign that her luck was changing for the better. Besides, the director had been at Chelsea's showing and maybe he wanted to discuss the future of Victorian art and the part she—and her gallery—could play in it.

She closed her eyes and made a fervent wish that she was right in her assumptions.

However, the minute she opened them again and found herself staring into Cooper's too-blue eyes she knew that wishes didn't come true. At least not to her.

'What are you doing here?' she spat out, gripping her bag tightly to prevent herself from swinging it at him, her first crazy impulse when she saw his handsome face.

'There's something you should see inside,' he said, his well-modulated voice raising her hackles.

Why couldn't he be more ruffled, more scruffy, less polite, less perfect?

She felt gauche and unworldly and flawed next to him and she hated it. If his mere presence here hadn't undermined her, his air of cool unflappability would have. Drat the man.

She stuck a hand on one hip and tossed him an 'I don't give a damn' look.

'And what would that be? A picture of you in all your smug glory because you've won?'

She paused and tapped her lip with a chewed fingernail, as if deep in thought. 'Though that can't be right. As high as the gallery ceilings are, I doubt they could fit a portrait of your big head in there.'

To her chagrin, he didn't react apart from a slight twitch at the corners of his mouth.

That very kissable mouth, the same mouth that had worked its magic on her and coerced her into believing a whole lot of garbage, mainly that she loved him.

She had to be nuts.

'Look, this will only take a few minutes. What have you got to lose?'

'Everything,' she muttered, casting longing glances at the departing tram she'd just disembarked from and shuffling uncertainly from foot to foot before shrugging and making a beeline for the gallery, not caring if Cooper fell into step beside her or not.

She waited till they'd entered the cool interior and moved away from the door before confronting him.

'The director's not coming, is he? This was yet another of your sick power plays to get me to jump to your tune.'

It was a statement, not a question, and she wondered why she'd followed him in here knowing that fact.

Because you love him.

Because you still harbour some crazy hope this is all a bad dream and you'll wake up to a perfect day.

Because you're creative and are way too good at building ridiculous fantasies of happily ever after in your own head!

The great dolt had the grace to look sheepish. 'No, the director isn't coming. I'm sorry about that. It was the only thing I could think of on the spur of the moment to get you here.'

'What for? To rub my nose in it? To make sure I'd meet your stupid deadline?'

The silly thing was, he *was* rubbing her nose in it; rubbing her nose in the fact she loved him. Loved the way his blue eyes shone with intelligence, loved the way his mouth quirked when he was struggling not to laugh, loved the way he filled out a suit, even if guys in fancy rags didn't usually do it for her.

Ariel grabbed for a curl and twisted it around her finger, hoping the sharp tug on her scalp might erase her thoughts. Instead, it made her focus on Cooper even more, the way he reached out to still her hand before thinking better of it and letting his arm drop to his side.

The truth of the matter was that she loved him, loved everything about him, and getting over him would be yet another burden while she tried to recover from the loss of the gallery.

'I asked you here to give you this.'

He reached into the inside pocket of his silk-lined jacket and pulled out a folded document.

'Don't tell me. You've made another amendment and demanded my soul as well.'

He didn't flinch, he didn't speak, but something about the hurt expression in his eyes made her feel lower than an ant's belly.

'Why don't you take a look?'

Rolling her eyes like an adolescent taking a lousy report from a teacher, she snatched the offending document and opened it, prepared to skim the print before folding it and flinging it back in Mr Big-Shot's face.

However, her nasty intentions went up in smoke the minute her eyes focussed on the new owner of the gallery.

'What the—'

She blinked, made a frantic grab at the recently released curl and wound it furiously around her finger over and over, seeing the print but not quite believing it.

'It's yours,' he said, shrugging his broad shoulders as if he purchased galleries for exorbitant amounts of money and bestowed them on needy artists every day.

She shook her head, read the final few lines of the document again, before lifting her head and staring at him in open-mouthed shock. 'This is some kind of joke, right?'

'Of course not. I know how much the gallery means to you. This way, you won't have to worry about losing it ever again.'

He spoke so calmly, so rationally, as if the *fait accompli* of presenting her with sale papers for the gallery bearing her name as owner were nothing out of the ordinary.

'I don't get it.'

Ariel took a deep breath and exhaled slowly, hoping the oxygen rush would clear her head.

It didn't.

She propped against a nearby wall, needing some support at her back before she crumpled in an undignified heap.

If the realisation that she loved Cooper had put her in a spin, it was nothing on the mind-numbing revelation that he'd bought the gallery for her. The big question was why?

'Look, I worked a few things out this afternoon and I thought you'd appreciate the gesture. As much as you want to deny it, I think we have a chance at being more than friends in the future and I wanted you to give us a go without worrying about business stuff.'

More than friends…more than friends…

Suddenly, the befuddled fog clouding Ariel's mind lifted and with a flash of blinding clarity she knew exactly why Mr Big-Shot had got so generous. And the resulting knowledge made her want to retch.

'I'm not for sale,' she said, each word uttered with icy precision as she handed him back the document that burned her fingertips with its treachery. 'So we had sex? Big deal. It doesn't mean you can buy me for a few more cheap thrills. Nice to know what you think of me, though.'

Anger flared in the deep blue depths of Cooper's

eyes, sending sapphire shards of fury outwards. 'Don't be ridiculous. I'm not trying to buy you. I just want this damn business sorted out so we can get on with things.'

'What things?' She kept her tone silky smooth when, in fact, she longed to knee him where it hurt the most.

He grabbed hold of her upper arms before she could react, his offer fluttering to the floor between them. 'Don't pretend there's been nothing between us. You feel the sparks just as much as I do. Is it so wrong to want to explore that further? To see whether there's a chance for a couple like us?'

Ariel tried to wriggle out of his vice-like grip but couldn't move, trapped in the intensity of his stare, wishing he still didn't have the power to make her pulse race and her heart turn over.

'There's no chance.'

And the knowledge stabbed her anew. They were too different, too conflicted and his actions today spoke for themselves. When the going got tough, he bought his way out of a situation.

For guys like Cooper Vance, money talked.

Unfortunately, she wouldn't listen. She couldn't.

She'd learned long ago, that no matter how desperate or hungry or cold, there was always a line you shouldn't cross. And right now, Cooper had unwittingly drawn that line and she wouldn't cross it.

If nothing else, she still had her pride.

Shrugging out of his grasp, she rummaged through her carryall till she found what she was looking for.

'Here. I think this is what you want.'

She slapped the signed proposal in his hand and closed his fingers over it.

Cooper shook his head and tried to give it back to her. 'This isn't what I want. What I want is you.'

Pain, fierce and deep, twisted her gut till she almost cried out with the agony of it. 'Like I already said, I'm not for sale.'

Without waiting a second longer, Ariel turned on her heel and walked quickly towards the exit, praying her tears wouldn't turn to sobs before she made it out the front door.

'Ariel, wait!'

Ignoring Cooper's desperate plea, she picked up the pace, wishing she'd worn her ballet flats rather than three-inch wedges today. That was all she needed, to break an ankle to match her broken heart.

'Please, Ariel. I need you.'

Her steps slowed as she reached the far end of the plush foyer. The front door was in sight and she could've made a bolt for it. Instead, the minute Cooper laid a hand on her shoulder, she swivelled to face him, unsure whether to swing it at him or rummage in her bag for a wad of tissues.

'What did you just say?'

She tilted her head up, ignoring the tears pouring down her face as she eyeballed the jerk responsible for them.

'I need you.'

He reached up and, with infinite tenderness, wiped the tears from her cheeks with his thumbs.

'I need you. I want you. I can't imagine my life without you.'

Once his thumbs stilled, he cupped her face, staring into her eyes as if he meant every word.

As if.

Looked as if he would pull out every weapon in his arsenal to win this contest.

If he couldn't buy her, he'd schmooze her, just as he had right from the very beginning.

'There's a word for what you're experiencing. Insanity.'

'You think I'm crazy? Fine.'

He dropped his hands to clasp hers, holding on so tight her fingers went numb. 'Tell me what you see.'

His soft, husky tone took her back to the exact moment she'd asked him the same thing, his disappointing answer and the realisation at the time of the yawning gap between them.

The sad thing was, nothing had changed since that day in the gallery when she'd done her best to show him what sort of a person she was, what was important to her.

Cooper only saw what he wanted to see and that would never change. For him, the world was black and white, a place filled with money and property and fancy cars, a world she could never belong or feel comfortable in no matter how serious his intentions.

'Let me go—'

'Tell me what you see.'

He squeezed her hands, his steady gaze not leaving hers for a second.

She rolled her eyes, knowing she had to put an end to this fiasco sooner rather than later. Her heart had already fragmented a few minutes ago when he'd thought he could buy her, no use letting it shatter altogether and do permanent damage to her insides.

'Fine. You want to know what I see? I see a big-headed, overconfident, pompous jerk who thinks he can buy everything he wants.'

He didn't blink.

He didn't flinch.

And Ariel found herself battling tears again at the cruel words she'd just uttered all in the name of severing all ties with the guy she loved once and for all.

'Want to know what I see?'

'Not really.'

Her defiant act would've worked better if her breath hadn't hitched and come out sounding like a pathetic sob.

'I'll tell you anyway.'

To her amazement, he smiled, a soft, gentle smile totally at odds with his usual arrogance and it almost undid her completely.

'I see a beautiful woman filled with fire and passion and conviction. A woman who gives her all to keep a promise. A woman who steals my breath away with how much I love her…'

He trailed off and for a moment Ariel wondered if her frazzled brain had conjured up the words she'd wanted to hear.

He tugged on their linked hands and she leaned towards him, powerless to stop the swift, fierce kiss he slanted across her lips as if branding her as his.

'You love me?' she murmured, pulling back to stare at his face while wishing he'd kiss her again and again till she didn't have to think any more.

He nodded, his blue eyes glowing with an emotion that could only be love, its warmth radiating towards her better than any roaring log fire and infusing her with a bone-melting heat.

'I love you. All of you, from that over-stressed curl you keep winding around your finger to the bottoms of those crazy shoes you wear and every delicious inch in between. I love you, Ariel Wallace. So what do you think about that?'

He placed a finger under her chin and tipped it up, his gaze drifting to her lips.

'I think you've been spending too much time at

the studio and those paint fumes have affected you as much as they've affected me.'

The corners of his delightful mouth twitched. 'Does that mean—'

'Yes. It does. I love you too. Don't ask me why because we're as opposite as two people can get but, somehow, I've fallen for you.'

'Such sincere words of love,' he teased, placing her hand on his heart with his hand covering it.

Ariel smiled right back, enjoying the fact his heart pumped as hard and fast as hers and wondering exactly how much faster their organs could take when they moved past the kissing part onto the good stuff again. The thought alone sent her into meltdown.

'You know I'll still paint and run the gallery and wear funky fashion?'

He dropped a slow, lingering kiss on her lips, the type of kiss that had her melding to him and wishing their clothes would disappear and they could find themselves miraculously in a private place.

'You know I'll still acquire land and develop properties and wear suits and ties?'

She shrugged, staring up at him from beneath her lashes. 'I suppose I can learn to live with it.'

'Ah-h-h…but can you learn to live with this?'

His hot, open-mouthed kiss had her hankering for more, a lifetime more.

EPILOGUE

'I NOW declare the Barbara Kane Art School officially open.'

Sofia cut the thick red ribbon stretched across the front of the new building with great aplomb before spoiling her regal act by grabbing a glass of champagne from Chelsea and guzzling it.

Ariel laughed and leaned back, content in the circle of Cooper's arms as they watched Sofia and Chelsea take charge of the milling crowd and guide them through the glass doors of the new school.

'You made this happen, you know,' she said, snuggling into her husband's arms further as a cold gust of wind blew up Brunswick Street.

'We both did,' Cooper murmured against her ear, hugging her tight as his hands skimmed the sensitive underside of her breasts and made her shiver more than any old southerly wind.

She turned in the circle of his arms and looked up,

amazed that the man staring down with so much love was her husband.

'Barb would've been so proud.'

He stroked her cheek with slow gentleness. 'She would've been proud of you.'

Ariel blinked back the sudden tears, remembering a morning years earlier when a compassionate woman had taken pity on a down-and-out street kid.

'She took a chance on me when no one else would. Barb saw something in me I never knew existed. I owe her so much.'

A flicker of remorse shot through Cooper's eyes. 'I had no idea about your past and how much the gallery meant to you or how hard I must've seemed, pushing you relentlessly, forcing you to sell—'

'Shh…' She placed a finger on his lips, a shiver of delight skittling down her spine when he nibbled it. 'Old news. Look how far we've come.'

He glanced around them, noticed the absent crowd and pulled her further into the shade of an old oak. 'Tell me, Mrs Vance. Exactly how far have we come?'

He kissed his way from her finger to her wrist and slid his lips up her arm till her head fell back in abandon, yearning for his masterful touch on the sensitive spot between neck and collar-bone.

'Oh…' she murmured, melting into his arms, knowing she'd never felt so safe, so treasured, as she did in his embrace.

A tooting horn disrupted their erotic encounter and Ariel chuckled at the mortified expression on Cooper's face as he straightened. 'What? Doesn't Mr Big-Shot get caught out necking with his wife?'

'I have a reputation in the business world to uphold,' he said, aiming for a haughty look, which fell flat considering the smug smile on his face.

'Yeah, you're a real toughie,' she said, gesturing towards the art school over her shoulder with her thumb. 'Not only do you throw yourself wholeheartedly behind the new and improved Colour by Dreams, you find this delightful row of old terrace houses, pay the owners ten times what they're worth and develop them into an art school for underprivileged kids in the area.'

Cooper smiled, a warm, tender smile that never failed to set her pulse racing.

'Hey, it wasn't all me. My dad's a toughie too. After all, it was his idea to get Vance Corporation's employees volunteering down here once a week as part of their better-employee-relations policy.'

Ariel noted the pride in Cooper's voice when he mentioned Eric and she couldn't be happier. She'd watched the two of them re-establish a strong father-son bond over the last few months and had been touched when Eric had included her in a boys' weekend away where the three of them had sat around and she'd learned more about her amazing husband from a man proud to tell a lifetime of anecdotes.

'What are you thinking?'

Cooper slid his hands around her waist and locked them behind her back, bringing their lower halves into tantalising contact and making her wonder how soon till they could escape to the cosy confines of her studio, one of their favourite places for making love.

It had all started there and, thankfully, Cooper had agreed to pose for her again, completely naked this time, though she never quite got around to painting him.

He had a way of distracting her that made every colour she'd ever imagined coalesce into brilliant, startling clarity as he took her to the stars and back every time.

Smiling at her adorable husband, she said, 'I'm thinking you and I are one heck of a team, Mr Big-Shot.'

'I love it when you call me names,' he growled, and proceeded to show her exactly how much.

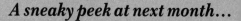

A sneaky peek at next month...

By Request

RELIVE THE ROMANCE WITH THE BEST OF THE BEST

My wish list for next month's titles...

In stores from 18th October 2013:

❑ In the Italian's Bed – Carol Marinelli,
Margaret Mayo & Catherine George

❑ Passionate Affairs – Kate Hardy,
Nicola Marsh & Natalie Anderson

3 stories in each book - only £5.99!

In stores from 1st November 2013:

❑ The Illegitimate Heirs: Luke, Zach and Jake
– Kathie DeNosky

❑ Bride Under the Mistletoe – Susan Meier,
Cara Colter & Jessica Hart

Available at WHSmith, Tesco, Asda, Eason, Amazon and Apple

Just can't wait?

1013/O

Come home this Christmas to Fiona Harper

From the author of *Kiss Me Under the Mistletoe* comes a Christmas tale of family and fun. Two sisters are ready to swap their Christmases—the busy super-mum, Juliet, getting the chance to escape it all on an exotic Christmas getaway, whilst her glamorous work-obsessed sister, Gemma, is plunged headfirst into the family Christmas she always thought she'd hate.

www.millsandboon.co.uk

1113/MB442

She's loved and lost — will she ever learn to open her heart again?

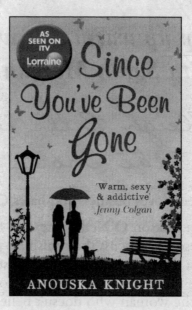

From the winner of ITV Lorraine's Racy Reads, Anouska Knight, comes a heart-warming tale of love, loss and confectionery.

'The perfect summer read — warm, sexy and addictive!'
—Jenny Colgan

For exclusive content visit:
www.millsandboon.co.uk/anouskaknight

A Royal Mistress!

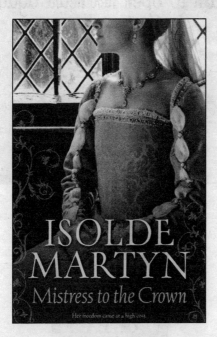

ISOLDE MARTYN

Mistress to the Crown

Her freedom came at a high cost.

Elizabeth Lambard was to become known as the notorious whore 'Jane Shore'—lover of King Edward IV. Facing scandal and a damaged reputation, can Elizabeth's beauty keep her out of trouble? Or will it lead her to the hangman's noose?

Available from:

www.millsandboon.co.uk

What will you treat yourself to next?

*Ignite your imagination,
step into the past...*
6 new stories every month

INTRIGUE...

Breathtaking romantic suspense
Up to 8 new stories every month

*Captivating medical drama –
with heart*
6 new stories every month

MODERN™

*International affairs,
seduction & passion guaranteed*
9 new stories every month

n o c t u r n e™

*Deliciously wicked
paranormal romance*
Up to 4 new stories every month

*Fresh, contemporary
romances to tempt all
lovers of great stories*
4 new stories every month